To Sheemu
Thank you for
Support !
D. Noe

KAU D'VARZA

A story in the ChaosNova universe

Written by David Noe
Edited by Karl Relf

David Noe

Find out more about the authors, the ChaosNova creative group, and stories set in the ChaosNova universe at www.chaosnova.co.uk

Huge thanks to Karl Relf (https://karlrelf.wordpress.com/) for editing this massive sci-fi adventure.

To Kieyotie McDermott and Drew Eckhardt, we've come a long way since the forum, what a ride it's been!

To Laura Loolaid, ChaosNova is now a cohesive story universe because of the work we've put into it together.

I'm so glad to be on this journey with all of you, and I can't wait to see what other stories we work on together in the future.

Finally thank you to anyone who has read our stories. We often publish snippets, stories, and news on our website; http://Chaosnova.co.uk

Contents

CHAPTER ONE- A LONG WAY FROM PARADISE

Elise Rivera sat alone, her pale face illuminated by a data-pad, its screen filled with denied requests and warnings. Her exasperated sighs and irritated screen-taps were the only noises in the otherwise silent observation lounge.

After a final rejection, she stretched out, yawned, and slid down the leather-covered bench. Her eyes drifted to the kaleidoscopic wall of vivid colours beyond the curved window. The colossal anomaly was known as the Void Cloud, and it still gave her a shiver of nervous excitement every time she saw it. Despite the distance, the Void Cloud provided a constant, and constantly varying, show for any willing to watch.

She felt her eyelids growing heavy, but a wisp of perfumed air stirred her from her reverie. The bench squeaked under her hands as she straightened.

A low hum came from behind her, followed by foot-steps. She watched a figure step up to the window and place his hand against it. He closed his eyes and breathed a sigh that clouded the surface.

"Are you alri-"

He spun round and stepped back. "Sorry... I..." He took a deep breath and straightened out his lavishly decorated tunic.

Her eyes lit up with recognition. "Arch-commissioner Nevos?"

"Only when I'm at the Office." He approached, studying her face. "Here, you can call me Gierre."

"Elise." She made a greeting gesture with her hand which he replicated.

He then motioned towards the bench. "May I?"

She smiled. "Aboard this station, *you* may do as you please."

"Not exactly." He sat down, but didn't relax. "Thank you."

"Something on your mind?"

"Always..." He focused on the Cloud, making it clear he wanted to change the subject. "Quite the view, eh?"

"Certainly something to think about."

"Oh?"

Elise had been ready to make the long trek back to her suite and settle in for a decent snooze, but upon Gierre Nevos' arrival, those aspirations had quickly vanished. It wasn't every cycle she got a chance to speak to the person elected to run Kau D'varza station.

"Yeah." Elise nodded. "It's been there for longer than we can tell, and yet we know nothing about it, what it is, what lies beyond. It's just there..." She turned to look at him. "That's what I think about. What about you?"

"I come here to clear my head, not fill it with more questions." He sighed. "I guess you could call it meditation. I don't often find people down here though. What is it you do for the station, Elise?"

"Long-term visitor." Her shoulders slumped. "Although the board occasionally contracts me for systems work."

Gierre raised an eyebrow. "Oh? You don't sound happy with the arrangement."

Elise tried to hide her frown. "It keeps me fed... I only put tech-support down because I had some experience. I really wanted to be a journalist."

"A journalist?"

She nodded enthusiastically. "Yeah, you know, document the events of an ever-growing station, investigate stuff, chronicle life aboard, that sort of thing."

"We have the Office of Public Relations to keep people informed." He spoke as though that was the end of the discussion.

Elise wasn't satisfied. "The O.P.R. doesn't report specifics... or anything that might 'damage morale'... but the people have a right to know what's going on."

"I'm afraid I have to disagree. The Office of Public Relations does exactly what it should. As long as Kau D'varza exists, information will be distributed on a need to know basis, and while people are happy, doing their jobs, they don't need to know." He made a sweeping motion with his hand. "It's all background noise anyway... cleaning schedules, meeting times, delivery records. You're not missing much. Besides, what's wrong with the on-board social network? If there's anything worth knowing, the citizens know about it before we've made any statements. Information already spreads like an infection, whatever format you had in mind for such an endeavour... it would be too slow compared to the existing system."

"It's hardly well-reported... just rumours and speculation for the most part."

"And the fiction is often more exciting than the eventual truth." He sat back and turned to look at her. "In reality, this station... it is a boring place to work and live besides the view. If the citizens want to make their own entertainment, that's fine by me. A little excitement to break up the monotony. I must say, I rather enjoy listening to the whimsical theories people come up with."

Elise couldn't hold his gaze, instead her eyes drifted back to the Cloud. A large bloom of amethyst had erupted from deep within, drowning out the surrounding ambers and turquoises.

"If you like..." Gierre continued, "I can see if there's any more systems work for you... bump you up the list a bit."

Elise felt herself replying before thinking. "Why?"

"Well, you have to pay your bills somehow."

She shot him a look. "I can pay my way. With or without tech-contracts."

Gierre raised his hands. "I didn't mean to cause offence. And I only suggested it because if you find yourself fulfilling work, you might prefer it over what you had planned. You seem like a, please excuse the term, 'useful' person. Kau D'varza needs people like you if it's going to keep functioning."

"I didn't come here to perform grunt work."

"If you don't mind me asking, *why* did you come here?"

"Why does anyone come this far out? Looking for a new life. An escape."

"And what did you need an escape from, Elise?"

"You ever hear of Paradise?"

Gierre shook his head. "I have not."

"Void Region local huh?"

"All my life."

"How'd you end up running this place?"

Gierre grinned. "A group on Windan Prime asked me to recruit a secondary wave of volunteers to boost the station's population. They told me I could stay if I wanted, and the volunteers seemed happy enough to have me around. Requested a place on the board. Fast forward half a *giga-sek*, and the elections rolled around. Put my name forward, did a bit of campaigning." His smile widened. "I talk about it like it was easy... maybe compared to what I've dealt with since, but you already know how this story ends: the people elected me, and the board made it official."

"And that was that?"

"And that was that." He replied, smirking. "So. *Paradise?*"

Elise nodded. "It's a small mining settlement on

Gira. It's in the Yurnto system. One of the last to hold out against businesses from Ar-Kaos, but when they finally gave in things started getting better. We suddenly had better healthcare, better education programs, and better infrastructure was under construction too." Her head slumped. "It was beautiful... really took Paradise' aesthetic into consideration..."

"What happened?"

Elise made a fist and hit the bench. "The Free Paradise Movement happened, started causing trouble, bringing in people from outside to disrupt Ar-Kaos' plans."

Gierre spoke calmly. "So you left?"

"Not straight away... I thought the security forces would deal with the problem. Then when they didn't, I considered signing on. Things just got worse. We needed more direct help from neighbouring cities, but it never came. Last I heard, the Movement had captured a ship convoy. Glad I left, didn't wanna get dragged into something like that."

Gierre studied her expression, then sighed. "You probably made the right decision."

"Came here looking for a fresh start. A way out. This is the farthest I could get from Paradise, so I booked it and took off. Haven't looked back since."

"Don't you have family, friends?"

"My family are a stubborn bunch, but they encouraged my decision."

"Do you stay in touch?"

Elise offered a knowing smile. "When the connection is stable, I send messages. Sometimes, on a good cycle, I get one back too. Haven't heard anything for a while, but that's expected given the distance. Probably a message out there right now, flying it's way across thousands of beacons just to get here."

"Would you ever go back?"

"I dunno. Maybe for a visit. Paradise isn't the same place I remember growing up. I don't think it ever will be."

Elise let the silence hang in the air.

Eventually, Gierre found something to say. "Have you been here long?"

"Long enough to know the layout, not long enough to make friends."

"You strike me as the sort of person that chooses her associates carefully."

Elise snorted. "Maybe a little too carefully..." She offered the Void Cloud one final glance and got to her feet. "It's been a pleasure, *Gierre*."

"I assure you, the pleasure has been all mine."

"Hope you work out whatever it is that's eating you up."

"Thanks." He nodded as she passed. "Good sleep."

* * *

As the door hissed shut, Arch-Commissioner Gierre Nevos felt calmed by the silence, and finally allowed himself to relax.

Any illusion of tranquility broke minutes later. He was roused from his thoughtless staring by a short, sharp cough. Once Gierre had gathered his senses and straightened up on the bench, he gave an irritated glance to the person standing beside him.

"You have news?"

Kaska Stone stood as straight as she could, despite her obvious tiredness. There was a darkness in her eyes that Gierre hadn't seen before.

"We still haven't received a response."

"And the scans?"

"Scans show no visible damage," Stone replied. "Their comm equipment should be functioning. It appears deliberate, Sir."

"No course change?"

"Only when we attempt to move the station. It sees what we've done, and alters course to match."

"How long do we have?"

"If they maintain current speed, half a mega-sek."

"And then what?"

"I don't know."

"What-" Gierre rocked forward. "What do you think they're likely to do?"

"If it really is just a ship with communication problems, then there won't be a problem. We will repair their equipment, remind them of the rules they should be observing and send them on their way."

"The alternative?"

"With respect, Sir, I recommend you discuss this with Defence Commissioner Zeled."

"He would simply blast them out of existence, consequences be damned. I want *your* opinion."

"If Kau D'varza can spare a vessel, we could intercept them and discover what the problem is."

Gierre sat back and took a moment to assess his options. His only alternative means of defence were the stations 'All or Nothing' cannon, but if the incoming vessel really was experiencing communication problems, he'd be giving the order to wipe out hundreds, maybe even thousands of innocent people.

"Do we have any active ships?"

"*Akonda* and *Vykpa* are undergoing repairs. *Mambaka* and *Kobra* are on the Gaitlin mission. I think *Bo'a* is ready."

Gierre frowned. *"Bo'a* is a transport ship."

"Yes, Sir."

Gierre closed his eyes and rubbed his forehead. *"Akonda* and *Vypka,* how close to ready are they?"

"I would need to speak to the engineers."

The bench creaked as Gierre stood. He took a deep breath and spoke with a firm voice. "Specialist Stone, find me a ship, preferably one with weapons, that can intercept that vessel before it poses a threat to this station."

Her head remained still, but her eyes searched the observation lounge. "Uh... Me, Sir?"

"Will that be a problem?"

Her eyes narrowed. "Ah... No Sir."

"Very well. Any questions?"

"If the intercept mission meets with difficulty, what will our alternative solution be?"

Gierre exhaled and shook his head. "That's what I'm going to see Commissioner Zeled about now."

* * *

As Kaska Stone stepped out of a personal transport pod, she realised that the early-risers probably wouldn't be too happy to see a specialist running around with concern practically oozing from every pore.

The freshly cleaned floors reflected brighter-than-necessary lights, while the walls were lit up with panels displaying adverts or picturesque scenes of somewhere else in the system.

She straightened out her uniform, and tried to display confidence as she strode away from the pod.

I told him I'd get it done. Why did I do that?

She felt uncertainty trying to claw its way in, but Stone took a deep breath and continued her confident stride until she reached the elevator.

As the otherwise empty pod rushed down the chute, lights whizzing by, Stone tried to push the tension from her aching bones. She'd been awake for two full cycles now, and although she did her best to hide it outwardly, she was feeling it internally. Taking a breather brought to the forefront all the sensations she'd been blocking out; tension in her stomach, a dry ache in her throat, the foggy haze that clouded her mind.

The smells from the engineering bay reached her before the doors opened, forcing her back into the fake posture of someone who knew what they were doing.

It was still early, but many of the engineers worked odd hours to accommodate the any-time visitors and fulfill the seemingly endless list of work orders. As she wandered between the huge bays, it occurred to her that there were many ships available, just none that fell under the stations control. She could ask Gierre to request a volunteer vessel, but that would show his trust was misplaced, and proving the Arch-Commissioner wrong rarely ended well. She also knew there was no guarantee anyone would step forward. She bit her lip, reminding herself that her failure could mean much worse than a demotion. It was close to bleeding as the office door swung open ahead of her.

"If you're here for *Akonda*-" A young, round-bellied man dropped down the step with a proud smile, "it's gonna be another three M-seks. Sorry, *Spesh*."

"What about *Vypka*?"

"She's gonna be even longer. We haven't even pried her open yet to see what the problem is."

"The Arch-Commissioner needs a ship."

"And I need a raise, more *sekunds* in the cycle. Can't always get what we want."

"What *do* you have?"

"Nothing." He smiled. Stone realised he was enjoying this little game.

"You can't provide the Arch-Commissioner a vessel, yet you expect a raise?" She raised her hand as he drew breath to reply. "Unacceptable. What if the security of the station were at risk, or we needed to transport someone to a medical facility?"

"I-"

"It's unacceptable," she repeated. "This station has five vessels for such jobs, yet you seem unable to keep them in service. You can't even keep the simplest of Transit Cores functioning properly. Have we promoted you above your ability? Is this too much for you to handle?"

His face contorted angrily. "I'm the only person who can keep this shed running!"

"Would you be willing to bet your job on that?"

"I-" He exhaled, his shoulders slumped. "We've got one ship. *Bo'a*. I can have it ready by lights out."

Stone maintained her cold stare. "*Bo'a*? That's it?"

"It's that or nothing."

"How long will it take you to equip a weapon?"

His face scrunched again. "A weapon? What exactly are you planning?"

I have to give him something.

"If-" she replied, firmly, unsure of where the words were coming from, "the Arch-Commissioner should travel on this vessel and come under attack, it will be more than your job on the line."

"You don't have to threaten me, ya know?"

She stood up straight, reminding the engineer that she was in charge. "I need a ship, I need it armed, and I need it in under quarter of a M-sek. Consider this your final warning. Failure to comply will result in my direct recommendation to the Arch-Commissioner that you not only be demoted, but arrested for negligence."

He fixed her with an icy stare and wrung his hands. "We'll get it done."

Stone's spoke with a hiss, emphasis on each word. "See to it that you do."

As she turned and started back towards the elevator, she was painfully aware that if he failed, he would be the least of Gierre's concerns. She positioned herself near the rear of the pod, away from the other workers. Her corner of solace gave her enough space to think.

Shouldn't have got so angry. She exhaled. *Too much stress. Not enough down-time. No sleep. Treating people like that though... ugh, I'll be lucky if he doesn't sabotage whatever ship he comes up with. And Bo'a? Oh, Bo'a...*

She shook her head. If the transport was all they had, it would have to do.

CHAPTER TWO- NEXT MOVE

Elise stared up at the ceiling of her modest habitation module, tired, yet unable to sleep. The so-called relaxation music the station provided wasn't helping. Piano notes sounded harsh instead of soothing, the drums were too loud, even the gentle chimes rung out just a little too long. It wasn't a mystery to her either; her conversation with Gierre had let loose some deep-rooted irritation that she hadn't been aware of before.

"Ugh."

She kicked off the covers and stretched out before slamming her arms back down into the mattress. Something in the dark registered her discomfort and set a gentle breeze blowing through the room.

"Didn't come all this way for a tech job..." she grumbled in Paradisian. "No guarantees you were gonna find work as a journo either though... damn it, Elise. You can't survive on a dream alone."

She rolled off the bed, a dim light barely illuminating

the room as she stood to full height.

"Music off," she ordered, walking over to the food processor. A few button taps later, a cup of water appeared behind the transparent hatch. It was refreshingly cool to the touch. She took a few seconds to press the chilled container against her forehead before downing the liquid in a few gulps and requesting another.

She leaned against the machine, her eyes coming to rest on the large screen on the opposite wall. During the station's day-cycle, it would show various vistas from around the system. When Elise looked at it now, however, all she could see was a dimmed star-scape.

"Display map."

She lowered herself onto the sofa and took a swig of her drink. The screen faded up, bringing with it a crude two dimensional view of the Windan system. A smiling cartoon face appeared in the bottom left, offering assistance should it be required. Elise flicked him away with a hand gesture and studied the image.

"Two habitable planets," she read. "Windan Prime and Exiss, modest populations, one public station - Kau D'varza..." She sighed heavily. "Zoom out," she ordered, her voice cracked. It took a couple of seconds for the view to escape Windan. As it continued, Exen, Heradim and Kandaha appeared at the edge. "Stop."

Heradim and Kandaha were systems in the Arabia sphere of influence. Elise had neither the credentials nor the desire to settle in that region. Her gaze swept to the other system.

Exen.

Her eyes narrowed. The system of Exen was less populated than Windan, had fewer habitable planets, only
a handful of research stations, and if the warnings on
the map were correct, was not a place many came
back from, likely due to its proximity to the Void
Cloud. Exen attracted a lot of 'Voiders', people who
thought they could breach or navigate around the
anomaly. Nobody had been successful, yet they kept
coming.

"Zoom out."

Two more systems appeared on the border: Gaitlin
and Arokia.

"Stop. Focus zoom on region…" She squinted, trying
to read the digits on the screen, "Er… Six, four… Two.
Stop. Display information for Gaitlin… Read."

"Gaitlin," the vid-system's flat, synthesised voice
stated. "Six planets: Gaitlin One; Gaitlin Two; Iskoda
- moderate population; Mallanix - medium population; Gaitlin Five; Gaitlin Six - large research facilities
at polar regions. Several moons in this system are
also populated. Gaitlin has one public station - Kisela
Dock. Records indicate a recent conflict on the surface of Mallanix. Caution is advised within this region. Additional information can be accessed via the
Win-Net."

Elise finished her drink and sat with the cup against

her lips, not quite staring at the information. Before long, her eyelids grew heavy, and she passed into a deep slumber.

**

"Hey, wake up."

Joseph Raffa lazily opened an eye to see his aide leaning over him. He opened the other and glanced around. He was seated on the back of a Personal Transport Vehicle, which waited at the entrance to the station's Administrative Core. He remembered why he'd been summoned and let out a heavy sigh. Something beeped ahead of them and the P.T.V. rolled forward.

Ikarus Brook occupied the seat beside him, flicking through a datapad full of information that Raffa dared not attempt to understand. The screen automatically adjusted as they entered the shadowy tunnels under Admin Core.

"Any additional info?"

Ikarus shook his head. "Regretfully, no. Arch-Commissioner Nevos is only willing to discuss the issue in person."

That can't be good.

"Any idea why he wants me, specifically?"

"Comcap Teq is leading the mission to Gaitlin, Comcap Rexon is on leave. You were the only one available."

Raffa grinned. "You sure know how to make a guy feel

special."

The P.T.V. stopped parallel to a large set of double doors. A security officers poked his head out of a hastily erected booth, realised who it was, and granted them entry.

Raffa had barely left his seat when the vehicle sped away.

"Eh..." He frowned. "People seem... tense."

"With that in mind, you should make haste."

Raffa nodded. "Perhaps I should. See you soon."

Arch-Commissioner Gierre Nevos looked up as Raffa stepped into the Admin Core Control Centre, or, as it was more commonly known, Command Core. Nevos said something to Kaska as she poked at a console, then turned to Raffa with a frown.

"Comcap Raffa."

Raffa raised his right hand in salute. "Is there a problem, Sir?"

"Unfortunately so." He shook his head and waved off Raffa's formalities. "Ease."

He visibly loosened up, but his face still held a look of worry.

"Yestercycle, Specialist Trast observed a vessel. Some kind of freighter, making its way towards Kau D'varza, direct course."

Okay, Raffa thought, *nothing unusual so far.*

"It isn't responding to communication, we've seen no distress beacons, and at their current rate they'll be here in under half an m-sek."

There it is.

"I take it we've already tried to move out of its path?"

Gierre nodded solemnly. "It adjusts course once it detects what we've done."

"That's not good. So what are my orders?"

"We need you to intercept the vessel, board it, and resolve the situation. We have no problem if they want to dock here, but as we are unable to determine their intentions, we need to prevent them from getting in range until we can be sure they aren't a threat."

"*Akonda* or *Vykpa?*"

"*Bo'a.*"

Raffa tilted his head. "I must have misheard you."

"You misheard nothing. The engineers are working to upgrade *Bo'a's* defensive capability."

"What defensive capability? It's got a shield. That's it."

"If I may, Arch-Commissioner?" Kaska said, turning from the console.

Gierre nodded, seemingly relieved. "Of course."

Raffa eyed her cautiously as she approached, clutching a datapad in her hands.

"I understand your concern," Stone said. "*Bo'a* isn't built for this sort of mission, but it is able."

"It's a transport."

"And we're asking you to use it to transport people."

"Into the proximity of an unresponsive vessel, which may or may not fire upon us."

"If they do," Gierre replied, "we'll know what their intentions are, and have the right to shoot them down with the station's defences."

"And what about the people on *Bo'a*?"

Kaska glanced at him. "Shields should hold against whatever they've got."

"Should? Specialist Stone, with respect, I'm not leading people to their deaths because something *should* hold but doesn't."

Gierre spoke with a cool confidence. "Need I remind you that failure to act could lead to the destruction of the station?"

"If they get within firing range and still don't respond, we have every right to defend ourselves."

"And what if it's refugees? What if they're people in need?"

"Then they should be doing everything in their power to telegraph their intentions. Even a flash from the emergency beacon would let us know they're in trouble. Instead, nothing."

Stone nodded. "Comcap Raffa's assessment is correct. However, we can't know what condition their emergency beacon is in."

"We can make a damn good guess. It's probably fine; they just have bad intentions, and you're sending, I take it, our only active bird out to meet them. Just blast it when it's in range. Disable, don't kill, then we can pull it in and flood it with security."

Stone shook her head. "We've run the simulations. Disabling the ship provides a greater than eighty-two percent chance that it, or the debris, will damage the station beyond our current repair ability. Destroying it outright would reduce that risk, but we don't want it to come to that."

Gierre stepped forward. "We also don't want to alert the citizens to what's happening."

Raffa punched his hand and pointed at Stone. "So let me get this straight: You want me to take a transport vessel out to meet a potentially hostile ship, hope they don't shoot us, board it, and provide aid if necessary. If they're hostile, you want us to turn them away; if they refuse, we're supposed to get rid of them. And, if anything happens to *Bo'a*, that gives you the justification to use the station's guns?"

Gierre and Stone both nodded.

"I want it on record that I think this is a dumb plan." His shoulders slumped. "But I get the feeling you won't take no for an answer."

"Comcap Raffa, we *cannot* take no for an answer."

27

He straightened and saluted again. "With your permission, I will put this operation into effect."

"Go ahead." Gierre turned to face Stone and glanced back over his shoulder as he continued, "Oh, and *Joseph*, I hope I don't need to remind you that this incident is of the utmost secrecy. The citizens will not find out unless the unthinkable happens and I need to order the evacuation. Is that clear?"

"Like trans-steel."

"Good. If you have nothing to add, Specialist Stone?"

"I do not."

"Then please, Comcap, do not let me keep you."

* * *

Gierre and Kaska glanced at one another as the door sealed behind Raffa.

"Your assessment?"

Stone considered her answer for a moment. "Comcap Raffa is capable, but only when properly equipped. His concerns about using *Bo'a* are well-founded."

"Once this is dealt with, I want a full audit and inspection of the workshop."

Stone's eyes widened and a smile crept to her lips. "Sir, I would appreciate the privilege."

Gierre eyed her with uncertainty. "You have some ideas on how to improve the situation?"

"I have some idea who the problem is."

"Is this a personal vendetta, Specialist Stone, or a legitimate concern?"

"A legitimate concern that has developed into a personal vendetta. The lead engineer is incapable, and through his failings, Kau D'varza, my home, is now at risk."

"A fair statement. And I appreciate your honesty. You will get your wish. However, I request that you undertake this operation with an aide."

Kaska closed her eyes just long enough for Gierre not to notice her irritation. "Did you have anyone in mind, Sir?"

"Which aides will be available?"

Kaska tapped at the pad and flicked through a couple of directories. "Aide Tannen is still undergoing treatment for Ice-bug... aide Yata has been sent to the surface as per our recruitment agreement, and everyone else is assigned to captains, commissioners or *executives*." There was a hint of spite on the last word.

"We'll requisition someone after we've dealt with this situation."

"That will not be a problem."

He nodded. "Very well, Specialist Stone, let us return our attention to the problem at hand. Please inform me if there are any changes."

She saluted, then turned back to her console.

* * *

Ikarus could tell from the look on Raffa's face the meeting hadn't gone well.

"What are our orders?" he asked, eager to get to work.

"Send a whole bunch of good folk to die when there are better alternatives."

Ikarus blinked. "Perhaps you should elaborate?"

Raffa shook his head and whistled down the tunnel. In the distance, a P.T.V. started up and rolled towards them.

"I'll fill you in on the way."

Before the vehicle could roll on, a broad shouldered man bundled into the seat beside the driver and turned to look at Raffa and Ikarus.

"Gentlemen."

Both men turned and raised their hands in salute.

"Commissioner Zeled."

"I hear G-Man has given you a mission."

"Yes, Sir," Raffa replied. "Classified."

"Don't worry, Comcap. I'm not here to turn you out." He sighed and tapped the driver on the shoulder, pointing forward. The P.T.V. started to hum, then rolled on.

"You boys are in for a hell of a job. G-Man's right to suggest we... investigate. Gotta figure out if... innocent parties are involved. But *Bo'a* isn't up to it."

"I'm hoping this is the part where you tell us you've got a ship hidden away somewhere."

"I wish." He sighed. "Truth is, it's all we've got right now. And it don't matter what weapon they glue on, your odds don't get much better."

"If you don't mind me asking, what was your recommendation to the Arch-Commissioner?"

He didn't hesitate. "Destroy it."

"But-"

"Listen, the people of this station expect a publicly strong Defence Commissioner. When the Office of Public Relations reveals our meeting, people won't want to see me sitting in a passive trance suggesting we should take it on the nose, they'll want someone to voice their anger: 'This is a threat to our homes! How dare they?' And then for all my shouting, G-man will be seen to pick the balanced route, calmer heads will prevail, and the people of this station will feel protected. Just business as usual." He pointed to the ceiling, a transparent window out to the system. "We have to do it for all of *them* too."

"Sir?"

"If one of those nutcase cults or hungry-for-war factions from the surface sees that the Defence Commissioner is overly aggressive, they might think twice. It's the reason our security force is so large."

"Won't they see that the Arch-Commissioner chooses an alternative?"

"Another bluff. If the station really does come under attack from hostiles, we won't need to worry about 'innocents'. The alternative will not prevail that cycle, and it will shock them."

Raffa shook his head. "Politics is all too confusing for me."

"Managing a ship full of people... That sounds like politics enough for me. All I have to do is stomp around saying stuff like 'Blow it up!' and my commitment is fulfilled."

Ikarus took a deep breath. "It is not often we get to enjoy your company, Commissioner Zeled. I sense this conversation has another purpose."

"Astute observation, Ikarus, as always." He grunted. "Don't take a full squad."

Raffa scoffed. "Sorry?"

"Listen, if you run into any trouble. *Bo'a* won't hold up. Throwing away security personnel is not part of your mission."

"With respect Sir, my *mission* will be difficult enough without reduced manpower."

"This isn't one of your training simulations, Raffa. If you encounter even the slightest resistance on your journey, you won't get a second chance."

"I am fully aware of that, but-"

"Comcap Raffa, what you are doing, honourable as it may be, only has two possible conclusions: peace or hostility. I must have the resources available should it be the latter."

"Hostility is more likely," Ikarus replied, "should we appear weak."

"We're sending a transport to do the job of a warship; we already appear weak."

The P.T.V. jolted to a stop outside a group of unremarkable office-like buildings. A heavily armoured door and two security personnel standing guard were the only things that made them stand out as different to most other constructions on the station.

Ikarus jumped up, scanned the area and nodded an All Clear.

Raffa stepped off the rear bench and turned to face Commissioner Zeled. "I will speak with my advisors, and take your... *recommendation...* into consideration, Sir."

"See to it that you do. I'd rather end your record with honours, not anger."

He got the driver's attention and spun a raised finger, indicating he was to turn around.

Raffa raised his hand in salute, and watched as the P.T.V. took off round the corner.

"I find my curiosity aroused," Ikarus said as they approached the door. The two guards offered the pair a crisper salute than Raffa had given Zeled. He nodded to them. "Report."

"Force Commander Winters arrived point five kilo-sek ago," the senior one replied. "He seemed in good spirits."

Raffa tried to hide his exasperation. "We'll see how long that lasts. Anything else?"

"No, Sir."

"Very well, continue."

The junior guard turned to a panel beside the door and pressed his face against it. After a series of clicks, the heavy metal aperture split in two and the halves disappeared into the thick walls.

Raffa nodded his thanks and stepped through with Ikarus close behind.

A series of defence-filled corridors led them to the Command Suite. A circular room, nearly-obsolete consoles and their operators situated around the curved inner wall. Raffa approached the large data-scape table at the center and nodded to the armored figure on the other side.

"Winters."

"Comcap."

"Alright, we haven't got much time so let's get down to it." He motioned for Ikarus and Winters to gather closer together. They offered one another subtle nods, then focused on Raffa.

He tapped the data-scape and brought up a top down, simplified view of the system. The view zoomed in on the space surrounding Exiss. Raffa adjusted it once more to show Kau D'varza station, and the incoming ship.

"Command Core's Specialists recently spotted a freighter on a direct course with the station. They are unresponsive to communications, and no emergency beacon or other such signal has been observed. When Command Core attempted to move the station, the ship automatically corrected its course. The manoeuvre was repeated, and the freighter changed course again. We've been given the unenviable task of taking *Bo'a* to intercept the freighter, determine their intentions, and either assist them or turn them back."

"*Bo'a*?" Winters grimaced. "For an intercept mission?"

"I know. *Vypka* would have been my first choice, but it's out of action."

"What about *Kobra*?"

"On the Gaitlin mission with Comcap Teq."

"What does he need a stealth vessel for?" Winters' voice had a sharp edge to it.

"That mission is confidential, and we've got our own problems to worry about."

"Sir..." Ikarus had been studying the datascape. "What do we know about the freighter?"

Raffa gave the simplified logo a tap. The view zoomed to the incoming ship.

Ikarus couldn't stop himself letting out a disappointed sigh as the spartan list of details appeared.

"Well," Raffa said, "we know how big it is, at least."

Winters shook his head. "That doesn't help. We need to know what weapons we're coming up against, what sort of numbers we're facing. If we get close to them in *Bo'a* and they open fire..." He frowned. "I guess we'll know their intentions then, but I don't fancy *our* chances."

"Me either. So we need to come up with something that maximises our chances, but still protects the station."

Ikarus looked up at Raffa. "In a best-case scenario it's a problem with the ship. You can board, regain control, bring it in safely."

"And worse case?" Winters asked.

"Worst case? They destroy *Bo'a* on approach and continue on until they either board or destroy Kau D'varza."

"We can't accept that," Raffa replied. "If the freighter's got weapons, what are they likely to be? Where are they likely to be positioned? And how can we get around them?"

"Hmm..." Ikarus rubbed his chin. "From what we know of the freighters that visit the station, weapons are short-range, concentrated along the sides, with a focus on the cargo hatches."

"That's a limitation," Winters remarked. "We can approach low, swing under them, backflip onto the underside and breach a mech corridor. The only risk is long-range or front-facing weapons."

"Backflip onto the underside?" Raffa replied, his face twisted in confusion. "Maybe in *Vypka*, but *Bo'a* can't perform a maneuver like that, especially not against a moving target."

Winters shrugged. "Best I've got."

"The Comcap is correct." Ikarus pointed to the icon for the freighter. "You need to approach alongside, match speeds, and dock. *Bo'a's* hull can't cope with high stress maneuvers, so that will be your only option."

"They're sticking a weapon on *Bo'a*. Won't be much, but maybe..." Raffa's eyes narrowed as he read back through the datascape. "What if... hmm... come in low, avoid the defences, pick off the guns on one hatch, circle back around as many times as we have to, then dock?"

"Time will be a factor. And this plan relies on the opposing vessel having lax front and rear defence."

Winters cleared his throat. "Why can't we circle back round, match speeds, then dock with the mech hatch? Maybe a backflip is too much, but a simple rotation might do the trick."

"Hmm..." Raffa tapped the display, an input window appeared. "Run simulation. Vessel one, *Bo'a*; vessel two, unidentified freighter. Acquire live information from current data feed."

The view zoomed out once more, giving them the top-down scene. An icon representing *Bo'a* appeared over Kau D'varza, another - the freighter - in the distance.

"Winters, please input your suggestion."

Winters rolled his eyes, exhaled, then leant over the data-scape with a disinterested frown. "You know I hate these things."

"I haven't got the time, spare ships or people for you to run a real life sim. This is the best you're gonna get until the run."

"Talking of people..." Ikarus said in a way that made Raffa's shoulders slump.

"An unreasonable request on Zeled's part," Raffa replied, a faintly masked irritation in his voice. "He commands four main security teams, two support teams, and can call on two volunteer squads, yet he asks me to break up my squads to leave some here. We need those troops."

"The request was to not take a full squad. May I suggest that, to appease Commissioner Zeled, you take the majority of both squads, but leave the least experienced, wounded or otherwise unable units to defend the station. This way, your commitment is fulfilled, however dubiously, and you still maintain a reasonable size force."

"How many people can we fit on board *Bo'a*?"

"With equipment?" Ikarus glanced at his data-pad.

"Two hundred. Not including crew."

"That makes my job easier." It didn't take Raffa long to do the maths. "Remove fifty people from both squads, station them here, load the rest onto *Bo'a*." He glanced over to Winters who was still trying to navigate the datascapes menus. "I need you to get me a list of the hundred staying. Once we're done here, I want the rest prepared and running exercises until the ship is ready."

"Won't take long to come up with that list," Winters replied flippantly. "Been thinking about making some cutbacks, use the funds to better train the ones who actually know what *security* means."

Raffa shot him a look. "That will need some discussion upon the completion of this mission."

"Oh, I know." He stood up straight and motioned to the datascape. "There. It's ready."

"Run it."

The trio watched, tense, as the simulation played out in front of them at twenty-five times speed. *Bo'a* raced away from Kau D'varza. The icon getting gradually smaller to represent it going low compared to the freighter. The two ships passed, *Bo'a* out of range of any potential weapons fire. The icon then rapidly grew in size as it arced upwards, then shrunk once more as it dipped and dove on the freighter.
Raffa sucked through his teeth at the drastic stunts, but according to the readings *Bo'a* held together.
The two icons eventually overlapped as *Bo'a* arrived

under the Freighter and latched on. The simulation proudly declared itself 'Completed'.

"I don't like that rear approach." Raffa said flatly.

"Why not?" Winters replied, irritated that his simulation hadn't impressed Raffa.

"The first approach needs to look for rear-facing weapons. If the crew can pull this off, I don't want them blasted on final approach."

"So the first pass should be a firing run."

Raffa nodded. "Only if we see weapons. No need to damage it if there's nothing there."

"The visual scanners will see what the freighter has from some distance. You'll be able to make a decision early," Ikarus said.

"Once that's done..." Raffa turned back to the datascape. "We breach the mech-corridor, then spread out in opposite directions, with a focus on the command center."

Winters nodded. "The sweep will be the easy bit. A layout would be nice, but with two-hundred soldiers a ship that size shouldn't take too long to clear and map out. Once we're in control, we bring it into dock?"

"That's the plan."

They watched the updated simulation and while the result wasn't perfect, it was better than losing the station.

Raffa took a deep breath as the 'Completed' notification appeared. "I really hope they don't fire on us. Is it wrong to hope for a ship full of civilians who couldn't keep life support running?"

Ikarus thought about it for a few seconds, then nodded. "Wrong, yes. But it would mean your entry aboard will be unopposed, swift, and execution of the operation will be successful, thus more lives would be saved in the grander scheme."

Winters stepped around the table, closer to the edge with the freighter. "Do we know where they came from?" He asked, eyes narrowing on the neighbouring systems. "I'd like to know who we're potentially up against."

"Command Core are probably looking into it, but best guess would be Exen, Hol, Clion or Grinda."

Ikarus shook his head. "Grinda and Clion are practically empty; there's no way they'd have the capability. If whoever this is came from either of those, it wasn't their point of origin."

"Exen and Hol aren't into losing ships either," Winters added.

Raffa sighed. "Truth is, we don't know, so assume the worst."

"Ah. Damnit." Winter's eyes glazed over as he whispered. "What if it's Beyema?"

"Reclaimers?" Ikarus frowned. "If that's the case, Kau D'varza is in for a difficult time."

The silence lingered just a few seconds too long before Raffa tried to calm everyone. "We can theorise all we like once this is over. Might be we find some clues while we're on-board." He stood straight and looked to his aide and force-commander. "Are there any questions?"

They shook their heads.

"Alright then. Winters, put those teams together and get 'em prepped. Ikarus, I need you to find out how long it's gonna take the engineers to get *Bo'a* lifting."

Ikarus nodded, while Winters gave a stiff salute. Raffa returned the salute, and watched as they disappeared into the corridor. After several seconds, he turned back to the display, his eyes slowly wandering over the simulation before him.

CHAPTER THREE-
FORSAKEN
COURIER

The sofa felt wet against Elise's cheek as she stirred from her impromptu snooze. She opened her eyes and wiped the dribble from her cheek, then sat up, focussing on the screen again and trying to remember what she'd been doing.

"Gaitlin?"

Her conversation with Gierre came rushing back: the long, thoughtful walk home, and the inability to sleep causing her to seek out an alternative.

Despite the rest, Elise could feel herself getting tired. She gripped the edge of the sofa and pushed forward, stumbling to her feet. After a moment of self-congratulation for beating her laziness, Elise half-walked, half-limped to the cleanroom on a leg stiff with pins and needles. After a clean and a change of clothes, she walked back into her habitational proper, now wearing a neutral-blue auto-button shirt and loose fitting trousers. She still felt the tiredness in her bones and silently cursed herself for not sleeping on the more comfortable bed.

She approached the machine in her kitchen, though any hope of eating was shattered by a loud bang on the door. The alarm rang out too, as though the cacophony of noise would catch her off-guard. If that had been the intended result, it worked. She stumbled toward the door and tried to shake off the confusion before pressing the panel beside the door. The vidscreen showed two people outside. Her eyes widened, partly in confusion, but mostly in fear.

Station Security? What are they-

"Citizen Rivera?" one asked, checking the panel outside and comparing it with his data-pad.

"What-"

"Citizen Rivera?" he asked again, as though it hadn't gone through the first time.

"Yes," she relented.

The corner of his mouth curled upwards. Something about it unsettled Elise.

"We require you to accompany us to Station Security Center Five."

"What? Why?"

"We will not make this request a second time, and we would rather not publicly debate the reasons for it."

"I..." Her shoulders slumped. "You got any I.D?"

He was more than happy to press his thumb to the external panel. Information appeared on the screen.

Kau D'varza - Security Specialist - Sif Raizen...

She took a deep breath.

Shit.

Another deep breath as she reached for the door controls and hit 'unlock'.

The door slid away, and both security specialists stepped through.

Sif stayed with Elise while his partner wandered deeper inside.

"Hey!"

"Citizen Rivera, please." He spoke in hushed tones. "Your datapad. Where is it?"

Elise shivered as a chill ran down her spine. Everything clicked into place in a gut-twisting instant.

"Bedroom." Her voice barely a whisper.

"Thank you." Sif nodded to his companion who strode over to the bedside shelf, snatching up the pad with a deft flick. He examined it briefly and smiled. If he said anything, Elise didn't hear it. She was too caught up in the whirlwind of thoughts racing through her mind.

She was brought back to reality with a thud as Sif tapped her on the shoulder.

"Hey, Citizen Rivera, I'd rather not have to restrain you for the walk, the rumours will already be bad enough."

She nodded, her face drained of all colour. "I understand. I will follow you without incident."

Sif's smile told her he wasn't enjoying this, not anymore. Now he acted more like a parent who had to reluctantly deal with a child they didn't really want to punish. The dispirited smile slipped from his face as he turned back to the corridor. Elise followed closely behind, not wanting to give them any reason to misinterpret her actions as anything other than compliance.

As the door closed behind his partner, a new whirlwind tore through her mind.

By the stars... This is it. I'm totally fucked.

* * *

"That's it?" Joseph Raffa looked deflated. "One railgun?"

Ikarus nodded and waved his hand in the direction of the ship bay despite nearly an entire station separating them. "The engineers tell me it's more like a mass accelerator."

"Great." Raffa exhaled and slumped into his chair. "And what of the shields?"

"I'm told they function 'as well as can be expected given the time available'."

"Sounds like engineer for 'It'll break when you most need it.'"

"That would be my assessment as well."

"Do we at least know something new about the freighter?"

"No, Sir." Ikarus pointed to the desk between them, the tabletop displaying a flat, spinning image of the incoming ship. "Command Core thinks that they've located weapon points, but we won't know for sure unless they start firing."

Raffa's eyes narrowed as he looked at the image. "Are they where we thought they'd be?"

"Yes. Your approach will not need altering. I also took the liberty of speaking with one of our visiting pilots."

"Oh?" Raffa raised an eyebrow. "About this?"

"I was most discreet."

"I hope so. What did our pilot friend have to say?"

"The weapons on the hatches are most likely for defence against boarders. His assessment was that any vessel like that would have the support of another close by, for defence and scouting." He pointed at the display again. "We haven't seen an escort, we looked. Command Core even applied what they knew about *Kobra*'s interference field to their scans. It is their assessment that the freighter is alone, and I would further speculate that it's defences will be minimal."

"We've got to be missing something." Raffa leant forward, resting his elbows on the table and his chin on his thumbs. "That's a big ship. People don't just give up investments like that."

"I also considered this."

Raffa noticed that Ikarus suddenly looked very tired.

"I believe," Ikarus continued, "and this is merely speculation, that this 'Region' of space, from Kandaha to Clion is becoming extremely dangerous to unprotected travellers. We spend too much of our time looking to the surface, preparing ourselves for the day when some faction or cult finally tries to claim Kau D'varza, but the threat is much larger than those small groups on Exiss." He lazily swept his arm toward the undecorated bulkhead behind Raffa, as if to draw attention to the many surrounding systems and their dangers. "Unless Kau D'varza meets some of these threats, you will be intercepting more than just drifting freighters."

Raffa studied him for a long moment before reclining in his seat. "We can't ignore the threats from the surface."

"I am not proposing a binary stance on the matter."

"*However*," Raffa continued, brushing off the interruption, "I would appreciate it if you compiled a report. Include your thoughts, and make sure it includes the most recent issues we've had to deal with."

Ikarus produced his data-pad and tapped a button,

forwarding an item to Raffa's desk. A notification popped up.

"I also went to considerable lengths to acquire data from neighbouring systems. Gaitlin were most forthcoming as they also share my concerns."

Raffa grinned. "How long have you been working on this?"

"About a mega-sek."

"I should have known. All without raising concern I hope?"

"I was most discreet."

"Alright, I'll review it when I get back and forward it to Commissioner Zeled." His eyes fell on the image of the freighter once more. "If I don't make it back, assume I agreed with your recommendations and get it to Zeled yourself."

"It is my sincerest hope that you return."

"No need to get all sentimental on me, Brook."

"It isn't that, Sir; merely the thought of having to deal with the Commissioner alone. It unsettles me."

Raffa's mouth curled into a smile. "You're more than a match for Zeled."

"Perhaps. Perhaps not. The Commissioner is... wise. Wiser than he lets on."

"Not sure I agree with that assessme-" The desk's comlink chirped. Kaska Stone appeared on the screen.

"Comcap Raffa. I am... *happy* to report that *Bo'a* is ready for your assigned 'training exercise'."

A glimmer of confusion crossed his face, then he nodded. "Of course, I understand. I will join Winters and the others immediately. Thank you, Specialist Stone."

* * *

Stone watched Raffa's image for signs of understanding, but apart from a slight frown, maybe bewilderment, his features remained impassive. He said he'd understood. She could only hope he had.

No other way to phrase it, though...

She realised she'd been staring at him when he asked, "Specialist Stone? Was there something else?"

She struggled for some appropriate words. "I... I wanted to wish you every success in your endeavour."

Raffa blinked. "Uh... alright, thank you, Specialist."

Stone hurried to cut the connection and felt her face flush.

Too tired...

After taking a moment to compose herself, she spun in her chair and stood up. Nevos was looking over another console as she approached.

"Arch-Commissioner, Comcap Raffa has been informed of the latest on *Bo'a* and is moving to join with the rest of his team before departing."

He straightened up, wearing a timid smile. "Then there is nothing else we can do but monitor the situation." He glanced around at the other tired, hopeful faces around him. "You can stand down. Have the day-cycle team take over. I'll brief those who need to know about the situation. I want the rest of you to get... hmm..." He glanced at the console again. "Twenty-Five k-seks of sleep. It's going to be a difficult few cycles so use the Krash-Beds if you have to. I need you at your best."

Stone felt a massive weight lifting from her shoulders. "Thank you, Sir."

Gierre looked as if he had just remembered something, nodded at her, then spoke to the room again. "I know this has been a stressful time, but you all performed exceptionally. Thank you."

CHAPTER FOUR-
ILLUSIONS

Despite the cramped conditions in the cell, Elise felt tiny as she stared at the floor, a vacant glaze in her eyes. Her thoughts had abandoned her, replaced by numbness. Goosebumps emerged across her skin as a breeze of just-clean-enough-to-be-legal air swept over her. She didn't feel it, nor did she smell the faint stench of recycling and the many people who had breathed it before her. Shadows flickered on the wall as a dim lamp swung in the draught. Ahead of her, barely an arm's length away, stood an oversized solid metal door with a hatch in it, meant to instill a sense of authority and the futility of trying to escape. Even the magnetic lock slamming into its housing didn't rouse her. However, the shout from the security specialist did.

"Citizen Rivera?"

She raised her head slowly, gazing into the silhouette surrounded by sterile white light. Her lip quivered as she nodded.

"We are still analysing your data-pad. It will take

some time. Meanwhile, would you like something to eat?"

She shook her head slowly.

"Citizen Rivera, I must insist."

The words caught in her throat. "Wha' do what you want?"

She hadn't meant to sound angry, though the specialist reacted with a sharp intake of breath. Elise could feel his displeasure, could almost sense his frown even though she couldn't see his face. He turned to someone or something in the corridor, then returned with a tray.

"You know how serious this is. You should eat while you can."

He knelt down, placing the tray beside her. He shook his head when she didn't move, then retreated into the corridor and closed the door behind him, leaving Elise alone in the dimly-lit cell once more.

* * *

"You think you should tell 'em the mission?"

Bo'a rattled as it broke away from the station and started on a low intercept with the freighter. Raffa pressed against the harness, hoping it would lift away, but it held firm, locking him in his seat.

"I want us to get farther away from the station. Right now, the citizens think this is nothing more than a training mission. If anyone hears what we're really doing, it'll cause panic."

"I wouldn't leave it too long," Winters replied. "Our boys and girls have to know what they're up against."

"And they will know. But right now, it isn't safe. I want us to be on that freighter, dealing with the problem before anyone on Kau D'varza knows what's up. That way, any rumors will be 'First and Second Squad are kicking ass', not 'Potential threat inbound.'"

"It wouldn't take a genius to see an incoming freighter."

Raffa grinned. "But that's all it is right now, isn't it?"

"Sir?"

"It doesn't look like anything other than standard system traffic from a neighbouring system. As far as they're aware, it's just some ship coming in to drop off supplies or refuel."

Understanding dawned on Winter's face. "Got it. Damn... we're lucky Command Core caught this."

"Finding threats to the station... that's their job."

"And it's our job to clear up the mess they find."

"Don't sound so disappointed. I can find you a nice job behind a desk somewhere if you'd prefer?"

"You know I wouldn't last the cycle," Winters said, smiling. "Besides, you need me. Getting too busy around here these days."

"Eh? You been talking to Ikarus?"

"Not since planning, why?"

Raffa moved to scratch his chin, was stopped short by the harness, and sighed. "He seems to share your concerns."

"Void Cloud's always attracted crazies, Comcap, but... I dunno. This is different, innit?"

"What's your assessment?"

"Ha, that's Ikarus' department. I'm just telling you what I'm seeing. Up to him to work it all out."

"And?" Raffa pressed.

"And what? You know as well as I do that between Beyema and the Void Cloud, there's been a lot of... *activity* recently."

"Ikarus seems to think if we don't deal with it, Kau D'varza could see a lot more incidents like this."

Winters blew the air out of his cheeks and pressed against his harness. "You know what that means; going to Beyema."

"You can't seriously blame the Reclaimers for everything we've seen recently?"

"Everything started happening when they moved in. Sure we had the occasional hit and run on the station, pirates, data-fiends... hey, you remember the hostile take-over those Pride assholes tried?"

"How could I forget?"

David Noe

"My point is, that was all routine shit. Stuff to be expected when you're running a seemingly defence-less station in a system full of cults and crazies. Then the Reclaimers move into Beyema and we start hear-ing about people going missing, ships disappearing... the crims in Gaitlin got nervous and came to Windan, started stirring up shit here instead."

"It's too simple." Raffa made a sweeping gesture. "There's more to it than that. The Reclaimers are easy to blame, we've made no efforts to contact them or engage with them in a meaningful way. Someone else might be doing all this, knowing they'd get the blame. It's too direct, especially for Reclaimers. You know they play the sides and pick up the remains."

"Regardless, they got no right to just float into Beyema and start operating without so much as a 'How do you do?'"

"I disagree. Beyema was never settled. Plenty had claims to it, but no-one had done anything with it."

"They say the Arabians were claiming it so they could justify war with Yor', if Yor' ever acted on their claim. Guess neither expected the Reclaimers to swoop in."

Raffa's eyes narrowed. "Same problem Kau D'varza's having. Too busy watching one thing, when we should be paying attention to everything else."

"That sounds like Ikarus talking. You've been spend-ing too much time with him." Winters bared his teeth in a wide grin. "He ain't wrong though."

"He rarely is."

A hiss sounded through the bay, followed by a series of clicks as people lifted their harnesses into position and stood up.

Raffa and Winters did the same, moving to the front of the immense space. Raffa scanned the dimly lit hold with pride in his eyes. Hundreds of men and women, all prepared for a fight. Lightly armoured; their faces a combination of determination, excitement and sweat.

"Kau D'varza First and Second Squads, your attention please."

The air in the hold was uncomfortably warm. Raffa felt his armour's cooling system rumble to life as silence descended and everyone turned to face him. He spoke clearly, and with an assured firmness.

"Forget what you think you know about this run."

That got several whispers that were quickly silenced.

"A few cycles ago, Command Core picked up a freighter, inbound to Kau D'varza. It isn't responding to our communications, isn't signalling any distress, and any time the station moves, it re-adjusts its course. We don't know where it came from, we don't know its intentions, we don't know a whole lot. Therefore it'll be up to us to board it, see if they're hostile, and if they're not, figure out what the problem is and guide them to the station in a safe manner."

He nodded to Winters, who took over.

"The way we're gonna be doing this is as follows: First and Second Scouts, head in opposite directions from the mechanics corridor access. Split at each crossroads, minimum team numbers of four. If you encounter people, have them surrender to you and direct them back to the Assault squads coming in behind. Assault squads, it'll be your job to secure the sections the Scouts have mapped out, and funnel the detained back to the Support squads." He took a deep breath before continuing. "Support squads, once Assault have fully secured a location, you'll be looking after it until we gain total control of the vessel. Our ultimate goal is to gain control, preferably via peaceful means, but if anyone shoots at you, you better shoot 'em back and make it count. Do I make myself clear?"

A chorus of 'Yes, Sir' filled the bay.

Raffa's earpiece chirped and he turned away to listen. After a few seconds he said, "On my way," and glanced at Winters. "We're approaching, scanners haven't seen any weapons at the expected points. I'm going up to talk to the pilots."

"I'll get everyone armed up."

As Raffa stepped off the ladder into the control center, he was struck by how cool it was. A light breeze rolled over the various consoles and controls centered around a large, empty chair.

"What's the problem?"

"No problem," one of the pilots replied quickly. "Our

first pass revealed no weapons and they're not evading, even though our intercept should have been clear a kilosek ago. We're coming round for our docking run now."

"What's that tell you?"

"If I were to guess? No-one's home. Ship's running on auto, low-defence mode. Waiting for someone to find it."

"Waiting for someone…" He grimaced. "Could this be a trap?"

"I… er… I wouldn't want to speculate, Sir."

"If it were a trap, what sort of trap would it be?"

The pilot glanced uncertainly at his companion. "Ship that size? We're not getting any life readings on the scanners, but you know how easy they are to fool." He pointed to the screen as a data sheet on the freighter appeared. "Best guess, if there really is no one onboard… power generator overload. Probably rigged to drop all fail-safes when your people trip a scanner."

"How long would it take to blow?"

"Eh… half a kilosek?"

"That doesn't leave a lot of time."

"Like I said, I didn't want to speculate, and that's all this is. We've got no indications this is anything other than an abandoned ship drifting through space on auto."

Raffa turned back to the ladder. "I hope you're right," he muttered under his breath, annoyed at himself for not seeing the potential problem earlier.

* * *

Kaska Stone sighed in exasperation and closed her eyes. Her data pad had been constantly chiming and buzzing for a while, disturbing her attempts to sleep, but then it had stopped. Now, just as she had dared to think she had succeeded in convincing the caller to leave her alone, the device chimed again, alerting her to an incoming communication.

Eyes still closed, she stretched her arms forward, bringing one down on the pad. "Stone."

"Specialist Stone."

Nevos.

"I apologise for cutting your rest short. However, I am facing some issues and would like your input."

She rubbed her eyes and sat up. After taking a few seconds to tidy her hair and make herself moderately presentable, she picked up the pad and blinked at the disheveled video of Nevos.

"With respect, Sir, you look... in need of rest."

"Your concerns are noted, Specialist, however I have neither the luxury of time nor the ability to... *rest.*"

"How can I help?" All irritation had faded, replaced by her usual professionalism.

"Command Core is unable to contact Comcap Raffa or any of his team. According to our observations, they had completed their first sweep and were circling back to board, but that happened a while ago and we haven't seen any updates since. It's as though the feed has paused."

The delay is understandable, but…

"Paused?"

"A static image. Neither ship has made any maneuvers."

"Have…" Kaska strained, searching for names. "Who's on duty?"

"I've got Lime, Echido and Seira with me at Command."

"Put Echido on. I think I know what's happened."

There was a rustle as Gierre passed his pad to Echido. As he did, Kaska climbed out of the Krash-bed and straightened her uniform. The room she was standing in held about twenty other beds, all arranged in rows and stacked two high on either side. All were occupied by people seeking an induced sleep: insomniacs, those who had to work again in a short while, anyone amped up on some stimulant or another looking for a quick come down… As she wandered between them towards the exit, her pad chirped again.

"Echido here. What's the go, Stone?"

"Have you tried viewing the freighter using an interference sweep?"

"What, you mean the *Kobra* protocols?"

Kobra was Kau D'varza's stealth cruiser, although stealth was something of a misnomer in this instance. Instead it relied heavily on fooling other scanners into thinking something else was happening, or that *Kobra* was somewhere else. Thanks to the development and study of such a vessel, Kau D'varza was better equipped to deal with similar threats from outside. Why such countermeasures might be present on a freighter was beyond Stone's current reasoning abilities.

"You know how to set it up?" Stone replied.

"Uh, sure. Just one sek'... and... done."

"Run it. But make sure you set the scan area to where you expect the freighter to be, not where it was."

Forgetting something?

"Oh. And take into account the time difference! The closer it gets, the nearer to real-time it is. Less delay in what's happening and what you're seeing. Calculate for that when you adjust your sweep area."

"Right."

Kaska stepped into the employee elevator to the Command Core, waiting on Echido to reply. Her impatience finally got the better of her.

"Well?"

"We're picking up... something."

"Is it *Bo'a* and the freighter, or something else?"

"Standby, Stone. Incoming message."

The doors opened on the Command Core. Kaska hurried to a vacant console and got to work.

"*... Mission successful. However, there is a fault with stealth system.*"

"That's Comcap Teq!" Echido seemed pleased he'd been able to help in at least some capacity.

"*Engineers suggest hardware as the cause. Have tried disabling system, however hardwire protocols and safety mechanisms are preventing such an action. Am returning to Kau D'varza for immediate repairs and to report on our mission. Comcap Teq, outsign.*"

"Specialist Stone," Gierre said, in a heavy voice. "Are we to assume that until Comcap Teq brings *Kobra* in and shuts it down, we are blind to the system around us?"

She pulled a control pad out from under the console. Her fingers danced over it and the touch screen in a blurred flurry.

"Not if I've got anything to say about it, Sir."

Echido slid up beside her and scanned her work. "What are you..."

"If we apply the interference sweep on an area around the station, we'll get limited visibility of the stuff closest to us. We can then boost the scanners to maximum to push the range. It'll still be limited, but we should be able to see the freighter and *Bo'a*."

"What about *Kobra*?"

"Hmm…" Her eyes narrowed, but her fingers continued their dance. "The interference will get worse the closer they get. There's not much we can do about that."

Apart from dump that damn engineer out an airlock! This is practically sabotage!

Any anger she felt towards the incapable repair bay overseer would have to wait. A bead of sweat rolled down her cheek as she glanced up at the main-screen.

"Close range scanners online, visibility limited to immediate locale." She slid her finger up a bar at the side of the screen. "Increasing power input."

A virtual bubble grew outwards from the representation of Kau D'varza on the screen. Eventually it grew so large that the view pulled out to show it all. Several blips appeared on the edge.

"Regular system traffic," she said quietly, continuing to slide her finger up the screen.

"What are they doing?" Echido asked.

"If they've got any sense, they're staying still. Stars only know what they're seeing right now."

"There!" Gierre stood from his chair in a single, sudden motion and locked eyes on the two dots that had appeared on top of one another.

Stone nodded. "Ident. It's *Bo'a*. She's docked."

"Excellent work!"

"Thank you, Sir."

Gierre motioned her over as he settled into his seat again. "I would hesitate to bring it up, but since you're here... No. I should let you return to your rest."

"Oh, don't worry about that, Sir. I wouldn't be able to sleep again anyway. How may I be of service?"

The Arch-Commissioner looked at her thoughtfully for a moment. "Well, if you're sure..."

She nodded. "I am."

"Then in that case I have another issue that requires your... special skills."

"Field work, Sir?"

"In a manner of speaking."

CHAPTER FIVE- ASSAULT

The airlock slid open without resistance and the Technician stood back, watching as the Scouts rushed in, standard issue Kau D'varza pulse rifles at the ready. They wouldn't damage the ship unless fired at electrical systems, although the downside was it would take several shots to 'peacefully' incapacitate a living target - especially one in armour.

Takk Winters led the second wave, the fast assault team following after the Scouts.

As Raffa stepped forward, he noticed the freighter was about as budget as they came. Flimsy panels covered precious systems, if they remained in place at all, while the grated flooring had the maximum size holes it could get away with and still be called a floor.

The tactical feed on the inside of his helmet's visor showed the Scout teams rushing through the vessel. For the most part it looked as though they were just running down corridors and splitting up any time they came to a junction.

As Raffa called back to the Support squad, he noticed the scouts had slowed considerably. It looked from their movements as though they were clearing rooms.

The Assault teams caught up, and an alert chimed at the corner of his vision.

"Raffa."

"Winters here."

"Go ahead." He waved the Support teams forward. Formed into two orderly lines, they descended into the freighter side by side, rushing to meet up with their comrades.

"We're not seeing any resistance."

"What about traps?"

"If it follows standard layout - and from what I've seen, it does - the Scouts should be reaching engineering in a few seks."

"Alright, stay alert and call me the sekund you find anything."

"I have a feeling you're gonna be waiting a while."

"For once, that's no bad thing."

His focus switched back to the task at hand. He led one group down several corridors and joined up with the Assault team that looked in the most need.

"Report," he demanded, drawing up with a small

group on guard at one of the cross-paths.

"All quiet here, Sir. No resistance."

"How do you feel about that?"

The soldier shook his head. "It's too easy. Feels like a trap."

Raffa nodded in agreement. "Stay alert, be ready to fall back if I give the command."

"Won't let you down, Sir."

"Never had any doubts."

He waved the Support team on, and once again they met up with the next group further down the corridor. Then another, pressing ever deeper into the vessel as the Scouts continued, followed by the Assault squad, and then finally the Support teams.

"Second Squad, Scout Tyra, reporting control of the command center."

As though not wanting to be outdone, another alert came in hot on the tail of the last.

"First Squad, Scout Alenki, engineering secured."

"Winters here, final sweep of cargo bay reveals no threats."

"Alright," Raffa replied. "Alenki, you got anything unusual where you are?"

"No, Sir. Scout-scanner shows no traps, listening devices, nothing that shouldn't be here."

"Have the support team check over the systems."

"Of course, Sir."

"Tyra?"

"Right here, Sir."

"How's it look?"

"Empty."

"Empty?"

"There's nothing here. No command crew, no automated defences. It's like whoever was here just got up and walked out the airlock."

Raffa suppressed a shudder at the idea. "Do you know why it's going to Kau D'varza?"

"The Techs... uh... Support team is looking into it now. They're not sure how it managed to Transit without a crew, but according to them it's locked on to the station's welcome signal. We were practically advertising that Kau D'varza is capable of providing aid and assistance to damaged or in-need vessels and their crews. Best guess is a failsafe kicked in as soon as the ship realised it had no crew, taking it to the nearest point of aid."

"Can you bring it into dock?"

"They're working on it, Sir."

"Good job. Alright, carry on." He glanced to the image of Winters at the bottom of his visor.

"Did you get all that?"

"Yeah. Makes sense I guess. Apart from the Transit bit. Do freighters have that ability?"

"This one seems to."

"So what's the plan now?"

"Run another sweep of the ship, I want this entire thing scrubbed from top to bottom."

"We'll get it done."

"Once you do, have First Squad return to *Bo'a*. I'll keep Second here to guide this tub back to the station."

Winters drew breath to reply but was cut short by a notification from Tyra.

"Sir, there's a problem."

"Do you have to be so ominous? What is it?"

"The systems... The Techs say... Yeah, that's what I'm trying to tell him if you'd give me a sek!"

"Tyra, report."

"Yes, sorry, Sir. It's the navigation system. We can't see anything."

"What do you mean, 'you can't see anything?'"

"It's like... er, the tech here keeps telling me to say 'Interference field?'"

"The freighter has a stealth system?"

"Er... no, Sir. It's being affected by one."

Raffa felt a knot tighten in his stomach. "Winters, I want First squad covering all points of access to the ship. Tyra, have the technicians lock the external entry points."

Another call, this time to the pilots of *Bo'a*. "Clear yourselves to undock and return to Kau D'varza immediately."

"No can do, Com'."

"Navigation systems gone wonky?"

"How did you guess? We're blind out here. Protocol states we stay where we are until the problem passes."

"There's no way to get back to the station?"

"Well... there is one way."

"But it goes against protocol, and as we all know, pilots just hate breaking rules."

"I'm offended at the suggestion, Sir."

"File a complaint." Raffa sighed. "What's this solution?"

"Solution might be putting it on a bit strong. We can get *Bo'a* back, but unless you've got a skilled pilot who can fly manual on that behemoth, your best option is to sit and wait."

"What if this is some kind of trap?"

"Then you won't be waiting very long."

"Can you guide us into range of the station's defences?" Raffa asked, ignoring the comment.

"Well... I guess so, but if the station is also being affected, they might not be able to see any targets."

"It's the best we've got. Clear for undock, patch into Scout Tyra of Second Squad and get her to put you on to their best pilot."

"Would you like a drink too? Maybe I can sweep down the passenger hold?"

Raffa ground his teeth. "Just get it done."

CHAPTER SIX-
BLINDSIDED

"Accessing confidential folders. Application of malicious software. Attempted bypass of cyber-security..."

Specialist Sif Raizen's monotone droned on as he read out the list of Kau D'varza's charges against Elise. She sat on the opposite side of the table, staring through it with unfocused eyes and slumped shoulders.

He finished the list and glanced up from his pad. "Citizen Rivera, these are serious charges. The sort we reserve for spies and saboteurs. Are you either of those things?"

She considered her answer, huffed a short breath and allowed her eyes to drift upward to Sif. "No."

He frowned. "Then what possible reason could you have for seeding our systems with bugs?"

"Access."

"To gain information?"

Elise exhaled and straightened up in the seat. "I had no intention of compromising the station. I live here too."

"That doesn't mean anything." He pointed at her with his free hand. "That information is secret for a reason. Our security network functions better when it isn't full of glitches, and we've got better things to do than chase malware. You might not have wanted to *compromise* Kau D'varza, but you did, however indirectly."

A flicker of realisation struck her. "I... I'm sorry. That was not my intention."

"What was your intention? To take the information and sell it?"

"No."

"Have you got anything to do with the malicious software currently affecting our ships' Transit systems?"

"No."

Sif seemed to get more annoyed with every question while Elise sat, staring dispassionately through him, answering in barely a whisper.

"You've seen my travel details?"

He nodded. "You came from Yurnto a while back."

"I did. Specifically, Paradise."

"What has this got to do with Kau D'varza?"

"The reason I'm here... I left Paradise to start a new

life. I was a systems technician but it bored me to tears." She bared her teeth in the first sign of anger since being arrested. "The *Free Paradise Movement...*" She nearly spat the words, "didn't look like it was going anywhere, so it was either them, or me."

"What has this got to do with Kau D'varza?" Sif repeated.

Her eyes narrowed, focusing on him. "I took off on a transport heading to the Void Cloud. Jumped off at Kau D'varza. Wanted to put my life behind me, sought out new work. Something different."

"You took up data-mining?"

Her lips twisted. "Not... no. It could be viewed that way I suppose, but I wasn't looking for information to sell to some shady enemy of the station." She made a sweeping motion of the world outside the interrogation room. "The Office of Public Relations does a terrible job of keeping people informed. They leave it up to rumours and whispers before sharing the official story. That's not how the citizens should be kept up-to-date with the goings on of their home."

"So you took matters into your own hands. To what? Share 'the truth' with people?"

She nodded.

"Did it ever occur to you that such information *should* be kept from people until it's been scrubbed of falsehoods?"

"I..."

"And further, if you believe, Citizen Rivera, that the rules aboard this station are incorrect, you can petition the Councils and their Commissioners to have them changed if enough people agree with you. I feel that, as you were unable to acquire this support, you took matters into your own hands." He raised an eyebrow. "In fact, you didn't even attempt to change the rules; you just dove straight in and broke them."

Elise shook her head. "I went about it the wrong way. But once people had seen an alternative to the O.P.R. I would have got that support."

"By sharing confidential, dirty-files with any and all who come to the station? Do you have any idea what sort of security risk that would cause?"

"I wasn't hoping to share missile launch codes! Just the interesting, recent-"

"But it's all on the same network. Let's say you're snooping around the Security network for... 'News', and you accidently trigger something. It could be a disaster, whether you *meant it* or not."

"I-"

"Further, what right do you have to decide what to share and what to keep secure?"

"It's-"

"A citizen with that much access would be extremely dangerous, and easy for our enemies to flip." He raised his hand to prevent Elise from interrupting a third time. "I will have to review this new information.

You will be returned to your cell."

Elise slammed her fist down on the desk. "If you're going to charge me, charge me. You've already made up your mind despite my intentions."

"The end did not justify the means. Regardless of intentions, this is a security threat. We can't just charge you and ignore it without fixing the root problem."

She slumped back in the chair, deflated. "Do what you want."

Sif studied her for a moment, then asked, "Would you want the station to know about this? About you being arrested?"

She didn't answer. Sif sighed, stood, and motioned for Elise to follow him back to her cell.

* * *

Gaining access to the security offices had been the easy bit. Most people knew Kaska Stone, and if they didn't, her uniform told them immediately that she worked directly for the Arch-Commissioner. It allowed her a great deal of freedom, going from office to office, planting little pieces of information. An entry in a computer here, an edit to some of the logs there, some falsified conversations... She projected a confidence that said 'I should be here. You would be unwise to challenge that.' It wasn't a role Stone took often, but when she did, she was a master.

The difficult part came when she tried leaving.

"Ah! Specialist Stone," Zeled said, his face displaying a wide grin but suspicious eyes. "To what do we owe the pleasure?"

"Good cycle, Commissioner." She presented him with her pad and frowned. "Arch-Commissioner Nevos has personally asked me to investigate the potential of a leak within the security forces."

Zeled's grin faded. "In the security forces?" he asked, in a hushed tone. He scanned the screen. "These are some… serious accusations, Specialist."

"Indeed. Which is why I was unable to inform you of my visit."

Oh… Too easy.

"We also believe that some elements of this station are… unknowingly sabotaging our vessels."

"Sabotage?" He couldn't help but raise his voice. "Against Kau D'varza?"

"That's what I'm trying to find out."

Divert the conversation now. Don't be obvious.

"I assume you've heard what happened to *Kobra*? We think it's all related."

Zeled's eyes darkened. "*Kobra*?"

"Yes," she replied. "The interference countermeasures are affecting any ship or scanner they can reach. Comcap Teq's engineers seem to believe the problem is a hardware fault."

"A shoddy repair?"

"Possibly, but we don't know whether it's deliberate or not, and if it is deliberate, whether they're working alone. In any event, any unusual communication would have been detected by Security."

"And since you haven't seen any reports confirming that..."

"The Arch-Commissioner and I concluded there may be some kind of agent covering their own or someone else's tracks, or leaking just the right information at the right time, or altering the repair manuals so that the engineers aboard Kau D'varza think they're doing everything right. *Kobra*'s systems are not common. The engineers need all the help they can get."

"You don't need to tell me about the difficulties of *our* ships, Specialist Stone. It is hard to project force when the Transit Cores only take us to the default waypoints!"

Good, he's angry, not paying attention.

"I apologise, Sir. I'm so used to interacting with the other groups, they like it when things are spelled out."

He replied through clenched teeth. "Did you find anything?"

"I will have to compile my report and seek Arch-Commissioner Nevos' advice on some of the things I have learnt. You will have that report shortly, Commissioner."

"See to it that I do." He turned to continue on to

the main doors. "Specialist Stone," he said, his voice adopting a cold edge.

"Sir?"

"I would appreciate a *warning* next time."

What are you getting at?

"I will ensure the Arch-Commissioner is aware of your wishes, Sir."

"It is not Nevos I am worried about, Specialist."

Kaska hurried back out to the street and boarded a personal transport back to the safety of Core Command.

Upon arrival, Gierre fixed her with a nervous stare. "I just had a very interesting conversation with Zeled."

"As did I." Kaska shook her head. "He knows I'm up to something, Sir."

"I got that impression."

"It will take him a while to figure it out. By that time-"

"You agreed with my assessment."

"There was truth in your logic, Sir. However, that does not absolve us of risk."

Gierre nodded, took a deep breath and reluctantly stepped out of his chair. "I believe it is time for my part in this little act."

"I should warn you, Commissioner Zeled is not in the best of moods."

"If I didn't know any better, Specialist Stone, one might assume you enjoy upsetting our friend."

Her mouth curled upwards and she raised her hands, feigning ignorance. "Sir, I'm sure I don't know what you mean."

He returned the smile. "I'm sure you don't, Specialist Stone, I'm sure you don't."

"I'll keep an eye on the *Bo'a* situation." She offered him a hopeful smile. "Good luck, Sir."

* * *

"And I said point four, what are you? Drunk or something?"

"That's enough, pilot," Raffa said, as he rotated his shoulders as best he could under the heavy armour. He'd taken position at the rear of the command centre while the specialists from Second Squad followed, or tried to follow, the instructions coming in from the pilots on *Bo'a*. Winters stood beside him, shaking his head.

"Flyboys are assholes," he said in hushed tones.

"Eh, they're under a lot of stress."

"Because taking a freighter is such an easy job."

"And they're probably not used to flying under these conditions." Raffa glanced towards the comm-specialist. "We had any luck contacting Kau D'varza yet?"

The operator returned a grim frown. "Sorry, no. Sir."

Raffa sat back, rubbing his chin. "What is going on?"

"What would Ikarus tell you to do?" Winters asked, a hint of sarcasm in his voice.

"Analyse the facts."

"And what are 'the facts'?"

Raffa sighed. "We're on a freighter, approaching where we assume Kau D'varza is."

"Right."

"Diagnostics have shown that every system on this vessel should work as expected."

"True."

"However, the scanners are not functioning as expected."

"They are not."

"The technicians therefore believe that the problem is external."

"And I would agree with their expertise."

"So what do we know of in local space with the ability to interfe-" Raffa blinked. "*Kobra*?"

"If Teq is back from the Gaitlin mission, then it's possible."

Raffa frowned. "But why would he be targeting *Bo'a* and the freighter? We're obviously together."

Winters grinned. "Unless Teq's planning a coup."

"If he is, he sure kept it quiet. Teq's the most loyal

out of all of us. If he's flipped, that was a long game he played." Raffa's forehead wrinkled into a deep frown.

"So," Winters said, "what other reason would result in us being targeted by *Kobra*, or a *Kobra*-like interference system?"

"Someone else has got a stealth system?"

"Not unheard of, but unlikely. Although…" Winters inhaled and shook his head. "Would Reclaimers use tech like that?"

"I wouldn't put it beyond them, but why would they come here?"

"Maybe it's their freighter?"

Raffa made a fist with his free hand. "This is stupid. Kau D'varza might need us. We're blind here and we've got no clue what's going on. Has anyone got any suggestions? I don't care how dumb or illegal they are, we need to dock with Kau D'varza and we need it done yestercycle."

The radio crackled. "We're holding position relative to the freighter because it's all we can see. Our mass scanners are going haywire. If you start moving though, we're staying put. No offence, but your pilots are shit."

Raffa exhaled. "If your situation changes, update us."

Winters shook his head.

"Something the matter?"

"Why are we still talking to them?"

"Because they're our only other chance of getting back to the station if this interference doesn't clear up soon."

"No, I mean, Uh... how?"

"How are we still talking to them?"

A shuffle at the front of the command center caught their attention. "Distance, Sir. *Bo'a* is extremely close in the grand scheme of things. Our connection to them is mostly uninterrupted."

"Can we use that?"

The tech shook his head. "*Bo'a* is-"

Another excited movement. "Hold that thought." Scout Tyra had made her way over and was examining the screen belonging to the technician.

"What's the range on that?"

"Uninterrupted?" He frowned. "Short-range only. I couldn't give you an exact distance."

"Can *Bo'a* use that to communicate with the station if they're in range?"

"In theory. But space is *really* big. Getting within range of the station would take some skill, an extraordinary amount of luck, and a little guesswork."

"But without the scanner, that's our best shot at interacting with Kau D'varza?"

"Hey," The radio crackled. "We've got a pretty good

idea where the station should be, we just can't see it. If you've got some cunning plan to get back in communication with them, let's hear it."

Tyra glanced back to Raffa, who in turn glanced to Winters.

"Don't look at me, I'm just here for moral support."

Raffa rolled his eyes, then turned back to Tyra. "Set it up."

CHAPTER SEVEN- PANIC STATIONS

Not knowing when her next interrogation would be, Elise had laid down on the cell's thin rubber mattress in a vain attempt to sleep. Tears stuck her face to the easy-to-wipe material and clumps of hair rubbed against her skin, but despite the discomfort Elise remained still and quiet, her eyes closed.

You're an idiot. What were you thinking? You had a home here. Had potential employment. You could have made something of yourself. You wanted more. You always want more. You're not special, Elise. The universe doesn't revolve around you. And it doesn't need any more journalists. It needs people willing to wake up early, do a solid cycle of work. Proper work. Didn't want that. And look where it's got you. Now this one mistake... you've ruined your life here before it even got properly started. They think you're a spy. An enemy agent. You're lucky this isn't Heradim. Lucky? You might not be executed, but you'll be dumped in a cell somewhere. Forgotten. The only mark you'll leave on this universe is in the records of some justice centre. Well done. You're an idiot. What were you thinking?

She must have dozed off, because the next thing Elise remembered was being shaken awake.

"Citizen Rivera?"

She blinked, and focused on Sif kneeling over her. He stood up as she yawned.

"Uhh...?"

"Please, come with me."

She sat up and scanned the cell briefly. Sif held out a hand to help her up, but she brushed it aside and pulled herself up along the wall. As she stood to full height, she took a second to compose herself, pulling her hair out of her eyes and wiping her face.

Sif motioned for her to step into the corridor. She raised an arm to block out the intense white light. She had no doubt it was set at such uncomfortable levels to disorient prisoners.

She was led down a series of walkways, doors spaced perfectly apart lined both sides. Eventually, just as Elise's eyes were adjusting, Sif stopped at one of the doors and glanced back at her. He looked as if he wanted to say something, then paused, shook his head, and pushed the door open.

As Elise stepped into the interrogation room, her eyes were immediately drawn to the figure on the opposite side of the desk. Her blood ran cold in an instant.

"C-Commissioner Z-Zeled."

His eyes met hers. The coldness of his gaze chilled her to the bone.

"Sit down. *Citizen*."

* * *

"The closer *Kobra* gets, the less we can see."

Kaska turned from her console and saw Echido help-lessly waving his hands.

"What are we supposed to do?"

"Specialist Echido, I would appreciate it if you could remain calm."

"With respect, Specialist Stone, it's madness out there! We've got time-sensitive cargo-haulers, incom-ing freighters, several small passenger ships, and none of them can see us - or one another - unless they're nearly on top of us."

"Are you done?"

"And *Bo'a*, *Kobra* and *Mambaka* are all out there some-where too!"

Kaska counted to five in her head and took a deep breath. "Specialist Lime, call engineering and have them squeeze everything they can into the stations scanning equipment. Specialist Seira, setup a pulse beacon warning everyone to stay put. Let them know that the interference is affecting us as well and we're working to resolve it as quickly as possible."

There were no affirmative noises, just work.

"Specialist Echido," she said, "I need you to watch that screen and tell me the second you see anything enter the scanner bubble. You need to tell me *immediately*, Specialist Echido. Do I make myself clear?"

He wavered, then nodded. "For Kau D'varza."

Kaska offered him an encouraging grin. "For Kau D'varza."

Echido turned back to his screen, his eyes widening at what awaited him "Surface Hauler *N-Wich* is approaching from sector fourteen!"

The console screen flared to life under Kaska's fingertips. She located the *N-Wich*, cleared her throat, and tapped the open communication channels.

"Kau D'varza station to Exiss Surface Vessel, *N-Wich*. Please reduce velocity and report your status."

A video popped up in the top corner of her screen, revealing a haggard looking pilot with sunken eyes. "*N-Wich* receives, Kau D'varza. Status green. Is there a problem?" he asked, in a soft voice.

"You're not suffering from scanner malfunctions?"

"Uh, no, Ma'am."

She turned to Echido. "Get me a status report on the other ships we can contact and find out if this is clearing up." He nodded as she focused back on the pilot. "*N-Wich*, be advised all vessels in proximity to vessel

Kobra are experiencing interference issues."

"Not here, Ma'am... although not surprising. *N-Wich*... she isn't a new ship. I suppose she isn't even an old ship. Ancient would be appropriate."

"Please explain."

He took a deep breath and made a motion with his free hand to the rest of the ship. "Old systems... Ping Feedback. *N-Wich* sends out a... pulse, I guess you could call it. Then when that pulse hits something, the system picks up that obstacle and feeds the data into the ship's systems."

"Kau D'varza's system uses the same technology."

He nodded. "Yeah, but it's advanced, right? Instead of just saying 'Oh there's an obstacle here', your system tries to interact with it, analyse it. We just fly between the surface and Kau D'varza; the most we gotta do is avoid crap pilots, talk to you or the surface, and stick to the timetable. Our scanners are more than capable of their little task."

Kaska brushed her hair back. "Do you think we could mimic those settings?"

"Dummy the system?" The pilot frowned. "It's possible. I don't know what software you're running, but if you can turn off all the interaction and just have it report on obstructions instead..."

A smile crept across her face. "Thank you, *N-Wich*, I'll transfer you to Flight Control."

"Appreciated, Kau D'varza. *N-Wich*, outsign."

She forwarded the connection, then tried contacting Gierre. No answer. Kaska bit her lip, inhaled sharply through her nose, and brought up the stations scanner controls. It took her several seconds to reach the top of the list where she found the preset for 'Dumb System'. She considered trying to contact Nevos once more, then shook her head and hit the button.

Kaska held her breath as the consoles in the Command Core flickered and died before coming back to life amid a flurry of warnings and alerts.

"Report!" Kaska demanded.

"A moment…" Echido rushed to make sense of the data. Adjusting view angles and zoom distances. "I've got a view of local traffic, but I couldn't tell you what any of it is. But at least now we can *see* it!"

"Alright, now see-"

A notification popped up on her screen, she felt a tug in her gut as she thought Gierre was calling to tell her she'd made a mistake, but it wasn't his image that appeared when she answered.

"Freighter calling Kau D'varza. Comcap Raffa reporting."

Kaska exhaled, feeling a weight she didn't know she'd been carrying disappear.

"Comcap Raffa, Kau D'varza receives. It is good to hear from you."

"Specialist Stone?" He grinned. "Good to hear from

you, too." He straightened up. "What's going on? Why is everything going haywire?"

"Hardware fault on *Kobra*. We're dealing with it as best we can."

"Can you dock us? The pilots on *Bo'a* don't seem to be enjoying our company."

"You gained control of the freighter then? What did the crew have to say?"

"There was no crew, at least not when we got here."

She frowned. "That is... unusual, Comcap Raffa."

"I had my suspicions, but it's always good to have them confirmed."

"As for docking... We can't bring you inside until our equipment is fully operational again, it's too big."

"Wait till you see it up close."

"Airlock A-Seven is the only area you can dock a ship that size."

His expression darkened. "External docking..." He rubbed his forehead. "Will we have some assistance from the station?"

"As much as we can provide. However, Comcap Raffa, that is not a lot in our current situation."

"What's the alternative?"

"Wait until *Kobra* returns and we can shut her down. But there are issues. You'll be waiting at least half a cycle until it arrives, and during that time, both you and *Bo'a* will be sitting targets. And the closer *Kobra* gets, the worse the problem becomes."

"Stuck on a ship with two-hundred jumpy soldiers and no real defence?"

"I'm not going to order you do this, but there are certainly risks involved if you don't. I'll leave you to consider your options. Let me know what you want to do. Kau D'varza, outsign."

* * *

Raffa stared at the empty space where Specialist Stone's face had been seconds before. "Well, okay then."

Winters lowered his head. "I knew a girl once."

"Just the once?"

Winters glanced over and fixed him with a stare. "You wanna hear this or not?"

Raffa raised his hands. "Go ahead."

"We were best mates, two soldiers coming up in the same unit, always had each other's backs. I had some pretty strong feelings about her, but never did nothing about it. Too scared, worried about rejection, ruining the friendship, whatever. Then one day, I find out she's dating this asshole from another squad. When she gets to asking me why I'm so pissed off, I tell her how I feel, and to my horror, find out she felt the same way."

"Why 'to your horror'?"

"Because by this time she was pregnant. I'd missed my chance." Winters looked thoughtful for a moment, then waved towards the image of Kau D'varza. "Look, the point is this. You either take the risk now and see what coulda been, or you wait and let the universe pass you by, and punish you for the inaction. It's your call."

"Couldn't you have just said, 'I think you should try docking to the station'?"

"It wouldn't have had the same effect. Besides, you're cheaper than the station head-doc."

Raffa shook his head, then turned his attention to the rest of the command centre. "Now you know where Kau D'varza is, how easy would it be for you to hit that airlock?"

"Er..." The pilot shrugged. "Well, it gets easier the closer we get... In terms of visibility anyway."

"Can you do it?"

"We're trained... we'd appreciate help from *Bo'a*, though."

Raffa felt another headache coming on. "Damnit... alright, put me through."

CHAPTER EIGHT- RESOLUTION

"We don't believe your... *story*, Citizen."

He's just trying to intimidate you.

Elise straightened up and stared directly into Zeled's eyes. Any fear she might have felt had been replaced with anger.

Nothing to lose. This is rock bottom.

"That's your hard luck."

"I beg your pardon?"

"You heard me." Elise pointed at him. "It doesn't matter what I tell you. You won't listen."

"We're offering you a way out. Given the circumstances, I'd say that was quite generous of us." He returned the stare, adding an edge of his own. "Tell us who sent you."

"Nobody *sent* me! You... you asswit! I just wanted some information and went about it the wrong way. I'm not a spy, not an enemy agent! I'm Elise Rivera, damnit!"

Zeled relaxed.

He's changing tactics.

"Okay, *Elise,* okay."

"I'll accept Citizen or Miss Rivera. Only friends call me Elise."

"Do you have many friends, *Miss Rivera?*"

"Enough."

"And what would they think about all this? Sneaking around confidential files and getting yourself arrested?"

"What my friends think is none of your concern."

"You'd like to see them again though, wouldn't you?"

"If you're trying to blackmail me, guilt-trip me into telling you what you wanna hear, you're gonna be here a long time." She leant forward, baring her teeth. "I am *not* a *fucking* spy."

"What did you intend on doing with the information?"

"I already told your other lackey."

"I wanna hear it from your mouth."

"Tough shit."

"Fancy yourself as a bit of a rough, Citizen? Grew up in Paradise, Yurnto system, correct?"

"Moving onto my home now, eh?"

"So you don't consider Kau D'varza your home? Interesting."

"I won't play your games, Zeled."

"I just find it interesting. No-one on this station would dare talk to me like that, and yet here you are, sat across from me, undergoing interrogation, and you're acting like you've got nothing to lose." He leant forward. "Well you're wrong. You've got everything to lose. So I recommend you start showing me the respect I deserve as Defence Commissioner, and start explaining exactly what it is you planned to do."

Elise drew breath to reply, another combative comment primed and ready to go. Zeled's attention turned to the door as it slid open, his eyes widening with a depth of fury that she hadn't seen before.

"I am conducting an inter-"

"That's quite alright, Commissioner."

"No, *Arch-Commissioner,* it is not."

Elise couldn't be sure, but it looked as though Gierre was giving her a sideways smile.

"It seems as though you have found yourself in a spot of trouble, Citizen."

"I-"

He raised his hand and turned back to Zeled. "You will release Citizen Rivera without further delay."

"I bloody won't!" Zeled snapped back.

"I'm afraid you don't have much say in this matter, Commissioner. Citizen Rivera is under direct orders from me to test and probe our network's defences. Of course, I couldn't tell you about such an operation; we needed to test the non-alert state." He grinned. "And I must say, your specialists performed excellently."

What the fuck?

"You can't seriously expect me to believe this, Nevos."

"I don't need you to believe me. Look at her work contracts: Unspecified technical work directly for the council."

"That's-"

"Furthermore," Gierre continued, "if you analyse the visitors' log to the observation lounge, you will see that I met directly with Citizen Rivera only recently to hear of her progress."

"This is..." Zeled sounded defeated now.

Elise tried to fight down the terrified excitement she felt.

Why is he doing this? Why is the Arch-commissioner helping me?

Gierre spoke with immense confidence now. "I would further implore you to check your logs regarding Citizen Rivera more thoroughly."

"Enough!" Zeled raised his hands. "Your little rat,

Stone, she was snooping around here earlier. No doubt planting this so-called *'evidence'*!"

"Commissioner Zeled, if you ever refer to Specialist Stone as anything other than her proper title again, I will see to it that your position suddenly becomes very untenable. Do I make myself clear?"

"Go to the Void, Nevos. This woman is a threat to Kau D'varza, and having you undercut me like this makes the entire station look weak."

"The station will see that you intercepted the threat, proving your anti-intrusion specialists are more than skilled with the station's defence. This will make you look extremely good, Commissioner. People will feel confident in trusting you."

"I-"

"The matter is settled then." Gierre smiled. "I thank you for seeing sense in this... *unusual...* situation, Commissioner. Had we not been dealing with the incoming freighter, I may have been able to inform you personally of my plans."

"Raffa," Zeled replied with a scowl. "Fine. Take your *pet*, Nevos. I have bigger concerns."

"Ah, yes. Comcap Raffa. If he successfully completes this mission, I'd like him sent to me for personal congratulations. There will also be a celebration to honour his success. Please let me know as soon as you hear from him."

All colour had drained from Zeled's face. He sunk his

head into his palms as he spoke to Elise. "Get out."

She didn't need telling twice, jumping up quickly enough to knock the chair over and darting through the door before she could be asked to pick it up.

Gierre followed behind, sealing the room behind him. "I believe we should give him some time."

Elise fixed him with a perplexed stare while she caught her breath. "Why did you-"

"We shouldn't talk about it here. Please, follow me."

* * *

Specialist Stone stood at airlock A7, pad in hand, watching as Raffa's pilots did their best to get close enough for her to extend the docking tube. As she waited patiently for the guiding lights to turn green, she felt tiredness creeping in once more.

It's been a long cycle. Hopefully it'll all be over soon...

Her mind switched to thoughts of *Kobra* and *Mambaka*, still out in the system somewhere, drifting ever closer and causing disruptions as they went.

That damn engineer. I should ask Raffa to lend me Ikarus. If anyone could bring the maximum charges...

She sighed, her eyes drifting between the pad and the airlock. If the readings were to be believed, Raffa's pilots had almost come to a complete stop and were taking their time to line everything up perfectly. *Bo'a* was close by, providing additional guidance where it could, and the Command Core was in contact with

Raffa as well. It wasn't an ideal situation for anyone, but with them all working together, the conditions were even better than a training mission. All Stone had to do was wait for some lights to change colour, see if they held that colour for a few seconds, and press a button. She spared a thought to all the people trying to make this work, and felt a tinge of anger that the universe just wouldn't leave Kau D'varza in peace.

The problems on the surface, and now this... things are going to get worse before they get better.

A notification appeared, a symbol of a speaker with *Bo'a* on one side, Joseph Raffa on the other.

Do I wanna hear this? Ugh, I suppose I should. Could be important. And how could I just expect anything to work around here without issue?

She tapped the button and immediately regretted her decision.

"... listening to me! I told you, you need to turn starward!"

That'll be Bo'a *then.*

"And I told you..."

Not Raffa. Probably one of his pilots.

"... we can't see the star. Just the station."

"And since you know where you are in relation to the station, you can work out the rest by..."

"Enough!"

That'll be Raffa then.

"Can you dock us without crashing the damn ship?"

"If *Bo'a* would stop-"

"Yes or no?"

"Yes."

"Then stop dicking about and get it done."

Sounds like I'm not the only one stressed out by all this.

"Right, just a little more. And... there!"

The lights on the pad flickered from orange to green. Stone watched them for a few seconds, then tapped the button. The station's automatic systems took control of the freighter and guided it to the airlock. She watched the entire process, hoping that everything would go as planned. Fortunately - for everyone, not least Stone herself - it did.

"Freighter docked and secured," she said.

"Copy," Raffa replied. "Thank the Void."

"Rough trip, Comcap?"

"I've had better."

She smiled, glancing down at her pad. "Pressure equalised. You're free to disembark."

He turned his head. "Hear that? Pop the hatches and let us off this damn can."

She watched, feeling strangely tense, as the freighter's

airlock hissed and a ramp extended.

Despite their tiredness, the soldiers of First and Second squad managed to form up and maintain two straight, orderly lines as they marched out of the freighter towards the elevator.

Kaska scanned the faces. They seemed to be in good spirits, but obviously worn. As she sought out Raffa, she sensed someone standing beside her.

"Specialist Stone."

"Ikarus," she replied, not taking her eyes from the airlock. The freighter had both doors open, spewing seemingly endless lines of soldiers back into Kau D'varza.

"I am relieved to see the operation was a success."

"As am I. I assume you helped plan this mission?"

"My role was minor, Specialist," Ikarus said, flatly. "Mostly research. I spoke to those who might know about such vessels, assessed what defences were most likely. I feel as though Comcap Raffa would have been able to complete this particular operation without my assistance."

She frowned. "You're extremely valuable to this station, Ikarus. Don't sell yourself short."

"The Specialist is quite kind to say so."

"While we're talking, how would you feel about joining me for some additional work?"

He didn't hesitate. "Are you poaching me, Specialist

Stone?"

"No. Your loyalty to Comcap Raffa is very clear. No, Ikarus, I'm just proposing that you assist me with an upcoming inspection of the engineering bay. I would like it to be... thorough."

She could sense him smiling just from his voice.

"Oh, indeed?"

"Indeed," she echoed, teasing. "I get the feeling I'm not the only one wants to know why Comcap Raffa had to take *Bo'a* instead of *Akonda* or *Vypka*."

"No, you certainly are not." He inhaled. "Your proposal is most interesting, Specialist Stone, I shall see to it that I am available for such a task. I have no doubt that Comcap Raffa would also prefer this investigation to be thorough. He has many questions."

"If I could have sent him in anything other than *Bo'a*, you know I would have."

"Specialist Stone," he said, "I have no illusions about the work you went through to have a weapon attached to the vessel just so they would have some means of defending themselves. That gesture, that extra thought, meant a lot to Comcap Raffa. Despite his protests."

Kaska shook her head. "It was inadequate. If they'd faced a real threat... I don't want to consider that alternative."

"Which is the reason you are now conducting an inspection of the engineering bay. You haven't just solved the smaller problem, but are looking to the root cause. Most would not bother; you are different. Comcap Raffa and I both thank you for that."

"That's..." She sighed. "Things can't go on like this. We face more threats each day. We need our vessels in working order."

As the last of the soldiers filed out, Takk Winters waved over to them both.

"Ikarus. Specialist." He nodded and gestured to the freighter as they approached. "Say hello to the beast!"

"The beast?" Kaska replied. "That's its name?"

"We don't know what it's name is. The techs haven't been able to crack the encryption, and everything else has been wiped." He whistled. "It's like... I dunno, someone wiped it and just set it drifting."

Ikarus' eyes narrowed. "And yet it was on a direct course for Kau D'varza..."

"Yeah, something to do with the station's welcome beacon."

"The aid system?" Kaska replied. "It was tracking that?"

Winters nodded. "Sounds about right."

Before Kaska could reply, footsteps behind Winters caught their attention.

"Specialist Stone." Raffa offered a crisp Kau D'varza salute. "I would like to report that our mission to intercept and recover the freighter went as perfectly as could be imagined."

"Ease, Comcap. On behalf of Kau D'varza, congratulations, and thank you."

He relaxed and smiled. "*You* are most welcome."

Winters glanced at Raffa with a poorly concealed grin. Kaska ignored it, and motioned for them to follow her down the corridor. As the elevator opened, a squad of Station Security flooded out and hurried towards the freighter.

* * *

Elise was staring at Gierre with wide, confused eyes. He sat behind a modest-sized desk, the screen-surface currently set to show a dark wood of some kind. Gierre's office hadn't been at all like she'd imagined. Instead of rich bora-leather or fur furnishings, she found herself sitting on a barely padded metal chair under the light from an undecorated lamp, surrounded by bare metal walls.

"I... I'm sorry," she finally stuttered, "run that by me again?"

Gierre smiled and settled back in his chair.

"It's very simple, actually. Kau D'varza doesn't have enough investigation specialists. Not for... larger issues. If someone commits a crime, the few specialists we do have can deal with it. But let's just say, for example, that an external force committed a crime against us. We can't send them to deal with that."

"I get that, but why me?"

"I have many reasons, not least of them being that one of my specialists saw a great deal of potential in you. I happen to agree with her assessment." Gierre weaved his fingers and rested them against his chin. "The first thing that caught our attention was the sophistication of your intrusions into our network. Such talent should not be wasted. Secondly, you have a desire to be a journalist, correct?"

Elise nodded slowly, her eyes remaining on Gierre.

"And am I correct when I say that journalism requires investigation?"

Another nod.

"So would I not be remiss to at least try and put these skills to use, for the benefit of Kau D'varza?"

"And you think the best way to do that, is to make me a... what was it? *Investigation Specialist?*"

It was Gierre's turn to nod. "I do."

"Okay."

He blinked. "Just like that?"

Elise shrugged. "Sure. I mean, my choice is either take this job, or end up back in Commissioner Zeled's hotel."

Gierre grinned. "I assure you, that particular matter has been settled. So long as you agree not to intrude in our network again without our permission."

"So what? I could turn this job down, walk out that door, and that'd be it? No worries?"

"It would be a great shame, but yes, that option is always open to you."

"Huh..." She took a few seconds to consider her choices, then glanced back up at Gierre. "When do I start?"

* * *

The Command Core seemed busier than usual as Raffa, Ikarus and Winters followed Specialist Stone through the flurry of people and toward the office.

"What's going on?" Winters asked.

"The interference from *Kobra* is causing a lot of problems."

Raffa frowned. "Any new updates?"

"Not really. They can send us messages occasionally, their communications system is built to get through the interference field, but it's also broken; they can't see what we're sending them."

"How in the *Void* are they supposed to dock?" Winters replied, his tone laced with anger.

"*Kobra* is smaller than a freighter, Force Commander. Once it gets close enough, we'll send shuttles out to meet it, at which point they can shut *Kobra* down, activate emergency life support, and bring it home."

They stopped outside the Arch-Commissioner's

office, the soldiers averting their eyes as Kaska tapped in an entry request. After a few seconds, the door slid open, and they were invited inside by a seemingly excited Gierre.

"Commander-Captain Joseph Raffa!" he said, in a booming voice. "And Force-Commander Takk Winters." Gierre stood from his seat and stepped over to shake their hands. He waved off their salutes. "Oh, relax. You've earned it."

As he stepped aside, Raffa noticed someone sitting in the chair. A woman; young, and from the state of her hair and clothes, it looked as though she'd had a rougher time of it than the soldiers. Kaska was also intently studying her.

"Would you like a drink? We've just had a delivery of Neska Vintage."

"Vintage?" Winters grinned. "It would be my honour to accept your most gracious offer, Arch-Commissioner."

Kaska moved towards the drinks panel in the wall, but Gierre raised his hand, stopping her in her tracks.

"Sir?"

"We have you to thank as well, Specialist Stone. I am not blind to the amount of work you have put into the last few cycles." He smiled and pressed the edge of the panel, a modest selection of spirits and glasses emerged. "Please, allow me. It is the least I can do."

"I…"

Raffa smiled. He hadn't seen Kaska off-step before.

"Y-yes, Sir, of course."

After filling and distributing six glasses way beyond what could be considered appropriate, Gierre settled back into his seat and raised his drink.

"To the men and women of Kau D'varza."

Those gathered repeated the toast with varying degrees of enthusiasm.

"Enjoy it." His expression hardened. "Unfortunately, our work must continue. I have read your report, Comcap Raffa, and am most troubled."

"I would be more than happy to fill you in on the details."

"Just a couple of things really stand out." Gierre took a sip of his drink. "You really didn't find a single person?"

"We swept the entire vessel four times, random pattern, heavy-duty sensors. If there was someone stuck to the hull of that thing, we'd have found them."

"And the ships logs?"

"Erased, Sir. Long before we arrived."

The young woman tensed. Gierre noticed and realised he hadn't introduced anyone.

"Ah! My apologies! Please, this is Comcap Raffa, Force-Commander Winters, Aide Ikarus Brook, and Specialist Stone."

They nodded and raised their glasses in greeting as Gierre continued. "Everyone, I'd like you to meet our newest Investigations Specialist, Elise Rivera."

Stone smiled. "I look forward to working with you."

Elise nodded. "As I, you."

"You had some thoughts on the data?"

"Gie-uh, I mean the *Arch-Commissioner* filled me in on the details. This is about that freighter, right?"

Stone nodded.

"And you're saying that it drifted all this way, with no one onboard, and all the information's been wiped?"

"Not all of it," Raffa admitted. "There's some deep-lock system aboard. We couldn't crack that, but everything else... yeah. Where it came from, who built it, even it's damn name. We've got nothing."

Gierre looked up. "Specialist Stone, what would you recommend?"

She considered her answer. "Legally, the freighter belongs to us now. Between locally agreed salvage law, the threat it presented Kau D'varza directly, violation of our space-debris laws, and the lack of crew to argue it, that particular point isn't an issue. Therefore, we can approach this however we please." She let out an exasperated sigh. "We could turn it over to the station's engineers, have them run the usual checks and scans. It'll take a while." Her eyes drifted to

Elise. "However, my personal recommendation? This would be a good test for our newest Specialist."

Gierre turned his attention to Elise. "What do you think? Are you up to your first mission?"

"What would my specific goal be?"

"Find out everything you can about the freighter: where it came from, how it ended up in Windan with no crew, and see if you can get a name."

"Nothing difficult then?" she replied with a grin. "And if I don't manage it, your engineers will figure it out sooner or later?"

"Indeed. This is ultimately of little risk to us; we won't lose that data. I also agree with Specialist Stone that this will make for a suitable test."

Elise looked thoughtful for a few seconds, then raised her glass. "To my first mission, then."

CHAPTER NINE-
VOID-STRUCK

The entire station was enjoying something of a celebration. Upon hearing of the potential threat they
had faced, and the prompt nature of Raffa's response,
Nevos had declared an evening-cycle of rest and en-
joyment for the citizens. His announcement was still
repeating as Specialist Elise Rivera descended towards the freighter. She was feeling a little woozy
from the drink, but had taken the time to tidy herself
up and try on her new uniform: a tight-fitting tunic
with a Kau D'varza 'Investigation Specialist' logo on
the left, and a pair of crisply-pressed trousers. Kaska
Stone had given her some basic pointers on how to
act, with the promise of further training later, but
Elise wasn't willing to wait around while she had the
tools to carry out her assigned duty.

The two guards posted on security detail noticed her
stepping out of the elevator and shifted nervously.
One studied her as she approached, while the other
mumbled something into his pad.

"Is there an issue, Specialist?"

Just like Stone told you. Confident. You're meant to be here.

"Elise Rivera," she supplied, feeling a twinge of pride. "I'm here to inspect this vessel."

Don't tell more than you need to, Stone's voice echoed in her head once again.

"Uh-huuuh... Rivera, you say?"

"Yes," she said, as firmly as she could manage without it feeling rude or too abrupt.

This is going to take some getting used to.

"Weren't you hauled into Sec-Core earlier?"

"A misunderstanding. I... er, *encourage* you to check my records."

His partner looked up from the pad with a confused nod. "Confirmed. Specialist Elise Rivera. Congratulations on your new job, Ma'am." He stepped to one side. "Our apologies for delaying you."

They're doing their job, thank them.

"That's... alright. You're doing important work."

They exchanged uncertain glances, then nodded slowly.

"Good luck with your inspection, Ma'am."

Calm. You are supposed to be here, Elise. This is your job now.

She smiled, trying to exude confidence as she stepped

into the airlock. Elise heard one of the guards speaking as she crossed the threshold. It sounded as though he was letting the security personnel on the ship know about their visitor, his voice fading as she reached a connecting corridor.

She pulled out her own datapad. Gierre had convinced Zeled to return it to her, and Kaska had upgraded her access so that the systems she had once tried to invade were now entirely open to her. She flicked through several options until she found the virtual map Raffa's squads had passively created when they'd boarded. The software found her location and, after a few more screen-taps, highlighted the route to the command centre.

Elise followed the rigidly straight corridors, paying attention to the plain, dirty panels and dim lights.

So dull... even the budget transport that brought me here had more decoration.

Several patrolling security personnel regarded her with questioning glances, but offered help all the same. Elise simply confirmed she was going in the right direction before wishing them well and carrying on.

After several minutes, she arrived at the command centre. It was a small, rectangular room made up of two levels; a higher platform for the command staff, with the lower section holding the controls for the pilots and systems operators.

Elise shrugged off the cramped conditions and settled

into a seat on the upper level. Tapping at the console screen brought it back to life with a grey flash, and she studied the list of options.

What did Raffa call it... Deep-lock? That's a variation on the...

"Ugh..." She checked her pad and found the information she was looking for.

Variation of Defence-Shield. Deep-lock is the ship version, eh? That's all I needed to know.

* * *

"Damn, man." Winters pulled his collar and tried to look relaxed. "Look at all this food."

He and Raffa were sat at one of the tables near the front of the announcements hall. The room was usually reserved for station officials to address the citizenry with mass messages, but on occasion, like this evening, it could be converted into something of a luxury dining hall. Several large circular tables surrounded the podium, while the soldiers of First and Second squads sat further back with their families and friends.

"We were just doing our jobs," Raffa replied, slightly annoyed that he'd been forced into his ceremonial uniform after a long day of work. "We've never had any parties thrown for us before, either."

"Ah, just enjoy it. Not everybody's got ulterior motives."

Raffa inhaled. "I guess you're right. I'm just on edge.

Still expecting that freighter to spring some trap."

"No chance," Winters said, with some force. "My people scanned that thing, top to bottom, back to front, several times. There's nothing there that shouldn't be. Only way that thing's gonna mess us up now is if someone overloads the reactor, and that would take such a long time to achieve we'd spot it easily." He waved his fork, then stabbed at another thin wafer of bora on his plate. "Besides, look at everyone... Haven't seen 'em this happy since we turned back that take-over, and that was a while ago."

Raffa looked up from the glass of water he'd been staring into and glanced around at the hundreds of gathered people. Winters was right; all of them were smiling, joking. They were happy, and getting the recognition he felt they deserved, despite his suspicions.

Winters started saying something else, but Raffa's attention had been fully seized by a figure in white walking down the steps towards their table.

Is that... Specialist Stone?

He hadn't realised he'd been staring until she was barely a few steps away.

"Something the matter, Comcap?" she asked, a playful smile on her face.

"I... Ah... Miss Stone..."

Winters nudged his arm and whispered, "Spit it out, boss."

"You, er..." He tried again. "You look stunning this evening, Specialist Stone."

She turned away, her cheeks reddening slightly. "Thank you, you don't look so bad yourself." She motioned to the empty seat beside him. "May I?"

Without really thinking, Raffa stood up and pulled the chair out for her. "Please, be my guest."

"Comcap Raffa, you are quite the gentleman when you aren't wearing that armour."

"Please, call me Joseph."

As Stone took her seat, Winters fixed Raffa with a smile that quivered on the edge of laughter.

"Oh," Winters said, over-exaggerating his words, "would you look at that? Empty glass. Well, I guess I'd better go get another." He promptly stood, winking at Raffa despite his boss's 'I will fucking kill you if you leave me' stare, and moved away to visit other tables.

Raffa, feeling suddenly lost and abandoned, returned his attention to Stone and was struck once again by the beauty he'd understood was there, but had never allowed himself to really see. He had little for her but a nervous smile as she pulled a plate of hors d'oeuvres closer to them.

"You have some interesting people in your force, *Joseph*."

"He's not so bad."

"Winters?" she said, taking a tiny mouthful of food.

"Isn't that who you meant?"

She swallowed. "Maybe. You know, I've read that report on the pair of you hundreds of times, but I've never heard it directly from you."

Raffa's face flushed white. "You mean the take-over."

"The *attempted* take-over. You and Winters made sure that's as far as it got."

"I..."

Damnit, Stone, why'd you have to bring this up?

"We protected the station, and the Defence Commissioner at the time felt it best to promote both of us." His expression hardened. "That's all there is to it."

"You're being too modest. If it wasn't for the both of you, we'd be speaking Pirate right now."

"Kandahese," Raffa corrected.

"You knew what I meant," she replied with a smirk. "The two of you are heroes, and you've done it once again this cycle."

Raffa motioned to the soldiers and specialists. "They're the heroes. Winters and I wouldn't be a damn thing without them."

"Maybe, and they'll be awarded the promotions you recommended, but don't forget the role you played."

Raffa felt like she was staring into his soul as her softened gaze settled on him.

"You're an important person to a lot of people on this

station."

A lot. To mean you?

As if reading his thoughts, Stone winked then turned back to her meal. He sat dumbfounded for a few seconds, then glanced back at her.

"Why do we never talk outside of work?"

"Because work is the only time we see one another." Her tone had taken a matter-of-fact edge.

"Would..." Raffa inhaled sharply and tried to focus his thoughts.

You can lead three-hundred people into the unknown, but talking to women...?

"Would you like for us to see more of one another?"

She looked to him with a coy smile. "What are you proposing?"

"I- ah, er..."

Damnit.

"Joseph, relax." Another smile. "Yes, I'd like that very much."

His shoulders dropped slightly in relief. "So...?"

"You could always try inviting me out for dinner, or to a show."

He nodded. "Sorry, I'm not very good at this."

"You must have had some experience?"

Raffa sucked his teeth and narrowed his eyes. "Some."

"Now that sounds like a story," Stone said, waving her fork. "So, you gonna ask or not?"

"Oh. Yes, of course. Specialist St-"

"Kaska."

"Very well, *Kaska*, it would be an honour and a privilege if you would accompany me to dinner, tomorrow night, at... ah... Caystein's?"

Thanks, brain. Twelve restaurants on the station and you automatically pick the most expensive?

"Don't feel as if you need to impress me, Joseph."

"It's the only one I know."

"Well, someone has expensive tastes! But perhaps we would fit in better at Miranda's Grill?"

Kaska Stone, you are a beautiful genius.

"That sounds... suitable."

"In that case, I would be happy to join you for dinner."

Well, Raffa thought as he sat back, *that wasn't awkward in the slightest.*

* * *

The blaring tone accompanying the notification on the console caused Elise to wake with a start. She wiped the dribble off her chin and glanced around blearily before remembering where she was.

Right. Probably don't wanna fall asleep too often when you're on the job.

The notification on the screen faded, revealing a 'Transfer Complete' window. Her datapad flickered with similar information. She scooped it up and settled into a more relaxed posture as she began to work through the now-unencrypted files.

Built at Fa'Gan... goods freighter between there and Ar-Kaos... No designation? Weird. Ownership transferred to private company after it was decommissioned, usual routes. Hmm...

She rubbed her eyes and tried again.

Usual routes were between Rayuel and Yor' regions, but no fixed route prior to arrival here... So where were they when they abandoned ship?

She shook her head.

No... that's not right. The escape pods are still attached and accounted for. Nobody abandoned this ship unless they were connected to another one.

She tapped through more options, this time discovering the crew manifest.

This'll be useful if we ever try to track these folks down. Wait... forty people to crew a freighter? That doesn't sound right...

As Elise read through the lists and details, it struck her that barely any of the crew had the skills needed to fly such a vessel.

One pilot, and a single doctor? That's it?

A voice called to her from the hatch. "Is everything alright, Ma'am?"

"Uh... yeah, yeah." She frowned, then glanced over. "I don't suppose you've got much experience with ships?"

"Not me, Ma'am, I've lived on Kau D'varza my whole life."

"You've never left the station?"

"Once, Ma'am. The surface world feels horrible."

Elise grinned. "Too much fresh air?"

"That, and the gravity feels different... and there's no movement."

"Well... there is," Elise corrected, "it's just that you can't feel it."

"The station has a certain hum to it as-well. I felt most... disconcerted, without it."

"Well, I'm certain the station is glad to have you."

An uncertain frown crossed his face, then he smiled. "Thank you, Ma'am." He turned to leave, then looked back. "What was it you were after again?"

"Someone who knows about ships."

"I'll see what I can do."

Elise nodded. "Thanks."

She listened as his footsteps faded into silence, then looked back down at her pad.

So what else? Typical cargo manifest... Nothing. Can't work out it's route. Can't figure out how it Transited without a crew... Nothing!

She was about to toss her pad when something on the screen caught her eye.

Where did that come from?

A few more taps, a few seconds to scan the information, then a frown. "Grinda? What the Void was it doing in Grinda? There's nothing there."

A sudden flash of clarity struck Elise, her fingers danced over the pad's screen.

Local map. Zoom out. Grinda... Clion, Hol, Exen...

Her eyes widened.

"Beyema."

She'd heard rumours of what had happened in that system. The transport that brought her to Kau D'varza had gone to great lengths to avoid it. It had added a couple of megasekunds to her journey, but the pilots had insisted it was better to arrive late than tangle with the Reclaimers who had recently started operating in the area. Elise, growing up in a system occasionally visited by Reclaimer Fleets, didn't fear them like so many others she'd met clearly did, but she couldn't deny the pilots concerns, and they seemed to have a very good reason for staying away from Beyema.

So why didn't you stay away too, nameless freighter?

"Ma'am?"

The same voice from before had returned, Elise shook off the mental cobwebs and stood up.

"No luck?"

"No, Ma'am."

"That's alright. I think I've got all I can from this thing." She pointed at the console with her thumb. "Thanks for trying though."

"Not a problem. Would you like an escort?"

"An escort? Back to the station?"

"It would be no trouble."

"Sorry, this whole specialist thing is new to me. I'll be okay, I can find my own way back."

"Very well. If you need anything, please let me know."

Why are security so... needy towards the specialists? It's kinda weird...

He disappeared once again. Elise gave it a minute or so, then followed, hoping she didn't catch up to him.

* * *

"I'm surprised Nevos gave you the evening off." Raffa waved to another group of revelling citizens as he wandered the station with Kaska. "Especially with the *Kobra* situation."

"That's practically resolved. I doubt Teq will get a party thrown in his honour though."

"Oh?"

"His mission was easier, and he had the right tools to do it with."

"He was still successful."

"Maybe, but he only had to collect six fast-attack craft, and we gave him a stealth cruiser and a destroyer to achieve it with. We gave *you* a transport to intercept what could have been another take-over, or a ramming attempt."

"At least if it happens again we'll have more firepower. Oh, and thank you, for making sure we had something to defend ourselves with had the worst happened."

They came to a stop at one of the viewing windows and watched the ever-changing colours and patterns of the distant Void Cloud for a few moments.

"I don't think I allowed myself to admit it before, but I've always been quite fond of you, Joseph, had something happened to you... Well, I don't know what I'd've done."

"Don't take this the wrong way, but I had a feeling you might."

"Oh, did you now?"

Raffa looked quite pleased with himself. "You stare."

"I stare?"

"You stare. Whenever you relay orders to me directly, you take your time, and you stare."

"Well maybe I do. But I didn't mean-"

"It kinda... I dunno, it gave me a boost. I liked it. A little reminder of why I put the armour on. Who I'm fighting for."

"For me?"

"For you, and everyone else who lives here."

"We're lucky to have you."

As Kaska looked into his eyes, Raffa felt something stirring inside. He'd felt it before during battle, an urge to act without thinking, to charge forward and rush the enemy or take a new position under a hail of las-rounds and pulsers. But this time, there was no enemy, no rain of projectiles, just Kaska. Her professional mask had fallen away, revealing a softer, caring expression made all the more compelling by those sparkling, hopeful eyes.

"Kiss her!" Winters called from behind a bench opposite. He flushed and tried to bury his head behind a data-pad when he realised he'd shouted it.

Kaska turned back to the view, trying to hide her disappointment and not doing an entirely convincing job. Raffa, suddenly angry with himself for not realizing - and at Winters for following them - glared at his subordinate with a scowl. Before he could tell Winters exactly how he felt, Kaska pulled her dress-jacket around herself and offered him a nod.

"Good evening, Joseph."

He stood, dumbfounded, as she turned and walked away. He was still struggling for words when she disappeared out of sight.

"You. Are. A. Fucking. Idiot. Boss."

"I didn't need your help!" Raffa spat. "I... I was handling it."

"Didn't look like it from where I'm sitting."

"Ugh. Why are you even here?"

"You're kidding right? I'm your wingman, your partner in crime, your brother in arms."

"So that means you sabotage my chances?" Raffa shook his head, gave a final respectful glance to the Void Cloud, and started walking back to his habitat. An aura of anger had engulfed him. Despite that, Winters caught up.

"Look, I'm sorry, alright? But as long as I've known you, you haven't had the best luck with women."

"I don't need your help."

"Oh give over, Raf'. The look in her eyes... how could you not see it?"

Raffa swung round and poked Winters in the chest. "I'm a soldier! I've spent my entire adult life shooting things, taking objectives, following orders, completing goals. That's how my mind works. And while I may not have had 'the best luck with women', I don't need help from the kind of person who sleeps with anyone and anything that so much as glances his way. Do I make myself clear, *Force-Commander* Winters?"

"Oh, go to the Void, Raffa. I was trying to help."

"And look where it got me! Stick to your job, and stay

out of my personal affairs."

"Alright, I'll stay out of your failing love life, but we're friends, Raf', I-"

"Is that was this is about? You think Specialist Stone would create a gap between us?"

"No! Fuck, Raffa, I want you to be happy! That's what friends want for one another."

"After this eveni-"

"If I wasn't here you'd still be trying to stare into her soul like a dribbling idiot! The next time it happens, you'll know what that thick fucking head of yours is trying to tell you."

"You better hope for your sake there is a next time."

Raffa gave him a final sharp nudge, then stormed off.

How in the Void am I supposed to even begin putting this right? That dumb...

Winters' voice broke into his thoughts - "Nicely done, Takk. Yeah, real good job, asshole." - the tone of regret enough to cause him to check his stride, but then he thought of the look on Kaska's face before she turned away - the disappointment, the regret - and the damage it might have done to his - their - chances, and felt his anger and embarrassment flare again.

He'd just better hope I can find a way to sort this. Maybe Ikarus might know? Yeah... Ikarus...

CHAPTER TEN-
STATE OF
CONTEMPLATION

The walls of Elise's apartment glowed with blue light from the room's screen. All the data on her pad was now available for review on the station's system and she was going through it at her leisure, a glass of Kandaha Red in one hand, the other hovering over the pad itself, using it as an interface for the larger screen.

There's something wrong here. Why does some data exist while other bits have been deliberately removed? Are we only seeing what someone wants us to see, or is this some kind of weird corruption?

The sensation that she was missing something only grew as she returned to the other files. Various sections, each with sparse details on things like cargo, routes and supplies filled the screen. She scrolled down, onto the sections marked Crew, System Logs and Misc., then sat forward suddenly, the sofa squeaking as she moved.

What's this?

An option she hadn't seen before appeared at the bottom of the list.

Recovered/Restored? Did the station fix some of the files?

She hurriedly clicked on the new section, and let out a sigh of disappointment.

One file.

A video. Three seconds long. Elise pressed the 'Run' button and raised the glass to her lips.
At first she wasn't sure what she was looking at, she set the video to repeat so she could get a better view.

Okay, corridor view... That's a pod of some kind... Rejuvenation maybe? Or cleanroom? No, too small. Someone falling towards it... Pushed towards it? Doesn't want to go in...

It repeated several more times until Elise hit Pause. The screen froze on the terrified face of a crew member.

"Cross-reference with files in section marked 'Crew'," she ordered.

Barely a second later, the system returned a match.

Litago J. Foxin, civilian. No skills of note.

Elise frowned, blowing air out of her cheeks. "Who are you? Where did you go? And why were you listed as crew when you're more like a damn passenger?"

She stared into the image taken when he'd signed on.

Sunken cheeks and eyes, dark circles, more wrinkles than someone his age would usually have.

Elise had seen this before, among the refugees who had arrived at Paradise.

Is that it? You signed on as crew to pay your fare from whatever you were running from? But if it's that, why so many? Surely the real crew would have lost money? And what is it exactly that you're running from?

She placed her drink on the table and leant forward, elbows on knees, chin resting on interlaced fingers, eyes fixed on the screen. After several minutes, she exhaled.

This is gonna drive me nuts. Every time I get a new slice of information, I just have more questions. I need to talk to someone.

"Show active personnel."

Eh... Stone and that Captain both in private mode. Winters too... Don't think he'd be much help though... Ikarus? He's the smart one. Raffa's quiet assistant. He seemed alright, and he's still awake.

She thought about it for less than a second. Downing the rest of her drink, she scooped up her data pad and stumbled out the door.

* * *

Kaska Stone was staring up at her ceiling, wide awake, and still fully clothed despite lying on the bed in almost complete darkness.

Why do I even bother?

Another voice spoke up; a thought, a memory. *'You always did have bad taste in men, Kassie.'*

"Yes, thank you, Mother," she answered aloud, though her mother - whether the remembered version or the real thing - would have been mistaken this time.

Raffa's not bad. He just... I don't know... He's not exactly the romantic type.

A pipe hissing in the distance made her look over despite the darkness, then slump her head back down onto the pillow.

And that idiot, Winters; good advice, bad delivery. Completely ruined the moment. If I want this to work with Raffa... Joseph... I'll have to help him. But then, do I want it to work? Isn't this just going to make things awkward at work? And what about when he gets sent away on missions? Winters is always going to be there, too. That's never going to change. They're too close for that.

Kaska let out a guttural moan and tried to stretch out, only to be restricted by her evening wear. She reluctantly got to her feet.

"Lights on."

The lighting came up slowly, until a soft warm glow bathed the spartan, open space. The few decorations that adorned the walls were the ones that had been there when she'd arrived: an abstract painting with lots of colored squares, another with circles. Her work console sat in one corner, the screen surrounded by a mess of data chips and other paraphernalia. The only things that showed any sign of a personal touch were the handmade cushions, given to her by her mother, and the hologram wall of service certificates for her continued contributions to the running of Kau D'varza.

Kaska, bare-footed, staggered into the clean-room and set about finding some comfortable clothes to sleep in. She struggled at first to climb out of the body-hugging evening-wear, but eventually she managed it and stepped into the all-clean booth in the corner. When she stepped out, her hair was straightened, her make-up gone. She lazily slipped into the plain grey, loose-fitting top and slid on some underwear before returning to bed. As the lights faded, she found herself staring up at the ceiling once more, lost in thought.

* * *

The door to Ikarus' habitat seemed slightly more armoured than his neighbours. Bare-metal panels welded in place, with additional spaces cut out of the bulkhead for the modifications to slide into. Elise double-checked that Ikarus' status still had him as available, and pressed her hand against the panel.

After a few seconds, the door slid open with a pained whine.

"How can I be of assistance," Ikarus said, paused as he realised who was standing before him, then added, "er... Specialist Rivera?"

Elise took a breath. Ikarus' demeanour was as calm as always, but there was something in his tone that suggested something else; annoyance, perhaps?

"Sorry, have I come at a bad time?" she asked. "I wouldn't have troubled you, but your status..."

"That is for the benefit of Comcap Raffa. However, you look troubled, so I am available should you need me."

Elise nodded. "Thanks, Ikarus. It's about the freighter."

"Indeed?" He stepped back from the opening and raised his arm to motion her inside. "In that case, you'd better come in."

Elise was struck by an unfamiliar smell as she followed him into his habitat and looked around. The most noticeable things, besides the smell, were the bookcases that lined the walls, each filled with tomes, pads and data-storage devices. A single bed jutted out of the wall, it too surrounded by various audio-players and books.

"This is... incredible." She wasn't sure where to look first. Every nook caught her attention, every item held immense intrigue.

"Thank you, Specialist."

"Oh." Elise turned back to him, Ikarus was weaving his way around the food-processor, pouring out drinks. "You don't have to call me that. Elise is fine."

He offered her a cup of something warm and motioned towards a small table covered in more archaic media.

"As that may be, I fear it may form a bad habit. For example, Specialist Stone would not appreciate me calling her Kaska when we're working with one another."

"Why not? You're friends aren't you?"

Ikarus grinned. "Colleagues."

"Hmm, fair enough. Well, you can still call me Elise if you like. It's going to take some getting used to, this whole 'Specialist' thing."

"In that regard, how is your first assignment going?"

"I... I know where it came from and who built it. I know the forty crew-members, and I know what it used to do before all this. But I still haven't got a name, and I found a video that... Well, I can't make much sense of it."

Ikarus cocked an eyebrow at her over the brim of his cup. As he set it down on the table, he took a deep breath and sat back.

"Let us start at the beginning. Who built it, and for what purpose?"

"It's a Fa'Gan vessel, some orbital shipyard built it, and after completion it *was* used as a freighter to haul goods between Fa'Gan and Ar-Kaos."

"A good start. What happened after that?"

"As far as I can tell, some private company bought it, but the details there are sketchy. Just an idea of the region they operated in. I don't know what they were transporting, but I've got a pretty good theory."

"Oh?"

"How many people would you say it takes to crew something like that freighter?"

"I'm not an expert in such matters, but Kau D'varza would assign eight to ten. At least two pilots, someone trained in medical matters, a commanding officer, his or her aides and a support team of three or four for maintenance."

"Hmm, but not forty?"

"Certainly not. A vessel built to transport goods would not waste money on a crew that size. Additional quarters, more storage for staff supplies... it would take away from the amount they could haul, which in turn would make them less profitable. They'd also have to pay those people." He shook his head. "No, forty people is far too many."

Elise's eyes drifted to the large screen present in all residential units. Some people covered them up. Ikarus, however, had decorated his with a fake-wooden veneer to bring it in line with the rest of the room's design.

"I think they were refugees."

"Why?" The tone wasn't accusatory. Rather, it was designed to make her think.

"If you look through the files, about thirty six of them look like they haven't eaten in weeks... or slept, for that matter. Their clothes are torn, chewed up, covered in dirt... I saw this back at Paradise, refugees from Setin and Kyrex trying to get away from environmental hazards ended up coming to Yurnto to start a new life." She turned back to him. "I think they signed on as crew to pay for their 'escape'."

"All of them? That doesn't make sense from a business perspective."

"That's what I thought. But if the people who ran the

ship had a connection to those people, then maybe they did it out of kindness."

"Have you discovered any such connections?"

"No. The crew details are... sparse. My concern is, besides the obvious, what were they running from? If I can figure out where they came from I can figure out what made them want to leave, and what their likely route would have been. So far, my best guess is that they came from Beyema, via Grinda... but that's all it is; a guess. I'm certain on the Grinda part, but we already knew that."

"Beyema." Ikarus sighed heavily and rubbed his eyes. "I was worried about that."

"I can't confirm anything right now. I could be wrong."

"It is unlikely that you are. Our new neighbours seem to be bringing no small number of troubles our way, however indirectly."

"Why is everyone so afraid of them?" Elise snapped. "They're just people, like you and me."

"I don't dispute that fact, Specialist, but 'people' are capable of some very unpleasant things."

"We can't blame them for all our problems, Ikarus. Kau D'varza was under attack long before the Reclaimers showed up at Beyema."

"But you cannot deny things have grown worse?"

"I... No. I suppose I can't."

I'll get evidence. I'll go to Beyema myself if I have to and ask them.

"Do not be disheartened. If it is any consolation, you are not the only one who believes the Reclaimers are an easy place to lay the blame, and perhaps I am the bigot for not seeing alternatives. However, I am a realist, Specialist Rivera, and from the data I've studied, there is a direct link between the Reclaimers at Beyema and the troubles we have faced in recent times."

"Can you show me that?"

"It is available to you on the Win-Net, you have access now," he reminded her, then, with a wide smile, he added, "And permission."

"Thanks."

"Specialist Rivera, it seems as though you have completed several of the goals assigned to you. I recommend that you send your report to Specialist Stone for review."

"What? That's it?"

"You are always welcome to make addenda or to reopen your case if new information surfaces. However, you have achieved most of what the Arch-Commissioner asked you to do. You have confirmed where it came from; you have discovered details regarding the crew prior to the ship's arrival in the system; you have even found out who built it and what it did until it drifted our way. If you later discover how it arrived here without a crew to operate the Transit drive, or if the vessel's name suddenly resurfaces, add that to your report. As it stands, however, the rest of this information is enough. It's thorough, it answers questions."

Elise sat, listening, and considering her answer. "There's more. I recovered a video clip. It's only short but I can't make much sense of it."

"Would you like me to link my screen to your pad?"

"If you wouldn't mind."

"Of course not. Please, activate the ping-back feature."

It took a few seconds to set up, but once connected Elise hit the run button and sat back. She let the clip play a few times, then paused it.

"Looks like he's tripping over, or being pushed."

Ikarus nodded. "I'd agree with that assessment."

"Do you know what that pod is? I thought it was a rejuvenator or a clean-pod, but it looks too small."

"It's a stasis pod."

"Stasis?" She glanced back to the still image on the screen. Ikarus hadn't taken his eyes off it, as if searching every pixel for information. "Why would someone..."

"He's being abducted."

"Abducted?" Elise blurted. "What? Abducted? Why? And why use stasis pods?"

"Cheaper than keeping your captives fed and healthy. You don't have to listen to them, either."

"So let me get this straight." She pointed at the screen. "Someone boarded the freighter, forced everyone into stasis, took them off the ship, then left it drifting?"

"I would agree with this assessment."

"But all those people!"

Ikarus finally turned from the screen and fixed her with a fiery stare. "Specialist Rivera, in this line of work you will encounter things you find most abhorrent but can do nothing about from Kau D'varza. It is most frustrating, I know. However, the things you've uncovered... You are more than capable of the job entrusted to you. The Arch-Commissioner was absolutely correct when he placed his faith in you. Do not let your emotions get in your way."

"We're just going to ignore this?"

He shook his head. "No, but the answer will not be found sitting around my table drinking Escafo. This needs to be seen by people higher up than ourselves. They will decide how to act, someone else will ensure justice is done, and if that isn't achievable, they will at least ensure Kau D'varza never suffers such a fate."

"Which is why you want me to compile my report. So they know about it sooner rather than later. So they can act."

"Indeed. I have a report of my own awaiting approval. Together, they would make a strong case to further increase Kau D'varza's defences, and for us to track down those responsible so they are no longer able to force their problems our way."

"Alright, Ikarus." She finished her drink in one and returned the cup to the food area. "This has been... enlightening. Thank you."

"Indeed." He smiled at her. "Perhaps Comcap Raffa isn't the only person I'd welcome at my door at all times. Just don't make it too frequent a habit."

Careful Elise, you might actually start making friends.

She grinned. "Thanks, Ikarus. Pleasant dreams."

With that, she slipped out the door and made her way back home.

CHAPTER ELEVEN-
CRITICAL MASS

The elevator hummed as it carried Kaska Stone down to the engineering bay. She was steadying herself against the rail. Every part of her body ached.

Didn't sleep a wink. So tired.

The doors slid apart. The bay was thick with smoke, and Kaska had to stop herself gagging at the strong fumes as she plunged forward, waving a hand before her face until she was clear. From the look of it, some las-engraving had gotten out of hand, sparking a small oil fire under the landing gear of a neighbouring vessel. One of the robot responders had put it out, but smoke still poured from the source.

Kaska fixed her gaze on one of the workers who didn't look particularly busy and motioned him over.

"Where's your boss?" she asked, flatly.

"Dunno... er, *Ma'am?*"

"Ma'am is fine." She indicated the rest of the bay with a sweep of her hand. "The six F.A.C.'s from Gaitlin. Where are they?"

"Er, this way... Ma'am."

The skinny, grease-covered engineer led her through the large vessel bay, past the sleek body of *Kobra* - currently undergoing repairs to the stealth system - then *Mambaka*, the heavily-armed destroyer. Though *Mambaka* was smaller than its neighbour by several meters and carried less armour, in combination the vessels worked extremely well together.

Further on, *Akonda* and *Vypka* were still waiting for attention. Indeed, the heavy cruiser and small, fast corvette still looked as though no one had so much as given them a glance since they'd been dragged in.

Seeing the ships together this way really brought the true size of the engineering bay home, and for a second Kaska felt sorry for the person running the place. Then she remembered who she was feeling sorry for, and it quickly passed.

"Has *anyone* been assigned to repair these vessels?"

"'*Konda* and *Vyp*'?"

She fought against the urge to sigh or snap in exasperation. "Yes."

"Not that I know, Ma'am. Customer vessels take priority."

"Who told you that?"

"Boss Jimba."

"I'm familiar with him. He told you customer vessels take priority over the ships used to defend the station? Why?"

"We get paid per vessel on customer jobs, get paid by time for Kau's ships."

"And no doubt, he's skimming off the top on such jobs…"

The engineer turned pale. "Ma'am! Don't tell anyone I said anything, please! I like this job!"

"Relax. If anyone's losing their job, it isn't you." She raised her hand. "Wait here a moment please."

"O-Of course, Ma'am."

She turned away and brought up Ikarus on the pad. As his image appeared, she had the feeling she wasn't the only one who'd had trouble sleeping.

"Aide Ikarus?"

"Receiving, Specialist Stone."

"Is everything alright?"

Ikarus smiled. "It isn't often you ask, madam specialist. Does something about my appearance offend you? I shall rectify it prompt-"

"It's alright, Ikarus, you just look tired. I wondered if something was troubling you."

He considered his answer. "Have you spoken with Specialist Rivera?"

Elise? Why would I have spoken to her?

"Not since yestercycle. However, she did send me some files to look over when I was on my way to Command Core earlier."

"You will be pleased to know that yourself and Arch-Commissioner Nevos have selected wisely. She is a determined worker. I feel she will be a most valuable asset."

Did Ikarus get lucky last night? Is that why he looks so tired? No... Surely not! It must be something else, something he's not telling me. I'm too tired to deal with this now.

"I appreciate your commendations, Ikarus, thank you."

"Of course, Ma'am. Now, how may I help *you*?"

"I know our partnership hasn't officially begun on the Engi-Bay audit yet, but I'd appreciate it if you could make an extra copy of the financial files before any-one has the chance to tamper with them."

"Would you also like me to... scrutinise... these par-ticular files?"

"I would."

"Barring any delays, I will have a conclusion to bring by lights-out."

"You've never disappointed me, Ikarus."

His eyes narrowed, as if suspicious..

Damnit, he thinks I'm talking about Raffa. And of course Raffa and Ikarus talked about it. Maybe that's the reason he's tired.

"Was there anything else, Ma'am?"

"Wha- Oh... No, thank you, Ikarus."

"Very well, I shall get to work immediately. Good cycle, Specialist."

"Yes. Good cycle, Aide."

She shook her head in a vain attempt to rid herself of the growing tiredness and returned her attention to the engineer, who had grown at least twice as nervous as when she'd last looked at him.

"Lead on," she commanded, whereupon he tensed, turned, and walked at a fair pace between the over-sized bays.

They passed through a set of double doors into the smaller craft bay, which currently housed a few shuttles and six fast-attack craft that had once be-longed to their partners in the neighbouring system of Gaitlin. The ships themselves weren't particularly impressive; crescent-moon shaped vessels with gim-bal-mounted weaponry above and below on the tips. Kaska studied each one briefly before moving to the next. The white paint on their hulls had faded, lend-ing them a tired, almost neglected look, but other than that they appeared to be in adequate condition.

"Any problems here?" Kaska asked as she finished her small inspection.

"Er... I wouldn't know, Ma'am."

"You haven't checked?"

He made a helpless gesture. "They're not *customer* vessels."

Kaska inhaled sharply, her nostrils flaring. "If the station came under attack this cycle, what would you be able to send out to defend us?"

"We've got *Bo'a*, Ma'am."

In a flash of anger, Kaska let her professional exterior

slip. "Does nobody in this damned place care? We're practically defenceless! None of our ships function, we're putting guns on transports, and any new vessels we get are just left unattended! What are we supposed to- No. You know what? Forget it! I'm gonna fix this." She stormed away and brought up the communication details for Gierre Nevos. "I'm gonna fix this *right now*."

* * *

"I am sorry." Raffa looked at his reflection in the vid-screen and tried again. "About last night, I just wanted... to say..."

Oh, who are you kidding? Winters is right. Just get your next assignment, leave the station for a spell, and forget this ever happened. We'll just go on being professionals any time we see one another and...No. Don't want that either.

He shut off the vid-screen, slunk out of the clean room, and fell onto the cushioned bench at the bottom of his bed. The familiar chirp of his data-pad rang out before he could get too comfortable, and he sighed. At least it was close enough for him to reach without moving.

"Raffa," he answered, face still pushed into the bench.

"It's Ikarus, sir. Is... now a bad time?"

"Yeah, but it's about as good as it's gonna get. What's wrong?"

"I wanted to request that you hold off on sending my report to the Arch-Commissioner, to allow him time to review Specialist Rivera's findings regarding the freighter. I believe her report will boost the relevance and strength of my own."

"Sure thing. How long are we talking?"

"Specialist Stone received Specialist Rivera's findings this morning, but has of yet been unable to examine them."

Raffa pulled his head out of the padding and looked at Ikarus. "You've spoken to Kas- Specialist Stone?"

He eyed Raffa suspiciously and nodded. "Yes, Sir."

"How is she?"

"My assessment is that Specialist Stone is healthy and eating sufficiently, though she could use more sleep."

"I meant her mood, Ikarus. I swear, sometimes you're like a damn machine."

"I apologise, Sir, I did-"

"Her mood, Ikarus."

"I sensed that Specialist Stone was upset, perhaps angry about something."

Fuck.

"Any ideas about what, exactly?"

"Specialist Stone requested that I copy and examine several files regarding finance from the engineering bay before they can tamper with it. I would assess that her mood is based on the failings of the engineering staff, in addition to the aforementioned tiredness."

"But you're not certain?"

"I am not." The suspicion had risen to levels even Ikarus couldn't hide. "Sir, is there some sort of issue I should be aware of?"

"No, I just-"

"Sir, please, I have been your aide now for as long as you've been Commander-Captain. I know when something is troubling you, and this looks as though it is particularly troubling. If there is anything I can do to help, it would be my pleasure."

Raffa looked away from the pad and sat up. "I was supposed to do something. I didn't do it, and now I don't know if I'll ever get the chance again."

"And this something relates to Specialist Stone?"

"That obvious, huh?"

"As I said, we've worked together a long time." Raffa was sure he saw Ikarus grinning. "Would I be correct in assuming this failed venture had something to do with romance?"

"You can't have got that just from this conversation. Even you're not that good, Brook."

"I didn't need to be. The way the two of you act around one another... it is most unusual, as though there is a barrier between you, yet each of you yearns to be on the other side."

"Is this your... professional opinion, Ikarus?"

"I merely state what I have observed."

"Alright, fine." Raffa blew the air out of his cheeks. "We were on deck sixteen, looking out that big window they got there. It was just the right time to see the Void Cloud, and it looked stunning, but... Ikarus, it was nothing compared to Kaska. It was like... I don't know. I can't explain it."

"Have you told her this?"

"I haven't spoken to her since last night."

"Forgive me, but it all sounds a rather splendid moment. If you don't mind me asking, what changed?"

"We were standing there, just staring into one another's eyes..." Raffa punched the bench at the memory. "Then that damn idiot, Winters... he's been hiding nearby, watching us. Shouts 'kiss her!' After that, she promptly said her goodbyes and left."

"Ah." Ikarus took a few seconds to consider his reply. "Force-Commander Winters did not do you any favours. However, I feel Specialist Stone might be a forgiving person outside of matters to do with Kau D'varza. Speak with her, but do it in person so she knows you mean it."

"You think I should keep pursuing this?"

"'Pursuing' is the wrong terminology. Perhaps one should stop thinking in terms of being a soldier, and more in terms of being the Joseph Raffa you'd like others to see. You are more than just a suit of armour, Sir." He smiled. "However, yes, despite this minor setback, I doubt that either of you could find happiness with anyone else on Kau D'varza. You might find another, but your thoughts would always drift to what might have been."

"Take the risk," Raffa whispered, remembering his conversation with Winters in the freighter's control center.

"Indeed. It is not always the best option, however, in this instance, you would be remiss to give up at such an early complication."

He sat thinking for a few seconds, then nodded at Ikarus. "Thanks. I needed someone else's perspective.

The fact that it's yours..."

"You are always welcome, Sir. And if I may make a further suggestion, perhaps a gift would be suitable? Something small. I can have the aquaponics lab send up some flowers?"

"Flowers? Why would-"

"A traditional gift, Sir. I believe the idea is to give something beautiful so that one might simply pause and admire it. Appreciate it."

"Isn't that a waste? Flowers don't last very long outside of the labs."

"I would imagine that also contributes to the beauty. It is fleeting, of the moment, but in that moment, eternal."

"How'd you get to know so much about all this stuff?"

"I will forgive my honourable commander for forgetting my once-husband was an aquaponics technician."

"You don't talk about him much."

"People rarely ask," Ikarus replied with a sly grin. "We had a number of good times, but as with many relationships, we wanted different things." The grin faded slightly. "*Talis vita est.*"

"And he'd get you flowers?"

"So many I had little space to read or study. I would recommend you take a more... relaxed approach. A single bunch, not too small, nor too large. Try to find something that reminds you of Specialist Stone."

Raffa's eyes widened. "By the Void, I think I'd rather be sent out to intercept another freighter!"

"I would remind the commander to be mindful of what he wishes for."

"This is ridiculous! A gift, one that exists for only a brief time, and not too big or too small, in a specific quantity, that reminds me of the person I am gifting them too." He exhaled. "I can't wrap my head around this!"

"Congratulations, Sir; I feel we have made extraordinary progress in helping you understand love, and some of the minutia it entails."

"Your sarcasm is noted, Ikarus."

"I assure you my tone is not directed at you, rather the concept as a whole. It would take a thousand scribes a thousand lifetimes to even come close to understanding the unique bond between two people." His smile was hopeful this time. "However, in your ignorance, you may surprise even Specialist Stone. I shall inform the aquaponics lab you intend to stop by." He turned to something off-screen, then back to Raffa. "Oh, and I hope the commander doesn't think I'm being too forward by suggesting that, even though you were supposed to do something, you should not rush to do what you should have done when you next meet. The opportunity will arise again; an appropriate opportunity, at which time you'll know what to do. I implore you not to rush to Specialist Stone now and... embrace her."

"I wasn't-"

"Then please forgive my assumption."

Raffa nodded. "Sometimes, Ikarus, I don't know what I'd do without you. All the time actually."

"I believe you would manage, Sir." He said a few words off-screen, then smiled. "The aquaponics lab informs me they are ready for your visit."

"I suppose I should find some clean clothes then. Alright, thanks, Ikarus."

"My pleasure. I wish you every iota of luck the universe can muster, Sir."

The screen faded. Raffa folded it away and sat for several seconds trying to make sense of everything he'd just been told.

"Flowers? I don't know the first damn thing about flowers. Ugh... what *the Void* am I getting myself into?"

* * *

The ride down to the engineering bay accompanied by a team of security officers and Specialist Trast had been the easy part, but as Elise stepped into the bay proper, she was greeted with a scene of total anarchy. The officers rushed to form a barrier between the Specialists and the angry group of thirty or so who came charging toward them. Upon seeing the security team raise their shields, the group slowed and resorted to throwing tools and bolts instead.

"Where is Specialist Stone?" Trast barked at a nearby worker.

One of the officers closest to Elise turned to her as his shield pinged and dinged, deflecting the mobs projectiles. "Madam Specialist! Please, stay low!"

Trast slid to Elise's side as she knelt down. "Kaska never said it was this bad. Sorry, kid, looks like we're throwing you in at the deep end."

"What is all this?" Elise asked, flinching every time something hit one of the shields.

"Kaska quietly tried to have the boss of this place come with her to Core-Com. She thinks-"

Something hit the shield with a thud and the line almost broke. Trast spoke hurriedly.

"She thinks he's skimming off the accounts, and no doubt all these assholes benefit from those little transactions. It's not hard to see why a couple of them would be upset."

"So they're rioting?"

"The specialists don't have the best relationship with the engineers. Look at what they gave us to deal with that freighter."

"*Bo'a*... Right. So what are we doing?"

"Can't go back to the lift: leaving this place in their hands is bad strategy. Can't leave Kaska either, though the Void only knows where she is. As long as they're focused on us, they're not tearing the place apart. I'd like to keep it that way, despite the obvious risks."

"So it's a stalemate?"

"Until Zeled gets off his ass to deal with it, yeah."

"You know," Elise said with a frown, "I'm starting to get a little sick of red-tape."

"Ha! Kid! Welcome to being a specialist!" She slapped Elise on the arm with a friendly grin, then turned to talk to one of the security personnel. Elise eyed the distant crowd through a crack between shields. Cautiously, she stood up and tried to push between them. The officers, unsure, just held firm.

"Let me through," Elise murmured.

"Ma'am, I'm not sure that's a wise course of-"

Be firm. Stone's voice echoed in her head.

"Officer, you *will* let me through."

"Uh... As you wish, Ma'am."

As difficult as it seemed, the officers parted barely enough to let Elise through. She held her arms up, trying to appear as non-threatening as possible.

"What are you doing, kid?" Trast called, but Elise kept her eyes on the mob. Apart from one or two, the volley of projectiles had ceased, replaced mostly by confusion and surprise.

"Is there someone I can talk to?"

"Get fucked, Spesh!"

"It's just a uniform. I'm a person, like you." She kept her gaze steady, despite the growing tension she felt in her stomach. "I need to know what you want, so we can come to a solution that doesn't involve violence. Nobody wants that, do they? You might have an advantage now, but when Commissioner Zeled bursts out of that elevator we're all in trouble, me probably more than any of you. So, I'm gonna ask again, is there someone I can talk to?"

She took a step forward, then another, putting distance between herself and the security forces. Elise heard them nervously shuffling forward and called back, "Unless Specialist Trast has given you specific orders to the contrary, remain where you are."

The shuffling stopped. There was no further movement.

I kinda like this talking with authority thing. Oh damnit, Elise, don't let it go to your head. Focus on the situation at hand.

The mob didn't contest her approach until she passed beyond the midway point.

"Hold it, Spesh." The one talking seemed to be the leader of this little pack: tall, young, constant look of anger.

"My name is Elise. What's yours?"

"Employee Sixteen," he replied. The mood dropped.

"Pretty strange name. You strike me as more of a Stev."

That got one or two nervous laughs.

"You tryna be funny, Spesh?"

"Better than us all throwing spanners and bullets at one another."

"Last I checked, that fight? Pretty one sided."

"You already know that won't last. Come on, *Stev*, let's talk; what is it you want?"

"We want you lot to stop interfering down here. We've got a good thing going on, don't need you coming here changing shit."

"Oh, well that's easy." Elise grinned. "Keep all the station's warships running properly, and we'll only be down here to give out bonuses."

"Nah, we earn more in a cycle from civvie vessels than we could earn working on four of your birds. It ain't worth our time."

"How could we make it worth your time? The continued existence of the station doesn't seem to be doing it for you, so... what? More credits? Better tools?"

"Credits would be a start!"

"Alright, fine." Elise shrugged. "And you'll keep the ships functioning as expected?"

"We want a proper contract, written up, signed. Four-hundred credits per vessel, base price, then time on top of that."

"I can't authorize that, but Specialist Stone will be able to. Speaking of, where is Specialist Stone?"

"Heh, your little rodent friend scurried into one of

those new F.A.C.s. Might wanna hurry up an' find her. No telling what the boss might do."

His tone sent a chill down her spine, but Elise held firm and fixed him with a stare. "I'm going to find her, and for everyone's sake... for our deal to be a success... you'd better hope she's okay."

"Oh, our deal will be a success, Spesh, otherwise we start dismantling this station piece by piece."

Elise frowned, then addressed the rest of the group. "Commissioner Zeled will be here soon with a large enough force to arrest all of you. Make that difficult for him by returning to your jobs."

The group shared a few uncertain glances, then promptly scattered. When they did, Specialist Trast strode over.

"Eh, good work, Kid. Now come on, we've gotta find Kaska."

"What about your team?" Elise replied.

"They'll hold the elevator until help arrives. They won't cause any trouble unless they need to."

"Alright." Elise nodded. "Lead the way."

* * *

The fast-attack craft was as cramped as ships came. Two large rooms with a walkway connecting them, and some small bunks in an area with a ripped curtain for privacy near the rear. Kaska could hear the airlock hatch tapping against the bulkhead, and cursed herself for not closing it when she'd taken refuge from that lunatic Jimba. A beam of light shone through the opening, the only source of illumination in the powered down craft.

Stone, currently crouched behind one of the control panels, watched it carefully for any signs of movement and listened. She thought she heard a whirring sound, then became certain as it grew louder. There was a clunk as something latched onto the ship and started pulling it up.

"Going for a ride, Spesh?" Jimba called out from below. Kaska leapt from her hiding spot and ran directly for the airlock, only to stop at the last instant upon seeing how high she was.

"What are you doing?" she yelled.

"You wanted us to check the new craft. I thought you'd appreciate a first-hand demonstration!"

"Have you lost your mind? Jimba, put this craft back down immediately! That is an order!"

"I wouldn't want to stop you enjoying the ride!"

He shunted the ship one way, then another, knocking Kaska back into the vessel. It was now tilting at such an angle that trying to climb up the floor to reach the airlock was impossible. She lay against the console and clung on for dear life. Her heart was racing, a cold sweat sticking her tunic to her back. She heard the internal small-craft airlock alarm blaring and her heart skipped several beats. Her breathing slowed to a crawl. The oversized doors ground open, the Fast-attack craft jolted forward, and her body went numb as she heard the tell-tale sound of the doors closing again behind her. Then came the hiss as the airlock started to cycle.

***

Trast had left Elise eating dust when she'd heard the airlock alarm going off. By the time she finally caught up, Trast was delivering the most devastating punch she'd ever witnessed straight at the control operator's nose. As he fell backwards, Trast followed, snatching up the remote and hitting the emergency stop button. Once the alarm ceased, Trast rolled off him and sighed.

"What was that about?" Elise asked.

Trast, out of breath, made a meagre attempt to point towards the ship in the airlock. "Doors open... I'd wager... Stone... onboard."

"He was going to space her?" Elise looked down at the crumpled, bloody, well-fed heap of a man and scowled. "Son of a bitch."

"Damn near... broke my hand, too. Here." Trast threw the controls over and sat up, recovering quickly. "Press back, then bring up the Return to bay option, it's all pretty self-explanatory from there."

Elise did as instructed and watched as the vessel re-entered the bay. She let out a relieved sigh "Can't believe he was gonna space her..."

"Yeah, well, the Void Cloud attracts all sorts of head-cases. Only problem is, not all of 'em reach the Cloud; Kau D'varza gets a fair share too."

"But this?"

"If Stone's right, this guy's entire world had just come crashing down around him. I'd probably freak out if I was losing my job, but being found out as the head of some racket? He was probably looking at exile at the very least. He won't have been acting alone either, so no doubt he'll be taking a few people down with him. Oh, and did I mention how much the engineers hate us Specialists already?"

Elise glanced at the soon-to-be-former engineering boss once more, then back at Trast and laughed.

"Something funny?"

"'Come on, tag along, it'll be fine, just some on the job training'." Elise winked. "If this is training, the real deal must be hardcore." Elise helped her to her feet. "You keep an eye on this guy. Even with a broken hand I think your swing is better than mine."

"Alright, I'll get medical down here. Go find Stone."

Elise nodded and headed for the ship. As she descended into the darkness, she tapped the emblem on her chest, lighting up the ship's interior with the embedded torch. She saw Stone straight away. She was sprawled on the floor, badly bruised and cut in several places by the loose equipment, but she was still breathing. Elise approached cautiously.

"Specialist Stone?"

No response. She tried nudging her.

"Specialist Stone?"

"Uhh…"

"Hey, hey, easy. It's okay. We're here."

"Here?"

"Oh… on one of those new ships. Some guy was trying to dump you out an airlock."

"I remember. Jimba." She scowled and tried to sit up, then sucked through her teeth and laid back down.

"Problem?"

"My legs and back… feel like they're…"

"Okay. Easy, just lie still for now. Looks like all this mess took you for a tumble."

"I'm gonna need medical."

"They're on their way."

Kaska lay quietly, looking up at the ceiling.

"You wanna talk?" Elise asked. "Might help pass the time."

"I'm... in a bit of pain. But you go ahead."

"It was you, wasn't it? The specialist who thought I'd make good in this job."

Kaska mumbled an affirmative.

"I... Well... thanks." She sighed. "I left Paradise because there was nothing I could do to stop what was happening, and signing on woulda just got me in trouble. But here? The problems are still manageable; there's still time for me to make a difference and help. I can prevent Paradise Two."

"Manageable?" Kaska replied. "Barely."

"Well... I hope the day never comes when I'm being carried out an airlock in an open ship, but compared to where I come from? This is a quiet day."

"You're joking."

"Nope. There're these guys... Free Paradise Movement. Last I heard they'd attacked a convoy hoping to get their message across."

"Damn."

"Eh, didn't used to be so bad. Maybe things'll improve, maybe they won't. I hope my family make it out if things get worse, but they're a stubborn bunch. Paradise could be a crater and they'd find a way to live in the cracks."

Kaska scoffed. "Heh, don't make me laugh."

"Well if the cracks ever get flooded, maybe you'll get to meet them yet. Might even need to find a few new habitats to put them in."

"They'd be welcome."

"I'll tell them to keep their noses out of the network too." She glanced towards the airlock as shadows flickered and footsteps echoed. "Looks like the med team are here. You're gonna be okay."

She stepped back to let them do their work. As she turned to leave, Kaska called out to her.

"Hey, Elise."

"Mhmm?"

"Thanks."

* * *

"What happened?" Zeled's face was red with anger as

Raffa stepped off the elevator. He was surprised to find himself surrounded by an entire squad, plus a security team.

"Er..."

"What are *you* doing here?" Zeled snapped, then stared at the bundle of flowers in Raffa's hand. "And what are *those*?"

"I'm looking for Specialist Stone. And according to the lab, these are tulips."

"Do they need to be quarantined? Why are you just wandering around with them?"

"With respect, Sir," Raffa motioned to the gathered squad, "is there something going on?"

He frowned. "Get out of my sight, Raffa. You and I will talk later."

"I look forward to it, Sir."

Easiest conversation I've got to look forward to this cycle.

He wandered over to the security specialists, who offered him loose salutes that he quickly waved off.

"Relax. Where's your boss?"

One of the senior ranking officers stepped forward. "Specialist Trast is with Specialist Rivera, seeking Specialist Stone." She motioned towards the far end of the bay.

"'Seeking Specialist Sto...'. What went on here? What's happened to Kaska?"

"We arrived after it had all kicked off. Something about someone getting arrested, and that causing a riot." She pointed to the dents in her shield. "I'm pretty sure that was a spanner. Jiffa got an omni-tool jammed in his. Set to weld mode."

"A riot? Is Specialist Stone alright?"

"We're not sure, Sir. We saw medical heading that way earlier, but Specialist Trast told us to stay here and make sure things didn't boil over again."

Raffa didn't wait to hear any more. He headed towards the end of the bay in a flat-out run, taking care not to damage his precious cargo as he went, and skidded to a halt outside the shuttle bay just as a medical team were bringing Coda Trast through it.

"Specialist!" Raffa seemed surprised. "Are you alright?"

"Broke my damn wrist smacking that asshole sideways." She jabbed a thumb back in the direction they'd come. "He'll be out for a few, medics saw to that."

"Where's Specialist Stone?"

She adjusted her thumb towards the fast attack craft.

"Last I saw, in that thing."

"Is she alright?"

"You'd be better off asking her that question. If you don't mind, I've got my own sedation to see to."

"Thank you, Specialist, I hope the wrist heals soon."

Elise and one of the medics were helping Kaska out of the ship, her cuts cleaned and resealed, her bruises already fading. She raised a hand to block out the bright light, and saw a silhouette approaching.

"Comcap Raffa?" she said, in a hoarse voice.

"What happened?"

Elise frowned. "Guy tried giving her an unscheduled fresh-air tour of space."

"By the Void, Kaska..." He fixed his gaze on her. "Are you okay?"

"I'll live." Her eyes adjusted enough for her to lower her arm. For a few seconds, she studied the concern on Raffa's face and saw it was genuine. Then her eyes fell to the strange bundle in his hand.

"What are those?"

"Er... flowers. Tulips." Raffa flushed "Is now a bad time? I can-"

Kaska blinked, studying him "What are they for?"

"They're... er, they're for you." He presented them, a look of worry on his face. "Ikarus suggested it would be... appropriate."

"Well," Elise said, walking away, "I'm getting the fuck outta here. Awk-waaard."

Raffa's worry only deepened when Stone didn't smile. "Have I made a mistake? Has Ikarus set me up? I'm going to-"

"Comcap Raffa." Stone's voice cracked as she reached out and grasped the stems, smiling despite the pain. "They're beautiful. Thank you."

The weight that seemed to lift from Raffa's shoulders could have crushed the station and the deep, trembling sigh he gave made Kaska laugh. She winced when she did it, that was true, but she laughed.

"Did you choose them yourself?"

"Er... yes," he said, mentally apologising to Ikarus. They... reminded me most of you."

"We don't often see tulips around core control. They're usually reserved for our richer citizens."

"The Aquaponics lab took great delight in telling me all about their trade. It was... unrelenting."

"They were probably happy to have someone new to

talk to." She started walking back to the bay proper, but another sharp pain sent her tumbling into Raffa. He caught her and propped her up.

"Here, let me help."

"Ugh. I could kill that asshole."

"Wouldn't that breach your contract?"

"I'm sure the Arch-Commissioner would understand."

He helped her forward as a group of security officers swept past. Raffa nodded to the one he'd spoken to earlier.

"Hey, can we have a word?"

She came to an abrupt halt, leaving her colleagues to go on without her. "Of course, Sir. How can I help?"

"I think that guy is some kind of saboteur. Can you have him delivered to my offices for interrogation once you're done?"

She grinned. "I don't see that being a problem, Sir."

He nodded. "Dismissed."

The security specialist, still grinning, turned on her heel and ran to catch up with her squad, leaving Raffa and Stone to continue on their way.

Kaska coughed. "Saboteur?"

"I'm guessing he's the reason I was in *Bo'a* and not *Vypka*?"

"Yes. Apparently, getting military vessels prepped wasn't lucrative enough."

"Ah, that'll be why Ikarus said he's going through some *interesting* files he recovered."

"Yes. Sorry, I wanted to speak to you about it first, but-"

"If you need Ikarus for anything, I am happy to allow it. He will be extremely thorough once he hears of this."

"He's always extremely thorough."

"True. It is perhaps best I do not elaborate on some of Ikarus' other skills, though. Suffice it to say, your friend won't be seeing the light of the Void any time soon."

"Thank you, Joseph."

The soldiers parted to allow them through. There was an awkward silence between them as they waited for the elevator. When the doors finally rolled open, Raffa helped Kaska over to the rail.

"Thank you."

"Where are we going? Medical?"

"I think I probably should. The medics patched me up, but I want a more thorough check."

He hit a button and the doors closed. As the elevator hummed towards its destination, Kaska looked down at the flowers, then back at Raffa.

"Why'd you really get them?"

"I wanted…" He sighed. "I wanted to apologise."

"Because of Winters? Joseph, that wasn't your fault."

"Perhaps, but I am not entirely blameless. I've been a soldier for a long time. It is difficult for me to…well, to wrap my head around this."

"You're doing a pretty good job. No one's ever given me flowers before."

"Ikarus' suggestions were thorough, but vague."

She couldn't help but smile. "Confusing, isn't it?"

"Indeed." He drew breath to say more, but paused.

"Something else on your mind?"

"I had concerns. We're still having dinner later?"

"Of course we are. Even in my condition, I wouldn't miss it for all the colours in the Void."

"Thank you, that is a relief. I will ensure Winters is

kept in his quarters."

"I have a feeling you will still hear his voice."

"My guards can be- Oh. You mean... Of course."

The doors rolled open. Raffa took his place at Kaska's side, giving her support, then led her towards the bright lights of the medical section.

CHAPTER TWELVE- IMPENDING CONVERGENCE

Kaska Stone's eyes scanned each word carefully from her bed in the medical section. The report Elise Rivera had submitted was thorough and, to save everyone a lot of trouble in translating, she'd gone to great lengths to write the whole thing in Standard as well as D'varzan. Kaska couldn't help but be impressed, and felt an additional nudge of vindication in her suggesting that Gierre make use of the other woman's unique skills. She tapped the approve dialogue, and sent it on to Core Command.

"Specialist Stone?"

She glanced up to see a nurse approaching.

"Our examinations have revealed no lasting damage. However, I'd like to check your arm, give that nasty bruise another go."

"Of course."

She felt relieved that, despite her ordeal, she'd come through relatively unscathed. Her gaze drifted to the huge screen at her side. It had been set to a tropical waterfall upon her arrival, but she'd quickly grown bored with that and switched it to a traditional field blowing in the breeze.

"I don't know where they find those scenes," the nurse said as she pushed a trolley up to the bed. "Certainly nowhere in this system." She picked up a handheld device, white with a thick handle and large head. "Arm please."

Kaska's eyes remained on the view as she raised the requested limb. "They're from Harmony. They were presented to us as a way to brighten the place up, but I think it's more to drive tourism."

"Oh. They're from the Harmony system? It looks beautiful."

Kaska cocked an eyebrow. "You didn't know? I thought it was common knowledge. We use them all over the place."

"No, Ma'am, I didn't know." The nurse held Kaska's hand up and slowly swept the device back and forth along the length of her arm. It emitted a faint hum, which had its own soothing quality.

Well that puts a hole in my tourism theory...

"And... Done!" The nurse smiled. "Miss Stone, I am happy to discharge you on the basis that you are fit, healthy, and at no risk from any further injury from existing wounds." She put the device down and tapped at a pad on the trolley. "I recommend you take it easy for a few cycles, but other than that, you'll be fine."

"Thank you."

"If there's nothing else?"

"No, I think I can manage from here."

As the nurse wheeled the trolley out, Gierre Nevos stepped in.

"Arch-Commissioner," Kaska said with a sly grin. She threw her legs over the edge of the bed and got to her feet.

"Specialist Stone. I am relieved to see you moving, and sorry for what you underwent."

"Where is he?"

"Head... My apologies, *Ex*-Head Engineer Jimba is quite in demand after this incident. I think it is currently Commissioner Zeled's turn, then Command Core, then the arresting security team. Oh, yes, and Comcap Raffa has filed a rather... *thorough* list of charges."

Helped by Ikarus, no doubt. Damn, glad I'm not dealing with that.

"His punishment?" She swallowed. "Jimba's, I mean."

"Some of the citizens... It is troubling, they have called for an execution."

Kaska raised her hand. "No. I wanted it earlier too, so I can see their point, and believe me there is nothing I'd like more than to stick him in an airlock... but that isn't our way; we can't simply start executing people, regardless of the situation."

"I agree. And if we execute someone for trying to kill a specialist, the citizens will be most upset by our treatment of previous, actual, murderers in their ranks."

"Exile," Kaska said flatly. "It's the only option. The people won't be happy to pay for his food and keep while he rots in one of our cells. It also gets him well away from Kau D'varza." She smiled, coldly. "Of course, that doesn't mean the security teams can't run their interviews."

"After they are done, I will see to it that he is taken far from here, and followed by one of our agents to ensure he harbours no desire for revenge. I still have my... issues... with such a proposal, however."

"It's a tough situation," Kaska agreed. "Exile him and waste resources keeping an eye on him for however long, or lock him up here and waste resources keeping him alive while the citizens call for blood. The prior option is still my preferred one; if he is out of their sight, he'll be out of their minds."

Gierre's eyes narrowed. "The laws regarding exile don't specify a minimum population for the receiving world, do they?"

"I feel the wording was made deliberately obtuse for this purpose."

"In that case, we can imprison *and* exile him."

"The world will need some kind of breathable air mix... and the ability to find shelter and sustenance. There's nothing saying it has to be too comfortable, though."

"Stars bless ambiguity."

Kaska nodded. "Indeed, Sir."

He pointed vaguely in the direction of the door. "Are you leaving? Would you like a lift?"

"Thank you, Sir. I'd appreciate that." She straightened her tunic, scooped up the flowers and turned to follow him out.

Gierre raised an eyebrow. "An admirer, Specialist Stone?"

"Ah... I suppose you could say that."

He raised his hands. "Say no more. I respect your privacy, Specialist."

Kaska was steadier on her feet as she followed Gierre through the door and into the corridor. They passed one of the nurse workstations, and Kaska paused.

"Sir," she began, her eyes on the nurse, "I would like to report that I was treated with the utmost respect and care by the staff here. We are lucky to have such people working for us."

The nurse barely registered the compliment. "It is merely our duty, Ma'am, but thank you."

Kaska continued to follow Gierre until they reached the P.T.V. waiting at the bottom of a short set of steps on what most described as a 'street'.

"Habitat S-forty-nine, please," she instructed.

As the vehicle hummed along, Gierre turned back in his seat and put his arm on the bar between them.

"I wanted to ask, did you have any concerns regarding Specialist Rivera?"

"None, Sir," she replied, quickly and firmly. "She's a breath of fresh air for this station. I have no illusions that without her, I'd... well, I..."

"It's alright, I understand."

"She stayed with me, kept me distracted until the medics arrived." Her shoulders slumped. "She told me about where she'd come from."

"Ah, yes. Paradise. It sounds like a most troubled place."

"More so than Kau D'varza," Kaska agreed. "She wants to make a difference here. Make sure history doesn't repeat itself. No, sir, I have no concerns regarding Specialist Rivera. In fact, I believe she would make an excellent Commissioner, given time."

Gierre laughed. "That's all I need. Competition." He turned to face forward and straightened in his seat. "Looks like your stop."

"Thank you, Sir."

"Don't mention it. After the cycle you've had, it's the very least I could do."

As Kaska hopped off the back-seat, Gierre smiled at her. "I hope you have a wonderful and... *successful* evening, Specialist Stone."

Before she could reply, Gierre had directed the driver forward. She watched with a growing smile as it made its way out of sight.

He knows. Of course he knows. Can't get anything past Nevos.

With a light, but still tentative skip to her step, Kaska turned and headed for her habitat to prepare for the evening ahead.

* * *

"Are you sure it looks alright?"

Raffa stared into the vid-screen in his clean-room, appraising himself with a fiercely critical eye, while Ikarus stood at the door.

"Sir, you cannot go to Miranda's Grill in a service uniform, regardless of whether it is ceremonial or not."

"But this?" He looked at the crisp, featureless shirt and dark-toned trousers. "It's a bit plain, isn't it?"

"Subtle," Ikarus corrected.

Raffa rolled his shoulders and gave himself a final glance. "At least it's comfortable, even if I don't feel it."

Ikarus stepped back as Raffa wandered back into his habitat proper.

"Any more advice?"

"Only to be yourself. But remember, this is a social event, not a military exercise."

"It'd be easier if it were."

"Indeed. However, you need experience in both if you, Comcap Raffa, are to have any semblance of what some might consider a 'normal life'. Not all problems can be shot at, blown up, or captured."

"Believe me, I know. It's just... I don't know. I really don't feel comfortable. And I've already messed up once."

"If I may, Sir, this sounds like nerves. If it is any consolation, you can rest assured that Specialist Stone - Kaska - is worrying about the same things at this very moment. Yes, a situation occurred in which you came out unfavourably. You have, however, made amends, and you now have the opportunity to correct your mistake. Remember, also; she *wanted* to give you that chance."

"I think that's the part that worries me."

Ikarus smiled. "Remember what I said before: you will know when the time is right - if such a time presents itself at all. I must prepare you for the possibility that this may simply be a nice meal with a colleague, and no more. Do not go into this expecting the evening to revolve around that singular act, or opportunity to act, as it may not even occur."

"This sounds like more of your 'flower' advice..."

"And I must say, the commander performed admirably. It was an... *interesting...* choice, but I can see your logic."

"Well, thanks. But that reminds me, I want you to be present when they interview that asshole - what's his name? Jimba?"

"Yes, Sir. And it would be a privilege. I have uncovered many interesting facts about our former Head Engineer. I believe my input could guide the questioning in a very productive direction."

"I have no doubts about that. What about his associates? Those other assholes who went along with the riot?"

"Commissioner Zeled is personally overseeing the arrest operation based on video footage and interviews are ongoing. However, it is unlikely they will be allowed to continue to work on Kau D'varza: a threat against the station was made directly to Specialist Rivera. Commissioner Zeled is taking it extremely seriously."

"So what? We're gonna lock them all up?"

Ikarus shook his head. "That would be an unwise solution."

"So what, exile? What if they come back?"

"It is that or termination. Nobody wishes to open that book again."

"It's a shame there isn't some sort of in-between.

Exile them on a ship that they can't leave until their term is up or something. I don't know."

"Many prison vessels operate in this region. However, paying for them to keep hold of our criminals has the potential to become very expensive."

Raffa sighed. "Exile might be even more expensive in the future."

"I cannot argue with that, but of all our options, exile is the best."

"For now." He sat down on the bench and pulled a pair of highly-polished, jet-black shoes closer. "And what of the engineering bay?"

"Under constant watch. Commissioner Zeled has deployed two full teams to sweep the place and maintain order."

"They're gonna love that."

"Actions, and consequences," Ikarus replied in a matter-of-fact tone. "While our departments might not always be on the best of terms, Specialist Stone is Kau D'varzan as much as you, I, or Arch-Commissioner Nevos. An attack on her is an attack on all of us. Retribution will be harsh, it will be unrelenting, and it will last."

"That won't work. I might be a thick-headed commander, but we need to start repairing the damage, not making it worse."

"I agree it is better to build bridges than it is to build walls, however a lot of people are angry. Some are on Specialist Stone's side; some, although quieter now, support the actions Jimba took as some sort of rebellion against what they see as an unfair system. I say quieter, because since *someone* leaked information regarding his various schemes, and seeing how much money he was making, those voices are all but muted."

"And you wouldn't know anything about that, I assume?"

"It seems as though Jimba sent some of his more incriminating documents to everyone on the station shortly before his arrest. I'm sure he had a very good reason." Ikarus smiled a toothy grin.

"I'm sure *he* did, Ikarus."

"I am certain I do not know what the commander means."

Sometimes, I get real tired of this danc-

"Dancing!" Raffa blurted, then stared at Ikarus. "What if she asks me to dance? I don't know the first damn thing about dancing!"

Ikarus looked at him confused for a moment, then smiled. "Sir, even Specialist Stone is not that cruel."

"Oh… By the Void, I hope not."

"Perhaps, if things go well, you might try learning some techniques from the Augmented Reality programs."

"You mean the training sims?"

"Ah, yes, the old terminology. The commander might find there's been quite an update since he last used the system."

"Trust the military to be a few versions behind…" He waved his hands, mimicking Commissioner Zeled. "*If it's secure, and it works, we're not changing it!*"

"Very good, Sir. I feel that with a little more work, you may even be able to fool the Commissioner himself."

"Oh, shut up."

"Sir."

With the shoes on and sealed up, Raffa stood and spread his arms out. "Am I ready?"

"Ready is… optimistic. However, you look most acceptable, Sir. I believe Specialist Stone will enjoy seeing you in something that is not a variation of your work attire."

"You always know how to make a guy feel special, Ikarus."

"The commander's sarcasm is noted."

Raffa inhaled, steadied himself, then made for the door. "Well... here I go. Wish me luck."

"'Luck' should not be required. However, if it helps... good luck."

"Thanks, Ikarus. I owe you one."

Ikarus accepted the sentiment with a slight nod. "Please give my regards to Specialist Stone."

* * *

The message notification marked 'To Elise Rivera, From Danto Rivera" put a wide smile on Elise's face. She'd been trying, unsuccessfully, to find more info on the freighter - an activity that had led to a sharp decay in her mood. That all vanished in an instant with news from her family.

"Hey, Elly!"

"Hey, Dad," she replied, despite it being a pre-recorded message.

"How's that floating cage treatin' ya?"

He seems in high spirits... Nice to hear the old tongue again, though...

"Hope you're doing well. Just a quick one this time, there's lots going on."

She watched him take a deep breath and mentally prepare himself to break some important news.

"Tayborn's been arrested. The F.P.M. were almost totally wiped out when they tried to take that convoy."

Elise's eyes widened. "Paradise *won*?" She was both shocked and impressed.

"They're rounding up the stragglers now. They likely won't be setting foot on the planet again, let alone Paradise." He grinned. "They picked the wrong fight. With Reclaimers of all people! Could you imagine?"

Reclaimers? What are they doing helping with something like this? That doesn't make sense...

"There were two of them, I'm told. Took out damn near the whole group when Paradise couldn't manage it with a hundred Enforcers. Makes ya wonder what we're paying taxes for, eh?" He waved his hand in front of his face. "Ah, sorry, not the time for politics. Just wanted to check in, tell ya the good news. Hey, maybe now..."

Don't say it, please don't say it, don't put me in this position, don't do it...

"... you could come home? We all miss ya, and well... me and your ma, we ain't getting any younger."

Damnit.

He smiled. "Just something to think about, eh kiddo? Have a good one, love ya lots."

"Love you too, Dad," she mumbled, already lost in confused, troubling thoughts.

The video had frozen on his image as he'd leant over to stop the recording. She looked into his motionless eyes and felt even more conflicted.

He's happy... Looking forward to a future without riots, or trouble... But I've just found my feet, something to keep me here. And while Paradise might be free from worry now, Kau D'varza is just starting to get its fill. I could go back to the life I knew, to my family, or I could stay here and make a difference...

She stood up from the couch and headed for the drinks machine. After several sharp mouthfuls of whatever the machine had attributed the 'Strong' characteristic to, she took her glass back to the sofa and sat down. As she did, another notification appeared in the corner of her screen.

What now? Oh. Gierre.

"Accept. Yes, Arch-Commissioner?"

"Specialist Rivera." He seemed concerned, although Elise didn't properly register it, she was so lost in her own thoughts.

"Yes, Sir?"

"This report, is this accura-" he said, then paused. "Is something the matter, Specialist Rivera?"

Her eyes jumped to the screen. "Uh, no, Sir. You have concerns about my report?"

"Not about the quality, you understand, but the content. Is this accurate?"

"To the best of my knowledge."

"Then this is most troubling. Most troubling... Do you believe Kau D'varza could suffer such an incident?"

Elise frowned. "I hope not."

Gierre's face took on a frown of its own. "Specialist Rivera, you seem most distracted. Is now a bad time?"

"It's... I'm sorry, Arch-Commissioner, I just had a message from Paradise."

"Oh? Well that's a good thing, isn't it?"

She nodded. "Yeah... Good. Very good, actually. Paradise doesn't have to worry about the F.P.M. anymore."

"Well that is good news. You, your family and friends, have my sincerest congratulations." He paused. "Your family *is* alright, I trust?"

"They want me to go back."

Gierre's face fell. "Ah." He settled back, lacing his fingers. "Specialist Rivera, as unhappy as I would be to see you leave, you are under no obligation to remain here. If your home has been liberated of its problems then it will surely be safer than Kau D'varza, and, if I were your family, I would wish you were closer. However..." His eyes narrowed. "I would obviously prefer it if you remained here. Besides your obvious abilities and experience, I find myself growing quite fond of you. Dare I suggest that we might even be good friends in future."

"Uh..."

"But all that is by-the-by. Suffice it to say, I won't hold your decision against you, whichever way you choose."

"That is... most kind. Thank you, Arch-Commissioner."

She straightened up and shook the incoming drunken haze from her mind. "You wanted to know whether Kau D'varza could be the subject of a mass kidnapping like on the freighter?"

He nodded. "Or if our vessels could be at risk. If we send trade out to far-flung regions, might this happen again?"

"That's always the risk with sending assets out, but I feel the station is sufficiently protected. In any case, seeking out the problem at its core should be our goal. Remove that, we remove the threat to the station. But surely Specialist Stone -

"Yes, yes. I will ask for her assessment in due course," he said, waving her intended objection aside. "Right now I am seeking your thoughts, Specialist Rivera."

She straightened. "Then you have them, Sir."

"So you think we should be more proactive, even though doing so could potentially mean more risk?"

"Uh…" She frowned. "If you want Kau D'varza to end up like Paradise, then doing nothing is exactly how that'll happen."

Come on, what was it Trast said?

"Sir, given what we know, I *cannot* recommend ignoring this problem."

"Spoken like a true specialist," he said. Elise wasn't sure if it was a compliment. "Alright, I will speak with my advisors and try and find a suitable solution. Good work, Specialist, I am pleased with the prompt and precise manner in which this has reached me."

"Not a problem, Sir."

"You know where to find me if you need anything."

As Gierre's image disappeared, Elise stared off into space, glass pressed against her lips.

* * *

The smell of Miranda's Grill hit Raffa before the door had even opened. It made his mouth water and his nostril hairs dance. The Grill itself was a small, cosy building, tucked away in the corner of the shopping district. The exterior had the typical holographic menus and signs advertising what Raffa considered to be reasonable enough prices. He said a little thank you to anything willing to listen in appreciation that Kaska had selected such a venue.

Raffa didn't know where to look first as he stepped over the threshold into the restaurant proper. The decor was tasteful, even stylish, but warm and welcoming. Deep red walls and understated lighting created a relaxed atmosphere, even one of intimacy. He glanced up at the ceiling, his attention immediately caught by the sturdy beams.

Is that real wood? It's so dark... And detailed!

"Joseph!"

His attention snapped back to the room as he sought out the voice, and he smiled as he spotted Kaska Stone waving to him from a small table near the back, tucked behind the central square bar.

If she's as nervous as I am, she's doing a damn good job of hiding it...

"Good evening, Spe-... Kaska."

Great start.

She studied him momentarily, then met his eyes with a smile. "Good evening yourself, *Joseph*."

"I hope I haven't kept you waiting," he said, and motioned to the empty seat. She nodded and he sat down.

"Not at all. Actually, I think we're both a little early." She leaned back and looked around. "What do you think?"

"Of the restaurant?" he asked, and could have kicked himself for asking such a redundant question.

She nodded again, without turning back to look at him.

"It's interesting, unusual for Kau D'varza. A good choice, I believe."

"Wait 'til you try the food."

I should have researched the menu...

"Speaking of which, what do you recommend?"

Kaska tapped at the tabletop, the logo faded into a menu. "The ribs are good, but messy. I like the Bora Steak Wrap."

Raffa's eyes scanned the display. "Barramundi?" He frowned. "They've got those in aquaponics."

Great conversation piece there, Raf', let's talk about damn fish!

"It's got a sweet taste. A little flat, but nice enough, for fish."

Can we please change the subject? I've heard enough about aquaponics to last a lifetime.

"Hmm... I think I'll stick with what I know. Bora is good. What's a steak wrap?"

I feel dumb asking... Don't eat out enough to know all this stuff.

"Chunks of bora mixed with salad, wrapped in a flat-bread. You get two per order."

"Sounds good."

That sounded convincing... Damn, she's gonna think you're a right idiot... Or you're being sarcastic... Move on.

"And to drink?"

"I like the firewine, it's spicy."

Firewine?

"Sounds a little too exciting for me. I'll take a beer."

"Which one?"

Raffa frowned. "There's too much choice here… How about… Windan Amber?"

Probably best not to make a habit of choosing drinks at random. I'll take the Kandaha Poison brew please…

Kaska's fingers fluttered over the display. Six taps later, she sat back with a smile. "Thirty seks."

"Really? Doesn't leave much time for conversation."

"Speaking of conversations…". She paused, smiling, seemingly at her choice of words. "Have you talked to Winters yet?"

Ah. I don't wanna talk about him…

"I haven't, but I will." *Eventually.* "Ikarus sends his regards, though."

"Oh? He could have said so when he sent that report in just before I got here."

Raffa frowned. "It's like he never stops working."

She eyed him carefully. "That sounds like a complaint, Joseph."

Eh. It was. Hard to fully relax around someone like that.

"An observation. People shouldn't work all the time."

"This, coming from Joseph Raffa?"

Great, she thinks you're a workaholic...

He forced himself to smile, hoping the strain didn't show. "Even I enjoy *some* downtime."

A slot embedded into the wall at the end of the table opened, revealing two thick wooden trays upon which was their meals and drinks. Kaska laughed when Raffa licked his lips as the tray slid into place in front of him.

"Sorry," he said sheepishly, "most of my meals come from work. I'd forgotten what real food even looked like."

"I know what you mean." She pointed at the contents of the wrap. "Look at all those colours, not a grey or dirty brown in sight." She scooped up one of the wraps with both hands and tilted it towards Raffa. "To an enjoyable evening."

Wait... It's going well? I guess I'd be enjoying myself too if I wasn't freaking out.

Raffa watched her delicately tear off a small mouthful and start chewing. He clumsily tried to mimic her, with limited success, but at least the food went in his mouth and he didn't look like a total idiot, so he was content.

"Hey!" he managed, before swallowing. "This is good."

Kaska grinned. "So, tell me, Joseph: what did you do

before all this?"

"Before I became Comcap?"

"No, I mean before Kau D'varza."

"Oh…"

"Is that a tough subject? We can talk about something else, if you like."

"It's not that. It's just been so long since… Ah, let's see… I grew up in Yor' controlled space, always travelling, moving with my family…"

"Hopper, right? We see a few at Kau D'varza every now and then. They tend to stop for a spell, then move on just as they seem to be laying down foundations."

"Sounds about right. Didn't have much of a stable childhood. Probably why I signed up. Looking for routine."

Kaska chewed, motioning with her eyes for him to continue.

"I first signed on with the Yor' Defence Fleet. A soldier of the federation. Guess too much of my parents rubbed off on me. I served the minimum term of engagement, got out as soon as I could."

"Then you came here?"

"Not straight away. I thought Gaitlin might have what I was looking for, then Arokia. By the time I reached Kau D'varza, I figured I'd never find whatever it was I was after, so I was determined to make it work despite my apparent inability to settle. Went to sign on with security forces, they liked my previous experience, so they snapped me up. A few thoughts of moving on started to creep in after a while, but I did my best to distract myself; signed on for more training, did additional courses, and filled the rest of my time trying to be good at my job rather than letting myself sit and think. I couldn't believe it when I was promoted. And again. Then the takeover happened, and I made Comcap."

Raffa took a larger mouthful and took his time chewing, hoping Kaska got the message that he wanted to enjoy his meal rather than talk about himself.

"If you don't mind me asking, do you still speak to your parents?"

He swallowed and shook his head. "They're with the stars now. Dad didn't last long after Ma went."

"I'm sorry."

"Don't be. They did what they wanted, lived happy lives..."

"And they raised you well."

For a second, Raffa flicked back into work mode. "Thank you for saying so, Ma'am."

She laughed, waving a free hand in front of her face. "If we're going to keep meeting like this, that's a habit you'll have to get out of."

Still talking like there's potential here. Maybe I haven't screwed this up...

"Of course. Sorry, Kaska."

"That's better."

"But what about you?"

"What about me?"

"How did *you* end up on Kau D'varza?"

"Oh, I'm a local girl. Parents helped put the place together." She grinned. "Ma always used to say I was the greatest accident she'd ever made. I am reliably informed that a half-built station full of engineers can be a little... exciting... Sometimes."

"I'd heard stories."

"Legendary around this part of space. Started all sorts of rumours. My favourite is one the pervs down in the sim-suite came up with."

"I think I know it, but go on."

"Most likely." She grinned again. "They say there's a

station out there, drifting, and only those with an invite can board."

"And the whole thing is just a never-ending orgy."

"Yeah! I mean, could you imagine it? I'd hate to be the person who had to clean that up. And if they're... ah... 'boinking', all the time, where does the food come from? What do they eat?" She blinked. "On second thoughts, perhaps we shouldn't answer that."

He raised his glass to hide his smile.

Ever the practical thinker...

"I'm sure the sim-suite personnel have given it a lot of thought," he said.

Kaska smiled, nodding her agreement. "Too much, no doubt."

Eventually, she finished her meal and sat back, contentedly cradling the glass of Firewine.

"You seem relaxed," Raffa said, as he pushed his empty tray to one side.

"I assure you, it's all a front." She winked. "I can see how nervous you are. I suppose I'm trying to put you at ease." She placed her glass on the table and leant over to hold his hands. He tensed automatically - which he saw her notice - then forced himself to relax. "It's okay. I can't begin to imagine how stressful this is for you. This isn't my first night out, and I can assure you, this one is going the best so far. You've got nothing to worry about."

Damn, my heart feels like it's gonna burst out my damn chest!

"Thank you, Kaska, that is... reassuring." He smiled. "I too am having a most enjoyable evening."

That smile... And those eyes... What are you doing to my head, Specialist?

She gave his hands a final soft squeeze and sat back again, lifting her wine as she went.

A notification appeared on the tabletop.

"Oh," Kaska said, glancing at it for a second before looking back at Raffa. "I'm pretty full, but if you want, you could get a dessert?"

He shook his head. "I think I've had my fair share this evening."

She smiled. "Then we should finish our drinks and get out of here. Any suggestions on where else we could go?"

"Forgive me, but social venues are something in which I lack experience."

"Well..." She puffed out her cheeks as if in thought, then her eyes widened with excitement. "We could go dancing?"

Raffa's face flushed white. "I... Uh..."

Aaarrrgh!

Kaska laughed. "Relax, Joseph. Ikarus notified me of some of your concerns. I'm only teasing."

"Ikarus?" He frowned. "Anything else I should know?."

"Don't worry..." She bit her lip trying to think of the words. "He was 'most discreet'."

"Oh, for crying out loud..."

Kaska laughed louder this time. "How about the garden-park up on B-deck?"

"That sounds nice." He glanced at the tabletop. "How do I... Er... Pay for this?"

"Oh. Here, let me set it..." Kaska's fingertaps slowed. "Huh..."

"What's wrong?"

"It says the bills already been paid. Courtesy of..." Kaska grinned."Courtesy of one Arch-Commissioner Gierre Nevos."

Raffa gave a wry smile. "I guess I should thank him."

"He added a note. Says 'Have fun kids!' I don't know

how, with everything he's got to do, he still finds time for things like this."

"So that's it? We can just walk out?"

"Oooh, I can go ahead if you like, scout it out, make sure it's safe first."

"That won't be necessary, I will gladly-" He frowned. "You're teasing me again."

Her smile was infectious. "Sure am. Come on, let's go."

* * *

The gardens looked different each time Kaska had visited. The plants wore different colours, the trees and bushes took on unusual shapes, even the smells changed. Her nostrils flared as she filled her lungs with the fresher-than-usual air, despite it's higher-than-standard humidity. Unlike the scrubbed, re-cycled air of the station, it was fragrant and refreshing; the smell of life.

"What do you think?" she asked as Raffa closed the transparent door behind them.

"I've never been here before." He studied the area, body tense as though scanning for threats, then relaxed. "It's calming... I like it."

Well that's a relief.

"See these?" She knelt by the vine-fence and gently

tilted a delicate crimson flower closer to her face. "Star Glory. They train them to run the length of the planters for natural protection. Although... I thought they were white."

"They don't look like they've been painted..."

"Maybe not in the sense you're thinking, but it wouldn't be difficult for the tenders to tweak something here, graft something there, introduce a nutrient or a dye."

"It sounds like a lot of work, but the results are certainly pleasing to see."

"Agreed. Come on, there's something I want to show you."

Kaska grabbed his hand without thinking and led him through the rising plants, bushes and small trees until they arrived at the middle of the gardens. Ahead of them lay a large pond, surrounded by ornate wooden benches. Raffa's eyes were drawn to the large tree that stood on an island in the centre its trunk invisible thanks to the thick mesh of overhanging branches and leaves, the tips of which brushed against the surface of the water. Small lights flickered in the naturally-woven greenery, and for a few moments Kaska and Raffa stood in silence, admiring the tranquil beauty.

Nice to enjoy this with someone for a change...

She glanced down, having forgotten she was still holding Raffa's hand, and smiled. Raffa turned to face her, and as they looked into one another's hopeful eyes, that window of opportunity reappeared. Kaska gently put her hand against his cheek and leant forward, allowing their noses to brush against one another playfully.

I've done the hard work, Joseph Raffa. You better...

Raffa leant in and gently kissed her before she could finish the thought. Her grip on him tightened and, as he tried to pull away, she gave him a coy, but inviting smile. "Just the one? Now who's teasing?"

She pulled him closer again, and there, under the flickering lights of the gardens, Joseph Raffa and Kaska Stone disappeared into a world of their own.

CHAPTER THIRTEEN- NOT ANOTHER PARADISE

The yawn went on long enough to make Elise's jaw ache. Another long night cycle, with not enough sleep to fill it. She considered staying in bed, but as the artificial sun crept up the screen, thoughts of time a-wasting snuck in. She forced herself to stretch out and, after another lengthy yawn, rolled out of bed.

After a quick visit to the clean-room, she squirmed into a crisp new uniform and settled onto the sofa, where she clicked through the various reports and information updates that had arrived while she hadn't been sleeping.

Nothing seemed particularly interesting: there was some news from the engineering bay and a notice from Gierre telling everyone he was impressed with their work, but the rest held nothing that concerned her. She switched over to one of the station's music channels and sat back, not quite allowing herself to properly relax, as low-level melodies filled the room.

So, Elise, what's on the agenda for this cycle? There's no work unless Gierre calls, but without that you'll be left to stew over all the important decisions you've been avoiding.

She sat forward, brushing her hair away from her forehead and scowling. "Great."

You know you've got to deal with this sooner or later. At the very least they deserve a reply. But what to say...

Elise brought up the message centre and opened a new file. She selected 'Long-range', spoke her father's address so it appeared in the top bar, then sat, staring at the 'Record' button. After a few minutes, she straightened up, pulling the creases out of her uniform.

"Begin."

The button changed from amber to blue and the music faded.

"Hey, Dad."

She allowed a few beats for a reply she knew she wouldn't hear.

"It's good to hear from you. Amazing news about

Paradise! Hopefully now people can get their lives back on track."

She looked away from the screen for a brief second. "The thing is, I... I'm not coming back, not right now. Kau D'varza, they gave me a job... I think my full title is External Investigations Specialist, and I report directly to the Arch-Commissioner. He's like the foreman of the station. It's my job to investigate problems and compile my findings so they can act on them. I'm... I think... or hope, or something... I'm doing important work."

She tried a smile, but it felt fake so she let it drop. "You know I miss you more than anything, and as soon as I get some time I'll come see you, but I can't right now." The message-limit light began to flash. "Ah damn. I gotta go, but I love you, and if you ever decide to leave Paradise, there's a place here for you. For all of you. Love you all!" She waved, just as the recording cut off.

"Damn." She sunk into the sofa to review the message. Beside a couple of awkward moments, it seemed fine. After finalizing the last of the recipient details, she hit send and silently watched as it loaded itself into the message system in preparation for its long voyage across several systems to Yurnto, where it would be sorted and sent on to her family.

Despite knocking something important off the 'to-do' list, Elise couldn't shake the feeling that she'd still accomplished nothing. With the music still playing, she checked the active personal list, jumped to her feet and headed out the door to navigate her way through the early-cycle traffic to a personal transport boarding area. It took some time, but she eventually found a free one and rode it all the way to the food district, where she homed in on one of the more hidden establishments and tried not to let too much frustration spoil her mood as she made her way between the food stalls and around citizens enjoying an early meal.

Upon finally arriving at her destination, she passed through a door of the kind that hundreds passed but barely noticed, down a flight of stairs, then made her way along a dimly-lit corridor - careful to avoid the steam venting from a side room as she went - to the quieter, but still bustling workers' canteen. The arched ceiling gave the mess-hall a cramped feeling. Ringed girders ran from bulkhead to bulkhead while clean white lights illuminated the space.

A few people stopped eating, pointing at her and speaking in hushed whispers: "That's the new specialist." "You mean The Talker?" "Saved another."

She bounced on her feet, her hands curling involuntarily into fists.

I should go. I can't handle this. All the attention... I need to get out of here. I can talk to him later, when it's quiet, or... or I can wait and track him down to... well, wherever he works. Maybe even wait until he's back in his quarters. But later. Yes... later...

Out of the frozen scene, a single figure, dressed

in something other than the usual work-clothes, walked towards her.

"Specialist Rivera," Ikarus said as he drew level. "Is something of concern?"

"No, Ikarus... I just..."

"Ah. I see. A talk. It would be my pleasure. Please, follow me."

He led her towards the rear of the room, past plain metal tables surrounded by workers who either made eye contact and offered her a solemn nod or kept their attention fixed on their meals. She couldn't help but wonder how many of these people were friends, and how many were potential enemies.

"Would you like something to eat?" Ikarus asked as they stopped by the central block of vending machines.

Elise nodded, waiting her turn behind one of the larger workers before tapping the screen.

"There isn't much choice..." She blinked. "Ah! Porridge. That'll do."

A few seconds later, with a tray of steaming food in hand, Elise followed Ikarus to a smaller than average table in the corner, beside a door. After settling into his seat, Ikarus motioned for Elise to take the one opposite.

"So, Specialist, what is it that is troubling you?"

She lifted the lid off her tray and inhaled the dull, oaty smell "I don't know."

Ikarus grinned. "That certainly makes things a little more difficult."

Elise pushed her spoon around the bowl. "You're telling me..." She glanced up. "Why do you eat here?"

"I don't always. However, getting a sense for how the workers are feeling, their morale, can help with security."

"Comcap Raffa ordered this?"

Ikarus shook his head. "No. I haven't been 'ordered' to do anything. This is simply something I choose to do. I would prefer to have the information and not need it, than the alternative."

Her eyes narrowed as she studied him. "Comcap Raffa is lucky to have you."

"I believe Kau D'varza is lucky to have Comcap Raffa, and I appreciate the opportunity to support him."

"Why?"

"Are you suspicious of my motives, Specialist?" He gave her a knowing smile. "There's no need. There's nothing very exciting about me, I'm afraid. Kau

D'varza is my home, Comcap Raffa is my friend, and I earn enough to be more than content. I am happy, Specialist Rivera; I like this job."

"That's it?"

Ikarus raised his hands. "That's it."

"You don't want anything more?"

"There may be one or two things. However, the fact that I have not got that which I desire is down to my own failings, not that of Kau D'varza or Comcap Raffa." He settled back and studied her. "But you did not come here to discuss my shortcomings. At least I hope not."

Elise shook her head. "No. Sorry, Ikarus."

"It is quite alright. Perhaps I would not have elaborated so much with another Specialist. However, I can already tell you are quite different to the others."

She glanced up from the porridge she'd been pushing around the bowl rather than eating. "Is that a good thing, though? Does Kau D'varza need things done differently?"

"Hmm... You have concerns?"

"I just... I guess I'm worried about what might have happened if Specialist Trast hadn't been with me at the airlock. That Jimba... I've been asking myself if

I could have done what she did. Truth be told, I couldn't assess the situation quickly enough, Specialist Trast could."

"I've seen the reports, both of you handled your individual tasks beyond expectation. You brought the riot under control, discovered the location of Specialist Stone and, between you, tracked her down and rescued her. Your mission - the job you undertook - was a success."

"But only because of Trast."

He shrugged. "Specialist Trast would have failed her own task had you not been there. And vice versa." He swept an arm in a motion intended to indicate the entire station. "This is only your third cycle on the job. With time comes experience. If you can temper your own approach with the lessons taken from that of Specialist Trast, you will become a most valuable asset to this station."

Something clicked in Elise's mind. "The big decision..."

"Ma'am?"

"This is the choice, isn't it? I either stay here, continue on this path and lay down roots, or I go back to Paradise and try to get my life back there. That's why I'm looking for problems, excuses, so I can justify either choice."

Ikarus frowned. "Has the situation regarding Paradise changed, or is this simply a case of missing friends and relatives? Or perhaps, a fear of committing to Kau D'varza has led to this?"

"I... Perhaps a combination of all three? Paradise... They won. The F.P.M. are no more. My family want me to come home, at least to visit. I'm also unsure whether or not a career in external investigations is something I want."

Ikarus' expression hardened. "I see..."

"I guess that's why I'm irritated. I've just sent a message to tell my folks I was staying here, that I'd visit when I got the time, but Paradise is... Well, it's a long way from here; you don't just plan a holiday to Yurnto from the Void Cloud."

"Then perhaps somewhere between systems - a neutral ground - would be preferable? Somewhere closer that still allows you to retain your job?" He leant forward. "Specialist Rivera... If I may speak plainly?"

She nodded.

"Kau D'varza needs you. The recent issues this station has faced require more skill and experience than we possess. When you came face to face with rioters, your experience from Paradise became extremely valuable. Your access into the freighter's systems provided us with information that we can now act on without waiting for the engineering bay to 'find time'. And your attempted intrusions into the main system have revealed vulnerabilities which we are now working to fix. Considering the short time you have been here, your influence on Kau D'varza has been huge." Elise drew breath to reply, but Ikarus continued, "I am not ignorant of your personal needs. Family is important, the place you grew up is important. But making your own path, a new home... a new life... I believe that will bring the happiness you seek, especially if you and your family can agree to meeting somewhere that allows you to continue working here, in a meaningful career, while still maintaining those relationships."

Elise sighed. "In a perfect universe, that might be possible. But we all know it isn't as easy as that."

"Then perhaps you need to approach this from another perspective."

"Oh?"

"That region of space, Yurnto... It is positioned between Leeshan, Yor' Space, and Ar-Kaos Space, is it not?"

She nodded. "It's the reason Ar-Kaos were so interested. Yurnto is a good hub. It's more or less central to a number of other populated systems."

"Then perhaps you would be wise to suggest that the Arch-Commissioner sends ambassadors and negotiators to such a system. It would, after all, be in Kau

D'varza's best interests. And of course you could go with them as a mediator between all parties. Once again, your personal experience plays into this enormously."

Elise sat and thought for a moment. She'd been so intent in listening to Ikarus, she hadn't noticed the mess hall had emptied. Apart from themselves and the cleaning machines zipping up and down aisles, grabbing trays, polishing tables and floors, the place was deserted.

"In terms of production, Kau D'varza is just a station. I'm not sure we've got anything they'd want."

"I would leave that particular challenge up to our negotiators, but it would be prudent to remember that material goods are not all that we, or they, can offer. Besides, this is merely a means to an end. You get to visit home, see your friends and family, and possibly find a solution to your dilemma. It is simply a nice bonus that Kau D'varza stands to gain from the trip."

She nodded. "Hmm... Alright Ikarus. I'll figure out how to word it, then ask Gie-... Arch-Commissioner Nevos if this is something he'd approve of."

"Perhaps it would be wise to share your concerns with him as well. He is more likely to approve of such an idea if it meant you remained with Kau D'varza."

Before they could continue, both Ikarus' and Elise's datapads beeped. They drew them out of their respective pockets and studied the screens. After a few seconds, Ikarus glanced back up.

"Arch-Commissioner Nevos has requested our presence at a meeting."

"Is... this a good thing?"

"I would assume that we are to discuss the freighter, although something new may have occurred."

"Alright..." Elise looked down at her mostly untouched, and now almost cold, porridge, then pushed the tray to one side. "After you."

* * *

Kaska Stone walked into the meeting room next to the Core Command Centre with a spring in her step and a wide smile on her face, and took a place next to Coda Trast. Ahead of them, Raffa was speaking with Commissioner Zeled, while the Arch-Commissioner sat alone, reading through his data-pad. She even thought she saw Winters skulking around in the corner somewhere, too.

"Holy crap, girl," Trast remarked in a low voice. "I can feel the warmth comin' off ya'. What's the deal?"

Kaska reddened slightly. "I had a... most enjoyable evening."

Trast blinked, momentarily confused, then glanced over at Raffa. "The flowers..." Realisation dawned.

"Kaska Stone, you sly-cat!" Trast bumped her on the shoulder and grinned. "So come on, tell me all about it!"

Raffa glanced over, noticed her and offered a smile of acknowledgement before returning to his conversation with the Commissioner.

"Maybe another time, Coda. Somewhere private."

"You're kidding!" She spoke in an excited whisper. "You went all the way?"

Kaska raised her hands. "No, no... we're taking it slow. And to be honest, I think it would have taken away from the magic some. Yestercycle evening was special for its own reasons."

"Aww, Kaska Stone, you ol' romantic, you."

"You've seen me after evenings out before..."

"Yeah..." Trast's grin widened. "Never seen you this happy before though. Musta been real special."

She nodded. "It was."

The door behind them creaked open, permitting Ikarus and Elise to step through and meet up with the others.

"Hey," Elise said tilting her head as her eyes fell on Kaska. "What's up with you?"

"Miss Stone here..." Trast replied, "had quite the 'magical' evening."

"Oh really?" Elise glanced at Ikarus. "Seems your boss is quite the catch: first flowers, then a good evening out? I guess miracles do happen."

"Indeed." Ikarus replied. "Sometimes, he surprises even me."

The Arch-Commissioner glanced up from his pad. "Ah! Everyone is here. Good. Please take your seats."

The group filed into the room proper, sitting on the front row of chairs. Commissioner Zeled scanned the group, his gaze pausing on Elise. After giving her the briefest of scowls, which went unnoticed by none, he took his place beside Arch-Commissioner Nevos on the platform at the head of the room.

"Thank you all for coming on such short notice. I won't waste anyone's time, so let us get to the matter at hand. Two cycles ago, Comcap Raffa intercepted a freighter bound for Kau D'varza and brought it in to dock. Specialist Rivera then accessed the encrypted files, revealing some very troubling information."He tapped at his pad, an image appeared on the wall behind him. "We believe this video shows a member of the crew being forced, against their will, into a stasis pod."

Those who hadn't seen it sat in stunned disbelief as the footage rolled. Once Kaska had composed herself, she raised a hand.

"Sir, if I may?"

"Of course, Specialist."

"How were we able to recover this file if so many others had been deleted or corrupted?"

Gierre glanced at Elise. "Specialist Rivera?"

"It wasn't there to begin with. I transferred everything off the ship that I could, then reviewed it on my home terminal. I found that at the bottom, Recovered Files."

Zeled slammed his fist down. "You did what? Do you have any idea what kind of security risk that could be?"

"With respect, Commissioner, I made sure precautions were in place."

"You could have destroyed the whole stat-"

"Commissioner Zeled, that is enough," Gierre cut in. "Without Specialist Rivera's expertise, we never would have found this. And this information is vital: it shows us what sort of threats we can expect, and how to plan for them. In this case, the ends justify the means."

Zeled bristled. "Nevertheless, if you feel you need to take such measures again, *Specialist Rivera*, I will require you to receive permission from me, or a member of my staff, first."

"No, that will not be necessary," Nevos replied. "Specialist Rivera answers directly to me; I will be the one to inform you of any such activities. Furthermore, I would prefer this meeting not to descend into my constantly having to defend Specialist Rivera simply because you hold a grudge. We have greater, more urgent matters to deal with."

"Focus on your bigger picture, Gierre. Internal security is *my* problem and I will address it how *I* see fit."

It was Elise' turn to slam down a fist, much to the dismay of her fellow specialists. "External threats will result in internal ones! How can you not see that?"

Zeled's face turned scarlet, though Ikarus cleared his throat before he could respond. "Despite her perhaps regrettable directness, Specialist Rivera is correct: failure to address the larger problem *will* result in greater issues at home."

"I regret nothing. I will *not* apologise for my attitude on this," Elise said. "Our home is at risk. We've got ships, empty ships, drifting in from neighbouring systems, their crews - who are already running from something - are being kidnapped from virtually under our noses. If we do nothing, how long do you think it'll be before those responsible move their operation here? How long until they start intercepting Kau D'varza traffic? How long do we ignore the criminal elements that have moved into Windan since these threats arose? How long until Kau D'varza itself is fighting off another hostile action, this one aimed at kidnapping everyone for who knows what purpose?"

"Specialist Riv-" Zeled began.

Elise flared. *"How long, Commissioner?"*

"That's enough," Nevos said, calmly but in a tone that brooked no dissent. "I understand your concerns, Specialist, but we won't fix any of this by arguing." He addressed the rest of the group. "The crucial points are these: Specialist Rivera's analysis is correct, and we need more information. I believe we are all in agreement on this. We simply *must* establish exactly what this threat is."

Winters, who had sat quietly with his head down during the rest of the exchange, finally looked up. "With respect, Arch-Commissioner, we know what the damn threat is. It's that fleet of Reclaimer ships floating around Beyema."

Gierre raised a cautioning hand. "We don't have proof of that, Force-Commander."

"Maybe not, but it doesn't take a specialist to figure out shit's been getting worse since they moved in, Sir."

Raffa frowned. "I disagree. I think this is someone else, using the Reclaimers as a convenient place to lay the blame." He motioned to the now-still video. "It doesn't take a genius, or even a lot of bodies, to overrun a freighter, especially if you're putting the opposing force into stasis. Their fear works for you, and their numbers dwindle while yours stay the same. That alone makes it easier to progress, and if you're trained - skilled in that sort of operation - then you'll know how to deal with resistance. Do this across numerous systems around Beyema, everyone blames the newly-arrived but already-unpopular neighbours."

"I'm with Comcap Raffa," Elise replied. "Back in Yurnto - which is a Reclaimer Patrol Zone border system - the Reclaimer fleets would visit all the time, but they never actively caused trouble. There might have been some cultural differences and misunderstandings once upon a time, but not anymore. And even when Paradise was threatened by the F.P.M., the Reclaimers refused to get involved. It's not in their nature to take a direct approach."

Ikarus shook his head. "I have some difficulties with this theory. If someone engages in operations which result in a negative effect on how people see, and deal with, the Reclaimers, surely the Reclaimers would react? In addition, what does anybody have to gain from starting such a fight with the Reclaimers? And thirdly, are we sure the Reclaimers at Beyema are operating with those in the Patrol Zone, or are they a breakaway group, an independent faction? The distance between the two locations suggests they receive their orders from elsewhere - if they are receiving such orders at all."

Gierre spoke clearly, gaining everyone's full attention. "And this is exactly our problem. Currently, we do not know the true nature of what is happening. To this end - and as has already been said - we need more information. The only way I see of obtaining that information is by travelling to Grinda."

Winters frowned. "That might have been where the freighter came from, but we're kidding ourselves if we believe it originated anywhere other than Beyema."

"If our investigation leads us to Beyema, Force-Commander, then we shall pursue that route when it is appropriate. However, I refuse to skip steps, especially if that could lead to conflict with a group far better equipped than we are."

Raffa settled back. "So... we're going to Grinda."

"That appears to be our only logical step. It is where the freighter came from, it is where we will find the next link in this chain."

Raffa glanced at Ikarus and Winters, then nodded. "We can put this together. But I need to know a couple of things first: who exactly is going, and is anyone proposing we go in *Bo'a*?"

Nevos laughed. "No, Comcap, I wouldn't be so cruel. You'll be taking *Vypka* and two of our new fast-attack craft. I believe their designations are *G-Claw* and *G-Stinger*."

"I thought *Vypka* was out of action?"

"As Jimba had us all believe. Do not worry, Comcap; I am assured the best engineers from Commissioner Zeled's teams have been brought in to turn the place around. They have re-prioritised our vessels and, after inspecting *Vypka*, discovered it was fully functional all along, apart from the drinks dispenser on B-deck. They're still experiencing some kind of unspecified problem with the Transit Core though. Our latest thinking is that he could have purposely seeded malware to cripple our systems."

Raffa smacked his open palm against the chair. "I'm gonna kill that asshole."

Commissioner Zeled and Kaska chorused, "Join the queue," glanced at each other, and smiled.

"Jimba's punishment will be... fitting," Gierre said. "As for who will be accompanying you on this mission, Specialist Rivera will join you in an investigative role. It will be up to you who else you take."

"Am I expected to board any vessels I find?" Raffa asked.

"That will be at Specialist Rivera's discretion."

"Then I'll need at least one of my squads." He rubbed

his chin. "And if we find hostiles?"

"That will be at your discretion. Suffice it to say, Kau D'varza does not wish for a fight, but we cannot allow the risk to the traffic in this region to continue."

Raffa leant over to Ikarus. "Can we get a full squad on *Vypka*?" he asked, in a murmur.

The Aide didn't even need to check. "No, Sir. Too small. Moreover, it is lightly armoured, built for fast attack and run."

Raffa nodded his thanks and turned back to Nevos. "With respect sir, I would feel better undertaking this mission with *Akonda* or *Mambaka*. Either of these would allow me to carry a full squad of troops."

The Arch-Commissioner tapped at his pad again "*Mambaka* will require two more cycles until it is operational again, and *Akonda* is... unsuitable for this mission."

"That won't be a problem, Sir; it will take me at least two cycles to prepare everyone for this. Double that, if we're trying to be discreet."

"Then I see no problems with giving you command of *Mambaka* for this mission." He cocked an eye at Zeled. "If there are no objections?"

"It's a destroyer," Zeled replied, using the terminology from his homeworld, "good in a fight and fast enough, but you'll need those F.A.C.s to cover your ass in a retreat. I've got no problems giving Comcap Raffa command of *Mambaka*, however..." He laced his fingers and sat back. "I hope it goes without saying that if you throw away one of our newest ships, not only will I be most upset, but Gaitlin will be unlikely to deal with us in the future. See to it that you return with *all* my ships, Comcap, otherwise there will be trouble. Do I make myself clear?"

"Like trans-steel, Sir."

"Then the mission is agreed," Nevos said, triumphantly. "Once your squad is organised and *Mambaka* is ready to go, you have my permission to head to Grinda in search of information on the recent troubles."

"I will see to it that the objective is completed, Arch-Commissioner."

"I have no doubts." He looked back across the group. "If there are no more questions?"

Elise raised her hand. "What is my specific goal, Sir? Finding information... That's a vague objective. I take it we're looking for more information on those responsible?"

"Anything that leads us to those responsible, anything we can use against them, or where they operate from, will be invaluable. Further evidence of their actions would also help our case when requesting aid from our neighbours, though at this point, we'll take anything we can get."

"I'll get it done."

He nodded. "Specialists Trast and Stone will assist in your preparations. However, I must insist that Specialist Stone remains here to continue her investigation into the... situation... in the engineering bay. If Ikarus is assisting in this matter, I would appreciate that he stays as well, but please make best use of their skills while here." He glanced over each of them again and nodded. "Good luck, everyone. For Kau D'varza."

They chorused "For Kau D'varza" in reply, then stood and made their way out of the room, creating the usual muddle around the doors as they went, until only the Commissioners, Kaska Stone and Elise remained.

"I would like to speak with Commissioner Zeled, if he wishes to hear me."

"Of course." Nevos replied.

"In... ah... In private, Sir."

Zeled raised an eyebrow. "I will allow it."

Nevos looked between the two of them, then stood up. "Very well. I trust your exchange will be civil."

"Of course, Sir."

"Very well. Specialist Stone, if you'll come with me…"

She nodded, falling in behind Nevos as he made his way, unhurriedly, from the room.

"I wonder what that's about," she said, once the door was safely closed behind them.

"Hm. Perhaps she hopes to settle their differences."

Kaska raised her eyebrows. "I wish her good luck with that, after the way she called him out."

"Yes. She clearly has some kind of issue with authority, and that won't sit kindly with our Zeled." Nevos sighed. "Or perhaps the problem is that they're too alike. Neither seems to understand the need for…"

"Diplomacy?"

A corner of his mouth quirked into a smile. "I was going to say 'delicacy', but I suppose it amounts to the same." He turned to face her. "Anyway, Specialist, I will leave you to attend to your duties. Good cycle - or what's left of it."

Kaska bowed her head. "Good cycle, Arch-Commissioner," she replied, and turned away, casting the closed door a final glance as she passed. "And good luck, Elise Rivera."

* * *

Elise turned to face Zeled as soon as the door clicked shut. "I'm sorry."

"I don't want your apologies."

"You and I... we obviously got off on bad terms. I made some extremely poor choices, I admit that, and I can see, now that it's been explained to me, that I put the station at tremendous risk. That was never my intention, and for that I am genuinely sorry. However, I have a sad feeling that nothing I will say will ever allow you to forgive me. But now, you and I? We're working towards the same goals. We both want to keep Kau D'varza safe. You might look at it as me trying to make up for my past mistakes, or simply a nice way for me to earn credits, for selfish reasons rather than out of a genuine desire to try to build a career, but, ultimately, if I want to stay on this path I need Kau D'varza to remain secure; a safe home for me to return to, somewhere I can remain employed. And if that's the case, then you and I need to start working together. I get it: I fucked up. But don't punish the station because *I* was an idiot."

Zeled inhaled, his chair squeaking as he sat back. "I don't know what it is about you, Elise, but you make me very angry. It's more than the security breach, more than the way Nevos covers your ass and allows you to flaunt the rules as well as question my authority. But I don't especially care about any of that. In fact, because of your little escapades, I've got a few new holograms on my wall celebrating the successes of my department, so no, it's none of that. I don't actually know what it is, and that's what angers me most of all. Who are you? Simply *the girl* from Paradise? Really?"

"What you see is what you get. This is it. A slightly naive girl from half a cluster away, trying to escape the problems of home."

"Yet you speak our language almost fluently, had the funds to travel here from so far away, and seemingly gave up much in the face of somewhat minor trouble."

"The Free Paradise Movement was most definitely not 'minor trouble.'"

"And yet here you are, bravely facing down mobs, rescuing fellow specialists from insane engineers... I have done some research into Paradise; what you've already done here is more than you would face there."

"Maybe... perhaps the constant barrage of it, day in, day out, seeing my home, my birthplace falling to ruins when so many were willing to improve it... is the reason I got away? The problem is, I see the same thing happening here, and I want to stop it. I don't want Kau D'varza to become another Paradise, not least because I don't want to run again. This is my home now."

"And you'd be willing to give your life to protect it?"

Elise closed her eyes, inhaled, then opened them again. "If that's what it takes."

"Then prepare for your mission, Specialist. The best

way you can help Kau D'varza is to follow Nevos' plan. You do have an undeniable talent for finding information. I have seen the results."

"And us?"

"I will consider your words, but words are just air; I will judge *you* on deeds. For now, let it suffice for me to say that you and I have some way to go to repair this relationship."

Elise nodded. "Fine. For Kau D'varza."

His eyes narrowed, looking for any trace of insincerity or even mere sarcasm. Finding none, he allowed himself a flicker of a smile. "For Kau D'varza."

CHAPTER FOURTEEN- THE LONG WAY ROUND

Raffa entered the command core to find Ikarus and Winters waiting for him. After acknowledging their presence with a gesture, he spent a few seconds chatting with Kaska before she gave him a peck on the cheek and wandered off with Trast.

"So," Winters began, "we've got another mission."

"So it seems. But first, you and I have got some problems we need to work out," Raffa said, then sighed and motioned for them to follow him as he started towards the main door.

"Look, if this is about the other night, I'm fuckin' sorry, alright? I was outta line, I shouldn't have been following ya."

"No, you shouldn't, and yes, it was the wrong thing to do," Raffa replied, "but I've had some time to think, get a little perspective." The door opened as they approached. Raffa summoned a P.T.V. and turned back to Winters. "It helps as well that the damage was minimal, and others have since helped allay any... issues." He grinned at Ikarus, who merely nodded back.

"So... we're cool?"

Raffa nodded. "Yeah. We're 'cool'. Just make sure you've been invited next time you join me and Ka... uh, Specialist Stone."

Winters seemed relieved. "I think I can handle that, boss. Uh, thanks."

A P.T.V. pulled up and the group piled on, Raffa taking the seat beside the driver.

"So, this mission," Winters said, waving his hands as they rolled on. "Seems like an unnecessary step if you ask me, but we're doing it so *how* are we doing it?"

"I think it's best if we handled the planning at headquarters. Suffice it to say, what we're taking should be more than enough unless we drop in on a fleet when we terminate Transit, but even so we should have plenty of time to scan the system and leave if it looks like trouble." He sighed. "Would be nice if the Transit Cores were working properly. We could hop in anywhere then..."

Ikarus grimaced. "You should prepare for such an

241

event in any case."

"I will. *Mambaka*'s got speed on its side, some heavy firepower, but that armour won't take many hits. Ideally, I need to make sure it doesn't take *any*."

They spent the rest of the journey in silence, each pondering on how best to approach the situation. It didn't help that they were mostly blind when it came to Grinda, with only a few older beacons providing any kind of intel on the system... and even that data required a ship to be sent out for recovery. Grinda had never been seen as a problem, or even the source of a potential problem, before. It was a backwater, desolate, with few if any resources that were worth the cost of exploiting, so Kau D'varza had never prioritised it - had ignored it, in fact - and now their wilful blindness had come back to bite them.

The P.T.V. arrived at their destination and came to a halt. The three men jumped off, passed through the series of security checkpoints, and arrived at the headquarters planning room, in all its dull familiarity.

Raffa approached the datascape and leant over the top of the table, Ikarus and Winters taking up their usual positions to either side.

"Zoom out," he commanded, watching as the view changed from a close-up of the region of space immediately surrounding Kau D'varza to that of the local area map. "Stop."

242

The view froze. Along the top edge sat the expanse of the Void Cloud, with Windan just below it. Further along the edge of the cloud, in a region of space hardly anyone ever looked at, lay Windan's farthest neighbour, Grinda.

"By the colours of the Void... how long is that gonna take?" Winters muttered.

Ikarus pulled his pad out from his tunic and tapped some calculations into the screen, then frowned. "It seems as if the Transit computers on the Fast Attack Craft are most antiquated. Their relative lack of capability will reduce that of *Mambaka*'s own core substantially, if you want the vessels to stick together. Best estimates suggest travelling the distance to the default Transit location will take roughly point two megasekunds, then another point six in Transit, then however long the investigation takes, and of course you then have to make the same journey back."

"So we're looking at a couple of megaseks at the very least... Alright. Winters, you can get the supplies we'll need, right?"

He nodded. "Sure can, Comcap. We taking a full squad this time?"

"As many as can fit on *Mambaka* and the F.A.C.s."

Ikarus shook his head. "The F.A.C.s will be ineffective troop carriers. I suggest placing squad members on those vessels only if you believe their crews will need some... persuasion... to follow orders."

"Is that likely to be an issue?"

"Some pilots may be looking to redeem themselves after the fiasco with *Bo'a*. I would certainly take it into consideration."

"I hadn't even considered that. Damnit, why would they be looking to redeem themselves? They performed well."

"They performed... adequately. The non-essential discussions with *Bo'a* could have been avoided."

"Maybe, but their skill as pilots is not under question."

"Then I would tell them that, Sir, and let them know that, in your eyes, they have nothing to prove, especially to themselves."

"Alright. I'll keep it in mind." His gaze settled on the datascape map again. "So... we take the ships out to Grinda... but we should Transit in from a different location, just in case someone is waiting for us."

Winters blinked. "You think they would be?"

"Given our Transit issues... only being able to use the default settings and the fact that we're blind to Grinda besides those low-tech beacons could mean that someone *sent* that freighter to us knowing we'd conclude that we had to investigate. Though of course that would mean they'd have to know about our problems in the first place, and I'm guessing that bastard engineer wasn't one to keep secrets."

Winters studied the map, and frowned. "Then it's an ambush."

Ikarus' eyes narrowed. "So it would appear. But for what purpose?"

"I can't be certain, but I'd sure be willing to trade a freighter for *Kobra* or *Mambaka* if I were them."

"That would be difficult. Not including our new support ships, an opposing force would need to be heavily armed and extremely well-trained."

"Yes. Difficult... but not impossible, and we still have no idea what we'd be up against." Raffa stood up straight. "Which is why we're gonna come at this from Exen."

"Exen?" Ikarus frowned. "That will increase your travel time significantly."

"But it also give us a better chance if we run into... complications."

"Then it would be wise to pay attention to your squad on such a journey. You may be gone as long as four megasekunds - perhaps longer if you encounter a problem. You should let them know before they leave, allow them time to prepare."

"Ikarus is right," Winters replied. "Like you needed me to tell you, but some of our squads… the rookies, the longest they've been off the station was two m-seks, and that was on something a bit bigger than *Mambaka*."

"When we return, I will construct new training regimes to deal with the new threats based on what we learn. For now, prepare them as best you can for a long ride, and the potential for combat and boarding operations at the other end."

"Consider it done. Some might be green, but after the party thrown in their honour, all of them are eager to keep earning those accolades. They won't let you down."

"I have no doubt. So we've worked out the route, the supplies we need to take." He turned to Ikarus. "Has anything else come from Grinda recently?"

"No, Sir. Heradim, Gaitlin, Kandaha and Arokia continue to be our main trading routes."

"What about Exen?"

"Minimal traffic. A passenger cruiser returning from a sightseeing tour of the Cloud, and two cargo-transports. Nothing of note. Or risk."

"Alright. Good. Our entry into Exen will likely be uncontested because of their inability to defend the system, but it's also likely they won't be happy about it. We should prepare an apology in advance, and explain our mission just prior to Transit to Grinda."

"Then you arrive in Grinda," Ikarus replied.

"Indeed." Raffa's gaze returned to the display. "Zoom on Grinda."

The pitiful system rushed into view. One uninhabitable planet, numerous asteroid belts, and several orbital stations. Most of these stations were the relics of several aborted colonisation attempts, and had been left in a state of disrepair or powered down permanently as they were abandoned, while the few that remained held the tiny population of Grinda.

"Ugh..." Winters said. "It's so fucking depressing."

"Agreed. We should be glad Windan didn't end up like that." He traced a line between the default Transit entry point from Exen to the nearest populated station. "We'll drop in on these holdouts, get as much information from them as we can, then circle back to the Transit for Windan, getting info from those beacons of ours on the way out."

"Should I prepare the squad to board the station?"

"Only a small group. We don't wanna frighten them or start a fight."

"I'll get four of my best to accompany you. Plain

clothes, armoured."

"Make it two, and overtly armour them. Have a few more on standby. I don't want any trouble."

"You got it, boss."

Ikarus studied the map. "Your scans upon entering the system will allow you to spot any traps, but what if you encounter a... *problem*?"

"We'll have to deal with any as they arise. We can't predict everything that's going to happen, but we're going in with three ships, a full squad, and we've got the backing of Kau D'varza. In most situations, we would be operating from a position of strength. Any ships we encounter will think twice before engaging us, and if we're looking weak, we can always come back through Exen."

"And if anyone wanted to engage you, that would force them to fight in Windan, where we can bring the full might of all our vessels to bear."

"Got it in one." He glanced between them. "Any holes?"

Winters shook his head while Ikarus mentally ran the plan.

"I see no alternatives," he finally replied. "This course presents the least risk, despite the length of time it will take."

"I'm with Ikarus," Winters said. "It's gonna take a while, but it's better that than Transitin' into Grinda just to get popped."

"Alright. Well we've got at least two cycles, so if you do figure out any problems, let me know. Other than that, your orders are as follows: Winters, you will organise a squad of your choosing and ensure they have enough supplies for the trip. Let them know we're gonna be gone a while so they should spend their off-time with family. *Mambaka* hasn't got the most room, so try and pack light."

The Force-Commander nodded. "I'll get it done."

"Ikarus, I want you to find Specialist Rivera and explain our plan to her. If she has any problems, I need to know immediately. Other than that, you are to continue working with Specialist Stone regarding the engineering bay."

"Of course, Sir."

"If there's nothing else?"

"I have news regarding another matter."

"Would you like to discuss it in private?"

"No, and while it doesn't concern Force-Commander Winters, I have no issues with him hearing it."

"It's all good, if it's all the same to you, I've got troops to prepare," Winters said, and offered Raffa a crisp salute. After receiving one in response, he turned smartly on his heel and made for the door.

"So... Ikarus?"

"Yes, Sir. I simply wanted to inform you that you may send my report to Arch-Commissioner Nevos now. I believe he has had the time to absorb Specialist Rivera's report."

"I'll have it done by lights-out."

"Thank you, Sir. I do not believe the information will change your mission, but it will alert him to the other risks we and our neighbours face."

"The more we know, the better. I'll make sure he sees it."

With that, Ikarus offered his own take on the Kau D'varza salute before following Winters.

* * *

"You're not worried?" Trast asked as she, Elise and Kaska made their way towards the vending machine outside of Core Command.

Kaska rolled her eyes and blew air out her cheeks. "Of course I'm worried, but... this is his job. And if he doesn't do it, what then for Kau D'varza? All we can do is make sure they're as prepared as they can be. Our best chance is also theirs, so... we focus."

"Of course," Trast said, offering a reassuring smile before turning to Elise and shaking her head. "As for you..."

"What about me?"

"I've never seen anyone face up to the Def-Com like that before. You're either pretty brave, or pretty stupid."

"Believe me, the two aren't mutually exclusive."

Trast laughed. "No, I suppose not."

The vending machine dropped a bar and a carton of nutri-juice into the hatch, which Kaska grabbed and stepped back, letting Trast take her turn.

"Trast is right, though," she remarked. "Commissioner Zeled is not someone to be challenged lightly. You got away with it this time, and as fun as it was to watch, a repeat could land us all in trouble. Don't forget Arch-Commissioner Nevos still has to work with him every cycle."

Elise felt a twinge of guilt. "Yeah, I... I didn't think of that." She waved her hand, dismissively. "Ah, it doesn't matter anyway. I apologised, I'm trying to build some bridges with him."

"Well, good luck, kid," Trast said, stepping back.

"Plenty have tried that before, and you're already working from disadvantage."

"Oh?"

Kaska nodded. "Commissioner Zeled puts people into two camps: Those who work with him, and those who are the enemy."

"And right now, he sees you as the enemy," Trast added.

"Well… I guess I like a challenge."

"You're fixing to do the impossible, kiddo." She raised her cup in mock salute. "But as I said, good luck."

Elise followed the example set by her companions and ordered an easy-to-devour bar and nutritious drink. A group of soldiers ran past as they headed back towards Command Core.

"Looks like First Squad are shipping out." Kaska sighed. "I don't envy them their future accommodation."

The trio settled onto a bench a few meters away from the large door and security booth.

"Speaking of which," Elise replied, "why did the Arch-Commissioner suggest taking *Vypka* if he knows it doesn't have enough room?"

"*Vypka*'s a good ship. Fast, with a lot of firepower... The simulations probably suggested it would be the best choice for a short operation, especially when paired with those new ships."

"The simulation didn't take troop numbers into account?"

"Not unless they were specified. It's also cheaper to run *Vypka* than it is to run *Mambaka* or *Akonda*. *Significantly* cheaper."

Elise shook her head. "I don't think I know enough about ships to understand all this."

"That's why we have meetings like that," Kaska replied. "They allow everyone to be heard, so all areas of expertise get to chip in and eventually work out the best solution. The simulations do a good job most of the time, but *Vypka* is usually assigned as an escort vessel to one of the larger ships. Now, it's got escorts of its own. Which reminds me, we'll need to update the system to show that this isn't a preferred formation."

"I'm glad I don't have your job."

Kaska smiled. "What about you? You're going off to Grinda. I'm glad I don't have *your* job."

"Ah, I'm not worried. As long as we don't run into any trouble, it'll just be like a holiday..." Her voice trailed off and her eyes took on a distant, distracted look.

Trast looked at her and frowned. "You alright, kid?"

"I'm fine. Just been doing some thinking is all."

"Well if ya ever need to talk, you know where to find me."

Elise nodded. "Thanks. It wasn't anything personal. Well, maybe it kinda is." She sighed. "My folks got in touch, want me to go home. I told them I'm staying, but I miss 'em. I don't wanna give up this job though, so I was wondering... maybe we could send ambassadors and negotiators to Yurnto and the surrounding systems to broker deals and protection pacts? It'd mean I get to see my people *and* the station benefits."

Kaska raised her eyes to the ceiling in thought for a few seconds, then nodded. "I don't see why not. We'll have to make sure the route is safe for our merchants, but otherwise I think it's a good suggestion. I'll speak to the Arch-Commissioner about it."

"Thanks, Kaska. I appreciate it."

"Don't mention it, the advantages to Kau D'varza appear obvious. I have to ask, though, because he certainly will... What kind of stuff does Yurnto produce?"

"I can't speak for the whole planet, because lots of different places produce their own things... But Paradise is a mining settlement: extraction and processing."

"Hmm... well, we'd need specifics, but considering we have to employ belt-miners for the same task, doing a deal might work out cheaper. I'll do some research, and if everything looks favourable..."

Elise smiled. "Again, thanks."

Ikarus approached along the tunnel as Elise knocked back the last of her drink.

"A pleasure to see you all again," he said, before addressing Elise directly. "Specialist Rivera, I have been asked to brief you on the proposed plan."

"Sure," she said, placing the carton down. "Let's hear it."

"Would you not prefer to do this in a conference or planning lounge?"

She frowned. "Am I supposed to?"

"It is... traditional."

She glanced at Trast and Kaska. "Would anyone be offended if I just listened to this here?"

They shook their heads.

"Okay then, that's good enough for me. So, what's the plan?"

The women's eyes widened as Ikarus outlined what he, Raffa and Winters had decided, and grew even wider when they heard the reasoning behind it.

"Is there any chance that Comcap Raffa is being a little *too* cautious about all this?" Trast said after he'd finished.

"Initially, I thought so too," Ikarus replied. "But after hearing his logic, I agree with his assessment. Trading a freighter for one of our vessels would be an extremely lucrative exchange; whoever sent it here knew we would not, and could not, simply ignore it." His shoulders dropped slightly, but not enough to be considered relaxed. "The precautions... the longer route through Exen... minimises the risk of falling into a trap."

"Alright," Elise replied, "if Comcap Raffa thinks this is the best route, and you agree with him, then I'll go with it."

Kaska nodded, half-smiling. "Your 'holiday' just got a bit more interesting."

Elise ignored her. "Do we have any plans in place if we encounter another freighter? Or a fight?"

Ikarus drew a deep breath. "There are the usual directives in place for such occurrences. However, Comcap Raffa will deal with each incident on a case by case basis, and will most likely seek your guidance in cases where obtaining information might be achievable."

She nodded. "Tell Comcap Raffa I like his plan."

"Very well. Will you require any special accommodation aboard *Mambaka*?"

Elise frowned. "'Special accommodation'? Will I be sharing with everyone or have my own quarters?"

"As a specialist, you will have your own quarters."

"Then no. That'll be more than adequate."

He nodded an acknowledgement. "Comcap Raffa also asked me to inform you that, should any problems present themselves during this planning stage, you are to seek him out and alert him immediately."

She raised her hands. "I'm no tactician, Ikarus, I just get to ride-along unless or until we find something interesting. I wouldn't know the first thing about all of this planning crap."

"Which is precisely the reason why you might see something we have missed."

Elise grinned. "Alright, I get your point."

"Very good. I have nothing further to add."

Elise glanced at Kaska uncertainly. "Er..."

Kaska smiled and shook her head. "That will be all, Ikarus. Thank you."

He offered a bow, then left as quickly as he'd appeared.

"I dunno if I can treat him like a subordinate. He's, like, the smartest guy on the station..."

Trast nudged her shoulder, a wide smile on her face. "You'll get used to it. I saw a flicker or two of Uniform Pride when we worked together."

"Uniform Pride?" Elise asked.

"Yeah. Did you never wonder why everyone's always 'Specialist this, Commissioner that?'"

"It had crossed my mind. Is that why the security forces are so needy around us?"

Trast nodded. "Yeah, it's a similar thing. It's all about reinforcing the hierarchy. That uniform of yours... it means something to people. When you speak, they'll listen - most of the time. Look at when Kaska here got herself into a spot of trouble." She grinned as Stone made a face. "Uniform Pride. People don't see Elise Rivera; they see that purple tunic and think *Specialist*. At the same time, they also think 'This one works directly for the Arch-Commissioner. She's important'. And the thing is, they're not even aware that they *are* thinking it. It's ingrained, as deeply as their own names."

"I don't know if I like that. I'm not an extension of Nevos or part of some faceless bureaucratic machine. I'm my own person... and I'm not meant to boss people around."

Trast shrugged. "So don't. Everybody has their own approach." She motioned between herself and Stone. "We know the importance of getting a job done quickly, so that's the approach we use. You know the importance of talking to people. Just use whatever feels comfortable."

Elise let out a heavy sigh. "Ugh... This... I've said it before, but it's gonna take a lot of getting used to."

Kaska smiled. "Don't worry. I think you're getting there."

CHAPTER FIFTEEN- REFLECTION

Joseph had read Ikarus' report three times already, and was onto his fourth when the door chimed.

"Enter."

It slid open, allowing Takk Winters to step through, followed by Scout Chal Tyra.

"Sir."

Raffa stood, waving away their salutes and offering them both seats. As he sat back down, he glanced between them. and frowned. "So... To what do I owe the pleasure?"

Winters shifted in his seat. "Tyra here would like to be re-assigned to First Squad for the upcoming mission."

"Oh?" Raffa raised an eyebrow. "Any particular reason

why?"

Winters nodded to her, and Tyra cleared her throat. "I've got family in Grinda, in one of the stations orbiting that rock they call a planet. One of the stations *that're functional*, I mean."

"I didn't suppose you meant the other kind," Raffa said. "But this isn't a pleasure trip, Scout. There won't be time for personal business or sweet family reunions."

"Oh, no, Sir, nor do I want one; they're dicks. But be that as it may, I do know how to talk to 'em, get 'em to share with us."

Raffa sat back in his chair, rubbing his chin. "I've dealt with Grindans before. They can be most... unforthcoming."

"You should try living there. You keep secrets from the outside so long, you start keeping secrets from the inside too. Every person on that station is an isolated vault of themselves."

"I admit having an *envoy* of sorts to aid our negotiations would be invaluable. We need any information they've got. However..." He weaved his fingers and tapped them against his chin, "jumping between squads just to get the pick of missions isn't something I can agree to lightly."

"As Force-Commander I am happy to agree to this reassignment, given the skills she can bring to this particular mission," Winters said.

Raffa nodded. "I also believe that it was thanks to Scout Tyra that we were able to make it back to Kau D'varza early on our last mission."

"That is correct, Sir" Winters agreed.

Raffa got back to his feet, causing the others to rise too.

"In that case, I will allow this temporary reassignment. However, Scout Tyra, I hope it doesn't become a habit."

She nodded. "Of course not, Sir. Thank you."

"Go and prepare, and if you've got anything on Grinda we should know about, please forward it to myself or Ikarus."

She promptly gave a smart salute and made for the door. Winters watched her go, then looked back to Raffa.

"Smart girl. You wanna watch Comcap Rexon doesn't try to snap her up."

"He won't be back from leave until we're on our way, and I'll be sure to have something prepared by the time we get back."

"You know she's only one promotion away from leading a Scout team of her own? Two more after that, and I'll need to watch out for my job."

Raffa grinned. "Some competition might do you good, keep you on your toes."

"It's already difficult enough competing with Ikarus. I don't need anyone else."

"Relax. If there's ever a time I think you need to worry, you'll be the first to know." He gestured for Winters to sit back down as he did so himself. "How are the preparations going?"

"Good. Easier to organise one squad than two, that's for sure."

"How do they feel about the mission?"

"Excited, nervous... the usual mix. You weren't wrong about the travel time being a factor, though. Hopefully whoever's claiming to be in charge of the stations in Exen or Grinda this cycle will let them stretch their legs on their stations a bit."

"I wouldn't count on it. I've been reading this report from Ikarus, and besides Gaitlin, we're becoming pretty isolated. If we exclude the meagre trade deals we've got with others and the occasional tourists from Exen, we haven't got many friends out there."

Winters stared at him. "We knew that already." He made a sweeping motion to indicate the entire station. "They knew it when they *built* this place. It was always gonna be under constant threat; that's why it's got massive guns and a damned Stealth Cruiser."

"And all so Void Tourists had somewhere to restock."

"Yeah!" Winter exclaimed, then seemed to realise who he was talking to and calmed down. "Yeah. I can't deny the economic benefits, but let's not kid ourselves; Kau D'varza has to look after itself. We *are* isolated, and we can't be relying on Kandaha to come to our rescue or for Gaitlin to swoop in and handle our problems."

"You think I don't know all that? We're bolstering the number of ships we've got, Takk. I know that won't do it, not if we do have to go up against the Reclaimers-"

"Ah, yes. The bomb in the room that no one wants to talk about."

"We don't talk about it because we haven't got any evidence. Not that they're in the vicinity, not that they intend us harm, nothing."

"But we should plan for it, in any event."

"Plan for what? If it comes to a fight against the Reclaimers, we'll need all the help we can get. And a miracle."

"Assuming there's no mysterious force from the Void

that magics them away, though... help from who? Arokia doesn't have the ships to commit to a defence force, and Gaitlin... they've got problems of their own. Replacing the ships they've lost in their... disputes... hasn't been a smooth transition in any sense."

"We could ask Yor'. They've got systems bordering Beyema."

"Yor'? Are you serious, boss? They ain't gonna wanna fight Reclaimers!"

"Maybe we don't have to fight them. Just turn up with a large enough force and get them to move on... IF they are the ones causing all the trouble."

"Well, let's say for a moment that they aren't. What's your plan then?"

"If it's just some pirates... we'll find whatever contingent they've got in Grinda and shut it down. It can't be a large force."

"Why not?"

"Well, look..." Raffa tapped his desktop and summoned the map for a view of the systems neighbouring Beyema. "We've had reports of trouble coming in from all these systems except... er... Fresta, right?"

"Right. So?"

"*So* if there's a group false-flagging, trying to make

it look like they're the Reclaimers, they're gonna be striking in all these systems. But we've had no reports of any huge fleets or convoys from those places, so it's probably just strike teams. Not the usual Reclaimer MO."

Winter frowned. "Small groups, operating as part of a larger thing from some kind of out-system base?"

"Exactly."

Winters thought it over and shook his head. "Might still be some new Reclaimer tactic; a double-bluff."

"It might," Raffa agreed. "Or it might even be a triple-bluff. But before we go disappearing down that ernub-hole, let's remember that the simplest solution is usually the correct one. In which case, we're dealing with a pirate clan or a small faction. If we can figure out who they are and where they are, they should be easy to pick apart and scatter. And once we figure out how they're doing this, we might even be able to convince other parties to help us. Then we can go hunting." He smiled. "Damn, if I'm right, even the Reclaimers might help us."

"I wouldn't count on it. You heard what Specialist Rivera said: they don't like to get directly involved."

"Maybe, but if she's right and they're not as bad as we think, they might not take too kindly to anyone damaging their - already not great, as far as we're concerned - reputation. But even if there is no double-bluff, there is a chance that this is a rogue group operating independently of the R.P.Z. fleets. The thing is, we can't know unless we ask them."

"Ohh... I do *not* wanna be there for that meeting."

Raffa bit his lip. "Me either."

* * *

Kaska Stone hurried away from the food processor carrying a bowl of rice and placed it on the table she'd borrowed from Trast for the evening. Raffa had called to suggest they see one another before he left, but since neither could agree on a venue, Kaska had invited him over to eat at her place. It was a decision she was starting to regret.

It'll be nice to see him, but a little more warning would have been nice!

Exactly four kiloseconds after she'd ended the call with Raffa, the door alert sounded.

"Come in!" she called. The door flickered blue, then slid open.

She smiled as Raffa stepped through the opening and crossed the room to greet him.

He looks even nicer than yestercycle... I wonder if this is Ikarus' doing?

"Good evening, Kaska," he said, softly.

She wrapped her arms around his waist and went up on tiptoes to give him a kiss.

"Good evening, Joseph. Did you have a good shift?"

"They're sending me to Grinda to find out information on kidnappers that may or may not lead me into conflict with Reclaimers." He grinned. "Couldn't be better."

"Yes, I'd heard." She broke away, turning back to the food processor. "Speaking of which, did you see Specialist Rivera at that meeting?"

"I did. The Commissioner certainly has his hands full with her. I think the words 'How long' are gonna be ringing in all our ears for a while." He approached the table, his eyes growing wide as he saw the size of the spread. The tulips he'd given her were sitting in a vase at the centre. "Kaska... you didn't have to..."

"I know I didn't have to. I wanted to." She waved him to a seat. "I'm not ignorant to what's going on. If you're going off on this escapade, you're not going on an empty stomach." She paused by his chair, resting her hand on his shoulder. "I'm glad you suggested it. I didn't want you going off without saying goodbye first."

"Me either."

Kaska slipped away, grabbing a couple of bottles before settling into her seat opposite. She passed one over and they raised them in a solemn toast.

"To the future," she said.

"To the future," he replied.

She took a pull from the bottle, then laid it down and scooped food onto her plate, sensing Raffa watching her every move. She glanced at him and smiled, to indicate that she was done and it was his turn to fill his plate.

They ate slowly, taking the time to enjoy each other's company and talk. Their conversation touched upon various subjects but invariably came back to the mission, or the new specialist, or Commissioner Zeled, or what was going to happen when Raffa returned until, finally, Kaska pushed her empty plate to one side and sat back, satisfied. She watched intently as Raffa finished eating, and smiled as his eyes met hers.

"Hungry?"

"I didn't think so, but that was delicious, thank you."

"Don't thank me, thank whatever genius came up with the food processor."

"Still, the selection was most enjoyable."

"You won't be getting that sort of service in Grinda."

"If we get any kind of service in Grinda, we'll be lucky. One way or another, I don't think our hosts will be too interested in our wellbeing."

"You'll be well-equipped. And if it looks like trouble, you can always turn and burn, right?"

He gave a single nod. "That's the plan, but..." He sighed. "I'd like to come back with *something*. The Arch-Commissioner is right: we need more information."

"And what about Winters? Do you think he's right?"

Raffa's shoulders slumped. "I don't want him to be right."

"That's not what I asked."

"I know... I know... But Kas, come on. We're not equipped to deal with anything like that sort of threat."

"If you return with evidence that it's the Reclaimers, I'll make sure our neighbours know it. I'll make sure we're strong enough."

"I have no doubt. But I really don't want that to be the case."

They sat in silence for a few seconds, considering the situation, then Raffa glanced up. "Would you like to dance?"

"Dance? I didn't know you could."

"Ikarus suggested I... take some lessons."

"Lessons? You mean on the simulator?"

He nodded. "I don't think I'm very good, but I'm happy to learn more."

"When did you find the time with everything that's going on?"

"If Winters isn't banging my door down, once the plan is set I get a while to myself before an operation starts. I could go inspect the squad, but unless I've got something important to tell them it just looks like anxiety on my part at best, or that I don't trust them at worst. Neither is good for morale... or my authority."

"So you spent the time learning how to dance."

"I did."

She laughed. "Alright then, Joseph, let's dance."

* * *

Elise tested the weight of her backpack, decided it was too heavy, sighed, and dropped it back onto her bed.

"You don't need all this stuff!" she told herself as she reached to unzip the bulging main compartment. She had barely touched the tab when the fasteners gave way, dumping the entire contents of her pack onto the bed.

"Oh, *great...*"

She looked over her intended inventory: several uniforms, her datapad, some quick-clean fluid, a packet of food bars and a drinks container. She eyed the pile critically and mentally went over what she needed again.

There's got to be food on the ship, and some quick cleaners for the uniform, so get rid of those... And if I can clean my uniform, I won't need all these...

She pushed her spare clothes to one side, keeping just one tunic, a pair of trousers and a small selection of underwear. She then set about the packet of food bars, taking out a couple before putting the rest on top of her discarded clothes.

Alright, that's better. Gonna need my pad for sure... Quick clean fluid in case I can't get to a clean-room, and somewhere to keep a drink. Lemme try...

She jammed the remaining items back into her pack, fixed the zip and tried lifting it again. It was much lighter this time, a comfortable weight she couldn't foresee any problems with hefting to and from whatever accommodation had been organised for her on *Mambaka*.

With that sorted, Elise tidied away the extra bits, grabbed a drink from the dispenser, and settled in to

Kau D'varza

watch some mind-numbing 'entertainment' show on
the screen.

* * *

As the music faded out, Raffa allowed Kaska to pull
him onto the sofa with a giggle.

"Well, you're no Rhine Lightstep, but there's hope for
you yet."

He grinned. "It is kind of you to say."

"I never expected this from you. I always imagined a
rough and ready military type who got the job done,
with no time for silly things like romance. I'm glad I
was wrong."

"You weren't that wrong. I'm still learning."

"You make it sound like you've never know another's
touch."

He frowned, Ikarus had warned him about this sort of
conversation.

"Well, that wouldn't be true, but it's fair to say none
made me feel the way you do."

"And how do I make you feel, exactly?"

"I can't explain it... I feel a nervous happiness when
I'm with you. And I miss you something fierce when
we're not together, but I get this feeling inside... It's

not nervousness, exactly, but it… well it's like an excited anticipation. I've not felt like this before."

"Sounds like nervousness to me. But why? I think we've earnt the right to relax around one another."

"I…" he began, stopped, then sighed. "I don't want to mess this up."

Kaska leant over, close enough that their noses gently touched, and searched his eyes with her own. She kissed him, and he felt the gentle rush and sweet taste of her breath as their lips touched.

"I don't think you've got anything to worry about," she murmured.

CHAPTER SIXTEEN- THE TOUR

Elise was already awake when the screen lit up to indicate the start of another cycle aboard Kau D'varza. She rolled out of bed, stumbled into the clean-room, and emerged shortly after in her uniform.

Come on, lots to do…

She scooped up her pack and, after taking one last look around the room to make sure she wasn't about to forget anything she'd need, jogged out the door.

The trip down to the engineering bay was uneventful, but if anything Elise might have welcomed a little distraction. With nothing to do but sit on a P.T.V. or stand while an elevator whisked her towards her destination, a little voice of doubt started whispering in her head, accompanied by a small knot of anxiety that seemed to gnaw at her stomach. Ridiculous, seeing as they weren't actually embarking yet, but she couldn't seem to help it. She wondered if this was what it was like for Raffa and the other soldiers, and if so, how they put up with it and why - though she'd be lying if she said she wasn't also looking forward to the mission ahead, at least a little.

The elevator finally reached the engineering bay and the doors rumbled open. A couple of security guards glanced her way as she exited and strode purposefully forward.

"Where's *Mambaka*?" she asked, without even bothering to break stride.

"Bay Four, Ma'am," one of the guards said, hurriedly.

"Thanks!"

Elise's eyes widened and drifted upward as she reached the designated bay, awed by the sheer size and appearance of *Mambaka*.

Damn... A ship of war indeed. I'm glad this thing's on our side...

"Specialist Rivera!"

She turned to the familiar voice. "Hey... Force-Commander Winters."

"Call me Takk." He grinned and waved towards the ship. "What brings you to *Mambaka* this early? We're not due to ship out until next cycle."

"Wanted to dump my bag, check out my quarters, start getting settled in. Less stuff to worry about then."

"Oh, sure. Ya need any help?"

Elise motioned to the vessel. "I don't know the first thing about this, so yeah, please."

As they started towards the rear of the ship, Winters turned into something of a tour-guide.

"*Mambaka* here's an upgraded replacement of a ship with the same name. To Kau D'varza, she's a Class Six, but I prefer the old classification system. This baby? She's a destroyer."

"What does that mean?" Elise asked.

"Destroyers? They tend to be fast and manoeuvrable, with a lot of firepower but not much armour. *Mambaka* here is no exception. Before we got those F.A.C.s from Gaitlin, she'd be assigned to escorting the bigger ships. Now, she is a 'big ship'."

"I don't follow..."

Winters smiled and shrugged. "It's not ideal. The reason ships like this make good defenders is because attackers tend to go for the bigger ships. That leaves things like *Mambaka* to cause havoc; sneak up and Pow! 'Ya'll forgot about me, huh?'"

"But now... it's the target?"

"More than likely." They came to a stop near the rear cargo ramp set between a large cluster of oversized thrusters. "Those F.A.C.s... they need to make up for *Mambaka*'s lack of armour, stop anything getting too close while still letting *Mambaka* break out her own weapons."

He started up the ramp. Elise gave the sleek lines and dark paint one final glance.

"That's why," Winters continued, "if it were up to me, I'd be taking *Kobra*. But Void knows what's wrong with that thing. Every time someone tries turning it back on, *Bam!* Whole damn network lights up like it's about to blow. The engineers are talking about taking it apart, piece by piece. Fuck that."

The cargo bay was in a state of barely-organised chaos, with soldiers setting up makeshift sleeping areas, hauling boxes back and forth, or sorting and stashing various types of kit. The air rang with the sound of shouted orders and the low rumble, almost a thrum, of boots on deck plates.

Winters paused, motioning at the bay. "As you can see, we've not much space on here. Enough for this bunch and the supplies we're gonna need, but hardly ideal conditions."

Elise shuddered, thinking back to the transport that had brought her to Kau D'varza. "Will the life support be able to handle this many people?"

"Oh yeah, no worries. The old *Mambaka* got used for troop transport all the time, so when they built this one, it was something they planned for. It's not the intended function, but they gave it serious consideration."

"If it wasn't meant to carry people, why such a large cargo bay?"

Winters blinked. "You were on the freighter, right? This bay is tiny. Besides, back in the day our squads numbered more like sixty-five. Old *Mambaka* could fit them in a cargo bay that was usually meant for additional munitions and supplies, so when our squads started getting bigger, they made the new one bigger to accommodate."

"So it's like a... destroyer-transport?"

Winters laughed. "Yeah. Yeah, I guess it is." He cocked his head, indicating a quieter corridor.. "Come on."

As he sealed the door to the cargo bay behind them, the noise faded into little more than the ambient sounds of the ship's systems tapping and clicking as they ran diagnostic checks and sweeps.

"Be honest with me... Takk: Is *Mambaka* up to this? I mean, could it do it alone?"

"Eh... We have a better chance than we'd have had in *Vypka*." He shook his head and his shoulders slumped.

"Look, Raffa's a good Comcap; he can use what little he's given to good effect, be it ships or bodies. But if those F.A.C.s get taken out, *Mambaka* will struggle. He won't engage if the odds look bad, and will look for alternative routes home, but if we're surprised out there... nah, the armour on this thing won't hold up to much. We have to be the ones to do the damage first, and it needs to be enough damage to eliminate any threats."

"Can it do that?"

"Sure. If we hit first, or manage to get some space between us. Fights in space... they're pretty rare; both sides have to want to engage. Otherwise, given the distance? Usually you can just retreat. But *Mambaka's* still stacked, right? The four heavy cannons, they just fire lumps of condensed material at the target. Just good, old-school kinetics." He waved a hand at one of the weapon control rooms as they passed it. "Then you've got the missiles... Smart missiles. Those things are quick as fuck. One of our weapon expert locks onto a target, hits 'Send', then sits back and watches it go flying off at stupid speeds. Six missile batteries, two on each flat side of the ship for maximum coverage."

"You weren't kidding when you said it was stacked."

"No. But that's not all."

A door at the end of the corridor opened as they approached, revealing an unpainted metal stairwell down to the next deck.

"We've got the defence system too, so if we get chased down by missiles ourselves, we can disable or confuse most of 'em. And if we can make enough room, we can deploy *Mambaka*'s assortment of mines. They're like her party-piece."

"There's no shield?"

Winters shook his head. "*Mambaka* relies on speed to outmanoeuvre rocks, and the AM system to deal with missiles." His face hardened. "If we come up against directed energy or antimatter weapons... well, we won't even know it."

"That's little comfort."

"Like I said, I'd have preferred *Kobra*. But... Well, you know." He sighed. "If it's any comfort at all, though, those sorts of weapons? Kau D'varza hasn't encountered them yet."

Another door opened automatically as they reached the foot of the stairs, revealing the head of a T-junction with three short corridors going to various rooms.

"C and C is up ahead. Raffa's quarters are over there on the right, end of that corridor. Yours are..." He wandered to the left, inspecting the name plates. He stopped at the furthest of two doors. "This is the one. Specialist E. Rivera."

She walked over and grinned. "Please, call me Elise."

"Sure thing. Here…" He pointed at the panel beside the door. "The techs have already calibrated it for you. Should just be a case of sticking your hand on there and *Pow!* This sucker will open right up."

"Thanks, Takk."

"No worries. If ya need anything else, I'll be bossing my people around."

"Sounds like tough work."

"You have nooo idea."

He smirked, winked, and disappeared back up the stairs.

Better be careful of that one… Too familiar, his type… Probably best not to encourage him either…

Elise looked back to the door and placed her hand on the panel. There was a chirp of affirmation and the door slid open.

The first thing to hit her was the sweet smell of fresh, clean air. She closed her eyes and inhaled deeply.

"Oh, man, that's good!"

She savoured the scents until she became dizzy, opened her eyes, and steadied herself on the door-frame.

Damn! Look at this place!

The quarters were small, just shy of feeling cramped, but contained everything she'd need and every piece of furniture had a specific place. She stepped past the clean-room door and into the cabin proper, noticing the way the transparent desk folded up against one wall to double as a screen and the dense blanket that rested on a super-thick single mattress. Elise dropped her bag and fell onto the bed face first.

Oh maaan... It's so comfortable! I could just lay here all cycle... Guess they like the Comcaps and Specialists getting a decent rest...

"Ughhh... Come on, time for sleep later..."

She dragged herself back to her feet, fished her pad out of her pack, and headed out.

* * *

"Where in the Void have you been?" Winters asked as he sidled up to Raffa at the vending machine.

Raffa closed his eyes, bit his bottom lip, and turned away with a tray of food.

"Seriously, boss, I came by your hab' earlier, but you didn't answer the door. Everything alright? We're still cool, right?"

"We're fine," Raffa replied. "I was... elsewhere. Had some preparations I needed to make."

Winters took the bench opposite. "Is that seriously what you're going with? I've been working with you long enough. What's really going on?"

"Leave suspicion up to Ikarus, Takk, you're no good at it. We're about to go on a long mission, to a system we've got no recent intel on, to figure out if Kau D'varza is at risk. Therefore, I was making preparations." He fixed the junior officer with a stare. "Why? What did you think I was up to?"

Damn. Maybe shouldn't have asked that...

"What do I think? I think you and our good friend the specialist were enjoying one last evening together before we flew this bird into a star."

"Into a... This isn't a suicide mission, Takk."

"Ah. My mistake. But you don't deny you *were* with Specialist Stone."

Raffa flushed red. "That's none of your damn business."

Winters grinned and sat back. "Lemme guess, you were working on the plan?"

Remember what Ikarus told you: A man - a gentleman - never gossips...

"Actually, yes. And you'll be happy to know we've got

additional orders." He pulled his pad from a pocket and tossed it over. "Third tab."

Winters jabbed at the pad, then frowned. "Merchant ships?"

"Yep. Four of them, set out from Windan to Kessic a while back. It's too soon for them to have returned, but if we find anything in Grinda that looks like them, we're to investigate and report it."

Winters cocked an eyebrow. "And you worked this out with Specialist Stone?"

"The Command Core is responsible for certain logistics. It is within her area of interest to investigate whether or not these ships made it to their destination. They had to pass through Grinda and Clion as it's the most direct route to Kessic. By the time we head out, if nothing's happened to them, they should be coming back home, again through Clion. If all goes to plan, we will meet them in Grinda and escort them home. If we don't see them, we're to leave a beacon with a repeating message for them to be on their guard."

"So now we're on convoy duty?" He pushed the pad away and crossed his arms. "Damnit... This mission just gets longer by the sekund."

"So perhaps you should focus more on it, and not on whatever it is you think I've been getting up to."

"Alright, point taken. Shit, man, I just wanted to say I hope you had a good time." He motioned to indicate the station. "We're going away from all this for a while; it's important to spend time with people you care about."

It was Raffa's turn to raise an eyebrow. "That sounds like Ikarus talking."

"Maybe we're just hoping you're successful. You and Stone? You make a good couple. She could teach you a thing or two, and you're big enough and ugly enough to look after her."

Raffa smirked. "Specialist Stone does not need me to 'Look after her'."

"Not like that, moron, not everything is about fighting. Sometimes... People just need each other, you know? A companion, someone they can open up to."

"Now I *know* this is Ikarus talking."

"Call it what you like. The point is, you're good together, the whole station stands to benefit from the two of you matching up, and both of you stand to have extremely happy lives into the bargain. I mean, shit, the Void knows you could do with lightening up a bit, and Stone does that to you. You've had a little hop in your step since the two of you got together. It's actually kinda cute."

"Cute, Force-Commander Winters?"

"Ha, yeah, whatever." He raised his hands defensively. "Look, I might not have the best record with relationships, but I know a good one when I see it. You two, that's one of the good ones."

"Your keen interest in my romantic affairs is noted and concerning, Force-Commander," Raffa said, and grinned. "But I think I can let you off. After all, you may even have a point."

"I sure hope so."

Raffa started to chew at the flavourless lump on his tray, then glanced back up when he realised Winters wasn't leaving.

"If-" he began, almost gagged, and swallowed. "If you're going to watch me eat, you might as well brief me on how preparations are going."

Winters nodded, suddenly all business. "We're almost ready to go. The troops have gotten a little creative to create more space, crate stairways up to the top of supply containers where they've set up bunks and bedrolls, and so on. Some of the skinnier ones even found space in the overhead structure."

"Is that safe?"

"I don't see why not. It's integral to the ship, and containers can roll over. No risk of that up there."

"I certainly *hope* there won't be any rolling containers. There'd better not be, at any rate."

"Don't worry. We're triple-checking the tethers. No one's keen on losing a megasek worth of food when ration bars are the punishment."

"That's wise of them. If we're going to be waiting around for those merchants, we might need every bite."

"We could always ask Exen and Grinda to top up our supplies?"

Raffa grimaced. "I think I'd rather starve."

Winters laughed. "No kidding."

"Well... we'll consider it as a last resort." He took a swig of drink. "And what about the F.A.Cs?"

"Sorted. Gaitlin sent them over in pretty good shape. A little tune-up here, load a few supplies there, and *Bam!* Those bad boys are ready to roll. Took a little while - had to break down all the food supplies to fit them in - but with the amount of people on board? They'll outlast us, easy."

"So a few more K-seks and we're good to go?"

"I'd say about twenty."

"And the squad is definitely ready?"

"Itching with anticipation. A little excited, some are

scared. I can't say I blame 'em."

"Scared?"

"Yeah. Sure. Why wouldn't they be? Half of them have never been outside the system, let alone into a potential battle they've got no way to fight in."

"This isn't our first run."

"Eh, training sims, little scraps here and there, it's nothing like what we could face in Grinda. Here's something I've been wondering..."

Raffa took another bite and nodded for him to continue.

"What if we get there, from Exen, and the Reclaim- I mean whoever sent that freighter floating toward us, has ships on all the default Transit entries?"

"Hmm..."

"Even if we do manage to turn and burn from that, where in the Void are we supposed to go? And what if they do enough damage to chase us down? Those engineers need to fix those damn T-cores. We're easy targets without full control over them."

Raffa washed his latest mouthful down with a gulp and frowned. "What are you suggesting?"

"I don't know. But you better hope for all our sakes

that if we do face something, we come out firing, and don't stop until the dust settles."

"Full battle readiness upon Transit termination?"

"That'd help, but... Damnit, if we had some more eyes in Grinda, this would be much easier."

"We've had traffic through from Exen, suggesting that system is still safe to travel through. We can check in and see if there's any news from Grinda there, see if there's any risk."

"And if there're no ships to ask?"

"Then that in itself would be very telling, wouldn't you say?"

"Damnit, Raffa. This mission... we need to be fuckin' careful."

"You think I don't know that? We're taking a full squad, plus the crews of three ships and a specialist farther than most of them have ever travelled before on a totally fluid mission into potentially hostile ground. You think I'm not aware we 'need to be fucking careful'?"

"Just so long as you're thinking about it. You ain't the only one with people to come back to." Winters got to his feet. "I'm gonna finish preparations. You wanna set off as soon as we're ready?"

"Yeah, find Specialist Rivera and tell her of the update. I'll let the Commissioner know."

"I get the feeling our Specialist is already prepared, but I'll clue her in. Sir." He gave a stiff salute, which Raffa acknowledged with a nod, then left, leaving Raffa to his flavourless meal and his thoughts.

* * *

The freighter seemed familiar, even welcoming, as Elise stepped through the airlock and hurried to the command centre. There was less security on board than there had been previously, but those that remained offered her smiles and nods as they passed.

She was mildly disappointed to find several people still lingering around the command centre, inspecting systems and running checks, but not surprised; this ship was still a mystery, and warranted checking out. The technicians glanced up from their work as she settled into a seat near the back of the room, shrugged or frowned at her lack of acknowledgement, then returned to whatever they were doing.

Elise placed her pad on the flat shelf of the console and stretched her fingers. She brought up the data she'd previously seen, and thoroughly checked every single sentence, every word, every detail.
The only thing that stuck out to her was the lack of 'recovered' files.

At least that answers one question. Repairing that video was Kau D'varza's doing. Must have transferred a bunch of corrupt stuff over... The station only managed to fix one though?

She sighed, the chair squeaking as if in response as she sat back.

So you've got a bunch of uncorrupted, untouched stuff that no one attempted to delete... then you've got all the missing stuff... the important stuff... and then every-thing that was corrupted... So there must be some kind of data storage on-board somewhere. I should have checked on my first visit. Damnit.

She glanced over to one of the workers. "Hey, is there a data-store on board?"

He finished tapping something into the console and looked over at her. "Yes, Ma'am. One deck below. Technical department opposite the engineer-ing wing."

"Thanks."

She scooped up her pad and headed out the door. After bringing up the map and following it down a level, she arrived at the Tech-Department.

The cramped room hummed with the buzz of the computers, consoles and data-stacks that lined the walls. The only light came from screens and flicker-ing status lights. At the centre, a large black col-umn reached into the ceiling, most of its components damaged or undergoing repairs.

A lone figure sat in the corner, her face illuminated by the glow of the console she was working at.

"Er... Hello?" Elise said, turning her head to hide her smirk as the technician visibly jumped.

"Oh! H-hello, Specialist... ummm..."

"Rivera." She waved a hand. "But so long as none of the bigwigs are about, you can call me Elise."

"Uh... yes... thank you, Ma'am." She smiled cautiously. "I'm Danya. Squad Three, technician. You're the one who found all those files, right?"

"Sure am. What are you working on?"

"Oh... nothing much. The system isn't cooperating."

"In what way?"

"Please don't take offence, Ma'am... uh, Elise... but I have a feeling this ship is hiding more than just the files you found."

Elise grinned. "No offence taken. I was thinking the same thing."

"That's why you're here?"

"That... and I wanted to test a theory."

"A theory, Ma'am?"

"You're familiar with this ship, right?"

"As familiar as it's letting me be."

"And would you say that certain files have been intentionally corrupted or deleted?"

Danya nodded. "That matches everything I've seen so far."

"But others... It's like they haven't been touched."

"Uh. So the files that were left, were left deliberately?"

Elise frowned, nodding. "That's what I'm thinking. Whoever kidnapped the crew clearly had all the time in the world to wipe everything, but they didn't. The big question is, 'Why not?'"

"The logical answer is that they wanted whoever found the ship to find that information," Danya said, then slumped back, frowning. "But why? What purpose does it fulfil?"

"Well, the ship seems to have been targeted at us, so it's probably safe to assume we were meant to see something... but what, specifically?"

"Well, whoever did this left the most information on the crew... though that isn't saying much. But there's another question: can we assume the ship *was* targeted at us by those who kidnapped the crew?"

Elise frowned. "Who else would it be, and why?"

Danya's sudden confidence evaporated, leaving her looking flustered. "Er... well, I don't know, Ma'am."

Elise nodded. "Mhmm... so let's keep it simple: if you were gonna kidnap a shipload of people, then send said ship somewhere it would be found... why would you leave information on the crew?"

"I... I don't know that either, ma'am."

Elise's frown deepened. "Neither do I, and it's driving me nuts." She turned away, tapping on her pad. She brought up the details for Ikarus and hit connect.

A waveform appeared on the screen. "Specialist Rivera. How can I be of assistance?"

"Hey, Ikarus. Have you got a sek'?"

"Certainly. In fact, I have been looking for you. Force-Commander Winters has asked me to provide an update on the mission, but I cannot locate you anywhere on *Mambaka*."

"Oh... I'm on the freighter," she said, and checked her settings. "Tracker is on and active, though, so..."

"Hmm. Perhaps the hull of the freighter is obscuring the signal. No matter, I will be there shortly."

"Alright. I'm in Tech."

"See you soon, Ma'am."

The waveform disappeared. Elise eased back against one of the consoles, absentmindedly tapping the pad against her lips.

"What if..." Danya started, then shook her head self-consciously and lapsed into silence.

Elise looked at her. "Go on. 'What if...?'"

"Well, we've checked those passengers out hundreds of times. Sent details to neighbouring systems looking for answers, but we've heard nothing so far..."

"Crew, not passengers," Elise corrected, staring blankly at the opposing rack of consoles.

"Right. Crew. Sorry. But we couldn't figure that out either. Out of all those on board, there were only two people useful enough to keep something like this going."

Elise's eyes narrowed as a new thought occurred. "Two that we know of..." She blew the air out of her cheeks and turned to Danya. "What if the information we're seeing on the crew is also misleading?"

"The cross-reference with the person in the video is a match, so unless that's been modified... edited, we know at least one of those profiles is accurate."

"But only so far as we know he was onboard. We don't

know if that name is accurate, if his recorded skills are correct..."

"Well, all I can say is that if it was changed, it was very professionally done." Danya stretched her arms out in frustration. "But again, for what purpose? Why go to all that trouble? What's the point?" She growled. "If only we knew who did this! We might be able to get into their heads, figure it out."

"So why not make a wargame out of it?" Ikarus said from the hatch. "Make an assumption as to who may be behind this incident, and go from there, repeating the process as often as seems necessary?"

Elise nodded to him. "Hey, Ikarus."

"Specialist Rivera."

"We've got a few ideas," Danya continued. "If it's pirates, then the Void knows why they'd do this. But if it was the Reclaimers..."

"'If it was the Reclaimers...'" Elise echoed, then shook her head. "I get that everyone here is terrified of them, but it's too direct! The Reclaimers at the Patrol Zone... At Yurnto..."

"I am assured that the Specialist does not need reminding that those at Beyema may be different to those she has previously encountered."

"Yes, Ikarus, I am aware of that. Still, though, it's all

wrong. What possible reason could they have for kidnapping people? And why would they delete some
data, but leave other bits intact for us to find?"

"Perhaps it is characteristic of something else Madam
Specialist has seen of the Reclaimers?"

"Hmm..." Elise rubbed her chin. "They like their secrecy. Not too keen on sharing much about themselves..."

Danya grunted. "You're not kidding. Just look at those
damned abilities of theirs. You don't know what's
coming until it's too late." Her voice took on an edge,
like something close to panic, as she became more
animated. "I even heard some can make your heart
explode without touching you! How are you supposed to fight something like that?"

"You're not," Elise replied. "My dad told me it took
just two Reclaimers to wipe out the Free Paradise
Movement. Security had been trying for... well, too
long. You can't fight something like that, even if
they're nowhere near as strong as you've just made
out." She grinned. "But that story you've heard is just
that: a story. It's an example of the other weapon in
their arsenal: Rumours."

"Rumours?"

"They let people talk about them, blow the stories out of proportion. Sometimes they seed a little
misinformation themselves, just to build fear, keep

people guessing."

"But what does all this have to do with the freighter?"

"I'm not sure. If it *is* the Reclaimers - and I'm not at all convinced of that - then this could be a new tactic, or at least one I haven't seen before. But besides the tampered-with data, none of this fits, it's absolutely *not* their usual way of doing things." She shook her head. "Like I keep saying, too direct."

"For Patrol Zone Reclaimers," Ikarus added.

"Yes. Okay. So let's say for a sekund that these Reclaimers are different. What do they want?"

"The most recent news from that region suggests they have set up in orbit around the largest planet, with a substantial force of unusual vessels," Ikarus said.

"Unusual?"

"They do not fit with what we know of Reclaimer vessels. It is possible, however, that these are a significant advance or modification on an older design."

"And what are they doing around the planet?"

"It looks like a mining operation, but we cannot be sure."

Danya frowned. "They'd need plenty of bodies for a mining operation."

"You think the Reclaimers are kidnapping people to mine a planet?" Elise shook her head. "No way. It'd all be automated from above. Robot miners and base camps, that sort of thing. They don't need people for mining. We even tried buying tech from R.P.Z. Reclaimers for Paradise, but they wouldn't allow it."

"It could be a front," Danya replied. "You know, like they show the universe they're mining, when really they're using it as a base from which to kidnap local travellers?"

Ikarus nodded. "That would fit with what I have seen, but what they are doing with their victims? It is unknown."

Elise stepped away from the consoles and grimaced. "Ugh. I don't want to believe it, but it certainly looks like all the stuff we've seen so far is pointing in one direction."

"Which gives even more reason for the Specialist to be suspicious."

She looked at him. "But not of the Reclaimers?"

"Of everyone. But if the simplest route is to find them responsible, despite your belief that they would prefer secrecy, I would trust my gut instinct in this matter."

Elise closed her eyes tight and rubbed the bridge of

her nose. "So, basically, I've learnt nothing."

"No, it will just take time to digest the new information."

"Damnit... alright..." She glanced at Danya. "Hey, thanks for your help. If you find anything else while I'm away, make sure it gets sent to my quarters on the station. I'll check it when I get back. In the meantime, you can contact me on *Mambaka*."

"Sure thing, Ma'am."

Elise motioned for Ikarus to lead the way back to the landing bay station. "Alright, what's this about the mission?"

"Force-Commander Winters wanted you to know that the mission timetable has been moved forward. I believe they will be ready to depart upon your return."

"We're leaving early? Does that normally happen?"

He gave a single nod. "If the mission allows. It is situational. If the vessel and crew are ready to go, there is little sense in hanging around simply to comply with an arbitrary timetable."

"Hmm... Sounds sensible."

"Indeed. The longer our vessels are used fulfilling one purpose, they cannot be used to fulfill another. Given that, and the fact we have a limited number of ships even under the best circumstances, it would be point-less - as well as highly illogical - to waste time."

"As I said, sounds sensible. But I've been meaning to ask: Why snakes?"

"You mean for the ship names?"

"Yeah. I mean, I recognise the root of *Vypka* and *Kobra*, and I know they're both snakes, so I assume the rest are too?"

He nodded. "Indeed. No doubt a quirk of the engineers who built the first models. Perhaps it is ceremonial. If you're interested, I shall look into it." They reached the airlock and stepped back onto the station. "It strikes me that many in Gaitlin also follow a similar scheme. I would imagine such a practice has existed for a while."

Stepping into the elevator, Ikarus' finger hovered over the button for the engineering deck and pressed it when Elise nodded.

"We didn't have any ships at Paradise. I mean, ships came down all the time - visitors, cargo haulers, con-tractors, that sort of thing - but there was nothing we could call our own. The ships that leave Kau D'varza are certainly quieter than the ones leaving Paradise ever were, though. I mean, *damn*."

"Ah yes. Thankfully I haven't had much experience with planet-based launch systems."

"Count yourself lucky." She gave him a sideways glance. "That reminds me. Where do you come from anyway, Ikarus? What did you do before serving Comcap Raffa?"

He inhaled. "Ah... I have lived on Kau D'varza for most of my life, and for most of that I have worked as an aide. Upon Comcap Raffa's promotion, I was assigned to him - an assignment I am most thankful for. Comcap Raffa is fair, and takes a very hands-off approach to my method of operation."

"I'm noticing that a lot round here. Free reign to handle things as people see fit."

He shrugged. "People work best when they aren't under constant micro-management. However, our approach could perhaps be improved. I would like to avoid a repeat of the engineering bay incident."

Elise nodded. "As would we all."

The elevator came to a halt and opened with a rattle. They stepped out and headed towards *Mambaka*.

"Seems quiet..."

"I am happy to report that most of the work has been completed. However, we are still experiencing issues with the Transit systems. I have faith the engineers and technicians will resolve the issue in time."

"Damn," Elise muttered. "Perhaps you should start cycling the squad engineers through here more often. They could treat it as training, and the work would still get done."

Ikarus thought about it for a few seconds, then nodded. "I will consider such an option before presenting it to Specialist Stone. There are many obvious advantages, but one must consider the alternatives."

As they reached *Mambaka*, Raffa waved to them from the rear cargo ramp.

"Specialist. Ikarus."

"Comcap," Elise replied. "How's it looking?"

"Now that you're here, I can alert the Arch-Commissioner. I think he wants to come see us off, then we can leave."

"Alright. Sounds good. I guess I'll hang around here then?"

He nodded. "As you wish, Ma'am."

* * *

Kaska Stone kept in step with Nevos and Zeled as they hurried through the engineering bay to where *Mambaka* was berthed. She felt a shiver down her spine and her breath turn cold as she laid eyes on the ship. She frowned, wondering why she would experience such a reaction when she never had before, then allowed her gaze to pass over Elise and Ikarus before lingering on Raffa. The shiver happened again.

That's why. I'm... afraid.

"Is everything set, Raffa?" Zeled asked, breaking into - and dispelling - her thoughts.

"It is, Sir. Just say the word and we're gone."

Gierre stepped forward. "I wanted to wish you good luck. Try not to get us pulled into any wars out there, Comcap."

"I'll do my best, Sir."

Kaska saw his eyes flick to the right and she smiled, hoping she didn't look as nervous as she felt.

"We look forward to your return, *Comcap*," she said, and was grateful that her voice sounded resolute, strong.

After everything, it feels weird to call him that again...

Raffa gave her a hopeful grin. "As do I, Specialist."

She nodded and swallowed heavily.

Please be safe, and hurry back.

"And you," Nevos said with a mischievous smile, his attention now on Elise, "do what you do best. Find us something we can use."

"If it's there, Arch-Commissioner, I'll find it. Don't worry."

"If there's nothing else..." Nevos glanced around, and saw no arguments. "I would like to wish you a speedy journey, a successful mission, and grant you permission to leave whenever you feel it is appropriate." He raised a salute. "For Kau D'varza."

Those assembled echoed his sentiments before disappearing into the ship.

A few minutes later, Kaska and Ikarus watched as *Mambaka* was pulled out to the ship-airlock and sent off to meet up with the two nearby F.A.Cs.

CHAPTER SEVENTEEN- THIEVES AND THEORIES

Elise had spent most of the journey in her quarters, scrutinizing every speck of data regarding Exen, Grinda and the freighter she'd been able to find. The biggest problem she'd encountered was that the further they got from Kau D'varza, the weaker the connection became, leading to some considerable frustration. By the second waking cycle, the distance had become too great for comfortable use so, lacking the ability to cross-reference her research with anything other than the stuff she'd already downloaded, and with a hunger growing to a point where it could no longer be ignored, she headed for the mess-hall.

Despite *Mambaka*'s ability to house hundreds of 'passengers', the eating area was tiny, capable of seating twenty-five at most.

Elise squeezed between the ranks of squad members, murmuring an apology here or an "Excuse me" there, and came to a stop at the machine embedded in the rear wall. Self-consciousness pricked at her, and she tried not to fidget or think of the soldiers watching her as she waited for her selection to arrive. After what seemed an age, but was actually no more than a few seconds, a tray slid into the slot, followed by a bowl of bright orange fluid and a carton of Nutri-Juice.

She turned from the machine, and was surprised to find that the others were paying her no mind at all.

Paranoia, that's all it is. You're not one of them and you know it, even if they don't really care. Just... be cool.

She spied an empty seat at the end of a nearby table and settled into it, glancing around at the troops seated closest to make sure it was okay. To her relief, all seemed to turn to her with smiles, grins and warm welcomes.

"Specialist," the one closest to her said, in a respectful tone.

"Alright?" Elise replied, before looking around the others again, this time with a toothy grin. "How's it going?"

"Not bad," the soldier said. "Kierov here was just explaining his theories on Reclaimers."

The person next to him straightened up, tense, and

looked at Elise with uncertainty in his eyes.

"It's alright, you can speak openly," she said. "I'm interested in hearing anything that might help with the mission."

Kierov didn't relax. "It's nothing really. There's just a feeling among the squad that we're gonna have to fight the Reclaimers."

Elise frowned. "What, on this mission?"

"Possibly... but if not now, soon. They're not gonna move on, or stop doing what they're doing."

Elise laid down her spoon and sat back as far as she could, sighing. "Look, we don't know it's them. Not for sure. How would you feel if I said there may be another faction out there... another group... causing all this trouble, just so Kau D'varza decides to pin the blame on the Reclaimers and gathers allies to deal with them?"

The soldiers reacted with surprise and glanced around the table at each other while, Kierov's expression darkened.

"That would leave both sides weak," he said.

"Exactly," Elise replied. "If we wipe ourselves out going after the Reclaimers, and if someone else is responsible, it'd put them, whoever they are, in a position of strength." She sighed. "But, if it *is* the Reclaimers and we've got proof to hand, it'll be easier to convince others to help us. We've got to do this carefully, step by step, and make sure we do it right." She looked around the table, making eye contact with everyone. "So that means no jumping to conclusions. Ikarus ran through every scenario before we left. What we need now is evidence, to discover which of those scenarios is correct."

The soldiers were silent for a moment, leaving Elise to wonder if she had gone too far and alienated them in some way.

"I really hope it is someone else," Kierov finally muttered. "I don't think I'm alone when I say fighting Reclaimers is pretty low on the list of things I want to do."

There were murmurs of agreement from around the table.

Elise offered what she hoped was a reassuring smile. "If it does comes to that, though, Kau D'varza is extremely fortunate to have people like all of you looking after it."

The soldier next to her shifted in his seat. "That is kind of you to say, Ma'am, but projectiles are only so effective against superhuman abilities."

Elise snorted in irritation. "They're tough, yes, but they're not superhuman! We all need to start viewing the Reclaimers as what they are: human... people just like you and me."

"People just like you and me... with freakishly weird,

almost superhuman abilities," a female soldier added.

Elise took a deep breath and sighed again. "Alright, they're different in that way, but all these abilities they have... if we just think of it as technology or weaponry, it takes away some of the fear." She paused and shook her head. "You know, this kind of fear doesn't exist on my world. We don't know them - nobody does; they don't allow it - but nor do we run for clean underwear whenever they're mentioned. The fact is, no one from Kau D'varza has even tried talking to them. it's no wonder we're so in the dark about all this."

Another awkward silence fell over the group as they looked to one another before Kierov finally spoke up again.

"Forgive us, Ma'am. We simply don't have the same experience with them that you do."

She shook her head. "I don't have any experience at all with the ones at Beyema, but it'd be something new if it was them. Either way, I'm not about to judge them without evidence. If it turns out to be them after all, obviously my opinion will change, but if we find it's not... well..." She grinned. "You might have to get used to counting them as allies."

Kierov's eyes widened. "Work... with the Reclaimers?"

"Something to consider, huh?" Elise smirked, and started eating, leaving the rest of the group to talk amongst themselves.

* * *

"One Kilosek' 'til we're good to 'Zit," the pilot announced.

Raffa yawned, shaking off the cobwebs in his mind. "Very good." He straightened up in his seat and tapped a button on the seat arm. "This is Raffa. In approximately one Kilosekund, *Mambaka* and her escorts will engage Transit to Exen. Best estimates suggest this should only take point six megasekunds. Those of you who haven't travelled via this method before may feel unusual, but that sensation is only temporary. Note that upon arriving in Exen, only messages approved by the Command Centre will be allowed out until such a time as I deem otherwise. Comcap Raffa, Outsign."

"Spoken like a true leader," Winters said, grinning as he tossed a ration bar Raffa's way.

"What was wrong with it?"

"Nothing. A bit serious, but other than that, at least they know what's what."

Raffa's eyes closed in bitter disappointment as he tore the top off the bar. "Yor' Cabbage flavour. Damnit."

"Better get used to 'em, Cap. At least four of the containers up there are loaded with 'em."

"Four? That's like..." His face scrunched as he worked it out. "Ten percent of our total food supply."

"Yeah. I checked with supplies. Seems Yor' did us a deal."

"Some deal! I can't believe we paid for this stuff!"

"Well, I'm told we didn't pay a lot."

"Damnit... they should be giving *us* credits to eat this garbage." He sighed. "Only give these to the freaks who actually want them. We'll try to trade them for something better at Exen or Grinda."

Winters laughed. "I think I'd prefer the cabbage bars over anything they've got."

Raffa waved his free hand in front of his face. "Eh, you never know; we might get lucky."

His eyes went back to the bar, a flat grey mass dotted with dark green chunks, and tried to work up the courage to eat it.

I would literally cut my arm off to be back in Kaska's apartment right now...

"Oh, just eat it," Winters said. "Seriously, the tension is killing me. They're not that bad."

Raffa fixed him with a frown, raised the bar to his mouth, and kept his eyes locked on Winters as he chewed.

"Damnit man, you look like a bora eating a nemora."

"Haven't you..." Raffa swallowed, reluctantly. "Haven't you got anything better to do than watch me eat? Which, by the way, seems to be a hobby of yours recently."

Winters smirked and shook his head. "Training is done for the cycle and all equipment is clean. I - and by 'me' I mean 'they' - have even had time to scrub down the cargo bay. Thought I'd join you for Transit."

"Your company is welcome, but don't sit there and advise me on my chewing technique."

Winters laughed, raising his hands. "Alright, alright. I'll let you enjoy your meal."

Raffa raised an eyebrow. "*Enjoy?*"

Winters laughed and turned to the screen on the edge of his seat just as the door to the Command Centre hissed open. Raffa knew from the sound of the footsteps that it was Elise.

"Hello, Specialist," he said, turning to face her.

She looked stunned. "How did y...?" she began, then shook her head as she settled in at the console to the rear of the room. "You know what? Never mind."

He grinned. "Looking forward to Transit?"

"Just another method of travel to me. Remember, I had to get here from the opposite side of Yor' Space." She grinned back at him. "This isn't my first long-haul."

"Maybe, but I suspect your method of travel was a little more luxurious than a warship."

"Actually, the transport I came to Kau D'varza on was a heap. I was still lucky to get it though."

Winters looked up from his screen. "There's something I've wanted to ask. Why Kau D'varza?"

"It was the furthest place from Paradise I could get to. That's why I say I was lucky. There aren't many transports going from Yurnto to Windan, let me tell you!"

"I've gotta admit, I'd never heard of Yurnto until I met you," Winters said.

"It's no Kandaha, I'll admit that."

"No, I mean it's weird. Kau D'varza's never done any business with them, and Windan sources all its shit locally. They're actually pretty proud of that. Anyway, it makes me wonder... Do you know what else was on that transport? And if so, was there anything that might be a risk to the station?"

Raffa frowned. "What are you getting at, Takk?"

"Maybe nothing, but all I'm saying is, it's weird. What if some of those nutcases on the surface were buying materials for a weapon or something, and they didn't wanna source it locally because it'd raise suspicions?"

Raffa sighed. "This is a bit of a reach, even for you. Ships come to Windan all the time, we always have one off ships coming from rare places. Just because we don't do business with them, doesn't mean they're a danger." He turned in his chair to face Elise. "Besides, that was ages ago, right?"

Elise thought for a few moments before speaking. "It was," she replied, "but I'll admit it was odd to see Windan come up on the list. I'd never heard of the place until then. In the end I checked my map, saw how far away it was, and booked my place onboard. The rest is history." She grinned. "Destiny was smiling on me that day I think."

"Smiling on all of us," Raffa corrected.

Elise acknowledged the compliment with a smile. "We'll see."

"And we are stabilizing," one of the command crew said. "Reducing speed... Support vessels *G-Claw* and *G-Stinger* are reducing speed to match, maintaining relative position."

The sound of the engines faded to a low hum, and the voice at the front of the command centre spoke up again.

"Vessel running on power-gen mode. Maintaining

nominal charge levels. Support vessels report velocity within acceptable parameters to initiate Transit." He turned to Raffa. "Comcap, *Mambaka* is ready to Transit on your order."

He inhaled, wrapped his fingers around the arm of his seat and nodded. "Do it."

Elise watched as almost nothing changed. The screens got a bit dimmer - the external cameras weren't showing anything at all - but besides that, *Mambaka* felt like she always had, albeit a little quieter.

The chair creaked as she leant back, stretched, and yawned. "Well that was exciting."

"Same as always," Raffa agreed. "Alright, Winters, you have watch. Call me if anything important happens."

"Will do, Sir. Going anywhere nice?"

"Only to get something *decent* to eat, then I might even treat myself to some sleep."

"Right," Winters said, nodding. He seemed to be on the brink of saying something else, clearly decided against it, and turned away.

Good man. Sensible *man*, Raffa thought, smiling to himself as he stepped into the corridor.

* * *

"It is my assessment," Ikarus said, from his seat opposite Kaska in the engineering bay office, "that since the removal of former-Chief Engineer Jimba, this department has increased efficiency by thirty-six percent. The restructured management has worked well and additional squad engineers have also done an excellent job. I would like to commend you on a very well thought-out approach."

Kaska nodded, absentmindedly. "Thanks, Ikarus. Still a long way to go yet though."

"Indeed. To this end, I have finished my review of the documents we have recovered, and am ready to present my findings to be used as evidence against Jimba and his associates when appropriate."

"One less thing to worry about…"

Ikarus frowned. "I sense that something is troubling you, Specialist Stone."

She closed her eyes and inhaled. "Sorry, Ikarus, I just… Engineering bay, right?"

He nodded his understanding. "Ah. Of course, Ma'am. We can move to another area of the station to continue, if you prefer?"

"No… no, that won't be necessary. Everything we need is here." She smiled at him. "Thank you for the consideration though."

"Not a problem." He glanced back to his pad. "The

final item I have that requires your attention at this moment... *Kobra* is still causing problems. The engineering staff have requested permission to do a full strip-down and rebuild. This course of action, while extreme, has been approved by the new managers. However, something of this magnitude requires additional sign-off by a Command Core Specialist or higher."

"If they think that's the best option, then I'll agree to it."

"I believe, in this instance, this is the wisest choice. However, I would remind the good Specialist not to agree to everything so lightly. Until a new bay overseer can be found, you will face many decisions like this. Not all will be so easy."

"We need *Kobra*... it's our secret weapon."

"I do not disagree, Ma'am. However, such a repair will require resources to be diverted from other places: person-power, time, tools and materials. Fixing *Kobra* is important, but one cannot allow other priorities to dwindle in comparison."

The door alert buzzed before Kaska could reply, and she checked the screen on her desk.

"Danya Alarez... Third squad technician," she said, glancing at Ikarus and raising an eyebrow.

"I know of her. Specialist Rivera believed she was worth listening to."

Kaska nodded. "Enter."

The door slid open, permitting a nervous woman clutching a data-pad to step through the hatch and offer a tentative salute.

Kaska studied her for a few seconds, then motioned for her to stand at ease. "Is there something we can help you with, Technician?"

"Uhh…" She closed her eyes and bit her lip, steadying herself. "Ma'am, I have a recommendation I have been asked to share with you."

"Hm? Go on."

"Yes, Ma'am," Alarez said, and tapped the screen on her pad to throw the image up on the room's larger monitor. "We have completed our assessment of the freighter and have discovered no new information. However, I have spoken with several engineers and we believe that should Kau D'varza make use of such a vessel…" She paused and swallowed, glancing between the senior personnel. "I… that is, we, are of the opinion that it could serve us as a repair ship."

Kaska and Ikarus both frowned. "Repair ship?" they chorused.

Danya tensed some more. "Y-yes Ma'am." She raised her hand to the image of the freighter. "We neither import nor export enough to make running such a vessel economical in its current configuration, but it also occurs to me that with the recent troubles, we have more use of a vessel that can repair other ships outside of Windan."

Kaska glanced at Ikarus. "Hm. I'm not sure. Your thoughts?"

"Technician Alarez raises some excellent points. However, this project sounds extremely resource heavy."

She nodded, vigorous in her anxiety. "Yes, Sir, it would be. However, while I cannot speak for people-power, our investigation into resources secretly stockpiled by Jimba have revealed our stocks to be greater than originally believed. My fellow technicians are working to have the updated information sent to you once they have established exactly how much we've got. Either way-"

Kaska raised a hand. "Wait. He was funnelling supplies? Where?"

"There's a ship at the rear of the bay, Ma'am, just before the shuttles and small vessels. Looks like an old Yor' transport. He's been storing the excess in there."

"That *asshole*..." Kaska spat, before Ikarus interrupted her by clearing his throat.

"I believe, Specialist Stone, that this is potentially of great benefit to us. We will have to look into where exactly these resources came from and whether there are any detrimental effects from such storage, but otherwise... this is a pleasant surprise."

Danya nodded some more. "Further," she babbled, "as the transport itself is in such bad condition, we can also reduce that to component parts for additional supplies."

Kaska weaved her fingers and sat back. "Ikarus?"

The aide remained silent for a few moments while he thought. "Firstly, I would like to see the resources available, and what sort of effect this will have on the repairs to *Kobra.* However Technician Alarez raises an excellent suggestion, and once such conditions are satisfied, I would happily give my recommendation to initiate the conversion." He paused, then looked to the image once more. "Of course, I may be biased. The availability of such a vessel would be extremely useful to Comcap Raffa at this time..."

Kaska swallowed. *Damn right...*

"Agreed. And if it'd be useful to him, it'll be useful to all of us." She looked to Danya. "Alright, have all information regarding this project sent to myself and Ikarus. We will assess it further."

Danya saluted. "Of course, Ma'am. T-thank you."

She stood there, seemingly uncertain as to what to do next.

"Was there anything else, Technician?"

"Er... no. No, Ma'am."

Kaska nodded. "Then return to your duties."

"Yes, Ma'am,"Danya said, looking slightly disappointed as she turned away.

Kaska turned back to Ikarus as the door closed again.

"She seems... nervous."

"It is characteristic of her, I think. But I assure you, when I met her the other cycle, she spoke most confidently once she had warmed to her theme, and I have to say I was most impressed. She has some good ideas, sees things that people would usually miss."

"This meeting, was it official?"

"No. I was meeting with Specialist Rivera on the freighter. Technician Alarez was merely present."

Kaska frowned. "I get the feeling Specialist Rivera is better at talking to people than I am."

"Your skills lie elsewhere. I hope Madam Specialist has not forgotten that without her talents, Specialist Rivera would currently be wasting away in a prison cell."

"Alright, Ikarus. Fair point. All the same, though, I should have seen that asshole was skimming materials. I wonder now how long it's been going on..."

"In fairness, none of us saw it occurring, and in any case, that problem is now resolved. It also provides another charge we can add to the already substantial list."

Kaska nodded. "You're right. We should get back to work. Have you got those numbers from four m-sek ago?"

CHAPTER EIGHTEEN- THE CALM

Elise paused before hitting the call tab beside Raffa's door, her hand hovering in mid-air as if gravity-locked there while she debated with herself.

He wanted to sleep.

Yeah, but that was kilosekunds ago. He's bound to be rested by now.

That's as may be. Even so...

Her internal dialogue was interrupted by the door opening and Raffa almost bumping her out of the way as he stepped out.

"Oh! Sorry," he said, a slight frown forming as he noticed her unusual hand position. "Something on your mind, Specialist?"

"Always," she replied, remembering a conversation she'd had back on the station. A smile crept to her lips. "I was about to..." She saw him still frowning at her hand and lowered it. "Never mind. Do you have a sekund?"

"Well, I was just on my way back to the Command Centre, but... sure, if you want to walk with me."

She nodded and looked around at the quiescent corridors as she fell into step. The noises vibrating through the hallways and staircases had all but ceased when they'd activated Transit. Now, a low, pulsing hum was the only evidence that an engine was still functioning. Elise felt herself breathing in time with the rhythm as she tried to think of how to start.

Damn... that's even kinda relaxing...

"Looks like things are going well," she said.

Raffa frowned. "That's it? That's what you wanted to talk about?"

"Well, no, but... are they? Going well, I mean?"

He glanced at her sharply, his eyes narrowing for a moment before he nodded. "So far, yes, but we haven't gone far yet. It'll become more difficult to maintain this level of discipline and morale once people start missing home and loved ones."

"Are you expecting problems?"

"I'm always expecting problems, but I prefer the ones that come from inside; they're more predictable." His eyes drifted to the corridor over her shoulder, then back to her eyes. His gaze was direct, arresting. Authoritative. "What about you?"

"What about me?"

"How are you finding things so far?"

She shrugged. "It's alright. Wish we could access the Netrix but... it's a small price to pay for seeing other systems."

"You like travelling?"

"I think so, yeah. I didn't do all that much before leaving Paradise. This is great though: my quarters are practically luxury, I'm getting paid for a trip to two other systems I doubt I'd have seen otherwise, plus it's all in the name of getting answers. What's not to like?" She grinned, though it soon turned into a grimace. "Apart from the mysteries. I hate mysteries."

Raffa laughed. "I never would have guessed. I hope you're not too disappointed. The view of the Cloud from Exen is unbelievable, but besides that there isn't much there, and Grinda..." He frowned. "Grinda's damn near lifeless. One functioning station, a few mining platforms... It's jarring when you come from somewhere like Windan."

"And Windan is jarring to anyone coming from Ar-Kaos space."

"Ah, yes, I forget that's where you're from. Yurnto, it used to be Independent, back when I travelled with my folks. Businesses from Ar-Kaos aggressively buying up land in the system, setting up stations, doing deals with settlements and factions..." He exhaled, long and loud. "We all knew where it was leading... inevitable really. Yor' wasn't too happy about it, but they had their own problems to deal with."

David Noe

"We're stronger with the backing of Ar-Kaos."

"'We'?"

She swallowed. "I mean, Paradise. Yurnto."

"Specialist Rivera, if that were true, that Free Paradise Movement you've mentioned would have been shut down before it got off the ground. Instead, it drove you to Windan. That doesn't sound to me as though Ar-Kaos is good for Paradise."

"They crept up on us," Elise explained, not liking a certain 'pity me' tone she detected in, and quickly removed from, her voice. "At first it was just info-drops and peaceful protests. Then Tayborn, that fucking asshole, started riling people up, causing problems, bringing in extra hands from outside to bolster his numbers. By the time anyone knew what was really going on, they were too strong."

Although not strong enough to stand against the Reclaimers. I really need to check into that...

"I guess that's why I like to know what's going on," she continued. "I don't like surprises."

Raffa arched an eyebrow and smiled. "You and me both."

Something in Raffa's tone told her that it was time to get the point.

"So when we arrive in Exen, what's the plan?" she asked.

"We're travelling straight through, quick as we can. If

you can get info on Grinda from their network, you have my permission to do so, but I'd appreciate it if you didn't tell them of our mission until we're about to leave."

"What... Why?"

"I don't want any messages reaching Grinda before us. I mean, yes, they could always guess where we're going from our direction of travel, but as far as they're concerned we could just be doing something routine."

She grinned. "We *are* on a routine mission. Meet up with Kau D'varza's merchant vessels to escort them home."

"That's true. Even so, I'd like to keep Exen in the dark as much as possible," he said, coming to a halt as they reached the door to the Command Centre. "They can't contest our journey through their system – they don't have enough of a defence force for that – but they'd sell us out in a heartbeat if they could."

"Hm. They sound like nice neighbours..."

"More like desperate ones," Raffa corrected. "Most Independent systems out here, except Gaitlin and Arokia... they're not in good shape. The standard is set pretty low when it comes to what they're willing to do to survive."

"What's the official relationship between Kau D'varza and the elements in Exen?"

"The mining operations... they're fine. Sometimes ships come to Kau D'varza with their excess materials. They need to get rid of one thing so they can store more of another, so they come to us and we usually buy it cheap."

"That sounds useful."

"Yeah. It can lead to some resentment on their part, though. They have to wonder, sometimes, if we aren't ripping them off. I know I would." He frowned. "As for the rest of it. The station there, Freedom One… It was originally called something else, then got sold on. Nothing happened with it after that, so refugees from Yor' and Arabia space resettled it. They've been running things ever since. Outwardly they're friendly to Kau D'varza, but I've seen more than enough reports to know they absolutely cannot be trusted. F-Oners only ever look out for themselves, almost on an individual basis. It's a small wonder that the station is still functioning."

"Do they have someone in charge? Someone I need to research before interacting with them?"

Raffa shrugged. "There might be someone running things, or even a group, but it changes pretty often. Unstable government, everyone wants a piece of power… It's the culture, which also means it's the type of people the place attracts, right? All these people dreaming that life will be better if they 'escape' Yor' or Arabia, but when they reach places like F-One and it's worse, it usually goes one of two ways: they either accept their fate and get on with life, or they try to change it. Hence, the power struggles."

Elise's eyes narrowed. "That might actually make my

job easier. If they're fractured, there won't be a concentrated effort on cyber-defence. I should be able to just slide right in, grab the data we want, and slide right out again before they see it as anything other than a standard communication."

"Is it easy to set something like that up?"

Elise shrugged. "Few K-seks?"

Raffa scratched his chin while he deliberated. "Okay. Well... if you're confident you can get it done, I'll allow it, though I would prefer it if you started your data-pilfering when we're at a location in the system where it would be difficult for them to protest. If you can grab all their data just before we Transit, for example, that'd be my preferred option. I am not, however, ignorant of..." He gesticulated with his hands as he struggled to find the best term. "'Computer Problems'. Factor those in, and proceed with your plan on arrival."

"How long are we in Exen for, exactly?"

"Ah, so it's not so easy after all; you *are* worried about running out of time."

"Well... it might become a factor," she said. "So... how long?"

"Point four megasek, if everything goes according to plan."

She nodded, and sighed. "Plenty of time then. I'll get it done."

"I'm sure you will," he said, then cycled the door

and entered the Command Centre. "How're we doing, Pilot?"

"Transit terminates in point three kilosekunds, Comcap."

Raffa settled back into the captain's seat and tapped a button on the arm. "This is Raffa. We will shortly be arriving in Exen. I remind you that all communication with any entity within the system is prohibited unless expressly permitted by me, so all requests should be passed to the Command Centre." He took a deep breath. "Furthermore, while we are not expecting to encounter hostilities within Exen, everyone is to report to their assigned station prior to Transit termination and stand-to until further notice. Our journey in Exen is estimated to take point four megasekunds. Keep up the good work, people. Comcap Raffa, outsign."

"Nice. Should have ended on a song," Winters said as he stirred in his seat.

"Maybe next time," Raffa replied, distractedly.

"What's up with you?" Winters asked.

"Just wondering how *Claw* and *Stinger* are getting on. I'd hate to be cramped up in a F.A.C. for all this time."

Winters made a dismissive gesture. "They knew what they were getting into. Besides, any problems and we can swap people out, reinforce the chain of command a little."

"I'd rather we didn't have to."

"Transit terminates in Point two kilosekunds," the pilot called out. "Preparing for core shut-down... Engines restarting... diagnostics on thrusters show green across the board. They're ready to fire as soon as we reach Exen."

"Acknowledged," Raffa said, watching the flurry of activity occurring around him.

"Weapons Stations Two, Three, Five reporting stand-by status. One, Four, Six, still show Trans- Cancel that, One and Six just came online," Winters said, then growled and jabbed a button. "Station Four, what's the problem?"

"Weapons console locked up, Sir," a male voice said.

"Have you requested a technician?"

"Not yet, Sir. We-"

"Get a technician down there, and get it fixed! You've got..." He glanced at the main screen, then back to his armrest. "Point one K-sek."

"Yes s-"

Winters ended the communication and slumped in his chair. "Well, someone's going to be on the cabbage bars for a few cycles."

"Beatings will continue until morale improves!" Elise said with a laugh, having retaken her place at the rear console.

"Something like that," Winters muttered, his face deadly serious.

"Point defence online, Sir," the voice broke in again. "Power draw... optimal. Controls online... prepared, locked until transit terminates... Weapon Station Four reports online and standing by."

Winters tapped the button again. "Sloppy work, Station Four. I want a full report later."

"Of course, Sir, our apologies."

"Save them for the mothers of the soldiers who're killed the next time you screw up. Winters, outsign," he snapped. He caught sight of the look on Elise's face. "I meant it. This isn't a game we're playing here, Specialist."

She raised her hands in mock surrender. "I never said a thing."

She saw Winters and Raffa exchange a glance before the Force-Commander turned his attention back to his screens.

"Transit terminates in... five, four, three... Controls active..."

The ship rumbled slightly. Loose panels in the command centre rattled, and screens flickered briefly before coming back to life while others came out of sleep mode. The hum of the engines grew again, pulsing through the ship.

"Transit terminated, no reported issues," the pilot reported, after a few tense seconds.

Raffa jumped out of his seat and headed towards the main screen.

"Show me what we've got out there, and get me an update from *Claw* and *Stinger*."

"Yes, Sir!" the co-pilot acknowledged.

The main screen flickered immediately, revealing a tactical view of the system. Raffa's eyes narrowed as he scanned it.

"Nothing at the T-Point at least," he murmured, turning away.

"Let's hope our luck holds up till we get home," Winters replied.

"Both *Claw* and *Stinger* report no issues. Transit of Investigation Flotilla was a complete success," the co-pilot said.

"Alright, have them maintain position relative to us and put us on course to Grinda, I want a smooth-"

An alarm rang out as new scanner information reached the ship.

"Report!" Raffa commanded, his attention returning to the screen.

"Known pirate vessels discovered!"

"Where?"

"Five of them, orbiting or docked to Freedom One Station."

"Any hostile behaviour?"

Elise coughed. "Hostile or not, it's not in our best interests to let pirates get a hold of that station, or influence its people." Her eyes narrowed. "Besides, these could be the people we're looking for. The ones who have been causing all the trouble."

Raffa glanced at Winters, who shrugged.

"She's got a point, boss. This could be what we're on this mission for."

"Right. So get me information on those vessels. I want everything: weapon points, armour thickness, cargo, crew..."

To his surprise, it was Elise who replied.

"Oh... don't you worry," she said, cracking her knuckles and connecting her pad to the console. "Pirates ain't nothing!"

Raffa smiled. "Specialist Rivera, I do believe your Paradise is showing."

She grinned. "Can't help myself sometimes."

The co-pilot spoke up again. "Size and mass scanners suggest one Class Three micro-frigate, Two Class Two fast-attack craft, and two Class One attack shuttles."

Raffa punched his open palm. "Pretty even odds. Alright, let's get this done. How far out from Freedom One are we?"

"Point two-five megasekunds, Sir. That's top speed if we wish to stay with our escorts."

"And if they come to meet us?"

"They'd be better off running..." Winters rumbled.

"Engagement could happen in point one-two, if they move to intercept us as soon as we're detected."

"Orient *Mambaka* to Freedom One, bring *Claw* and *Stinger* up to seventy-five percent burn, and have *Mambaka* keep that speed."

"Seventy-five?" Winters frowned. "Why not just charge?"

"I want them to think we're slower than we actually are. And I want to see how they react… and if Freedom One have anything to say about all this."

"Eh. We ain't here for them."

"Maybe not," Elise replied. "But I'd rather have the refugees in charge over some pirates. They are our neighbours after all."

"Yeah, I know," Winters replied, flatly. "My point was, we ain't here for Freedom One; we're here to figure out what's going on around Windan. Helping them would just be a nice bonus." He frowned. "Or would it? No doubt they'd still be assholes…"

"Enough," Raffa said. "We've got a limited amount of time, and I refuse to spend it arguing. Winters, you're with me, we're gonna work out a formation. Specialist Rivera, keep working at that info on the 'rats."

"You got it, Comcap."

"Very well. Winters, with me."

The pair of soldiers huddled over a tactical console, where Elise could hear them quietly but animatedly discussing formations, fields of fire, and various contingencies for if or when something went wrong. To her admittedly untrained ear, it sounded like they thought of everything, which gave her comfort, even if it still didn't bring calm to her racing, tumbling mind. The jumble of thoughts and feelings, mostly accompanied by either excitement or fear, made her fingers clumsy and her focus unclear. At least, that was how it seemed to her. It came as a surprise, then, when Raffa suddenly appeared at her shoulder and she realised not only that the soldiers' work was done, but that she had also managed to lose herself in her work after all.

"You're handling this pretty well for someone who's never been in a ship fight before," he said.

"Ah... you might not have said that a few kilosekunds ago, and I don't think combat was in my contract, but if I don't do my job we'll be in worse shape. And besides, if we don't do something about this now, it might be it haunts us down the line."

"You're not afraid?" He sounded mildly surprised.

She glanced up at him and smiled. "Of course I am, but..." She shook her head. "No matter how this pans out, we're doing the right thing."

He gave a single nod. "We are. Still though... thank you for not making this difficult."

"Don't mention it. I guess it helps that, right now, I see Paradise in Freedom One. We obviously can't know the truth of the situation, but some group trying to impose their will on others is what it looks like. So yes, I'm afraid, Comcap Raffa, but I'm nowhere near as afraid as I am angry."

"If they stick around to fight, we'll punish 'em. Don't worry."

"They still haven't moved?"

Raffa shook his head. "If they've got the station under their control, they're backed up by additional defences. It's their best strategy."

"Have we tried talking to them?"

"Wouldn't do much good." He sighed. "We know they're pirates. We know they're pirate vessels. Unless they're surrendering, we are obligated to destroy or disable any that could pose a threat to Kau D'varza. These idiots have already shown they're willing to interfere with a station, so unless they message us to offer their surrender, we're not talking to them." He pointed to Elise's screen. "Besides, if they're marked up as pirates it means they've been to Windan, or we've had interactions with them before."

The console beeped and the screen lit up with a myriad of details, drawing her attention. "Ha! Got you!" Her smile only grew wider as she scanned down the lists. "Your Command Crew were right. One Class Three micro-frigate confirmed. System type suggests it was built somewhere in Kaiser. Looks like it's armed with two fixed rail guns and four swivel-mounted... mass-accs?"

"Mass accelerators. Ha!" Winters nearly exploded, his gaze locked on the representation on the main screen as it updated with Elise's data. "You really should run. Just run."

"It'd be better for us if they didn't, actually." Elise motioned to her screen. "If we take them down here, disable them as best we can... Even if they're not responsible for the freighter, you can bet they've been travelling this region for a while."

Raffa nodded, understanding. "Which means they might have info on whoever *is* causing problems."

Elise's attention returned to her screen as more data came through. "Scans suggests they're running a shield, but the armour appears flimsy."

"Makes sense," Winters said. "The smaller vessels create a screen for the larger one. They're not expecting the C-Three to take hits, not any decent ones anyway."

"What are their point defences like? Anything we should be concerned about?"

Elise shook her head. "Looks like heavy reliance on the shield. I'm looking through their system lists now, can't see anything, not even shut down."

"Can we interfere?" Winters asked, a hopeful smile on his face.

Elise shook her head. "Sorry, *Mambaka* doesn't have the sort of equipment I'd need. Perhaps next time you put a ship together, you should build an Interdictor."

"Interdictor? What in the Void is that?"

Raffa grinned. "Ar-Ka'en for Scramblers."

"Oh!" Winters nodded. "Well, *Kobra*'s a scrambler..."

"Not in the same sense as the Ar-Ka'en term" Raffa replied. "*Kobra*'s a stealth cruiser. A true interdictor... or Scrambler... is built to break through a ship's e-security and give remote control of engines, helm, weapons and defensive systems, and, er, other things too. *Kobra* just blinds scanners and targeting systems. It wouldn't let us switch stuff off."

"Hm. These 'Interdictors' sound useful," Winters murmured.

Raffa nodded. "Very. And very expensive, too, which means such a vessel is a bit outside our capability at the moment. Alright, what do we know about the other ships?"

"Hmm... Two Missile F.A.C.s. Design suggests they were built in... Kyrex, somewhere." She shook her head. "Damn, these assholes get around..."

"Missile F.A.C.s, eh? Alright... we might need to change up our formation plans, Takk."

"Not likely," Winters replied. "Those things will have such limited ammo they're almost not a threat, and our point-defence can handle any missiles they throw our way."

"You willing to risk *Mambaka* on that assumption?" Raffa replied.

"Wouldn't be much of a risk. Look, Missile F.A.C.s are fundamentally flawed in their design. Half the ship is taken up for launch equipment and munitions, the other half is used for control and comfort. It's poor design. Our F.A.C.s are much better equipped. Four swivel-mounted energy-based weapons? Are you kidding me? As long as the power generators hold up, we can fire indefinitely."

"Yeah, as long as we get close enough." Raffa looked back to Elise. "What about defences? What sort of armour are they running?"

Her eyes narrowed. "Seems thin. Here, take a look.".

She sent the data to the main screen.

"Damn. That *is* thin. Thinner than I'd expect," Raffa said.

Winters nodded. "Makes sense, though. Not enough space for decent armour when you gotta fit in all that extra shit."

"And..." Elise continued, "it Looks like M-F.A.C two's launch tubes are offline, undergoing repairs."

Raffa smiled. "Excellent. Let's hope they don't get them back online before we knock on the door."

"Cap, we've got movement," Winters said, tapping at the screen on his seat. Seconds later, the co-pilot at the front of the command centre confirmed what they were seeing.

"The Class Three, now designated M-Frig One, has undocked from Freedom One and is moving to meet up with orbiting ships."

"Speed?"

"Slow, Sir. Very slow."

"Slow?" Winters said, surprised.

"Yes, Sir. It appears they don't intend to leave the safety envelope of the station."

Raffa clenched his fist. "Which means they've left people on-board the station to man the guns... damnit." He took a deep breath and released it, slowly. "Alright, I wanna know when they get into position, and what formation they're taking. If we can blast straight through to that m-frig and force the rest to scatter, we'll be in good shape."

Winters growled. "I'll come up with something that means none of them get away. I don't like people with vendettas."

Raffa turned back to Elise. "What about those attack shuttles?"

"The Ident data is screwy, can't get a read on who or where they were built, but their profiles suggest Yor', or Kaiser again."

"What about weapons?"

"Uh... *Mambaka* has designated them as... plinkers? What are they?"

Winters laughed. "In-atmo weaponry... like a vehicle mounted gun."

"Can they use them in space?"

Raffa nodded. "Sure can, won't do much but scratch the paint, but they can use them."

"A decent weapon specialist can use 'em to clean up minefields," Winters added. "Slow work, but it can be done."

"Slow, *painful* work," Raffa corrected. "Alright, if they're atmo craft, then we can reduce their threat level."

"We have to be wary about ramming though, boss. You know what some of these 'rats are like."

"Incoming message!" the co-pilot said.

"Run it," Raffa ordered, turning back to the main screen, where the image of a severe-looking woman appeared.

"Forces of Kau D'varza, your intrusion into our system has been noted."

Elise glared at the screen, her jaw clenched.

'Our system'. Oh, for fuck's sake...

"My name is Tylir Enista, acting controller of Freedom One. I have been asked to inform you that should you engage with the forces here, the station will be destroyed."

"Whaaat?" Winters recoiled. "Those fuckers!"

"Furthermore, outsider vessels will no longer be allowed to journey across this system without our prior consent. We recommend, for everyone's sake, that you turn around and head back to Windan, then continue your voyage via another system. Enista out."

Elise frowned. "They want us to go back to Windan?"

"You noticed that, eh? I thought it was pretty obvious, myself," Winters replied.

Raffa shook his head, also frowning. "No, she's right. If they simply want us gone, they'd have said so. By ordering us back... They clearly want us to go to Grinda straight from Windan."

"What? Why?"

"Why do you think?"

Elise nodded. "Whoever those pirates are, they must have something to do with what's been going on." She eyed Winters, whose mouth had fallen open slightly. "I thought that was pretty obvious, myself."

"We can't let them get away. Not now," Raffa said.

"So it's really not the Reclaimers after all..." Winters mumbled.

"I never said that," Elise said, frowning. "I just said that right now, it seems like these assholes have got something to do with it."

"Pirates and Reclaimers working together?" Winters shook his head. "No way... not in a million cycles."

"You like to read a lot into what I say, Force-Commander Winters."

"Alright, you two," Raffa said, and sighed. "What are our options?"

"I believe..." Elise began, "they've still got friends on the station, people loyal to their cause."

"Clearly, since they'd need someone to operate those guns," Winters said.

"Right. But if they blew up the station like they said,

they'd lose those people. You've got to ask, are those people worth not blowing it up?"

"I can't believe the people of Freedom One aren't fighting back."

"They might be," Raffa replied. "We're only seeing what Enista is telling us. For all we know, she's holed up in a storage locker somewhere while F-Oners are breaking down the door."

"If that were the case, they'd be firing whatever station defences they did control on the 'rat ships." Winters shook his head. "No, the pirates are in control, which means they've got numbers on the station, significant enough numbers to keep it."

"Which should still mean they'd be less likely to blow it up, but I'm not keen on calling their bluff."

"Me, either," Elise agreed. "Even so, I hate the idea of leaving the F-Oners to whatever the 'rats have in store. So what else can we do?"

"Do?" Winters said with a growl. "Nothing! We've thrown a wrench in whatever plans they had by coming this way and we've learned their ships are no threat to Kau D'varza. We're not here for Freedom One."

"Force-Commander Winters," Raffa said, "I refuse to sacrifice the lives of so many just because they are not the mission priority."

"Well, you'd better come up with something then, Cap, because they know we've seen that message. It's only a matter of time before they see we're not altering course, let alone preparing to Transit back home."

Raffa rubbed his chin, then called over to the Command staff. "Notify *Claw* and *Stinger*. All ships are to prepare for full stop on my order."

"Oh, you're kidding!" Winters exclaimed. "I respectfully advise the Commander-Captain that a stalemate situation is not in anyone's best interests."

"Your concerns have been noted, Force-Commander."

"But ignored. Look, I know I've said it before, but I'll say it again: we're not here for them! And for all we know, that's a pirate station now."

"And if it is, there are still innocent people aboard. I refuse to continue down this path until I can be sure they are safe."

"Oh... fuck 'em! When has Freedom One ever done anything for Kau D'varza that wasn't entirely lopsided in their favour? Those pirates would be doing us a favour shooting that damn shithole into the Void."

Elise's eyes widened. "He's right."

"I am?"

"Not about the blowing up the station, that was a bit extreme… and I don't feel comfortable hearing that sort of thing. But if Kau D'varza has no love for Freedom One, why not tell them that?"

"That sounds a lot like calling their bluff," Raffa said.

Elise shrugged. "If what Force-Commander Winters says is true and they see we don't give a shit about the station, if they've got people on board they'll see they stand to lose more."

Raffa grinned. "Alright." He raised his voice and called to the Command deck once more. "Disregard previous order. Advise that all ships are to maintain course and speed." He returned to his seat and brought the screen around. "Prepare a message, to be sent to Freedom One and all vessels local to it."

"Setting channels… You're good, Sir; just hit the button."

Raffa cleared his throat, and spoke clearly. "This is Commander-Captain Joseph Raffa of the Kau D'varza Investigation flotilla. Your protest and advice have been noted. However, as Kau D'varza has no agreements in place with the current ruling body of Freedom One, and as we have our own interests in the pirate element currently active in this system, we must decline your instruction, citing our own interests as paramount." His mouth curled upwards slightly, though the smile got nowhere near his eyes, which became hard and cold. "Furthermore, the history between Kau D'varza and Freedom One suggests that, should Freedom One be destroyed, Kau D'varza stands to benefit. Because of this, you should be aware that we will not try to defend Freedom One in any way while pursuing our intended targets. Simply put, we don't care who is in charge there or for what purpose. However, any hostile actions on the part of Freedom One will be met with appropriate force. I *wholeheartedly* apologise for any inconvenience this may cause. Comcap Raffa, Outsign."

He pressed the button and sat back. It would take some time for the message to reach its intended target, but they would already have seen Raffa's flotilla maintaining its course.

"You're a cold motherfucker, boss," Winters muttered.

Raffa grinned. "Thanks. Do we know their formation yet?"

Winters consulted his screen. "It's as we thought earlier. They've formed up a square with their smallest vessels: M-F.A.C.s on the bottom, A-Shuts on top. The M-Frig remains behind it. They're moving relative to the station, keeping front-on to our approach." He glanced up and smiled. "It's hardly any defence at all. This is too easy!"

"Oh for... why? Why would you say that?"

"Because, when I say shit like that, you wonder why it's too easy, then see something I've missed, and save the day." He lazily saluted with a finger then pointed to Raffa. "Just like the take-over."

Raffa stood up, walking towards the main screen. "Just like the take-over," he replied, absentmindedly.

"What? You seen something?"

"No. But if we were gonna hit that formation, we'd aim for the top or bottom."

"Bottom would be my choice. Come in low, under the M-F.A.C.s, blow 'em away, then turn all guns on the C-Three. The A-shuts are no threat at all. *Claw* and *Stinger* can handle them. Or maybe we can take a few prisoners."

"Yeah, if they let us, which I doubt. They'll either break and run if they still can or they'll go down swinging." He shook his head. "That's all fine either way, but what do we do about the station?"

"Rely on speed, counter-measures and armour?"

Raffa shook his head. "It's not enough. F-One uses swivel-mounted mass-accs. We either need to draw the 'rats away, or ensure F-One doesn't - or can't - fire on us."

"Then you better hope they listen to your warning, because drawing them off will be a problem. My suggestion? Hit that Pirate formation as hard and fast as possible, split, and if the station has fired on us during the first run, turn our attention to them."

Raffa rubbed his chin. "It's risky... we're likely to take some hits."

"If the battle plan included speeding up just prior to contact, then F-One's targeting systems would have trouble hitting us. It's our best option, but if they've got any sense, they won't fire on us and we won't have to fire on them. F-One gains a lot from Kau D'varza, it's in their best interests to play as nice as they can."

Elise sat forward, eyeing them both. "Aren't you forgetting something? That station is most likely in pirate hands. You've said as much yourselves. So why are you talking like it's still independent?"

"Because it might still be," Raffa said. "And because, even if it isn't, it might suit the 'rats to pretend it is. A station is a bigger asset than a few ships, even if we ended up destroying the shuttles and M-F.A.C.s. They know the M-Frig would get a bit shot-up, but if they signalled their surrender, or ran..."

"We'd have to treat Freedom One as though it was liberated," she said, sitting back.

"Well, perhaps not quite that, but... yes." Raffa glanced to the icons on the screen ahead of him and took a deep breath. "So let's see... The run would be this: We come in low, while our F.A.C.s are a few seks behind; we engage the M-F.A.C.s at the bottom of the formation, wiping them out, then our F.A.C.s come in high, dealing with the A-Shuts. *Mambaka* continues her run, using disabling fire on the targeting scanners and weapons of the C-Three. The F.A.C.s target propulsion on their run, before *Claw* turns starward and *Stinger* goes edgeward. We go up, come back down in an arc, then all converge on the C-Three to finish the job of pacifying her before boarding. If F-One fires on us during our primary run, the alternative plan is to deal with the station's weapons systems, eliminating all threat, before re-engaging the C-Three."

"Sounds like a plan," Winters said. "So what are they gonna do to fuck it up, and how are we going to disguise what we're up to?"

"Well... what if..." He turned back to Winters. "Set up the formation so it looks like we're going straight for the C-Three, then just as we close to engage, have our F.A.C.s drop back. We dip, hit the M-F.A.C.s as *Claw* and *Stinger* accelerate again and go over the top to wipe out the A-Shuts."

Winters frowned. "Feign it? That's uh... well, yeah, it's possible, assuming they don't change their formation... Could lead to some crashes."

He glanced forward to the command team. "Alright, new orders. Formation change. Flat triangle, *Mambaka* leading. I want *Claw* closest to the star, and *Stinger* on the opposite point. Prepare for transmission of a battle-plan."

The command centre became a flurry of activity once more as they sent messages between the vessels and worked up vectors and course changes.

Winters leant into Raffa as he sat back down. "What if we destroy the C-Three?"

"Specialist Rivera, is it possible to download the information they have aboard?"

"Not from this range. They'd detect the intrusion and shut it down, data transfer would take too long as well. We need to be a little closer."

"How much closer?"

She shrugged. "The closer the better."

"Nice." He turned to the command crew. "How long until we're in range?"

"Eight kiloseks' til engagement at current velocity," the pilot advised.

"Still a little ways out... alright, Elise, let us know when you feel it's safe to start transfer."

"Will do."

"Comms reports that Freedom One and surrounding vessels have received your message, Sir," the co-pilot said.

"Good. Let's see how they respond."

"I can keep an eye on that," Winters replied. "You need to get to work on war-gaming that battle plan, see if there's anything we overlooked earlier on."

"How generous of you..." Raffa replied, his forehead creased with sudden worry.

CHAPTER NINETEEN- THE STORM

"How are you feeling, Specialist Stone?"

Kaska looked up from her console to see Nevos standing behind her.

"Sir?"

"You've had a busy few cycles, I wanted to ensure your wellbeing."

She blinked. "I... I'm fine, Sir. Thank you for asking."

He leaned over and peered at the screen. "Still working on the engineering bay situation, I see."

Kaska nodded. "Yes, Sir. We're currently chasing down all the funds Jimba misappropriated, and indexing the additional materials we discovered."

"Ah yes. That was quite the surprise."

"I'm trying to figure out how he got it past us. We should have seen it. *I* should have seen it."

"It is... of concern, Specialist Stone, but please do not blame yourself. People can be cunning, and they can be desperate. It is a shame it got to this point, but now we are aware such things are possible, and that means we can better detect them in the future."

"Of course, Sir. I will ensure it doesn't happen again."

"And that's the important thing, isn't it?"

"Sir?"

"The armour was dented, Specialist Stone, but now you are taking great strides to polish it out and reinforce it."

Ship metaphors. Right...

"Specialist Stone?"

"Uh... yes, Sir. Thank you, Sir."

He grinned. "Keep at it, I think you need the distraction."

She nodded, and turned back to her console.

What was- right. Inventory.

Her eyes narrowed.

Is this right? Scrapping the Yor' ship gets us... By the Void... are those Kobra *components?*

She straightened up, summoned Ikarus' details and hit connect.

"Specialist Stone?"

"Is this information correct?"

"You may need to be a bit more specific, honoured Specialist."

"About the Yor' transport. Was he seriously trying to build his own stealth cruiser out of that thing?"

"Ah. The evidence certainly suggests as much."

"Right. Where is Jimba now?"

"I believe it is Commissioner Zeled's turn to ah... question... the prisoner this cycle."

"Thank you, Ikarus. If you find anything else like this, let me know."

"Of course. The engineers tell me they are making slow progress on *Kobra*. Perhaps these additional components will aid them in their goal."

"I hope so."

"If there is nothing else, Specialist Stone?"

"Nope, that's it. Thanks again, Ikarus."

His image vanished and she tapped the screen again. Seconds later, Commissioner Zeled's broad, unnerving smile appeared.

"Specialist Stone, to what do I owe the pleasure?"

He's in a good mood.

"I have an update from the engineering bay, Sir."

"Oh?"

"An inventory of the equipment from the Yor' transport Jimba was using to store his skimmed goods indicates that he was also taking components from Kau D'varza ships. Most notably, *Kobra*. We believe he was trying to create a stealth cruiser of his own, though for what purpose we cannot be sure. One thing that is certain, however, is that his actions are responsible for the poor state of *Kobra* in recent times."

"Oh, indeed?"

"I would appreciate it if you approached Jimba with this new information, and sought to ascertain exactly what it was he had planned."

"Oh, don't you worry about that," Zeled said, his

smile widening and becoming even more disconcerting. "It is actually quite difficult to shut him up. And he has quite a distaste for you, I might add."

"The feeling is mutual."

"No doubt," he said, and nodded. "Alright, Specialist Stone, *thank you* for this additional information."

The commissioner's image faded and Kaska sat back with a frown.

I wonder what else that asshole Jimba has caused? Ughhh Kobra's just the beginning, I bet...

* * *

"Comcap Raffa!" Enista's angry, terrified face filled the main screen. "You are endangering the lives of hundreds by your continued intrusion! Regardless of your personal feelings towards Freedom One, you cannot allow a massacre to occur, yet pursuing your intended course of action will result in such! I have to insist that you turn around. Now. Enista, out."

"Ooh, she has to *insist*," Winters muttered, glancing at Raffa and smirking. "What do you say to that, Cap?"

Raffa shook his head. "Nothing. Whatever happens is on them. I've got nothing else to say to these idiots."

Elise sucked the air through her teeth behind them. "You mind if I send something? I've got some... extra packages to be delivered. They're already freaked out by our last response, so hopefully they won't be looking too closely at things like file sizes and bandwidth, just the messages."

"Be my guest. Just... take care."

"It's all bollocks anyway," Winters said, as Elise got to work. "We're six kilosekunds from engagement. If they were gonna blow the station, they'd have done it long before now. We just gotta hope their guns stay quiet."

Raffa rubbed his chin. "Hmm. I hope you're right, Takk. A lot depends on who's really in charge over there. Take this Enista, for example. Is she a pirate, or someone they're using as a mouthpiece?"

"Does it matter? It comes out to the same either way, doesn't it?"

"Not necessarily. Enista's scared, and she has every reason to be. But what is she scared of? Us, or being blown to smithereens along with the station?"

"Why not both?"

Raffa shook his head in frustration. "Come on, Takk: think! Does she seem suicidal to you? Because she doesn't to me. So, if she's a pirate, we've called her bluff and she knows it. Her fleet is outgunned and she daren't use the station's defences if she wants to hang on to their prize. On the other hand, if she's a hostage, there is still a chance that the station can be destroyed remotely by whoever the pirate leader really is. It's even possible the 'rats have left a core of fanatics on board to maintain control until the thing goes ka-blooey."

"I say she's not a 'rat," Elise said. "Remember what she said in the first communication? 'I have been asked to inform you...'. She even identified herself as acting controller. That says she's a hostage, to me."

Raffa nodded. "I agree."

"I still don't see what difference it makes," Winters said. "If the 'rats destroy Freedom One, so what? We've still got those ships to face, and if they do have the station fire on us we'll blow it out of the stars in any case."

Raffa ignored his Force-Commander and turned to Elise. "Specialist Rivera, is there any way - any at all - that you can scan the station for... I don't know, *strange* signatures - unusual transmissions, carrier signals between the station and those ships, things like that - and block them?"

She blew air through her cheeks. "I can try. But if there are any, I should have detected them before... and even if I find them, I don't like the chances of being able to pin down the frequency, or frequencies, well enough to block them. Like I said before, *Mambaka*'s equipment isn't sophisticated enough for systems hacking and remote takedowns."

"Alright," he said, and smiled. "All I ask is that you do your best."

She nodded, and he and Winters stood listening as Elise cleared her throat and began her message to the station.

"This is Investigation Specialist Elise Rivera speaking." She paused, drawing out the message while her fingers flew over her screen. "I find myself confused. Freedom One opened its doors to pirates, has aided and assisted them, and our reports show that no damage has been sustained by their vessels. Therefore, we must assume that Freedom One is now under pirate control, or at the very least has allied with them. Be advised that Freedom One will be treated as a direct threat unless and until we have clear proof to the contrary. Such proof - for example your defences remaining silent as we begin the inevitable engagement with the pirate ships in close proximity to you - would significantly improve your case. It should also be noted that Comcap Raffa has already made it very clear that, should Freedom One fire on any vessel in this flotilla, Freedom One will come under retaliatory action, and that we shall engage in such action without hesitation. I would also like to remind you that due to the... fluid... nature of Freedom One's governing structure, no overarching agreements exist between our two groups, and we therefore have no responsibility to ensure your protection. If Freedom One is no longer autonomous and is forced to act against its occupants' will, we can only offer our sincerest regrets. But in the event that Freedom One is still under autonomous control, and is acting voluntarily and continues to act in concert with the pirates... then just such an outcome is something you should have considered before willingly opening your doors to such elements. Investigation Specialist Elise Rivera, outsign."

"Damn, you dragged that out," Winters said as soon as she'd hit the button.

"I had to. Too short and they'd have noticed the extra stuff. The longer the message, the larger the file size and it doesn't raise suspicions as easy."

"I think I'll stick to ships," Raffa replied. "Any sign of weird energy signatures, signals from the ships, and so on?"

She flashed a glance back at the screen and shook her head. "Either they're not there, or *Mambaka* can't detect them."

His face screwed up in disappointment.

Mambaka *can't. Not I can't... Nice distinction there, Specialist.*

"Then we'll have to hope it was only a bluff. Good job with the message, though; let us know what you get."

He barely had time to register her nod before the co-pilot's voice rang out from the command deck.

"Enemy vessels, formation changing!"

"Acknowledged!" Raffa said, as both he and Winters headed for their seats, glancing at the main screen as they went.

Raffa felt a familiar knot of tension form in his stomach as he strapped himself in and reached for his seat arm.

"Raffa speaking. Elevate battle status from Standby to Ready. Bring weapon stations fully online. You will be receiving battle plans with designated targets. To the command crew of all vessels: if your vessel operators are tired, have the alternate shift take over. All pilots and other essential ship's personnel are to be at peak performance. Freedom One could present a threat during our primary engagement, requiring extreme attention." He paused, licked his lips. "This is what we came out here for, people. We may be far from home, but make no mistake, this is *For Kau D'varza*." He let the words hang for a few seconds. "Comcap Raffa, outsign."

"Enemy vessels have settled into a reverse formation. Class-Three sitting behind a triangle of smaller vessels. Missile F.A.C.s making up the point, attack shuttles to either side of the C-Three," Winters said, already hard at work drawing up a counter-strategy.

Raffa called up the plan on his screen and frowned. "What are you up to, Takk? This plan's no different to what we already had."

"No, boss, because it doesn't have to be! Their new formation actually works out better for us!" Winters exclaimed. "Look, they've set up thinking we're going to stick to this formation for the engagement. They've not figured on us making a last-minute shift to take us above and below them. We can hit more of their ships! Granted, we'll need to widen the gap between *Stinger* and *Claw*, but now they can hit the M-F.A.C.s and the attack shuttles while *Mambaka* hits the M-F.A.C.s and the C-Three!"

"That reduces our fire-power against the C-Three."

"Yes, but it also improves our chances of wiping out the M-F.A.C.s and A-Shuts on the first pass, making subsequent runs against the C-Three much easier, and if we can still deal it enough damage on the first run there's a good chance the thing'll be defenceless by then. This is great! They've played right into our plan!"

"And if you want more good news," Elise added with a grin, "I'm in the station's systems. Compiling data now. I've also found and shutdown a core override. Must have been added quickly and coded by an idiot, but it was there and now... it's gone."

Raffa and Winters exchanged a glance and beamed.

"Great work, Specialist Rivera," Raffa said. "I'll be sure to include *that* in my mission report."

"Incoming message," the co-pilot called. "From... 'Yosif Mendi?'"

"Acknowledged," Raffa said. He glanced at Winters and rolled his eyes. "I know that name."

"You and me both, Cap." Winters said. "Gaitlin Raiders. Must have moved up here to get away from Beyema."

"This is good!" Elise said, causing the soldiers to look at her. "When we reply, I'll get into his systems too!"

Raffa smiled. "Play it."

Mendi's image appeared on the screen. Raffa didn't know what he should have expected, but Mendi managed to live down to it, and then some. The prematurely aged visage was pale from a lifetime spent out of the sun, and seemed to be made up entirely of angles due to the man's overall leanness combined with high cheekbones and strong jaw. Several scars - some no more than nicks, others pointing to more serious injuries, most of them completely healed - gave him a typical pirate look, and the cold, grey-brown eyes were almost the same shade as his dingy teeth.

"Listen to me, you sly fuck," a deep, harsh voice began.

Winters grinned. "How delightful."

The voice continued. "I don't give a shit what your 'mission' is. This station? It's ours now. We own this system, so turn around and find another way or I swear on the G-Star, we'll turn you into dust!" Fleckles of spit distorted his image. "Comply, or die!"

The screen faded to black, then reverted to a tactical view of the area around the station. Silence reigned for a few seconds.

"What a melodramatic asshole," Winters said as he straightened up.

Raffa frowned. "I wonder why he sent a recorded message when we can communicate in almost real-time now?"

"Who cares? It works for us," Elise replied. "I've got some more treats, more data to extract from them before we engage."

"You wanna send this message too?"

Before she could reply, Winters said, "I will. This guy's a real asshole, and I can't let you have all the fun."

"Okay," Raffa said. "Get the message made up, then transfer it to Specialist Rivera so she can work her magic."

As Winters turned away to calmly speak some obscenities of his own into his armrest, Raffa looked back to the main screen.

"Four point five K-seks to go... If we change formation when there's only point one to go, it'll give us enough time to execute our plan without giving them time to react to it."

He tapped at his own screen and updated the battle plan. *Mambaka*'s computer did most of the fine work and, after a few seconds, he turned his screen to Winters, who cast an eye over the simulation as he completed his message and forwarded it to Elise.

"Looks good to me, Cap," he said.

"Alright..." He studied his work one final time before

hitting 'Send to Flotilla Vessels'.

* * *

As the time to engagement counter ticked away, the tension in the command centre grew. Elise kept scoring small victories in her data capture, while Winters sent antagonistic replies to both the station and Yosif Mendi as new messages came in. Raffa, meanwhile, kept his attention confined to the updates coming in from *Claw* and *Stinger* as well as *Mambaka*'s weapons batteries as they reported their combat readiness. Up on the command deck, one of the pilots and a comm-controller had been replaced, while a handful of support staff had arrived and were busily, but calmly, settling in.

"Point three kiloseks to engagement," a new voice said from the command deck.

"Raffa speaking. Battle stations. Strap yourselves in, everybody. Command centre, lockdown."

"Yes, Sir!" another new voice replied and the locks cycled shut as the lights dimmed, then turned red. A few seconds later, all weapon-stations were reporting they were combat-ready, with the operators at Station Four leading the pack.

Elise swallowed, hard, and tried to focus on completing her work. There wasn't much data left to gather up, and she thought she had already captured all the important stuff, but she was nothing if not a perfectionist. And besides, what else was she going to do?

It wasn't too long before she found she ran out of data,

though, and she sent a note to Raffa's chair-screen to say she'd captured as much information as possible.

Something else I can stop worrying about…

"Looks like they're holding formation," Winters muttered.

"Good. Unlikely they'll change now, takes time to maneuver that many ships," Raffa replied.

Elise turned, looking at the main screen as the pair of soldiers selected targets and built a fire sequence.

"You ever wonder what they're thinking right now?" she asked.

"All the time, every engagement," Raffa replied. "And if the truth's known, it's probably the same as us: we both think we can win this fight, but we both still hope we'll get to walk away. We're both confident: they've got the numbers, we've got the weapons. It's a question of which side has read the situation best and got their tactics right. That station is going to be a deciding factor, though. Will they fire or won't they? If they do, that tips the odds."

"Well, we'll know soon enough," Winters said, his face hard as he nodded toward the counter. "Point two to go."

Elise turned back to face her console. There was nothing left for her to do, but she couldn't bear to look at the unusually tense, taut faces of the men she had come to know. She might never completely understand their mindset or even come to see their worldview, but in all the time she'd known them they still seemed... *human*. Now, faced with a combat situation, the kind of stuff they had trained and might even say they lived for, they seemed different, not in the sense of being odd, but more in that of being cold, efficient, more like machines - or automatons - than men. She wasn't sure she liked it.

"One hundred sekunds!"

Elise felt *Mambaka* shudder as the pilots altered their approach vector and her eyes were drawn to the main screen again as *Claw* and *Stinger* split further apart and tilted upwards.

"Flotilla increasing speed. F.A.Cs going to full burn."

At first, the F.A.Cs seemed to race away from *Mambaka*, but then, as the low hum in the ship grew, it caught up and overtook them.

"Maintaining two sekund gap."

We're really doing this. Damn, didn't properly hit me 'til just now. Everyone else has been waiting for this for ages... hope we survive long enough to learn my lesson.

She wiped away the sweat and focused.

Out of my hands now. I've done my part.

"... a few sekunds for them to realise what we're doing.

And if they change up, it'll take time to come up with that plan and put it into action. They'll be out of position to fire on us... doesn't look like they're changing though..."

Winters coughed, causing Raffa to glance at him.

"You're thinking out loud, boss."

"Was I?"

Winters nodded.

"Sorry. Just vocalizing my thoughts."

"Well, as long as you know that, to some, it might sound like doubt. Either way, we can't know if they've second guessed our plan. Until we peel apart, it's out of our control."

"Still good to be prepared. Now pay attention."

"Fifty sekunds!"

Claw and *Stinger* were aiming their run above and between the smaller vessels, through the gaps between the inner M-F.A.C.s and the outer A-Shuts. *Mambaka* would hit them just before the F.A.C.s, then carry on to bombard the C-Three. At the speed they were going, it would all be over in a second. It would be down to the weapons specialists and their targeting computers to ensure a job well done.

"Twenty sekunds! Missile Batteries One, Two, Five and Six all prepped. Launching in five... four... three...

two... one..."

"Main screen, visual!" Raffa ordered.

Elise felt *Mambaka* shudder again as the ship sent four of its smart-missiles spiralling away. She watched as they corrected course and streaked at frankly alarming speed towards their targets: one each for the M-F.A.C.s, the other two aimed for the C-Three. There was no time for the pirate ships to break and run, and it wouldn't have done them much good in any case: the missiles could travel at speeds far in excess of anything a human-crewed ship could manage, at least without killing everyone on board.

The missiles reached their targets and detonated in blindingly bright, silent blooms, but before Elise could assess the damage *Mambaka* tore through the clouds of dust that had appeared, all weapons locked onto the C-Three. Behind them, the F.A.C.s had torn through their own targets, hitting the A-Shuts hard, just as Raffa had predicted, and too far out of range for the C-Three to retaliate.

"Five sekunds to contact with the C-Three!" A voice said, then, after a pause. "Station weapons coming online!"

"Damnit! *Brace!*"

The opening salvo from the station tore into *Mambaka*, and Elise gripped the edge of her seat as the warship rocked, rattled, trembled, and shuddered under the weight of the bombardment as well as the recoil from pouring their own fire into the C-Three. It was over almost as soon as it had begun as the ship arced out of range, and she was only aware that she had squeezed her eyes shut when she opened them again.

How in the Void did we survive that?

Her thoughts were interrupted by Raffa leaping out of his seat.

"Engage Course Plan Two! Bring us about and retarget weapons on those station defences! Damage report!"

"Armour breach in Sector Three, eight casualties. Sensor Suite One is offline. Weapon Station Three is reporting three casualties from a reload fault. We are able to re-engage," a voice said, in the same moment as *Mambaka* fired it's underside thrusters and started on its upward arc away from the fight. The ship shuddered and metal groaned under the strain, while Elise ground her teeth together and closed her eyes once more, her knuckles turning white as she gripped the arms of her seat.

"Alert medical and have the casualties taken care of-" she heard Raffa say, and her eyes snapped open again.

I can barely think! How are these people still functioning?

"*Stinger* is reporting significant damage to her starboard weapons systems. Three casualties..." The voice lowered. "And one... One fatality."

Elise's face turned pale.

We lost someone?

She watched as Raffa took a few seconds to steady himself before bowing his head and murmuring, "Go peacefully, honoured fallen."

"Go peacefully," Winters echoed. "Thank you."

I should have been expecting this, or known it was going to happen. Raffa and Winters didn't pay it much mind, though... or is that their way of dealing with loss: mark it now, mourn later?

Raffa looked up, his face fixed in a look of fierce determination. "Right. Time to make that count. How long until we're in position to make our second run?"

"At current speeds, we'll enter our new attack vector in one hundred and eighty sekunds, Comcap," a voice from the command deck advised. "However... you may want to reassess the situation first, Sir."

Raffa frowned. "Reassess the... Engagement playback, main screen."

The screen lit up with pieced together sensor data and footage from the three ships, and Elise watched as *Mambaka*'s missile salvo turned the M-F.A.C.s to dust. One managed to get a missile of its own away just as it was destroyed, though the subsequent explosion sent it spiralling well off-course. At the same time, impacts registered against the C-Three and bloomed with debris clouds of their own. As *Mambaka* went on to engage the C-Three with its heavy cannons, the Kau D'varza F.A.C.s fired volleys of their own into the debris fields where the M-F.A.C.s had been - the computers neither knowing nor caring that their targets had already been destroyed - as well as at the A-Shuts, wiping them out. At that point, *Claw* peeled away towards the system edge without receiving a hit, while *Stinger* passed too close to the C-Three and sustained the damage that had cost a crew member their life.

"Stop, and rewind to where the F.A.C.s break off," Raffa said. The image on the screen jumped, and the A-Shuts reappeared. "Play, and focus on *Mambaka*'s engagement with the C-Three."

The screen jumped again, this time centring on the micro-frigate.

The missiles launched by *Mambaka* had clearly done the pirate ship some serious damage already, but not enough to prevent a return strike as they swung by. Three of *Mambaka*'s four heavy cannon fired, with all projectiles finding their marks. The C-Three, by contrast, had only managed to score two hits, both with kinetic rounds into *Mambaka*'s sensor suites. The image on the screen flickered and the data stream disappeared entirely, before Suite Two took over and restored the feed. Mere millionths of a second later, two unidentified projectiles from the station struck *Mambaka* towards the rear.

"Damn that station!" Raffa said, turning to Winters. "What's the status of the C-Three? We did them a tonne of damage, but it looks like they're still-"

"Raffa, look!" Elise said, pointing at the unfolding events on-screen. Freedom One's weapons, instead of tracking *Mambaka*'s arc away, had sent several shots that *Mambaka's* systems only identified as 'energy rounds' into the already-stricken C-Three.

"What in the Void...?"

Winters clapped his hands once and laughed. "They weren't firing on us after all! Either their systems are crap, or we just happened to get in the way!"

They watched as the C-Three lit up, then tumbled away.

"Fucking beautiful!" Winters exclaimed, turning to Elise with a broad, infectious grin.

She grinned back, despite the sensation of something rising from deep in her gut.

Oh, God. Don't let me puke. Please don't let me puke...

She breathed deeply, trying not to swallow as she focused on Raffa, watching in grim, queasy silence as he tapped at his screen.

"I don't believe it. All primary targets eliminated," he said, as though he couldn't quite believe it. "Have flotilla vessels converge on *Mambaka* and take formation flat triangle, *Mambaka* leading."

"Incoming communication," a command deck voice said."It's Freedom One."

"Hm. I wonder what they have to say for themselves. Play it."

A man appeared on his screen, looking as though he'd

David Noe

come through a battle of his own. His clothes were torn and his face sported a large bruise, while blood ran freely down one of his arms even as someone tried to clean him up.

"Comcap Raffa!" he said, smiling broadly and throwing his arms up in relief, knocking his friend away. "You are a sight for sore eyes, *my friend*."

"'My friend'? I don't know you," Raffa replied firmly. "Explain yourself."

"Ah! Of course, of course. Please, forgive me." He motioned to his wounds. "As you can see, it's been a busy few cycles." He straightened up. "My name's Harrison. Just Harrison, if you don't mind. I am... was... am... kind of in charge here. You probably already know we don't have much in the way of a formal structure. And that kind of brings me to why... or how... we're here. See, a while back Enista started leading a group of people, claiming that Freedom One needed a government. But things don't work like that around here and, to cut a long story short, we basically ignored her, let her get on with her mad schemes. Then those damn 'rats show up from Grinda, and just as we're preparing to shoot em down, Enista busts in and arrests us all, then goes on to let them dock 'for repairs'. Next thing we know, the damn station's crawling with 'rats. Some people loyal to me and mine busted us out. We took to fighting, but only managed to regain control just prior to your little dust-up out there. We had to do some pretty quick retargeting work, so you have my sincerest apologies if some of it was a lit-

378

tle off. And congratulations by the way. The way you took those M-F.A.C.s out... wow, man. Just, wow."

Raffa waved the sentiment aside. "You say these pirates came from Grinda? Do you have any information regarding that?"

"Anything we know, your tech people already grabbed."

Elise felt a swell of pride as Raffa and Winters glanced in her direction, and she grinned.

Yeah! You daaamn right!

"Given the circumstances, we don't mind, but in future, we'd... prefer... you didn't do that," Harrison said.

"Your wishes are noted," Raffa replied. "And your assistance in this matter is appreciated." His expression hardened. "However, I will not pretend that we are friends. Or allies. Enista was wrong in her actions but right in her sentiments: this situation could have been easily avoided if Freedom One had a proper ruling body in place. You need someone to enforce rules, maintain defence and order. In short, to govern. How many of these incidents - these *takeovers* - are you willing to struggle to turn back before there aren't enough of you left to fight, or there's no station left to fight for? By the Void, man, even at your strongest you almost lost the station completely! And what strength do you have left?"

Harrison swallowed and looked downcast. "I... we... lost many. Too many."

Raffa's voice softened. "And for that you have my deepest sympathies. But you know what must be done to prevent further tragedy. Don't let their sacrifices go to waste."

"The people here... they won't be happy, especially not now."

"If you're being honest, if you fought for what they wanted, and if you're trustworthy, then they will follow you. They will see the damage wrought by a lack of government. Moreover, if you have proper representation you may find some powerful friends and allies. After all, it is in Kau D'varza's best interests that this station, and by extension this system, remains out of pirate hands."

Harrison nodded, slowly. "I can see the sense in that." He looked directly into the screen. "Comcap Raffa, on behalf of Freedom One, thank you. If there is anything we can do to assist-"

"There is nothing, thank you. Since we've got all the information you have, and with the pirate threat having been eliminated, we will be continuing on our journey."

"Well, if it's anything to do with chasing down any more of those guys, I wish you the best of luck. Uhh...

Harrison, out sign?"

The connection cut and Raffa turned to face Elise. His mouth opened, but he was interrupted before he could speak.

"Another message coming in. Audio only."

Raffa turned to face the screen again, scowling. "Damnit. Who's this one from?"

"Mining Platform E X Two-B."

"Who?"

"I'm on it," Elise announced, her fingers already flying over her console in gratitude at finally having something useful to do. "Mining Platform E X Two-B. Primary purpose: ore, mineral and precious metals excavation in the asteroid belt. Population, estimated to be around one hundred and fifty based on last formal count, which was... " She gave a low whistle. "Let's just call it a long time ago."

Raffa frowned. "What do they want? Okay. Run it."

"Message for Commanding Officer of Kau D'varza vessels. Thank you for ridding this system of the pirate threat. We are about to send a shipment to Kau D'varza, and were wondering if you'd like to send any information back. This invitation is time sensitive, but we will do our best to delay. Platform E X Two-B, out."

"Send an acceptance back immediately, then get a

full report put together. I need it yestercycle, is that clear?"

"Already on it, Sir!" a voice said, and he turned to Elise with a smile.

"You too, Specialist. I want everything you downloaded compiled, copied and ready for analysis. The sooner Kas... Specialist Stone can get to work on this, the better it'll be for all of us."

"Right," she said, turning back to her console again.

Footsteps behind her signalled his approach and he took up a position next to her. She noticed he stood with his back to the bulkhead, though whether that was so he could keep an eye on the rest of the deck or whether it was down to good old soldierly paranoia, she couldn't tell.

"So, how was it?" he asked.

"How was what?"

He laughed, gently. "You know. Your first taste of real combat."

She turned away from her console. "Frankly... it damn near made me sick. But I'd appreciate it if you didn't tell anyone. Especially not Force-Commander Winters."

Raffa's eyebrows shot up. "Takk?" He leaned closer, lowering his voice to not much more than a whisper. "I'll let you into a little secret: the first time Takk and I went into combat together, he... er... well, he had a little accident, shall we say? The kind that left him needing clean trousers and new boots. As for his socks and underwear… I think he had to burn them."

She snorted laughter. "You're joking."

He grinned and shook his head, then became serious again. "That was a long time ago now, though. You understand?"

She nodded. "You don't want me saying anything that might… well, upset things."

"Right. And remember, I only told you because, compared to some… compared to most, actually… you handled it very well."

"Thanks. But you'll forgive me if I say it's not an experience I want to repeat very soon."

He smiled again and nodded, before moving away.

"All ships in Investigation Flotilla are in formation Flat Triangle, Sir, and stand ready to move out on your command," the co-pilot said.

"Acknowledged. Alright, no need to mess around this time. I want the F.A.C.s up to three-quarters burn, *Mambaka* to match their speed. Get us to that Transit point." He paused. "And bring us alongside *Stinger*. There's something Force-Commander Winters and I need to take care of."

There was a heavy pause before the pilot replied. "Yes, Sir."

So they do feel the weight of their loss, or at least something. Good. I'd hate to be aboard a ship commanded by

David Noe

psychopaths...

Feeling both relieved and satisfied, Elise set about her task. It was a massive undertaking and one she doubted she could complete before the message had to be sent, but even a partial set of data plus a summary or informal report would at least prove useful, and the more she could get done, the happier she'd be.

CHAPTER TWENTY- INSIGHT

"His name was Laniz Rotik," the captain of *Stinger* said, as the three of them looked down at the body. "Can't say any of us knew him well, seeing he was only a rookie, but his team had nothing but good things to say: stand-up guy, worked hard, never shirked his duty..."

Raffa nodded. "A good man." He looked up, glancing around the narrow confines of the ship. "All that potential... What a waste."

The others stood in silent agreement until Winters finally spoke.

"Perhaps a promotion is in order, boss. It won't do him any good, but his family..."

"Yes, of course," Raffa said, looking down at the body once more. "In my capacity as commanding officer of this mission, and as permitted under the responsibilities and privileges befitting my rank, I hereby promote you, Laniz Rotik, to the rank of Energy Weapons Technician Second Class." He swallowed. "May you go peacefully, honoured fallen, and thank you."

"Go peacefully, honoured fallen, and thank you," Winters and the captain echoed.

"Let's get him over to *Mambaka*," Raffa said, waving a couple of waiting soldiers over to take the body to the storage area that had been set aside solely for dealing with fatalities. "As for you, Captain... good work. Please pass on my condolences to Rotik's team, and commend them for their bravery and dedication."

"I'll be sure to do that, Sir. Thank you."

Raffa shook the man's hand, with Winters following suit, then followed the bearers back to *Mambaka*. The airlocks hissed shut behind them, the connecting tunnel was withdrawn, and the two ships parted again. With a final glance in the direction of Rotik's body, Raffa and Winters headed back to the command centre.

"How long to the Transit point?" Raffa asked, almost before his boots had crossed the threshold.

"Approximately point three megasekunds, Sir," came the reply.

"And how long to convey our messages to E X Two-B's transport?"

There was a lengthy pause.

"The transport indicates it is scheduled to enter Transit to Windan in twenty-five kilosekunds, Sir."

"Right. Do we have everything compiled and ready to send? All messages, mission-critical data, progress reports, and so on?"

"Er... Yes, Sir. All bar your final update, the data from the station and a report of Specialist Rivera's findings, Sir."

"Pass a message to Specialist Rivera reminding her she has limited time, and remind her again at ten kilosekunds, then seven k, then every one kilosekund after that until the cut-off point at two kilosekunds to the transport's departure. I want to make sure absolutely every scrap of information we can provide is safely received."

"Acknowledged, Sir."

Raffa ran a hand over his face. He felt drained, tired to a point beyond simple fatigue. "Alright," he said. "Takk, you're in charge. I'll be in my quarters."

Winters nodded. "Right you are, boss."

Raffa left the command core and walked slowly along the corridor.

Void, I wish these were Kaska's quarters I was heading to.

He entered the room, removed as much of his uniform as he dared, and slumped onto the bed.

After all that worry about the troops, I'm the one who's pining for home...

He closed his eyes and put his forearm over them. He began to feel himself slide towards sleep, a sensation not entirely unlike falling - or more correctly, moving backwards - in zero-g, yet he couldn't quite make it all the way. He willed it to come, tried to force himself into sleep's welcome, and welcoming, embrace... yet the more he tried, the more it slipped away. Yet still he lay there, trying...

* * *

Elise jumped as her cabin's internal comm squawked.

"Message from command centre to Specialist Rivera. Comcap Raffa advises you are to have all data and your final report ready for transmission within twenty-three kilosekunds."

Fat chance!

"Command centre, please tell Comcap Raffa that there's no way I'll have even looked at 'all data' in that time, and he'll be lucky if I can put together much in the way of a preliminary report. Over."

"Message received, Specialist. Do your best. Command centre, outsign."

Elise's hands clenched involuntarily into fists and she ground her teeth.

What in the Void *do they expect from me? Miracles?*

She got to her feet, pacing in what little free space she had until she felt calm enough to return her attention to the screen, which was crammed with lists of the files they'd taken from the C-Three and Freedom One.

"So..." she said out loud as a way of re-focusing her thoughts. "The pirates definitely came in from Grinda. They headed to F-One for repairs... which means they were likely damaged in Grinda but managed to Transit out. But how were they damaged, and by whom?" She closed her eyes and shook her head. "And what part did Tylir Enista play? *Was* she a 'rat all along, or just someone who thought they could do a deal and got out of their depth? *Stars*, if only there was some way I could know!"

But the truth was, Enista had either been killed or she pretty soon would be. Either way, Kau D'varza, in the embodiment of Comcap Joseph Raffa, had no authority or jurisdiction here, and the new acting station commander, Harrison, could treat his people - and his prisoners, if that's what Enista currently was - however he chose. Even if that meant Elise, and Kau D'varza, had to live without knowing... or go to the trouble of finding out the hard way.

She felt a ball of anger rising at her lack of power and control, and forced herself to take a deep breath.

Okay, Elise: focus on what you can *know...*

"So... they were in Grinda... and they were in communication with other pirates there. They also took damage and ran, so... maybe they fought?"

She spent the next few k-seks scrolling down the the communications logs via her pad, searching for messages most likely to correspond to the pirates' time in Grinda, then chose the message at the foot of the list, closest to their departure time for Exen, and listened. She struck gold on the one third from bottom.

"... And I don't give a fuck," a deep voice said.

She frowned.

That'll be that asshole pirate, Mendi...

"Listen, you've got more than enough here to handle whatever pile of shit Winda' sends this way. We're going for repairs, and I'm not hearing another word about it!"

Elise stopped the playback.

Oh... oh damnit! They didn't fight the other pirates in Grinda; they're allies with the other pirates in Grinda...

She swept back a finger up the screen and selected another recording a couple of messages before.

"Can you believe this place?" Mendi's voice said.

"What happened here?" asked another.

"Doesn't matter, this looks like an opportunity. What's out there?"

"Nothing we can use... Oh. Wait. Freighter!"

"Useless! We're pirates, not haulers!"

"We could use it to draw someone else here... ambush them."

A pause. "Oh?"

"Wouldn't be difficult to set up a remote link. We should get in touch with our friends on that station."

"Friends? Does he mean Enista, or..." Elise frowned as another possibility occurred to her. "Or Jimba?" She sat back heavily against the bulkhead. "Son of a bitch..."

She staggered towards the hatch, nearly fell through it as it opened, and ran towards the command centre.

"You were right!" she said, slamming her pad down on the desk next to where Winters was standing.

He blinked, either surprised to see her or surprised by the vehemence of her outburst. "Specialist?"

"Where's Raffa?" she asked, looking around.

"In his quarters, resting," Winters replied, frowning. "Now, what's this about?"

"The pirates. It was them who sent the freighter through to Windan. It was abandoned, drifting... they found it, then set up a remote link to control it. They mentioned friends on a station. *That* station. At first I thought they meant Freedom One, because they mentioned going for repairs on a later message, though I listened to that one first-"

Winter's face creased with confusion. "Hold on... *what?*"

Elise took a breath and blew it out, slowly. "Alright. I

listened to a message where Mendi, at least I think it was Mendi, says he's taking his ships for repairs. After that, I listened to an earlier exchange from when they found the freighter. On this earlier message, they mention getting in touch with 'our friends on that station'. Because I'd previously heard them talking about going for repairs at F-One, for a moment I assumed-"

"That they were always talking about Freedom One," Winters said, nodding. "Yes, I follow." He looked at her. 'But...?"

"*But...* what if they weren't talking about Freedom One? What if these '*friends*' are on Kau D'varza?"

Winters looked thunderstruck. "Wait here. The 'cap needs to hear this."

He bolted from the room, returning mere moments later with a bleary-eyed Raffa in tow.

"Sorry to disturb your sleep, Comcap," Elise began, but he waved her aside.

"You didn't," he said, still re-fastening his uniform. "So... what's the story?"

Elise went back over everything she had already told Winters, adding, "They wanted to draw our ships to them so they could ambush them. The only way to be sure of catching them would be at the default Transit point in Grinda."

"And given the issues with our T-cores, along with F-One's insistence we go back to Windan and head to Grinda from there..." Raffa said, nodding. "Makes sense to me. They send the freighter, knowing we'll investigate. They leave breadcrumbs of data, again knowing we'll find them and send an investigative flotilla to Grinda, and in the meantime their friend Jimba screws with our cores and makes sure our best ships, including - perhaps especially - *Kobra,* are offline. All of which means we have no choice but to 'xit at default system entry points using whatever ship, or ships, we can make available at short notice. Either way, we Transit in all unawares, and find ourselves outnumbered and outgunned."

Winters grimaced. "Now that's not a comforting thought." He looked at Elise. "How bad is it? How many they got?"

She shrugged. "I don't know, but that asshole pirate says 'more than enough', so..."

"And you're sure they're only on the Transit point from Windan?"

She sighed again, not bothering to hide her frustration. "No. I can't be *sure* of anything, beside a few facts."

"Fair enough," Raffa said, "but based on what you do know...?"

"Based on what I *can* know... yes, they're only on the Transit point from Windan. That is, unless their friends in this system got a message to them."

Raffa sighed. "We didn't see anything leaving the system... no ships, no beacons..."

"Even so, we shouldn't count it out," Winters advised.

"No, we shouldn't."

"We need to be prepared for anything when we reach Grinda." Elise looked to the map. "If they've got ships stationed at the T-points from Windan and here, we're in trouble as soon as we arrive."

"But not as much trouble: If their forces are split, they'll be easier to deal with."

"That's a big if, Winters."

Raffa nodded. "I'd rather we got the drop on them, rather than the other way round." He looked around at them both. "But we'll be going in blind. So, any suggestions?"

Elise sighed. "No."

"Takk?"

Winters folded his arms and shook his head.

"Then we've got point six megaseks to think of a plan, and execute it before we arrive in Grinda."

"Bearing in mind that getting orders to the F.A.C.s in Transit will be all but impossible," Winters said.

"Anything specific, anyway," Raffa agreed. "Alright. We still have time until we hit Transit. Let's have a plan by then. Elise, if nothing else we need to get that information back to Kau-D'varza. Make that your top priority. The data, your analysis, and a full report *must* be sent with that transport, even if it means bumping personal messages to limit the file size. You have..." He glanced at a screen, "thirteen kiloseks to get it done and compiled for transmission, along with any other pertinent data you can find."

"I'll get it done."

"I know you will," he said, then as she headed for the door, he added, "And thank you, Specialist. This information is extremely helpful."

"I hope so," she said over her shoulder, and set off to work in peace and quiet.

* * *

Raffa and Winters watched Elise go, then, as the door closed behind her, they let their true feelings be known by exhaling, loudly.

"This is bad," Winters said.

"Agreed. Knocking the 'rats out of this system won't mean a thing if they're so strong in Grinda that more just turn up. Our effort here will be wasted, and Kau D'varza will be in greater danger. We need to deal with this."

"And preferably before they deal with us."

"Hm. The question is, what can we do?"

Winters shrugged. "Besides getting that info back to the station and a formation change, there isn't much."

"Again, agreed. Leaving the info side to Rivera, though, the question we face is what formation?"

"You've only really got two meaningful choices here, boss. We haven't got enough ships for anything fancy."

"Shame Freedom One couldn't spare anything..."

"They only had a shuttle. Nothing we coulda used."

"No. Okay, then. Let's see..." Raffa tapped the screen, waking it, and selected the option that showed the system in 2D form. The icons that made up the flotilla drifted further and further from Freedom One, the graphical representation showing them moving at a crawl despite the ships' incredible speed. He zoomed in, bringing up the tactical display, then flicked away the overabundance of details so they could focus solely on the three vessels at their command.

"My preferred method would be to spread those suckers out. Might only buy us a few seks, but they might be all we need," Winters said.

"I was thinking the same," Raffa agreed. "If we bring the F.A.C.s above us, maintain triangle formation but spread it wide, it should confuse their targeting systems enough to buy us some time."

Winters nodded. "We should engage retros on termination, too. Have the flotilla go backwards, not forwards, and if we encounter any hostiles... well..." He grinned. "*Mambaka*'s always got mines and missiles. We create space, drop some mines, then regroup and form a proper plan of attack."

"*If* we have time and *if* the odds aren't too badly against us. We have to try to do something if we can, but throwing three ships away would only weaken Kau D'varza at the time it needs them most. If things are too bad, we'll have little choice but to cut and run, maybe come back with pretty much everything we've got once we've got *Kobra*, *Akonda*, and *Vypka* back."."

"Right. But in the meantime, I think that's about as good as it's gonna get, boss."

"Yeah. Perhaps. But let's sit on it for a few, see if anything better comes up."

"Don't take too long. You know how people hate last sekund changes."

Raffa grinned. "Those pirates certainly would have had some complaints, if they were still around to make them."

"Damn right, too. And if I've got anything to say about it, we're about to space some more!"

A notification popped up on the corner of the screen.

A message from Elise that simply said 'No out-system communications found.'

* * *

Kaska stands in the gardens. She senses that someone is at at her side. It feels like Raffa. She inhales, and the scent of flowers and living, growing things fills her nostrils and is drawn deep into her lungs. She exhales again, slowly, but she can still detect the traces of perfumed miasma. She smiles, inhaling deeply again.

Everything here, now, is so perfect, she thinks. Why can't it always be like this?

She frowns, disliking the intrusive thought. Who says it isn't always like this? Why wouldn't it be? What other life is there?

A station, set against a pair of voids: one, the star-speckled vastness of space; the other, a chaotic kaleidoscope of rampant, vivid, ever-shifting colour.

Her frown deepens and she turns to face Raffa, but he isn't there. Or at least, she can't see him. All that is there instead is a blanket of stars and blue-black space. A single tear slips from one of her eyes.

Joseph? she says, calls, though her voice is soft, almost lost amid a strange humming. A device in his top pocket - where his top pocket would be - lights up, and she looks at it, frowning, unsure, until realisation dawns...

Kaska opened her eyes and stretched. Her datapad was flashing and humming beside her; the source of the final sounds and images in her fractured dream.

Damnit...

Her yawn lasted only a few seconds before she scooped the pad up and answered.

"Specialist Stone," she said, her eyes sliding shut again involuntarily.

"Ah, Specialist. I apologise for waking you. However, your presence is required in the Command Core."

She didn't answer. Instead, her breathing deepened and she let out a snore.

"Specialist? Specialist Stone? Are you still there?"

Her eyes snapped open. "Yes, Sir. Here, Sir. My apologies." She rubbed her eyes and sat up. "I'll be there shortly."

"Thank you, Specialist."

The pad went dark as Kaska swung her legs round and climbed out of bed. After a few moments in the clean-room, she emerged wearing a fresh uniform and hurried for the door.

When she arrived at the Command Core, she found Gierre Nevos and Coda Trast standing over a console, concern on their faces.

"Sir?"

"Ah! Excellent, you're here," Nevos said, though he

looked, and sounded, distracted.

"Is there a problem, Sir?"

He looked around at her, though his eyes were distant and unfocused for a moment. "Hmm? Oh! We've just received this from a transport coming in from Exen."

He restarted the video, and hit Play.

Kaska's heart skipped then started racing when Raffa's face appeared, though she frowned, feeling something like a stab of pain at how stressed and worn out he looked, though he had made an effort to tidy himself up. She straightened her back, giving herself a mental shake. This wasn't the first time she'd seen one of the comcaps look this way, and as long as she worked her current job it wouldn't be the last. The fact it was Raffa shouldn't make any difference. If it did - or rather, if it continued to - she would face a choice: change her job, or end things with Joseph. She wanted to do neither.

"This is Comcap Raffa of the Kau D'varza Investigation Flotilla reporting."

Her heart seemed to swell within her even more.

By the Void and all the stars, it's good to hear his voice...

"I do not have a lot of time as the transport due to deliver this message will leave shortly, therefore, I will be as brief as possible." He exhaled. "Upon our arrival to Exen, we discovered hostiles, known Pirates, in close proximity to Freedom One. Due to our belief that they had some connection to the problems originating in Grinda, and because of the threat their prolonged presence in Exen would cause, we engaged their forces. I am happy to report that our engagement was a success. It is, however, with regret that I must report that we took casualties, the most notable of which was a fatality aboard *Stinger*; a weapons technician named Laniz Rotik. I would appreciate it if you could inform his family and pass on my personal condolences. I will, of course, be happy to meet with anyone upon my return, should they wish it. Furthermore, while *Mambaka* received some damage, we see no reason not to continue on to Grinda as planned. We don't know what to expect there, but we have discovered that a significant force, allied to the Exen hostiles, is in-system, and we strongly suspect that they will be lying in wait at the default T-point from Windan. More information - all that Specialist Rivera had time to recover - and as full a report as she had time to complete, are attached, or should accompany, this message. It is my sincerest hope that those at home are well, and can make use of this information. For Kau D'varza. Comcap Raffa, outsign."

His image faded, and a deep sigh left Kaska' lips that caused both Trast and Nevos to look to her.

Damn...

"Pirates. In Exen?" she said, trying to disguise the bulk of her concern and knowing from the looks on their faces that she had failed. "We're not getting many breaks."

"*Were* in Exen," Nevos corrected. "Thanks to Comcap Raffa, that's not a problem anymore. I'm far more concerned by what he expects to find in Grinda. 'A significant force'... that could mean anything! If they encounter a group of frigates or destroyers, there's a real risk of losing our ships!"

"I don't think it would come to that, Sir," Trast said. "Raffa's experienced and savvy enough to cut his losses and run if the odds are too heavily against him."

"Yes, I'm sure he will... *if* he gets the chance to run at all. In any case, unless they're shuttles or little more than hulks, which I doubt, they're going to be up against it."

Kaska closed her eyes. "We... We need to send more ships. Now, and direct to Grinda to back him up."

Nevos raised an eyebrow to Trast who turned to her console.

"Simulation suggests... *Vypka*... *G-Barb*... and *G-Nail*. Commanded by Comcap Teq."

"Specialist Stone?"

"*Vypka*'s one of our fastest. The Fast Attack Craft will slow it down, though."

"And *Kobra*?"

"Still undergoing repairs. Engineering Bay says it'll be another megasek before we can even think about switching her back on."

"You're starting to sound like an engineer, Specialist," he said, smiling slightly, and turned back to Trast. "If we send those ships within the next six k-seks, when will they arrive in Grinda?"

"According to this... point eight megaseks."

Nevos spun away and pulled out his datapad. After several seconds, Kaska heard the tired voice of Comcap Teq.

"My apologies for waking you, Comcap."

"Not a problem, Sir; I am here to serve. What's the problem?"

"I need you, and however many troops you can fit into *Vypka* and two fast attack craft, prepared and ready to go in six k-seks."

"The mission, Sir?"

"Your mission would be to Transit to Grinda and assist Comcap Raffa in mopping up a flotilla of pirate ships, number and type of ships unknown."

Teq's eyes seemed to light up, and he almost smiled. "It would be my honour to assist, Sir."

"Somehow, I knew you'd say that. Alert your people, then meet me in Command Core."

"It will be done. For Kau D'varza."

While Nevos finished his communication, Kaska stepped up to beside Trast and ran her fingers over the neighbouring console.

"If Teq takes *Vypka*, *Barb*, and *Nail* that only leaves us with *Akonda*, *Bo'a*, a disabled *Kobra*, and two fast attack craft, *Tooth* and *Fang*."

Trast shrugged. "We've defended the station with less."

"*Comcap Raffa* has defended the station with less," Kaska corrected. "With Teq also gone, we'll be left to rely on Comcap Rexon."

Trast made a face. "Yes, but if we don't do this and Raffa runs into something in Grinda that they can't handle, which seems more and more likely the more of this info I read, we stand to lose *Mambaka* and two of the F.A.C.s."

"Listen, I know you're not wrong. But what if the threat from Grinda comes to Windan?"

"*Akonda* can deal with it. That ship alone will be more than a match for anything these pirates have."

"And what if the threat isn't pirates?"

Trast took a deep breath at the prospect. "Then we'd be unprepared whatever ships remained here. Look, I don't wanna send our defences away anymore than you do, but I don't wanna lose *Mambaka* and the people on it either." She eyed Kaska a little slyly. "Something I'm sure you of all people can appreciate."

"Oh, don't start. I'm trying to detach myself from my personal connections. I don't want it to affect my judgement."

"That's fair enough, but don't become so detached that you start overcompensating."

Kaska nodded. "Thanks. I think I needed reminding."

Trast winked. "Hey, Kas, It's what I'm here for."

* * *

Elise Rivera had again spent most of their time in Transit sealed away in her quarters, only emerging for one meal a cycle if that, as she tried to make sense of the wealth of information they'd gathered, most notably from the C-Three, and assemble it into a precise timeline.

The evening before they were due to terminate Transit, with her task finally complete, she stood outside Raffa's door. A drop of sweat, a sign of nerves, ran down her cheek as she raised a hesitant finger and pressed the buzzer. Raffa opened it himself and smiled.

"Specialist Rivera. Nice to see you've decided to rejoin us. Please, come in."

She attempted a grin, felt it fail, and stepped inside.

Raffa closed the door and turned to her with a frown. "You look… extremely troubled, Specialist Rivera."

Winters turned in his seat to look at her as she stepped across the room to the screen.

"I *am* extremely troubled, Comcap Raffa."

"Alright. Explain."

She linked her pad to the screen and brought up the timeline. "I've gone through all the data we took from the C-Three, and cross-referenced it with the information we gained from Freedom One as well as what we already knew."

She broke off as Winters gave a low whistle.

"Sorry," he said, noticing her look. "It's just that… well, I know that's no small task. I'm amazed you've got it done, let alone so quickly."

She nodded an acknowledgement, then got back to her briefing.

"There was a lot of stuff that wasn't relevant. I also ignored everything from before the point where the pirates arrive in Grinda." She paused again and swallowed. "What I discovered is, their initial fleet was twelve strong."

"*Twelve?*"

She nodded. "We dealt with five at Exen, meaning seven remain in Grinda." She watched as the soldiers exchanged a concerned look, though neither spoke. "Anyway, the ships arrived in Grinda. Next, they moved to this..."

She tapped her pad and an image bloomed onto the screen.

Winters frowned. "What in the Void is that... a ship graveyard?"

"Yes. And that's where the pirates picked up the freighter. The audio file I found before mentioned their plan, but I've found other, definite proof that it was them who sent it to Windan. The beacon from Kau D'varza then brought it to us. The records also show that seven ships followed the freighter until it activated Transit, while the five we destroyed went to Exen for repairs."

"What in the Void is a damn ship graveyard doing in Grinda in the first place?" Winters asked.

"That I don't know. The pirates speculated the Void Cloud had something to do with it, but I disagree with their theories. It's something we'll need to figure it out once we arrive. The point is, while the pirates might have sent that ship our way, it *wasn't* them who kidnapped the crew. They're not responsible for whatever created that... ship graveya- I'm sorry, is there seriously not a better term for that?"

Winters shrugged. "It's just what it looks like. Sorry."

"Okay. Whatever. The essential fact is, it wasn't them that created it; they just used it to their advantage, to lure us into Grinda so they could ambush us. Which confirms that they also knew in advance about the problems we're currently having with the Transit cores."

"So we've got two issues," Raffa replied. "Figure out what caused the ship gr... I mean, the debris field... and deal with seven pirate vessels. At least with Jimba locked up, I think we can assume that their source won't be leaking anything else."

"*If* he was their source, and if he was, assuming he was the only one," Elise said.

Raffa nodded. "Yes, true, but let's not start seeing hostile actors everywhere when none might exist. Do you have any info on the ships the pirates have left?"

Elise nodded and tapped her datapad again. "Here."

Winters couldn't help himself laughing. "A war-tug? Are you kidding me?"

"Why? What's a war-tug?" Elise asked, looking in confusion from Winters to Raffa, who likewise couldn't suppress a grin.

"Well... a tug is a ship used to pull other ships... but they're small, right? Not like ship-haulers or mega-tugs," Winters explained, to which Elise nodded.

"Well, a war-tug is a tug that's been retrofitted with weapons. Don't see many of them these days; tugs seem to be dying out. They're usually Class-Sevens, but..." He leaned forward, squinting at the screen. "*Mambaka*'s decided that one is a Class-Five. Hmm..."

"What does that mean? Might it be a problem?"

"No problem. In fact this is good news: a C-Five is much easier for us to deal with."

Elise frowned. "What, they *downgraded* a ship? Why would they do that?"

Winters shrugged. "Could be a whole bunch of reasons, but it's possible *Mambaka* might have calculated the mass and size of the ship based on the data and come to its own conclusions."

"What about the others?" Raffa asked.

"Looks like... two cutters, two M-F.A.C.s and two A-Shuts. The M-F.A.C.s and A-Shuts are C-Twos and C-Ones, respectively, same models as the ones we encountered in Exen, while the cutters're C-Fours," Elise read from her datapad.

"Hmm... Cutters. Usually tend to be extremely weak. A few well placed missiles will take them out if experience is anything to go on, eh, boss?"

"Let's hope so. Either way, they'd be a significant force for anyone caught with their guard down." Raffa put his elbows on his desk, laced his fingers and rested his chin on his thumbs. "Yet, since we know about it, we've got a better chance. Especially if they're still sitting on Windan's T-point."

"They should be," Elise replied. "That asshole, Mendi, made it very clear that he'd 'turn them to dust' himself if they moved before he got back."

"Well that helps. We'll just have to see how good they are at following orders... or how scared of Mendi they really were."

"The only thing that worries me..." Winters chipped in, "is that war-tug. I know I laughed before, but the more I think about it..." He shook his head. "We really need to figure out what weapons and countermeasures that thing is packing before we engage, even if it also gives us an advantage."

Raffa smiled. "Speed."

"Right. That thing gonna be slow as all get out, and the rest of the fleet will have to provide some sort of protection. We scatter that force, they won't stand a chance."

Raffa stood and made his way to the screen. "Alright. If our arrival in Grinda is uncontested, we'll head directly for the debris field. If the pirates want to engage us, I want them to come to us, and that field might provide us with some useful cover. We'll broadcast the fact we destroyed their friends in Exen, taunt them a bit, and hope that does enough to cause some to run or turn to engage us. That way we'll fight them on our terms."

"Then if we slice off the edges of whatever formation they adopt, or target the dub-tug directly... Oh, damn, this might actually be fun to see on the sim."

"Dub-tug?" Elise frowned. "I think it's going to take me some time to get used to all these little names you throw about."

Winters laughed. "Just be thankful we haven't come across any assault destroyers yet."

"Your language is certainly a colourful one... Regarding these forces though, can't they just Transit out?"

"A valid point," Raffa said. "But I don't see many places for them to run to. Do you?"

She straightened up. "I will continue my research into the debr-"

"No," Raffa said, in a tone not of suggestion but of friendly command. "You are to get something to eat, and then you are to rest. You look burnt out, and I will need you at your best when we hit Grinda."

She drew breath to reply, but felt weariness creeping in.

Damnit. He's right...

"Alright. I... alright."

Raffa smiled, and nodded. "That's that, then. And thanks again, Specialist Rivera, as usual your thoroughness has yielded extremely useful results. Now, food and rest. I'll even say 'Please'."

CHAPTER TWENTY- ONE- SERENE PREMONITION

Kaska Stone was feeling restless. Her eyes felt heavy and sore, yet every time she closed them her mind would race and the bed - usually so soft and comfortable - would feel like a mass of humps and hollows. A still image of Raffa from the video illuminated her habitat as she tossed and turned in bed, trying to get a tiny sliver of rest.

She rolled onto her back, sighing, and closed her eyes.

Try again...

As before, her mind kicked into high gear and her thoughts turned to Raffa, on his way to who knew what, and Teq, whose flotilla had left four cycles ago, but which would still be hundreds of kilosekunds away from arriving in Grinda. She imagined *Vypka's* arrival. Imagined the look on Teq's face when he reported back saying they had arrived too late, that they had found debris clouds - all that remained of *Claw* and *Stinger* - and the drifting, heavily-damaged hulk of *Mambaka*; empty, seemingly abandoned, but with buried data files showing the pirates removing occupied stasis tubes...

She opened her eyes again, her tiredness and frustration at her inability to sleep combining to almost make her weep.

Why in the Void can't I just sleep? Just a couple of K-seks. That's all I ask... Maybe if I just breathe deeply, focus only on that, the sound of air going in and out...

She closed her eyes once more and forced herself to ignore the thoughts and swirling, ever-shifting, Void-like patterns that started to form.

In... and out. In... and out. In... That's it, Kaska. Just... like... tha...

Just as she began to settle, her mind finally ready to switch off, the lights in her habitat hummed to life, indicating the start of another long cycle on Kau D'varza, and she reluctantly - almost tearfully - opened her eyes.

Oh, damnit...

"Make reservation... Krash-Bed, Kaska Stone... light's out, this cycle," she mumbled. A chirp indicated the space had been booked as she edged towards the end of the bed and lazily half-fell, half-stood out of it. It wasn't long before she was clean, fully clothed, and leaning against her food processor as it dispensed a cup of Escafo. The fragrance was almost overpowering as she raised it to her lips and took a sip. When she swallowed, a warming sensation ran through her. It helped. Not much, but enough, and this cycle, she decided, she would take what she could get. Still barely awake, Kaska headed out the door.

"Good cycle, Madam Specialist," Ikarus said as she arrived in the engineering bay, still clasping her now mostly-empty cup.

"Nothing good about it so far, Ikarus," she grumbled.

"Oh," he replied, half-smiling as she caught up to him and they started walking towards the office.

"Anything new to report?" she asked.

"A great deal, actually. All materials and components from the Yor' vessel have been properly catalogued. The ship itself is also nearly fully dismantled; a team has been working through lights-out in the hope of freeing up some additional space down here."

She frowned. "Is space an issue?"

"Not a pressing one, but I believe it would be wise to have more, just in case. Clearing the bay also serves a second purpose: it makes organisation easier."

"I see... what else?"

"The delivery we received from Exen has been assessed and placed in storage. We currently have no need to tap into such resources, due to the aforementioned breaking down of the Yor' vessel."

They reached the office overlooking the engineering bay, whereupon Kaska settled into her chair and tapped at the screen, bringing up an overview of the night-cycle's work along with several message notifications.

"Looks like it's been busy..."

"Indeed," Ikarus replied, maintaining a stiff posture as he remained by the door. "I am happy to report that the engineers are finally re-assembling *Kobra*. They estimate that with the 'rediscovered' components, *Kobra* will fly again in under point five megasekunds."

Kaska sighed. "That *is* a relief... I had some real concerns about that."

"As did I. However, between the loyal engineers, and those that Commissioner Zeled brought in, I believe our concerns were misplaced."

"Agreed. Funny how removing a few bad components can make such a difference."

A grin crept onto Ikarus' lips. "In addition, work has finally begun on stripping down the freighter."

"Oh? We didn't sign off on the conversion yet."

"This is simply to acquire materials. The hull, propulsion and other main systems will remain untouched until the best course of action has been decided."

Kaska nodded and scanned the screen again. "Looks like our stockpiles are filling up nicely... are we at risk from overflow?"

"Not currently, Ma'am, but if we continue at this rate, it will take roughly three megasekunds to reach that point. However, we have also started to use this excess. Therefore by my estimates, it should level out, then begin to decline again shortly afterwards."

"Keep an eye on it," she said.

"Yes, Ma'am."

She turned from the screen and sat back in her seat. "What about the other matter we discussed?"

"A shortlist of candidates has been forwarded to your system, Ma'am."

"Alright, Ikarus, thanks." Her lips formed a word. She paused, then tried again. "The situation with our Transit cores. Can it be fixed?"

"We believe so. It is being treated as a top priority, Ma'am."

She nodded. "Good."

"If there is nothing else, I will return to my duties."

"What are you doing?"

"I will continue my organization and 'tidy up' of the bays."

Kaska nodded. "That sounds appropriate. Please." She motioned for him to go.

She sighed as he disappeared from view, feeling tired, worried and run-down.

I need a break. Or at least to get back to doing just one thing. I can't do this job forever. I'm not an engineer; I'm not qualified to make all these decisions... and Command Core needs me. Joseph is going to need Ikarus back too... Been lucky so far. Had him to watch my back, balance my thinking... but with everything else that's going on... damnit... it's all too much. If only we'd seen this sooner, if only we'd caught Jimba and his schemes. None of this would have...

She sat forward, her eyes widening as one of the message files caught her attention. It was from Commissioner Zeled.

What's this?

She tapped the screen, causing his face to fill it instantly.

"You'll be happy to know..." he began, as though he wasn't speaking to anyone in particular, "that Jimba has admitted all the charges laid against him by the Security section, and is being held in high-sec until such time as punishment can be administered. It also appears there's been some sort of mix up with the prisoner's food. Nothing but cabbage bars, could you imagine such a thing?" He grinned. "I'm sure we'll get around to investigating the... 'problem'... shortly. Nevertheless, I wanted to *thank* you and the other specialists for all this information. Although I hope you don't mind me saying, if you never send me another report, it'll be too soon."

Even Kaska laughed at that. Zeled nodded to the screen. "For Kau D'varza, Zeled outsign."

Amazing. Zeled... in a good mood. And we got Jimba. I mean, the alternative would have been impossible; I've never seen such a long list of charges before, and if he's admitted to all of them... Damn, might as well send him into the Void for all the good his life is gonna be after this...

CHAPTER TWENTY- TWO- COMING JUDGEMENT

The screens in the command centre flashed back to life and began filling with information as *Mambaka* terminated Transit. Raffa felt the ship judder as the retro-thrusters fired at full, sending them backwards, and hadn't realised he'd been holding his breath, waiting for the icons for seven ships to appear around them on the screen and open fire, until the scans were complete and indicated nothing in the local area.

"Report."

"Transit to Grinda successful. *Claw* and *Stinger* accounted for and maintaining position. Evasive maneuvers successfully completed, no threats detected close by," the co-pilot said. He paused for a second to check something before continuing. "Two vessels en-route to Hol. Awaiting identification. Seven vessels in ambush position around default Windan entry point." There was an audible sound of relief. "Scans indicate two stations in orbit around Grinda One... six asteroid belts... Wait. No, five asteroid belts and... something..." Another pause, this time accompanied by a sharp intake of breath. "Specialist Rivera's report is confirmed; there's an extensive debris field. Scanners are picking up multiple contacts, but the field... it's so dense that it's impossible to get an accurate number. "

"But it's safe to say there's a lot?"

"Yes, Sir. Force-Commander Winters was right; it's a real ship graveyard out there!"

"Alright, let's not get carried away. Anything else?" Raffa asked.

"Uh... one moment, Sir... Yes. Oh. Sir? It seems as though the mining platforms in this area have been abandoned; we're not seeing any activity."

Winters frowned. "Probably for the best. Pirates, an expansive ship gra- er, debris field, no security... This system's a damn mess."

"What little system there is..." Raffa replied. "Alright, have *Claw* and *Stinger* take position left and right of *Mambaka*. Line Formation Two. Orient *Mambaka* towards the debris field and be ready to set off on my mark. *Stinger* and *Claw* are to maintain seventy-percent total burn, *Mambaka* to maintain speed relative to them."

"Another slow ride?" Winters asked, shaking his head.

"Yes. I want them to think they've got a chance. If we look like we're limping, they might think they can take us out. If we also send them footage of the fight in Exen, they're bound to try. They wanted a ship from Windan... well, we're right here, limping along, but still over-confident and boasting. I intend to make us look as enticing as possible."

"So we're going to talk to them this time?" Elise asked.

"Yes. Regardless of what happens, we need them off that T-point for Windan's sake; no traffic using default settings is safe. I suggest we send them the details of the fight, let them know their boss is dead, and that surrendering or fleeing is within their best interests."

Winters frowned. "Fleeing would put them back in the system we just cleared. We need to stop them from Transiting."

"Yes, Takk. That's why I want them to think they stand a chance of taking *Mambaka*. If we look juicy enough, they won't run."

"I think I can make sure they can't," Elise said, and grinned when the soldiers looked at her. "Kau D'varza ships have been afflicted by Jimba's malware for some time now, right? So let's turn it on them, make it so their cores behave how *we* want them to."

Raffa's eyebrows shot up. "You can do that?"

"It'll take some time and I'll need a little help from one of your techs, but yeah, it shouldn't be too difficult. Jimba didn't strike me as a particularly smart person. Let me put some kind of proposal together."

Raffa smiled. "Alright, do so."

As Elise flicked through various files, Raffa turned back to the screen. "Have we got an ident on those two ships heading for Hol?"

"It's just coming in now, Sir," the co-pilot replied. "Profile indicates Gaitlin... and... yeah, they're flying Gaitlin codes."

"Gaitlin?" Winters said. "That doesn't make a lick of sense. Safer to get to Hol or the Void via Exen..."

Raffa shrugged. "As long as it's not pirate reinforcements, I don't care. Alright, let's figure this out. We've got about point seven m-seks 'til we reach the debris field at this speed. If they move off the Windan T-point to engage us, it's likely to happen around..." He circled an area on the map with his finger. "Here, given what we know of their potential speed. Hmm..." His eyes narrowed as he focused on the debris field. "You think we can use that to our advantage after all?"

Winters shook his head. "Looks way too dense. We might be more nimble than they are, but fighting 'rats and trying to navigate a debris field? Ehh, it takes a lot out of the computers at the best of times, and the co-ordinators. Harder to get shots off, harder to navigate, you name it. With a field as packed as that…"

"So our best bet is to engage them before we get there."

"Our *best* bet is that half of them wanna flee, the other half don't wanna let 'em, and they wipe each other out."

"A bit optimistic, don't you think?"

Winters shrugged. "I suppose. A guy can hope though, right? Pirates don't become pirates out of a sense of community and team spirit. Self-interest's the name of their game."

"True. But since I don't build my plans on hope, let's figure this out."

"*Stinger* and *Claw*, in position. Ready to engage thrusters on your command," the co-pilot reported.

"Alright, let's go. Keep *Mambaka* between them until I say otherwise."

"Yes, Sir!"

* * *

The screen listed several files. Mostly still images of ships caught mid-explosion or videos of the event in real time plus the aftermath. Elise made a final check, cleared her throat, and hit record.

"This is Investigation Specialist Elise Rivera, Kau D'varza Investigation Flotilla, to the vessels currently blockading the Windan Transit point to this system. Your action has failed. However, we are willing to give you this single chance to surrender. Failure to comply will result in the *absolute* destruction of your vessels upon completion of our objectives within this region. I invite you to view the attached files *very closely,* and think *extremely carefully* about your response. While I think we would all appreciate a peaceful outcome, you will see that we are not adverse to using severe force if necessary. Specialist Rivera, outsign."

That should give them something to think about.

She hit transmit, then turned back to the Command Centre. Raffa and Winters were standing with their heads together, presumably discussing some aspect of the plan or other minor detail, while ahead of them the main screen showed the flotilla crawling towards the debris field. It would take some time for the pirates around the T-point to see they'd arrived, and a little while longer before they received her message. It would then take even more time before the pirate flotilla reacted, and *Mambaka*'s sensors relayed it so they could *see* that reaction.

Elise frowned.

Space is just too fuckin' big...

Raffa, seeming to sense her eyes on him, turned to face her. "I assume our friends have a delightful ultimatum headed their way?"

"Surrender or die," Elise replied. "Damn... that makes us sound like that pirate asshole."

"Yeah, well don't feel too bad," Winters replied. "Spend a sek' thinking about what they're doing, what they've already done, why they're hanging around our T-point."

"Could they really have taken one of Kau D'varza's ships?"

Raffa nodded. "Yeah. We have no kind of momentum when we terminate Transit. We're just sitting there, effectively dead in space, until the computers and what-not come back online. It might only take a few sekunds, but if they targeted the weapons in that time, we're defenceless. We could try to run, but without having any fear of return fire they could close in, pick apart our propulsion before we get up to speed. Then they make enough breaches, wait for the crew to..." He sighed. "You get the idea. I guess that's why they've got the war-tug; they want to pull whatever they catch until it's easy to take over."

"Well any remorse I might have felt just flew out the airlock," Elise muttered, and frowned. "I was just thinking, though... Space is big, yet we keep running into assholes."

Winters and Raffa both laughed.

"Don't matter though," Winters replied once he'd recovered. "We keep running into pirates like this, the local area's soon gonna be a bit tidier."

"What we did in Exen... that was right," Elise said. "But we can't give the impression to everyone that Kau D'varza will turn up to save them at the first sign of trouble. You were right when you said 'We're not here for them', although I didn't quite understand it at the time."

"You're right, it's not up to us," Raffa replied. "But we can't in good faith let pirates hold ground in neighbouring systems, especially when those systems can't defend themselves. Plus, if we want to trade with them, or just have good relations, they have to know they can rely on their more powerful neighbour. If we don't look to them, they'll look elsewhere."

"Like I said, you'll get no arguments from me on that. My concern is Grinda or Exen might get used to calling on us the sekund there's trouble. That's two problems in one: right now they *can't* defend themselves, but if we let them get the idea that we'll come racing to the rescue every time, they *won't* build up their own ability to defend themselves, and that means we might get pulled into something that puts Kau D'varza at risk."

"And..." Winters added, "if they've got expectations and we break 'em, that leads to its own problems."

"Damnit..." Raffa rubbed his forehead. "This sounds too much like politics for me."

Elise cocked her head, looking thoughtful. "Yeah.. I suppose I just don't know enough about these places: Grinda, Exen, Hol... but it seems that if they did form governments and some kind of defence flotilla of their own-"

"They'd probably just use it to fight each other, or themselves," Winters growled. "There's always going to be some asshole running a station or platform who wants a bigger piece of the system. But Hol isn't a problem... it's just a bunch of scientists studying the Void."

Elise nodded, slowly. "Yeah, I suppose there is that..."

"One thing is for certain," Raffa said, with a note of finality. "As long as this system is full of pirates and an unexplained debris field, it isn't safe for vessels coming to and from Windan via this route. We need to deal with the problem at hand, then worry about any issues that come with stabilising this place, so I suggest we get on with it."

* * *

"Kaska Stone," she announced. The door to the Krash-Bed lounge opened onto darkness. A dim light came on near a cavity in the corner to indicate which bed was hers, and she crept quietly past the others. All were occupied, all by people looking for a decent night's sleep regardless of the potential side-effects.

Kaska slipped into her pod, rolled the door down, and squirmed out of her clothes, forcing them into the tray beside her head. As she relaxed on the super-soft mattress, a small screen dropped down by her left hand. Kaska studied the options for a few seconds, selected 'Twenty-Seven Kilosekunds' and 'Deep sleep'. The warnings were flicked away as soon as they appeared. Her attention then turned to her datapad.

I deserve a decent sleep. I deserve some rest! Coda can handle anything Nevos needs. I just...

Her body felt like it was fighting her as she reached for her pad, but she managed to slip a finger over the off button and hold it down. As the screen faded, Kaska's head dropped onto the pillow with a thud. She closed her eyes, and fell asleep.

* * *

Raffa had been on his way to the mess hall when he'd received Winters' message calling him back to the Command Centre. His stomach rumbled as he entered the room, but it seemed food would have to wait.

"What is it?" he asked as he slid back into his seat.

Winters barely afforded him a glance before returning his full attention to his screen. "Their A-Shuts tried taking off, started running."

"Tried?"

"They didn't get far. The war-tug opened fire. Kinetic projectiles, wiped them out in sekunds."

Raffa exhaled. "Why couldn't the damn C-Fours have been the ones to run..."

"We'll get the chance to ask them soon enough," Winters replied. "They've broken the blockade and are moving to intercept us, should meet just short of the debris field." He looked up and flashed a grin. "Looks like they've taken the bait, boss."

"Which formation?"

"Open Gates. Flat."

"What?"

Raffa brought his screen round and found the information he was looking for. He studied the diagram, then looked back to Winters. "C-Fours up front and wide, M-F.A.C.s slightly in and behind them?"

"With the dub-tug sitting at the rear."

Raffa frowned. "It just looks like reverse triangle to me..."

"It would be, except the M-F.A.C.s need to be further out. They've got options: they can bring the F.A.C.s forward, close the gate, build a screen; or they can open them up, drop back, make that dub-tug more enticing."

"Assuming they stick with that, what's our best option?"

"With the C-Fours out on the edges like that, they're super vulnerable. They might protect the tug in the first two engagements, but once we've sliced the edges off 'em, it'll just be sitting there."

"And the M-F.A.C.s?"

"Hmm... they present a problem. If we can score a few hits while we're stomping the C-Fours, that'd be great, but our F.A.C.s will be at risk if they get too close."

"Alright..." He tapped at his screen. "If they don't see sense, I want us set up in right scalene formation, flat, *Mambaka* leading."

"The perfect formation to slice edges off an opponent. I love it."

"Line One might have worked too..."

"Nah, too many opportunities for them to hit back. They'd see a line formation coming."

Raffa grinned. "Oh... what if we..." He looked over to Elise's empty chair. "Damn."

"What?"

"I hope she didn't send too much info about our movements prior to the engagement, that's a trick I'd like to use again."

"Go in, straight line, then change up at the last sek'?"

"Any poor formation. We'd look vulnerable, they'd plan for that, then as we bring *Claw* or *Stinger* out to the point, they'd have to recalculate for the loss of target. They wouldn't have enough time to adjust, not if we left it 'til the last moment."

"We won't be able to use it again after the first clash. We'll have to maintain Right Scalene if we can't get space between us."

"We can outrun them, get the space we need..."

"And if we can turn quick enough, the dub-tug will be vulnerable. Super vulnerable."

"Hmm..." Raffa rubbed his chin. "That would require some extreme maneuvers."

"Only from *Mambaka*. *Claw* and *Stinger* can curve round, swap places while we spin and light off."

"This isn't *Vypka*, we can't pull those sorts of maneuvers."

"Not as smoothly, not as quickly, but we can do it. And a damn sight quicker than a dub-tug."

Raffa was silent for a moment.

"We're gonna have to give this some thought. How long 'til engagement?" he asked.

"At current speed? Point five m-sek."

"And we hit the debris field in..."

"Point six-five, approximately."

"Right."

Raffa stood up and headed for the hatch

"Where are you going?" Winters called.

"To the mess hall to get something to eat, then I want to pay our Specialist a visit."

Winters opened his mouth to reply, but a flash on his screen diverted his attention. "Er, boss, you might wanna hold on for a sek."

"What is it now?" Raffa asked, impatiently.

"Incoming message."

"From the 'rats?"

"Yeah, audio only."

Raffa blew the air out of his cheeks and reluctantly returned to his seat. "Someone let Specialist Rivera know I would like her present for this."

"Sir!" a voice from the command deck responded, then, after a few seconds, "Specialist Rivera is on her way."

Raffa's stomach rumbled again. "Damn, I'm hungry." Winters presented a protein bar, but Raffa instantly brushed it away. "Not that hungry. By the Void, if I never see another one of those damn bars, it'll be too soon."

"Oh, give over. They're not that bad," Winters replied, tearing into the packet.

Raffa shook his head, watching his subordinate eat with a growing pain gnawing in his belly. He was stirred from his near-trance by Elise stepping into the Command Centre.

"Problem?" she asked, settling into her seat.

"We got a reply from our friends. They're moving to engage us."

"I take it this reply isn't a surrender notice?"

"Probably not. We haven't heard it yet."

"Alright," Elise said, "ready when you are."

Raffa nodded. "Run it."

There was silence for a few moments, though breathing could be heard. Then a throat was cleared and a male voice spoke up.

"Is it...? Oh. Alright, alright..." There was another cough as the throat was cleared again. "To the Kau D'varza investigation flotilla"he said, speaking as though he were reading from a script. "A lot of my friends were on those ships you destroyed, so there will be no negotiations. You will pay for your actions, and if I have to die in the act of punishing you, so be it. Frey Aludac, out."

Winters frowned. "Seems like a nice, reasonable chap."

"Idiots," Elise muttered. "They haven't even tried to Transit yet. Do they *know* what they're up against?"

"Presumably. At least, they should do by now," Raffa said, then called up to the command deck. "Signal source for that message?"

"Er... It didn't come from the... uhh, dub-tug, Sir. It came from the cutter... the C-Four closest to the star."

"Oh?" Raffa said, raising his eyebrows. "Well, that changes things."

"Makes things even easier," Winters said, then frowned. "But you gotta ask why. Is he hoping to make some kind of quick escape?"

"I don't know," Raffa said, as his stomach growled again. "And I'm not gonna figure it out right now. Let me get something to eat, then we'll work it out." He turned back to the hatch. "Specialist Rivera, if you'd accompany me."

* * *

Elise followed Raffa to the mess hall, allowed him to order his food first before getting her own, then sat opposite him on a bench that had recently, and mysteriously, been cleared.

"Weird how a seat always just becomes available for the Comcap, isn't it?" she observed.

He smiled. "It's a privilege of rank. Takk and I usually find we have a table to ourselves too, no matter how large a crowd." He shovelled food into his mouth, chewed, and swallowed. "I blame Takk's personal hygiene, myself."

She grinned, then became serious again. "Is everything alright?" she asked, keeping her eyes off him as she stabbed a straw into her carton of juice.

His chewing slowed, then stopped. "Besides the upcoming fight, the unexplained debris field, and systems full of pirates? Yeah, things're great and I'm fine."

Elise snorted, wiped the drink from her face and smiled. "I'm serious. I mean, c'mon... there's got to be something."

He gave her an even stare. "You mean Kaska? Are you asking if I'm missing her or worried I'll never see her again?"

"Well, it's not exactly what I meant... and you seem to be handling it okay."

He poked at his meal. "I'm doing my best. Truth is, yeah, I'm missing her like crazy. Things seemed to just be..." He broke off and shook his head. "Never mind. I'm missing her, end of story. As for anything else... well, that's out of my hands, so why worry?" He lifted another forkful of food towards his mouth and glanced up at her before piling it in. "What about you? Find anything new?"

"Nothing your command team isn't already picking through. They know ship profiles... types, capabilities, and so on... better than I do."

He swallowed and nodded. "So there's nothing more about the debris field?"

"Not really... It's like the scans said: there's too much out there; could be five massive ships got blown up, or a hundred small ones for all I know. We have to get closer, do some digging."

"Yeah. But if the scans are right, the field is dense but it's also spread out, which means there's an awful lot of stuff just drifting about. It's gonna take gigaseks to clear it up."

"Maybe, but, thankfully, that isn't our job. We just need information. No doubt the people on Grinda Station can make use of it all anyway. No, our main concern is who or what created it in the first place."

Raffa swallowed again. "If it helps, I can send you one of our weapons specialists to review the information, see what kind of weapons were used."

"Actually, I already spoke to someone. They said it looks like generator overload. They weren't picked apart by weapons fire as far as we can tell."

He nodded, slowly. "That fits with the kidnap angle. Capture everyone, overload the generator, send it drifting, get away before it detonates and takes all the evidence with it."

Elise grinned. "So those pirates actually did us a favour when they stumbled on the freighter."

"Hmm... It's a bit mixed. They certainly alerted us to issues in this system, but if we'd come the way they wanted, we'd all be dead."

"Still though, it's pretty lucky if you ask me."

"What? That it wasn't destroyed? For all we know they're the ones doing this, and once word got out that Grinda was dangerous, they needed something to lure people here."

She shook her head. "That doesn't match with the footage I've seen. They found it, re-engaged the failsafes remotely, then sent it our way. As I mentioned before, the freighter's crew had already been abducted by the time the 'rats entered the system."

"I hate mysteries," Raffa muttered, shaking his head. "Are we likely to encounter any more overloads?"

Elise shrugged. "I couldn't tell you. Since the debris field is too dense to see any vessels, we can't get scans that are accurate enough, and even if we could, we don't know what the timescale is. Say someone's just come through here and got raided, it might be a while before they blow, but if it had been longer..." She sighed. "It's possible that one or more might pop."

Raffa closed his eyes and exhaled. "Great. I really don't want any more surprises."

"Me either. I'm getting annoyed with all these loose threads." She motioned to the system outside the ship. "Everytime we run into something, I think 'Oh, this'll be the answer'. But pirates in Exen, more in Grinda - who the Exen lot just happen to be allied to, - the debris field... every answer just seems to raise more questions."

"We'll get the answers we need. We'll chase them to the end if we have to. "

Elise sighed. "We're starting to sound like those lunatics who go out to the Cloud."

"Not every obsession is a bad thing. Solving this will be extremely helpful to Kau D'varza."

"And if we're gonna find those answers... this is where it'll be."

Raffa smiled. "That's more like it."

She grimaced at him. "You think we'll get that far?"

"Let me worry about that…" He gave her a knowing smile. "I have a feeling that everything is going to be just fine. Fight-wise, anyway."

"If you say so. I'll try not to lose any sleep over it."

Raffa nodded. "Best not; we'll need you at your best. I just hope I'm right."

CHAPTER TWENTY-THREE-TACTICAL WISDOM

"They're altering course!" the co-pilot announced, trying - and failing - to hide his excitement. "Vector change suggests... default Transit point to Exen."

"Acknowledged," Raffa said, and gave a sly grin. "Now why would they do a thing like that?"

"Sounds like you already know the answer, boss," Winters replied.

"Maybe I have an idea. Either way, we can't let them get to Exen space."

"Thank the Void for Specialist Rivera's version of the malware," Winters muttered. "They'd be free to Transit to anywhere from anywhere without it."

"Indeed," Raffa said, then raised his voice to address

the command crew. "All vessels in Kau D'varza Investigation Flotilla are to pursue pirate vessels. I want *Claw* and *Stinger* brought up to full burn, *Mambaka* to maintain relative position. Formation..."

"I'd go with Flat Triangle, *Mambaka* leading," Winters advised.

"For the engagement, sure, but right now... Hmm-"

"Detecting signatures at the safe entry point from Windan!" a voice from the command centre said. "They're ours! Early scan indicates vessels... Corvette, C-Four, *Vypka*. Accompanied by two Fast Attack Craft."

Raffa sighed with relief.

Thank you, Kaska. I knew you wouldn't... couldn't let me down.

"Sir, *Vypka* and the F.A.C.s have set course and are en route to engage the pirate vessels."

"You're damn lucky we pulled those 'rats away from that T-point," Winters murmured.

"Oh believe me, I know," Raffa replied, looking to the front of the command centre. "Formation, line two. Don't wait on my mark, just get after those damn pirates."

"Yes, Sir!"

Winters smiled. "You reckon it's Teq, or Rexon?"

"I hope to the Void it's Teq. If they've sent Rexon..." He shook his head. "Alright, what's our intercept looking like?"

"At current speed, approximately point three M-seks until we can engage."

"And it's the same for *Vypka*?"

"Yes, Sir."

"And how far are the pirates from the Transit point?"

"At current speed, the pirate fleet should reach the Exen T-point in point two-seven-five megasekunds."

"Damn..." Winters replied. "That's too close..."

Raffa nodded. "And if they can fix the Transit malware, they'll be in Exen by the time we're anywhere near weapons range..."

"Uhh..." Winters hummed, tapped his screen, then looked back to Raffa. "If we want any chance of stopping them, *Mambaka* and *Vypka* need to go alone."

"And leave the F.A.C.s?"

"Only until we can stop those assholes escaping. Besides..." Winters face flared with anger, "we're relying on these new ships of ours too much. *I* remember a time when you took on a lot more with a lot less."

"Yes, so do I. I also remember there were times where it didn't look like we'd be getting home. That's all in the past. We shouldn't push our luck."

Winters made a face. "It was never luck, it was skill." He spun the screen for Raffa to see. "We leave the F.A.C.s, we cut the time to point two to intercept. We'll catch them."

"What's going on?" Elise asked as she entered the command centre and settled in to her seat. "I felt movement. Are we going somewhere?"

"Friendlies just arrived from Windan, pirates changed course, we're moving to engage," Raffa said.

Elise tapped at her screen and narrowed her eyes. "They're going to Exen?"

"Trying to, we think," Winters replied. "The Comcap was about to give an order."

Raffa closed his eyes, took a deep breath, and frowned. "Send a message to *Claw* and *Stinger*, let them know *Mambaka* will be breaking formation to pursue the pirates. They are to join up with our other F.A.C.s in this system and await further orders."

"Yes, Sir."

Winters nodded. "Good choice. Might wanna let your fellow Comcap know the plan."

Raffa stared at him. "You know, that thought had never occurred to me. Thanks, Takk."

Winters looked suitably abashed. "Sorry, Sir. You know what I'm like; the excitement gets me carried away sometimes."

Raffa made a gesture to indicate no apology was really necessary, then sat down and tapped a button on his seat.

"Comcap Raffa, Kau D'varza Investigation Flotilla to commanding officer, *Vypka*. We are extremely glad to see you. The situation is this: the pirates in this system have recently changed course and seem intent on going to Exen. We cannot let this happen. Unfortunately, remaining with the Fast Attack Craft is reducing our ability to catch up before they have the chance to activate Transit. I therefore suggest *Vypka* and *Mambaka* break and go to full burn, while the remaining F.A.C.s group up and await our return. Comcap Raffa, outsign."

He hit send, then looked to the front of the command centre. "Get us to full burn, Pilot. We've got 'rats to catch."

"Sir!" the pilot replied.

Raffa felt the buzz of excitement growing within him. He may not have got as carried away as Winters - not anymore, at any rate - but there was no denying the thrill of the hunt. Judging by the reaction of the crew up on the command deck, he wasn't alone in feeling it. There was also a palpable sense of relief.

Perhaps limiting ourselves so we could stick with the F.A.C.s has worn them out. We'll need to be careful of that in the future...

"Incoming message, *Vypka*."

"That's too quick to be a reply..." Winters said quietly.

Raffa nodded his agreement. "Run it."

Winters and Raffa gave audible sighs of relief as Comcap Teq's face appeared on the screen.

"Thank the Void!" Winters murmured to himself, just loud enough for Raffa to hear.

"Comcap Teq, Kau D'varza support flotilla to Comcap Raffa, *Mambaka*. I am in command of *Vypka*, *G-Nail*, and *G-Barb*. We have orders to assist you in any way necessary. To this end, we will drive the pirate elements from this systems before joining with your forces. Upon grouping, I am to give command of the support flotilla to you, for integration into the investigation flotilla. For Kau D'varza. Comcap Teq outsign."

"Well we dodged a fucking missile with that," Winters said.

"Yes, I doubt Rexon would have been so keen to hand over command, no matter what his orders."

"Good ol' Teq," Winters said, smiling. "Remind me to get him a drink when we're home."

"You'll have to wait your turn. The first round's on me," Raffa said. "But let's plan the celebrations later. Right now, we need to come up with some kind of plan for how we're going to take down five ships with our two. Damn, I wish those F.A.C.s weren't so slow!"

"Yeah," Winters agreed, "but they are, so what other choice is there? Besides, you never know; the 'rats might play into our hands yet."

Raffa looked at him. "What do you mean?"

"Just that they're going to see us coming, and that tug of theirs has got to be slowing them down. It's unlikely they'll want to divide their force, but...

Raffa rubbed his chin. "*But* if they're desperate to get to Exen, they may leave the war-tug behind... They have to know they'd lose it, but... if Enista *was* one of them, or at least a sympathiser as it appears, they might assume that they're still in control of Freedom One despite Mendi's ships being destroyed. If that's the case, and if they break and run for the station at full speed on exiting Transit, Freedom One should be able to deal with the C-Fours easily enough, and we'll probably catch up with the M-F.A.C.s-"

Winters was shaking his head. "We can't trust F-One to do anything," he cut in. "As for the 'rats, we know their commanding officer is on the C-Four closest to us. That should be our target, not the dub-tug. If we can destroy or capture the flagship-"

"Yes, *if.* We need to think long-term, plan for what happens if they manage to overcome the malware and Transit out. If we can eliminate the war-tug here, and maybe the M-F.A.C.s too, the C-Fours won't be a powerful enough force to push anyone around whether they manage to Transit or not. But if we focus on the command C-Four and the tug jumps away, it'll be more of a threat."

Winters frowned. "I disagree, but let's get some kind of battle plan together and see what the sims suggest."

"Alright. Good. Let's -" He stopped as he caught sight of Elise staring blankly at her console. "Is everything alright, Specialist?"

"There's... something out there."

Raffa frowned. "Yes. We're chasing them-"

"Not them. Look."

She pointed at the screen. Raffa approached, scanned the information, then adopted a similar look of confusion.

"Is that... what is that?"

"Whatever it is, it's been hiding out in the debris field since we arrived."

Raffa turned to the front of the control centre. "We've got something leaving the debris field! I want to know what it is, now!"

"Yes, Sir!"

The flurry of activity stepped up a notch as scanner operators danced between consoles and read-outs.

"Sir... we're not detecting anything."

"Well runs the scans again, full sweep. There's *something* there; Specialist Rivera and I have just seen it!"

"Yes, Sir!"

Winters sat forward in his seat, frowning at his screen. "Whatever it is, it's definitely messing with our sensors. There seemed to be something, just for a tenth of a sekund or so, and then..."

"Activate interference protection!" Raffa ordered, a hint of anger in his voice. He stepped away from Elise and returned to his standing position at the fore of the command centre. "Well?"

"It's... we need to wait for the protection to come fully online, then for the scanner data to update."

"Get me a line to *Stinger*."

"Main screen, Sir?"

"Yes!"

Seconds later, the captain of *Stinger* was on screen, staring at Raffa with a slight, uncertain frown. "Problem, Sir?"

"Have you got eyes on the debris field?"

"Yes, Sir."

"Anything strange to report?"

The officer glanced off screen, spoke to someone, then returned his attention to Raffa, shaking his head. "No, Sir; our scans are... well, they're strange, but they're indicating nothing unusual or different in that area." His concern grew. "Why? Should we be seeing something?"

"*Mambaka*'s scanners detected an unidentified vessel heading away from the field."

"Sorry, Sir. We're not seeing it."

"Damnit." Winters said quietly. "Makes sense though. They're Gaitlin vessels, not Kau D'varza. They don't have the same equipment we do; not as sophisticated. And short of doing a full refit..."

"Alright, *Stinger*, you and *Claw* are to avoid that vessel and group up with Comcap Teq's F.A.C.s as quickly as possible. Keep your distance and regroup with *Mambaka* when it's appropriate."

"Will do, Sir," the captain said. His eyes narrowed. "Uhh... We can't avoid what we can't see, though, Sir, so we'd appreciate it if you could remote-share your scanner data with us."

Raffa nodded. "We'll do that for as long as we feasibly can. For Kau D'varza. Comcap Raffa, out sign."

The image faded, returning the screen to the 2D tactical map of the system. Raffa watched as *Mambaka* left *Claw* and *Stinger* behind, charging towards the predicted intercept point with the pirates. Comcap Teq's squad stayed together, it would be a little while yet before he received Raffa's orders, and longer still before they knew how he was going to react. Meanwhile the unidentified vessel was going much faster than either of them, but in the opposite direction.

"Man... And I thought *Vypka* was fast," Winters murmured, awestruck, as Raffa returned to his seat.

"Could be more misleading scanner data. Don't pay it any attention until the interference protection is fully active."

Winters shook his head. "I sure hope they're friendly. There aren't many groups in the local area with that sort of equipment. And we're one of them."

Elise cleared her throat. "Who are the others?"

"Hol have a couple of interference vessels, some places in Arabia space are rumoured to have some but..." He gave a wry smile. "We've never seen 'em."

"And the Reclaimers," Raffa added.

"Yep, them too," Winters said.

Elise sighed. "Here we go again; 'we don't know who it is, so it must be Reclaimers'."

"I'll just point out, Specialist, that what I saw on your screen didn't match any known Hol, Arabia or Yor' ship I've ever encountered, or even heard of," Raffa said.

"So that means it's a Reclaimer ship? You can be positive about that?"

He frowned. "No... but-"

"Listen, I know it doesn't look good, but even if it was Reclaimers, they might have good reason for keeping a low profile. For example, they could have been scavenging, realised what was going to happen between us and the 'rats, and simply decided to get out while they could. "

"I think you're deluding yourself," Winters said. "I get it: Reclaimers are people too. But everything we've seen, and the fact they're trying to get away under cover of an interference field... I mean, come on! You can't deny they're involved somehow!"

"I know what it looks like, Force-Commander Winters. Which is exactly why I'm not willing to jump to conclusions. Until we get to that debris field and do some proper digging around, we can't know anything for sure. " She looked at Raffa imploringly. "Comcap Raffa, tell him…"

Raffa sighed heavily. "I think he's right."

"What?"

"They've got their interference system active, so they think we can't see them sneaking away. If we'd come here with just the ships from Gaitlin, something from Arokia, or Yor', we *wouldn't* have seen them. Then there's the unknown ship type-"

"That we saw for all of a few sekunds before the interference field kicked in!"

"Specialist Rivera… Elise… I hear what you're saying, but there's no reason for it to be anyone *other* than the Reclaimers."

"I… they…" Elise rubbed her forehead. "Damnit…"

"I still want that debris field picked apart for evidence," Raffa said. "I know we've been reluctant to blame them because of what that means, but if it is them, I'm not doing this half-assed. We get proof, we show it to our neighbours, we gather allies, then we deal with it."

"Deal with the Reclaimers," Winters said, incredulously. "Deal. With. Reclaimers. Like it's that easy."

"I'm hoping if we turn up with a large enough force, they'll be willing to negotiate. We can't let them operate around here, kidnapping people, destroying ships, it's not acceptable."

"And you think waltzing into Beyema with an army of ships is going to make them negotiate? That's an act of war. If we bring fire, we better be prepared to use it."

"Force-Commander Winters is right," Elise added quietly.

"Twice in one cycle. Damn, I should quit while I'm ahead," Winters muttered.

Elise glanced in his direction but continued as though he hadn't spoken. "As much as I'd hate to fight them, if they refuse to stop doing what they're *allegedly* doing, then there's only one option." Elise shook her head. "And that's not a good position to be in."

"Couldn't we appeal to Arabia? Yor'?" Winters asked.

"They've got no stake in this as far as we know," Raffa said. "If the Reclaimers are smart, they're not doing this to Yor' or Arabian vessels. No way do they want to give any of the true powers a reason to join forces against them. Gaitlin, Hol... Arokia? They're where we'll find friends."

"Where all the people are too fractured, too unable to look after themselves."

"Maybe," Elise replied. "That's your problem. Why

hasn't Kau D'varza reached out to these places before now? Before it was too late?"

Winters threw up his hands. "Here we go. 'We shouldn't encourage others to be dependent on Kau D'varza, but why hasn't Kau D'varza reached out to them before now'. We can't win, can we? If we reach out, we're wrong for making them dependent, or we're wrong for encouraging them to look after themselves if - or rather, when - it comes to them going to war against another minor system or themselves, but if we *don't* reach out-"

"We get the idea. That's enough, Takk," Raffa said.

"I just don't know what people want, Cap! Do they want us to reach out and be a protector, friend, whatever, or do they want us to stick to Windan so we can't get accused of interference and imperialism?"

Raffa glared at him. "I said 'that's enough'." He blinked, slowly, as he turned his attention to Elise. "The fact is, we did reach out to them. We've got an alliance with several groups in Gaitlin - which is how we got the new ships - but we're not on the best of terms with Arokia, and Hol... groups there like to stick to themselves."

Winters nodded. "That's right. We couldn't bring them together unless we had something bigger to unite against. Now we do, they probably still won't go for it. We need something else."

"We do" Raffa agreed. "But what?"

"Well... after we trounce these assholes, we'll have plenty of time to think about it."

"Alright. Well, since we've still got some time before that happens, we should get some rest and see if we can work out some kind of battle plan with only two ships. Command team, you are to maintain current orders. If the situation changes, alert me, and have Comcap Teq's reply sent to my quarters. Any information regarding the unidentified ship should be sent directly to Specialist Rivera." He nodded to Winters. "Let's go."

* * *

As they disappeared from view, Elise looked back to her console, sighed, then got to work.

Don't know enough about these interference systems... I should do some research when we get home...

"Ma'am?"

Elise looked to her right and blinked away her confusion, her eyes settling on the source of the voice; a young man with a tired face and creased uniform.

"Yes?"

"With our interference protections now in place, we've been able to capture a silhouette of the mystery ship." He motioned to the console. "May I?"

Elise nodded. "Of course."

She got out of his way as he leant over the screen and tapped a few buttons. A shadowy image appeared, barely anything but darkness visible. He tapped another button, then stood up straight as the computer drew a line around the darkest patch at the middle of the screen. Elise watched, her eyes widening as the computers started detailing the straight edges and sleek design of an advanced looking vessel.

"Our closest match..." the young man said "is to a vessel Kau D'varza has designated as 'Reclaimer Clipper, Model-Two'. However, this particular model seems to be highly upgraded, and is using an extremely powerful propulsion system. At current estimates, it will be less than point two M-seks before they reach a safe location to Transit to Beyema."

"That's... impressive." Elise frowned. "Would you say these vessels have been upgraded in different ways to the Reclaimers at the R.P.Z?"

He shook his head. "I'm sorry, Ma'am, but I... we... don't have enough information on the Reclaimers in that region. Our extremely limited experience with them usually comes via travellers from those regions."

"All this data comes from third party sources? How do you know it's accurate?"

"We don't, Ma'am. It has been gathered over a significant amount of time and from various sources, though we've also rejected or questioned information that can't be corroborated or confirmed by other data."

Elise seemed satisfied by the answer. "If it's the best we've got, it'll have to do. They're a secretive bunch, so we're probably lucky to have this."

Her fingers swept across the screen, shrinking the wire-frame image of the Advanced Model-Two into the top left corner. She quickly made use of the new space by bringing up what little data they had on its equivalent from the R.P.Z.

She blew the air out of her cheeks. "A grainy image, and some estimated speed stats. You sure like to make my job difficult, eh?"

He flushed red, raising his hands. "Uh, Madam Specialist, that was not my inten-"

"Relax, I was joking. I should be thankful we've got this. Now let's see... Can you make it do the line image on this one too?"

He nodded. "Yes, Ma'am."

Elise watched as the outline appeared just as it had with the previous vessel. She then brought both images together, side by side, and tried to compare them.

"The angle makes it difficult to see similarities..."

"Ah, I mean no offence, honoured Specialist, but to a trained eye… the similarities are obvious." He pointed to a flat edge on the lower section in the second image, then to its matching counterpart at the top of the first. "Lower hull, follow it round to fore weapons… gets a bit trickier as we move along the upper hull, some major differences there… and the rear-ends are completely different; the correctional thrusters alone are twice the size. That would explain their speed capabilities."

"Wouldn't that much thrust…" Elise trailed off as she realised she didn't know what she was asking.

"If you were about to ask what I think you were, then yes; if we put thrusters like that on a Kau D'varzan vessel, it'd be torn apart in sekunds. But with the correct materials, computers running most of the systems, and a skeleton crew issued with the right equipment… it's feasible."

"Oh." She rubbed her eyes. "So, we can be pretty certain that this vessel has some connection to the Reclaimers in Beyema."

"I would say so."

"But why is it here?"

"Cutters… they tend to be scout or reconnaissance vessels. Their speed, even without the added equipment, makes them valuable for roles where getting in, getting information, and getting out are the main objectives." His shoulders dropped, just slightly. "They also work well as sentries. My best guess would be that that is this one's role."

"Sentries?"

"To watch the system. They can then take news to forces in other systems."

"In this case, Beyema." Her expression hardened. "They're going to tell the Reclaimers there what happened, and they don't think we know..." Her eyes widened. "Can we send them a message?"

"The interference may make it difficult. However, I would be willing to try, given Comcap Raffa's permission."

Elise didn't waste time bringing up the link to Raffa.

"Specialist Ri-"

"I want to send the Reclaimers a message."

Raffa coughed, nearly choking. After a few seconds, during which he visibly struggled to recover, he replied, "I'm sorry." He cleared his throat a final time. "Run that by me again."

"The unidentified ship, we're pretty sure it's Reclaimer, and they're heading back to Beyema to tell the others what happened here. If they think we can't see them but we send them a message, it'll hopefully unsettle them enough to reconsider their actions, at least for a short while. I also believe trying to get a dialogue going between our two factions is an option we need to explore."

"If we message them, they'll know we can see their ships. We lose our current tactical advantage, and they will also try to buff their systems prior to any future engagements. I'm sorry, Specialist Rivera, but from a strictly military standpoint, I cannot in good conscience approve such an action."

"What about from a diplomatic standpoint?"

"I believe the Arch-Commissioner made it very clear that in such instances, you are to use your best judgement. I will - reluctantly - approve the action on diplomatic grounds if you, as a Specialist, deem it necessary."

Elise rolled her head along the back of the seat, letting out an exasperated sigh.

"Specialist... I am reminded of an incident not so long ago, aboard a station called Kau D'varza. I think it was in the engineering bay." He spoke with a wry smirk.

"I... what's your point?"

"Specialist Trast would have held the line until reinforcements arrived, as we are taught. You took a different approach, and in so doing, saved Specialist Stone while also quelling the... issues... there."

Elise shook her head. "Specialist Trast still had to punch a guy."

"Very true. Which should serve to temper your decision. The question is, is this the time to talk, or should we be preparing to punch?"

"And if we talk..." Elise replied, "we risk weakening our punch if it comes to that."

"Got it in one."

"Damnit."

"I certainly don't envy your decision."

Elise closed her eyes.

Risk weakening one of the few positions of advantage Kau D'varza has... or attempt communication with someone who doesn't want to be - and thinks they haven't been - seen? We can see them, they don't know that... perhaps we should keep it that way.

She opened her eyes and fixed Raffa with a stern glare. "Alright. No messages will be sent."

His face took on an expression of pure relief. "Thank you. If there's anything else, please let me know."

"Of course. Enjoy your... well, whatever it is you're doing."

"Ma'am?" the technician beside her interrupted before Elise could cut the call. "I am informed that *Vypka* is accelerating. The Support Flotilla's F.A.C.s are also moving to to meet the ones we left behind. It appears as though Comcap Teq has received our message."

"Comcap Raffa? Did you get that?" Elise asked.

"I did," Raffa said, nodding. "Very good. Maintain current orders. We'll catch those damn 'rats yet."

"Yes, Sir," the technician said, and turned away while the screen went blank, leaving Elise alone with her thoughts once more.

CHAPTER TWENTY-FOUR- FOR KAU D'VARZA

"Enemy forces are coming about and changing formation... and we've got incoming communication from *Vypka*, real time"

"They're turning to fight?" Winters asked, seemingly surprised.

"Apparently so," Raffa said, as he got comfortable in his seat. "What formation?"

"Pentagon, flat. M-F.A.C.s at front, C-Fours at widest point. War-tug making up the rear-most point."

"It won't help them," Winters said, more to the command crew than to Raffa, and grinned.

"Accept communications with *Vypka*," Raffa ordered.

Teq's face instantly filled the little screen on his seat arm. "Comcap Raffa, I have reviewed the battle plan.

It is elaborate, but you have my trust. Is there anything else we should be aware of?"

"Just make sure you get the timings right, and keep your distance from the war-tug until the return run."

"It will be done. For Kau D'varza."

"For Kau D'varza," Raffa replied. The image disappeared, revealing a close up tactical view of the upcoming battle and the engagement countdown. He studied the icons, their positions, and frowned. "If they'd kept running they'd have that thin asteroid belt as a back wall. We would've been severely limited."

"They're pirates, not tacticians," Winters replied with a wave of his hand.

Raffa's eyes narrowed as he focused on the pentagon of opposing vessels. *Mambaka* was coming in at an angle, almost on direct course with the front of the furthest M-F.A.C., while *Vypka* was approaching from the opposite side at a sharper angle, aiming for the M-F.A.C. closest to *Mambaka*. *Vypka* had slowed to match *Mambaka*'s speed, and was on course to engage barely a few seconds after *Mambaka*'s initial strike.

"All weapon stations ready to engage," a voice from the command desk said. "Countdown to engagement, three hundred sekunds."

Raffa nodded an acknowledgement to Elise as she entered and found her seat with mere moments to spare before the lights switched to deep red and the command centre locked down.

"Alright," he said, addressing the command team, "if these pirates make it back to Exen, there's a good chance all our work there will be undone, and not only would that mean big problems for Kau D'varza, it also means we'd likely get tasked with going back to finish what we'd started. I don't want any of that to happen, so when we hit these assholes, I want it done quickly, cleanly, and I want them hurting so bad they'll be lucky to make it to the belt to become rock hermits, let alone Transit to another system. You have all done a phenomenal job so far, and I know you want to go home. I want to go home too, so let's make it happen by continuing to focus on getting the job done right." He paused, then delivered the salutation: "For Kau D'varza."

The command team echoed those last few words. To some, they held an important meaning; to others, it was simply a way for commanders to end their rallying speeches. Either way, Raffa's determination spread visibly around the crew, causing them to refocus. Even Elise seemed to have felt a stirring of pride.

"I have some interesting news," she said.

"Oh?" Raffa replied.

Elise nodded. "I managed to intercept some communications between the pirate vessels. It seems as if Frey is having some trouble maintaining command. They seem to agree that they 'need to deal with us', but after that I imagine they'll tear themselves apart in a power struggle."

"That might explain why those A-Shuts took off," Winters surmised. "Probably more loyal to that asshole in Exen than to whoever this Frey character is."

"Loyalty," Raffa scoffed. "Between pirates?"

"They're loyal to whoever can get them the largest paycheck," Winters said. "If that was Mendi, once Elise sent her message and they saw their plan had fallen apart, that paycheck disappeared." He waved a hand. "They all should have run at that point, to Beyema, Ekurana, Clion, Hol... but instead they went for us, and then thought better of it and tried to run for Exen." He shook his head, frowning. "Even if they figured on still controlling the station, I can't quite figure that one out."

"It's simple, really," Raffa said. "Three of those systems are a risk to their kind - especially Beyema - and there's nothing in Clion. Exen makes the most sense. With a force that size, they could retake the station once they realised they'd lost it, initiate repairs and bolster their numbers, then come for us later."

"And don't forget, when we arrived in this system, we limped along, showing them a limited capability" Elise added. "Next thing they know, they've got

Vypka to deal with and we turn to start chasing them down. They're probably still amazed that we were able to catch up so quickly. They probably thought they had plenty of time."

"One hundred sekunds!" a voice called out.

"Acknowledged!" Raffa called back.

"There's still something that doesn't add up," Winters said, abruptly. "These supposed command issues... even when it was just *Mambaka* and the F.A.C.s, we had a good chance of beating them. It wasn't guaranteed, but likely, yet they all moved to engage us on an attack that would have most certainly led to a few deaths. There was no deviation, no hesitation. *All* ships broke the blockade and burned, it wasn't a case of breaking up in ones and twos... but now you're telling us they've got command issues?" He shook his head. "People don't follow weak leaders into suicide missions. Something isn't right."

"They probably thought they had a chance when they all broke to pursue," Elise replied. "It wasn't until Comcap Teq arrived that they reconsidered, so I'd speculate that the command issues have arisen recently. They were all probably angry, but as our force's capability has grown, and time has passed, they've thought about what they're doing, what they'd been ordered to do."

Raffa nodded. "Too little, too late. Now they've been forced to fight."

"Good." Winters replied. "The more pirates we wipe out, the better. But it still doesn't make sense, boss: they have command issues, yet they *all* turn to attack, they *all* break the pursuit and run for the Exen T-point, and now they *all* turn and form up to fight..."

Raffa frowned. "What are you saying, Takk?"

Winters glanced in the direction of the command deck as a voice called, "Fifty sekunds!"

"Acknowledged!" Raffa called, scowling now as he glared at Winters. "Well?"

The Force Commander shook his head. "I don't know, boss. Probably nothing. It just seems... strange."

"You mean anything about this business hasn't been?" He straightened in his seat. "Alright. Time to see if our plan holds up."

"You can fire me if it doesn't," Winters said.

Raffa frowned again. "I doubt that'll be an issue."

"M-F.A.C. One launching missiles! Targeting... *Vypka!*"

"Number of missiles?"

"Two, Sir."

"Teq can handle a couple of missiles," Winters said. "Between evasive maneuvers and countermeasures, they'll be fine. That was just a waste of ammo."

"I wonder why they launched so early..."

"Desperation," Elise and Winters replied, in unison.

"Hm. Maybe..." Raffa's eyes were drawn back to the main screen, where the countdown timer ticked ominously.

Ten... Nine... Eight...

"Missiles targeted on *Vypka* have missed," a command technician reported, in the same moment as the pilot called "Initiating final burn!"

The ship shook slightly as *Mambaka* increased speed and alarms rang out as targeting systems recalibrated. Sweat-covered command staff worked furiously to clear warnings and adjust their settings. The sea of flashing red boxes on the screen disappeared as the time wound down. Just as it hit Zero, a large green 'Confirmed' box appeared. Raffa exhaled, unaware he'd been holding his breath.

"Weapons firing!" a voice said.

He would have berated Winters for cutting it so close, but his eyes remained transfixed on the screen as the icons flashed by one another.

Mambaka shuddered as she unleashed her payload, then suddenly shook violently, nearly throwing Winters from his seat. Raffa caught him and slammed him back down, winding him.

"Cheers, boss," Winters wheezed.

"Report!" Raffa roared, as more warnings and sirens blared out. The main screen faded, then came back online.

"Damnit!" Elise shouted, her fingers flying over her screen. "Missile Bays Four and Five appear to have been wiped out. There are hull breaches... three compartments venting atmosphere..."

"Those damn cutters were packing some serious shit," Winters said, coughing and still trying to catch his breath.

"Get the emergency crews down there, follow 'em up with medical. Re-route air flow to bypass those compartments!"

"Sir, reports confirm severe structural damage and mass fatalities in Bays Four and Five," one of the command crew reported. "They're..." She looked over at Raffa, her face pale and waxy. "They're *gone*, Sir. They're just..."

Raffa inhaled, his breath catching in his throat. "What's your name, Technician?"

"Syl, Sir. Beka Syl."

"Ever been on a combat hop before?"

She nodded. "Yes, Sir. Well, I mean..." She paused for a moment, frowning, then gave her head a quick shake, as if to clear it. "Yes, Sir. But never one like this, where... where we've..."

"Okay, Beka, I understand. Listen though: I know how

you're feeling right now, but I need you to focus. We've *got* to finish this so their sacrifices weren't in vain. We're not losing another person on this ship, but I can only keep that promise if I know what I'm dealing with. Is that clear?"

"Yes, Sir." She looked back to her screen, still visibly shaken. "Er... we have... " She shook her head, frowned, and seemed to find some kind of focus. "There's a reload issue in Missile Bay Six, reporting offline. Connection between command centre and Power Generator Two, offline. Auxiliary connections holding." A pause, then an exhalation. "Both enemy M-F.A.C.s and one cutter appear to have been eliminated."

"Alright. Very good."

"Commencing stage two," the pilot announced.

The ship twisted around on the start of a wide arc that would bring them down on the war-tug, throwing them all against their harnesses.

"Oh, *stars...!*" Elise groaned, fingers curled around her seat's arms in a death grip.

Raffa made eye contact and gave her an encouraging smile. "Still getting used to it, eh?"

"I'll never get used to this," she replied.

"*Vypka* is reporting light damage," Syl said, thrown against her harness like everyone else yet somehow unhindered by the sudden lurching. "Secondary scans indicate both enemy M-F.A.C.s and one cutter have been destroyed. One enemy cutter and the war-tug remain, though the cutter is heavily damaged and unable to continue combat."

"Four down, one big bastard to go," Winters said.

"We took a real battering there," Raffa said. "What in the Void happened?"

He pulled the screen round and brought up the playback feature. His eyes tracked *Mambaka* as it passed by the M-F.A.C. at a much reduced speed than it had in reality.

"The M-F.A.C. didn't even fire on us..."

"Probably reloading," Winters said.

Raffa then watched as they tore by the cutter.

"Damn..." he said, frowning at what he saw. "They really didn't hold back. Three mass-accs, sync-fired."

"Three? On a single side of a C-Four cutter? Someone went heavy on the upgrades."

"Yeah, you could say that. But how didn't we know what to expect? Did our scanners malfunction or something?"

"You thinking more malware?"

Raffa shook his head. "No. Maybe... Oh, I don't know. Perhaps it was a glitch caused by that interference field. Either way, that was rougher than we had any reason to expect."

"Yeah. Three mass-accs? No wonder we're aching," Winters replied, angry. "We should use our missiles, blow those bastards out of the stars..."

Raffa thought about it for a second, then nodded. "I don't see any reason to preserve munitions. In fact, we risk more by not doing so. Work up a targeting plan."

Winters turned his screen and worked for a few moments. "Done."

Raffa checked it over, then nodded. "Right. Send it to *Vypka*. Let them know what we're planning."

Winters' fingers worked some more. "And done," he replied again.

"Stage two complete! Going to fifty-percent burn to engage," the pilot called.

Winters smiled viciously and tapped his screen a final time. "Orders delivered and acknowledged, boss." He glanced at Raffa and gave a sly grin. "I fucking hate pirates."

"You and me both."

The countdown timer on the main screen ticked down again, before *Mambaka* rumbled, releasing its missile payload barely a few seconds prior to the following shakes of return fire. This time, there was no-one thrown from their seat, no loud bangs or sudden shocks. On screen, the icon for *Mambaka* swept past and away from a marker showing a heavily damaged ship, before *Vypka* crossed over their path and finished the job.

"No additional damage to report," the still-waxy-looking technician said. "Enemy cutter destroyed. Scans also indicate the war-tug is too damaged to continue fighting. All enemy vessels disabled." She paused, listening to something, then sat back and smiled. "Sir, war-tug indicates their unconditional surrender."

Elise punched the air. "Yeah!"

Raffa grinned. "Signal our acknowledgement, and secure from battle stations."

"Yes, Sir," she said.

After a few seconds, the lights returned to their normal sterile white glow and the locks cycled. Raffa was unsurprised to see Syl rise from her seat and stride quickly, if a little unsteadily, through the door.

Poor kid...

"Excellent work, team," he said, looking around them and making eye contact where he could. "Force-Commander Winters, get down to the weapon stations and get things organised. I want a full assessment. I'll be down as soon as I've wrapped up here."

"Sure thing, boss," Winters said, unbuckling his harness and heading for the door.

Raffa pulled his screen round and brought up a link to *Vypka*.

"Well executed, Comcap Teq."

"Thank you, Comcap Raffa," he replied, though he didn't look happy. "Scanners indicate you took some serious damage in the first engagement. Is there anything we can do to assist?"

"Repair your own damage first, then we'll talk."

"Very well. And what of this remaining ship? I'm told they've indicated their surrender."

"*Mambaka* will try to recover as many survivors as we can - if we can - then eliminate the ship at range. It's drifting, defenceless... Even I could hit it, and you know how bad my aim is."

Teq grinned. "That I do. Very well, we shall follow you back to the F.A.C.s and await further orders."

"Thanks, Teq. I owe you one."

He nodded. "The pleasure is all mine."

Elise glanced over as Raffa sat back and sighed. "You two have a history?"

"Some. A few missions. Teq's an old hand at this...

loyal to Kau D'varza. Good bloke at heart."

"So I keep hearing... but if he's the more senior, why was he told to relinquish control to you?"

Raffa shrugged. "I suppose Kau D'varza saw this as my operation. His given mission was clearly to support me. Besides..." He sighed. "Teq is extremely good at *following* intricate... uh... complex orders, but he hasn't got much vision to come up with that sort of thing on his own. It's a shame really: Command usually sends him off to pick up ships or protect convoys, but he's worth more than that. His loyalty alone deserves more than that." He glanced back to Elise, then tensed. "Sorry, Ma'am, I... I sometimes forget you're Command."

Elise smirked. "Oh, you can talk freely around me Comcap, I consider us friends. Besides, you've got a stronger ear than mine if you wanted to change things in Command."

"That is true, but fortunately for them, I don't want to change anything. I just wish Teq got the respect he deserved."

"If it helps... he's a hero in my eyes."

Raffa thought about it for a few seconds, then smiled. "And mine. Alright... let's wrap this mess up and get to that debris field. I want answers." He pointed to the main screen, specifically at Windan on the stellar systems overview. "And then, I want to go home."

CHAPTER
TWENTY-FIVE-
THANATOS
CALLING

"It's... by the Void..."

Elise closed her eyes, unable to keep them on the screen. The debris field ahead of them was truly vast, almost beyond comprehension.

How many ships? How many people have been kidnapped? This is terrible...

She felt a wave of fear washing over her as she realised they were getting ever closer. For a brief second, she worried that *Mambaka*, *Vypka* and the four F.A.C.s wouldn't be able to defend themselves if they were chosen as the next victims.

No. We've got a powerful force. And the best way I can help is by doing my job. This is part of why we're here. To get answers. And that... that mess out there... is where we're gonna find them.

She opened her eyes again, focusing on her console with renewed conviction. Her fingers danced across the screen as she brought up the reports being fed to the command core via the remaining sensors and scanners. She tried to ignore the looming ships on the larger screen as she scanned report after report.

"No doubt about it," Raffa finally said, "most of these are gen-overloads."

"How can you tell?" Elise asked.

"I've seen it before, a long time ago. See it enough times, you start to recognise patterns. It's the easiest way to destroy a ship once you've taken control. No waste of munitions, no risk to nearby ships because they've got time to get away, and best of all, it doesn't leave much evidence behind, just a hulk and several million small pieces, endlessly drifting."

Elise felt something cold crawl down her back and shivered. "Thank the Void and all the stars you didn't become a doctor," she muttered. "With a bedside manner like that..."

He grinned, but turned away quickly as Syl called out.

"Sir! We're detecting an unusual mass!"

"Another ship?" he asked.

"Yes, Sir, on the edge of the field." She leaned forward,

squinting at her screen, before sighing and sitting back. "Further scans indicate it's powered down."

Elise blew the air out her cheeks. "Is it safe?"

"Maybe, Ma'am. We won't know until we power it back up."

"It could be a trap," Winters said, quietly.

"It could, but it could be a trove of information," Elise replied, her voice equally quiet.

"Either way, we've got to check it out," Raffa said, returning to his seat and bringing the screen around. "Profile?"

"Frigate, Class Five. Profile indicates... Thanatos?"

"Thanatos?" Raffa frowned. "Where in the Void is that?"

"It's beyond Ar-Ka'en space," Elise replied. "Leeshan, Rystar, Thanatos. Parts from each have formed an independent alliance of sorts."

Another cold shiver ran down her spine, but this time, she didn't know why.

"Something the matter, Specialist Rivera?"

"I guess..." She stopped, shook her head. "Look, that ship is a long... *very* long, way from where it was built.

You'd be lucky to see Thanatosian vessels at Yurnto, so to find one in Grinda..." Her face flushed with sudden anger. "More questions! Always more. Fucking. Questions!"

"Wait," Raffa replied. "Thanatos... the Independent Alliance... if we presented this data as evidence of hostile Reclaimer activity..." He held up a hand to forestall Elise's immediate and inevitable objection. "*Assuming* it *is* the Reclaimers... Would they help us?"

Elise shook her head. "No clue. We take this ship back to them, they'd probably appreciate it and give us something in return for our efforts, but Rystar... They're the sort of 'leading part' of the alliance, and they've got a great relationship with the Reclaimers at the R.P.Z. They're like Yurnto: on the edge, just on better terms with their neighbours."

"Squeezed between the Reclaimers and Ar-Kaos." Winters lowered his head. "Sounds like a nightmare."

"It isn't so bad, really," Elise replied, with a hint of coldness in her voice. "If... *if* these Reclaimers at Beyema are a 'rogue faction', then the Reclaimers at the R.P.Z. might be willing to get involved, especially if Rystar asked them... but you'd need to convince Rystar first, who would then need to convince Leeshan. And that's always assuming you've already got Thanatos on-side, and ship or no ship, it's far from certain that you would."

"Politics," Raffa mumbled with no obvious emotion.

"I say we try. This alliance might be our only hope."

"Maybe," Winters said, squirming in his seat. "But if this profile is correct, that ship... damn, boss, it's an absolute weapon. If we take this back to Thanatos and they *don't* help us, we'd have gone a long way for nothing. I say we salvage it and keep it, if we can; use it to bolster our own forces."

Elise rolled her eyes. "Perhaps we should figure out if we *can* take it before making all these grand plans. I hate to say it, but what happens if you turn that thing on and the generator suddenly overloads?"

Raffa shook his head. "It takes time. First the ship needs to power up, then the engines need to reach max output, even if they're disconnected from the thrusters and main drives. Safety features then need to be disengaged, before a slow climb to an overload."

"But, we shouldn't ignore the fact there's other stuff we need to look out for," Winters said. "Traps, other ships waiting for us to take the bait..."

"Is there any way for us to drag it away from the field?" Elise asked.

"Unfortunately not," Raffa replied. "*Mambaka* isn't equipped to tug. Neither is *Vypka*."

"Almost seems a shame we didn't try to salvage that war-tug then, right? Instead of just using it for target practice, I mean."

Raffa shook his head again. "Wouldn't have done any good. There's no way we could have repaired it enough out here, nor could we have towed it to Grinda Station - as I said, we're not equipped to tug. As for putting a skeleton crew aboard to Transit it home... forget that. No one would have volunteered even if I'd asked them to, and I certainly wouldn't have *ordered* anyone aboard."

"So, we need to send forces," Winters said, summing up. "I'll get a team put together. Send them over on a F.A.C."

"And while you're doing that, we'll keep scanning this field for any more surprises."

Winters nodded and headed for the door, an action which prompted Elise to get to her feet.

"Wait up, I'm coming too."

Winters turned in surprise, then looked at Raffa. "Boss?"

"You're sure you want to be part of this, Specialist? I'll remind you we have absolutely no idea what to expect," Raffa said, his eyes fixed on Elise.

"No," she said. "But I... now I've come this far I *need* to be there; I have to know what happened, and why."

"And what if there is no 'why'? What if you find the Reclaimers - or whoever - did it just because they could?"

She took a deep breath and blew it back out, slowly

and evenly, with her eyes fixed on a neutral point on the deck between them until she was ready to meet his gaze again.

"Then I'll know you, and especially Winters, were right, at least as far as this group of Reclaimers were concerned. It doesn't change the fact that you've figured the others all wrong."

Raffa looked at her for a long moment, long enough for her to feel distinctly uncomfortable.

And this is how he can make me feel as a Specialist. Imagine how it'd be if I was a raw recruit...

"Alright," he said, "you go. *But* you are not to interfere with Force-Commander Winters' plans or second-guess his orders, and you're to stay safely behind the firing line at all times. Have I made myself fairly clear?"

Her mouth quirked into a smile. "Yes, *Sir!*" she said, tossing a mock salute.

"Very well. Then I wish you every success." He smiled, wryly. "*Ma'am.*"

* * *

Raffa stood on the command deck, his eyes on the patchwork of grainy, too-dark images being fed from the force's helmet cams as they breached the airlock onto the frigate. They entered, cautiously and quietly, and Raffa could just make out the perfectly aligned panels and hex-panel flooring as their weapon-lights danced over the various surfaces.

"Okay scouts, do your thing," Winters said, his voice slightly distorted by the mics. "Tyra, head forward, try to find the command centre. Alenki, you look for the engine room. Randa, Nomez, take your teams and check out any storage areas, generator rooms or secondary ops centres. Assault squads, watch their backs. Support, make sure you fill any spaces and stand ready. We check and double-check *everything*. All clear?" There was a pause, and Winters' camera panned around as he looked for gestures of assent. "Alright then people, let's move."

There were slight sounds of movement and nervous, but controlled breathing as the scouting teams spread out, accompanied by more grainy shots of Thanatosian concepts of attractive design.

Obviously human, but in some ways, so alien. It's enough to give you a headache, Raffa mused.

"Damn..." Winters said through the headset, his voice sounding slightly muffled. Raffa's eyes automatically shot to the feed from Winters' camera, but there was nothing save more Thanatosian design.

"What is it?" Raffa snapped.

"Oh... er, nothing, boss. I was just thinking, Specialist Rivera wasn't kidding; these guys know how to build a ship."

"You've been there about five sekunds..."

"Yeah, but quality speaks for itself. Pretty damn

loudly too from where I'm standing."

Raffa ground his teeth. "Just find the power, and stay alert."

"You got it, boss."

"The thing that's bothering me is, it doesn't look like they put up a fight," Elise said, sounding worried. "*Any* fight."

"Not much you can do once they're on board... especially Reclaimers," Winters replied.

"I've seen their abilities. There is truth to some of the rumours in that regard," she conceded.

"The real question is, why didn't they scuttle this one like the others?" Raffa said.

"That's bugging me, too," she responded. "I was thinking maybe Thanatos built it so you *couldn't* blow it up."

Raffa frowned. "You mean they built in failsafes the Reclaimers couldn't override?"

Elise's camera feed bobbed, an indication that she had nodded. "That's my best guess. Doesn't explain why they didn't blow it with missiles though."

"Evidence. It would have been extremely difficult to find, but missiles leave an easily read story," Winters said.

"Can we set the scanners to look for that sort of thing?"

"They've been looking for that and much more since we arrived. If there's something out there, and if the debris field isn't obscuring it too badly, we'll find it."

"That's a lot of if's."

"Unfortunately, it's the best we've got," Raffa said. "Which is why it's so important we capture this ship intact. Regardless of what we do with it, it should have information we can use."

"That freighter should have had more information too," Elise replied. "If they've done the same here as they did with the freighter…"

"Force-Commander Winters. It's Scout Alenki. We've found the engineering department, Sir."

"Right. Good work. I'm on my way," Winters replied.

Raffa watched the feeds as Winters, Elise and a pair of engineering technicians headed aft, occasionally receiving pointers from watchful soldiers *en route*, until they arrived in a large, almost cavernous room.

Winters, ever the soldier, looked around with his weapon raised. "Looks pretty different to our ships," he muttered. His light danced over a console with a flashing light. "Looks pretty different to everything actually. Get me those techs in here!"

Raffa held his breath as the technicians strode forward, Winters' feed displaying excited faces covered in sweat behind their visors. One approached the console, checked it out with a handheld scanner, then pressed the flashing button.

Every soldier stood to as the lights came on, preparing for automated defences and warning sirens. Of which there were none.

"Report," Winters demanded.

"Engineering department looks good, Force-Com. We're not seeing any problems."

"Okay," he said, looking at the smiling technicians. "Techs, see what the deal is with the engines."

"Sir," they replied, in unison.

Elise shook her head, the camera blur forcing Raffa to look away from *Mambaka*'s main screen in a hurry. "It can't be that easy."

Winters glanced at her and smiled. "Why not? It's about time we caught a break." His face became serious again. "You're right, though. That *was* a bit... well..."

Raffa scratched his chin. "Specialist, do you remember when we were in that meeting, and you suggested that someone left the data on the freighter for... someone, us or otherwise, to find?"

"I do. You think this is more of the same? Follow the trail, find another ship, see what they want us to see?"

"Why not?"

"Because if it is, this ship's a powerful thing to risk giving to potential enemies," she said.

Raffa's eyes narrowed. "Possibly. But let's not forget we don't know enough about it yet. Could be the first time we take it into real combat, our 'enemies' take control and use it to destroy us without having to fire a shot."

"True." The audio turned staticky as she sighed. "If I were you, I'd go over this thing with a micron scanner."

"A sentiment which I share. Don't worry though; Winters will be thorough."

"No doubt, but as you've just pointed out, we can't take anything for granted. If this thing has been left deliberately and does contain more info, we need to seriously consider why we're being shown certain things."

"Er, we're having a little bit of trouble…" one of the technicians said. "Neither of us can read Thanatosian… or whatever this is."

"Show me," Elise replied going to the console.

Winters also approached and made sure Raffa got a

clear shot. The console, now lit up brightly, was displaying a welcome screen of sorts.

"What in the Void is that?" Raffa asked.

"Writing of some sort, boss, but what sort... only the Void knows," Winters replied.

"Specialist Rivera, can you make anything of it?"

She studied it closely for a few seconds, then nodded.

Void, I wish she'd stop doing that!

"I think so," she said. "It's close enough to an Ar-Ka'en language, as well as Standard, that I can figure it out. Hit the second option down."

"What's that?"

"Settings... or 'Opshuns', as they have it."

Winters nodded to the tech. As he tapped the second option, a new menu appeared.

"Okay... fourth one down... 'Langch.'"

"What's that?"

"Not sure, without pressing it and finding out."

She extended a finger and tapped the option. A list of words, some appearing in very different scripts, unrolled down the page.

"Whoa! Whoa! Easy, Elise! Be careful with what you're pushing, there! One mistake and you could easily vent the atmosphere!"

"Force-Commander Winters, I appreciate your concerns, but I *do* know the difference between changing the interface and turning off the life support. But since you clearly don't trust me, I'll hand it over to you. Press the button. Fourth one down."

Raffa could sense Winters rolling his eyes even without seeing him.

"Do it, Takk" he said.

Winters sighed. "Right, boss." He took a breath. "Well, here we go, then."

His finger jabbed the button Elise had pointed out and another menu appeared.

"Right…" Elise said, peering at the screen. "Top one. It's for Standard."

"Oh… right, thank you, Specialist."

She feigned a smile. "You're very welcome."

"You're pretty good with languages," Raffa said, watching the monitor as the technicians worked away.

"Some of them," she replied. "Ar-Ka'en is easy. Thanatosian and Rystari… I think a lot of their settlers came from Ar-Kaos and surrounding systems. It's a bit of a mess, but most of their words are similar enough."

"And Kau D'varzan?"

"A little trickier... I made it a priority to learn it when I moved there."

Raffa watched in silence as Winters and his teams conducted another sweep of the ship, this time with the power on. Access to new areas had opened up, allowing a much more thorough search. Raffa was able to see the ship from several angles, and soon understood what Winters had meant by quality. He studied the crisp white and grey corridors in awe, trying to estimate what it would cost Kau D'varza to build such a vessel. The answer, of course, was too much.

Suddenly, Elise started to laugh.

"What?" he asked.

"Zeled was all 'Make sure you bring my ships back in one piece.' Now look at us."

"Ha. Yeah. All ships will be going home, and now it looks like we'll be taking them another one. At this rate, we're gonna run out of places to put them all."

"Not a bad problem to have given the current situation."

Raffa looked at Winters' feed as the force-commander spoke up.

"Winters here. All scouts report zero activity. Vessel is secured, no hostiles found, nothing unusual outside of a missing crew. Awaiting orders."

"Can any of our pilots fly it?"

There was a rapid exchange between Winters and the pilot crews back on board the F.A.C.

"They're willing to give it a try," he finally reported.

Raffa sighed. "Then I suppose that's the best I can ask for. Force-Commander Winters, I am placing you in command of that vessel. Return to the formation and await further orders."

"Yes, Sir. Thank you."

Another small victory...

"Comcap Raffa, I'd like to remain here, too. I can help with translation, if any more is needed, and I can look for, and hopefully find, a lot more information."

"Yes, that would be nice. But are you sure you really want to be stuck on that thing for a while?"

He could hear the smile in her voice. "Positive. I'll return to *Mambaka* once I've done what I can here."

"Very well," he said, then raised his voice to address *Mambaka*'s pilots. "Alright, take us to Grinda station once Force-Commander Winters signals he's ready to join us."

"Yes, Sir!"

"Sir," Syl said. "We're registering ships at the default Transit point for Clion."

He glanced at her and raised an eyebrow. "Number? Profile?"

She squinted at her screen. "Our scanners aren't yet at optimal performance, Sir, but it looks like... four. Signals indicate they're from... Kau D'varza? Merchant vessels?"

Raffa grinned. "They made it. Alright, broadcast a message welcoming them to the system, then inform them they are to rendez-vous with us at the station prior to being escorted back to Windan."

Syl looked up and gave him a relieved smile. "Yes, Sir!"

* * *

"No, you listen to me." Tyra's face was red with anger as she spoke to the poor unfortunate who had answered the communication from *Mambaka*. "This system is in bad shape. You won't survive out here much longer. I don't care what your boss says, either you send that data, or the next time pirates or whoever else parks up here, scaring off your traffic, Kau D'varza will sit back and watch." The harassed-looking man saw his chance and drew breath to reply, but Scout Tyra waved her hand dismissively. "Save your air. I'm not interested in what you've got to say. Get me Rulf Tyra, and get him *now*."

Elise was standing beside her, tense, as the station administrator scurried away. Tyra turned to her with a grin.

"Threats," she said, almost proudly. "Practically all they understand. It's why I left, you know? Always had to watch your back, couldn't trust anybody, not even your own family, friends... Kau D'varza isn't like that. It's better."

Elise nodded in agreement. She'd known nothing of Grinda's inhabitants or their society, but this one conversation had been enough to convince her that Kau D'varza was, indeed, infinitely preferable.

Another face appeared on the screen; older, harder, with enough similarity to the Kau D'varzan Scout for Elise to surmise that she was looking at Tyra's father.

"What the fuck do you want?"

Tyra smiled sweetly at Elise and turned back to the screen. "Some pocket money, and a unicorn."

"If you're gonna make jokes, I've got bet-"

"Yeah, yeah. Good to see you too. Look, this isn't a social call. Kau D'varza just fought off a group of pirates, and there's a debris field out here that puts colliding planets to shame. What's the deal?"

Rulf blinked. "They're gone?"

"Who?"

"The pirates."

"Yeah. We crippled their T-cores and chased 'em down." Her expression hardened. "Lost a lot of good people doing it, too, so..." She paused, and grimaced. "We need your help. Surveillance data, scans, sweeps, anything you can provide."

He sighed, the hard outer shell falling away. "I... I'm sorry to hear about your friends, Chal. Sincerely, I am... But we got problems of our own, and while I appreciate you getting rid of those dicks, if we send you anything... well, a handful of pirates'll be the last of our problems."

Tyra frowned. "What are you talking about?"

Rulf merely looked at her for a moment, then sighed."If we send you anything, this station won't be here the next time you visit. In fact, we'd probably be part of that debris field."

"If that's true, you need to get out. Come with us, back to Kau D'varza."

"I thought you said this wasn't a social call?"

Chal huffed. Elise decided it was supposed to be a laugh.

"It isn't, but the more you talk, the more I'm hearing emergency. I can't leave you here if you're in danger."

"You of all people should know you're never out of danger, here."

Tyra blinked, slowly, her patience clearly running out. "Under threat, then. You know what I mean."

He nodded, any hint of amusement leaving his expression. "I do. There's been some talk of... escaping... for a while, but nothing's ever been decided, let alone done." He straightened up, preparing to rise. "I'll ask the others. Are you... Are you sure about this, Chal?"

"I'll need to talk to the Comcap about it, and if we take you back to Kau D'varza you will have to adjust, but... yes, I'm serious."

"Leave the station..." Rulf said, almost to himself.

"You have to," Tyra replied, firmly. "Even if it's just for a little while. You can always come back when things calm down."

"I... I will discuss this with the others. Please let me know what your commander says."

"Good luck. Scout Tyra, outsign."

Elise sighed as the conversation ended. "It's going to be cramped..."

"Not with our new ship it isn't," Tyra replied, "and those merchants can pick up any slack in return for our escort services. But that's not my concern. He said they were in trouble from something other than pirates, something that obviously scares them."

"You sound like you've got some theories."

"Maybe, Ma'am, but it isn't my place to speculate."

"No..." Elise said, thoughtfully. "Perhaps that Thanatosian ship can provide the answers the people on that station aren't willing to. Or maybe if we get them back to the safety of Kau D'varza, they'll talk." She grinned. "Package it like that to Comcap Raffa, as though helping them would get us the information we might need to piece all this together, and I'm sure he'd jump at it."

"I'm not good at selling anything," Tyra said, shaking her head. She looked up at Elise, hopefully. "Will you come with me? You know how to speak to him, and as much as I might dislike the people and the culture on that station, this is my family's lives we're talking about here, plus whoever wants to come with them."

"I think I can do that," Elise said, with a smile. "Come on, before your dad comes back."

* * *

Raffa yawned, the monotony of reviewing after-action reports and information relating to their time in the system tiring him more than the actual battle had done. He had just finished reading through another dry analysis when the door alarm buzzed.

Thank the Void for small mercies...

"Come in," he called.

The door opened, permitting Elise to step over the threshold.

"Good evening, Comcap."

"Good evening to you too, Specialist. To what do I owe the pleasure?" He glimpsed at Tyra lurking in the corridor. "Scout Tyra? Don't just stand there, come in, close the door."

Tyra did as she'd been told and took up a position beside, and slightly behind, Elise, doing her best not to shuffle self-consciously.

Raffa looked between the pair of them. "So, what *can* I do for the two of you?"

"We've made contact with the active station here in Grinda," Elise replied. "Unfortunately, they're not willing to give us any information, since they fear that doing so will result in their destruction. Therefore, we'd like your permission to bring those who wish to leave aboard our vessels, so we can offer them aid and shelter at Kau D'varza. If we talk to them once they're in a place of safety, we might get more information out of them. Something scanners can't tell us."

Any relief he'd felt at the interruption had vanished. He blew the air out of his cheeks and frowned. "I didn't want people, Specialist Rivera, I wanted information." He raised his hand as Elise went to reply. "However, I cannot deny that they will be useful, and we certainly can't leave them here if they face a mortal threat. How credible…" He stopped mid-sentence. "What a dumb question that almost was. Anyone who's seen this system knows how credible the threat is." He sighed. "Alright. I will make preparations. How many people are we looking at?"

Tyra bit her lip. "It could be as many as fifty, Sir."

Raffa raised his eyebrows and stared at her. "Fifty?"

"Yes, Sir, but… my recommendation would be to send additional forces to the Thanatosian vessel, and potentially to the merchant ships too, in order to create the necessary space aboard *Mambaka*."

"Thank you, Scout Tyra, let me worry about the logistics." He sat back in his seat, rubbing his chin thoughtfully. "Alright, I'll get it sorted. Make sure they're ready to go as soon as possible. The merchants arrive in less than point two M-seks, and I want to be ready to leave by then."

Elise nodded. "We'll get it done. Thank you, Comcap."

"Specialist, I really hope this is worth the trouble."

She frowned. "With respect, Comcap, saving lives is *always* worth the trouble."

* * *

Mambaka's airlock opened with a hiss, blowing cold air onto Elise's face and hands. She shivered and tried to focus on the small crowd of people crammed into the small space. Two of Raffa's soldiers motioned them forward to a hastily erected check-point. She watched as they sheepishly approached and were signed in and checked by more soldiers.

"Welcome," she said, smiling as the first of the refugees passed by to gather at the other end of the short corridor. Tyra stood beside her, nodding the occasional welcome as she looked down the line, scanning faces until she finally saw the one she was looking for.

"Hey!" she called, pushing through the crowd toward Rulf.

"Hey kid," he replied, his voice carrying a note of defeat.

"Look, I know this isn't easy, but Kau D'varza... it's a good place. We can protect you until the threat is over."

He looked at her dubiously. "That's a tall order, kid."

Tyra flashed a determined smile. "You know me. We'll get it done."

"Well if anyone can..." His eyes wandered the corridor, finally resting on Elise. She gave him a respectful smile then turned back to welcoming the others, pretending not to have overheard the conversation.

"Who's the suit?" he asked, indicating Elise with a nod.

Tyra glanced around. "Oh, that's El- I mean, Specialist Rivera. Good person. Probably the only reason we're able to do this. She spoke to the Comcap for me."

"Then I guess I owe her my thanks."

"You can worry about all that later. Right now, you need to get checked in, then join up with the group at the end to be taken to your... uh.... 'quarters'."

"That doesn't sound like it's going to be too comfortable."

"It's just until we get back home."

Rulf afforded her a sidelong look and half-smiled. "Home, eh?"

Tyra nodded. "Yes. Home. Finally found that place to put my head down... Somewhere to call my own."

Her father's face softened, a genuine smile on his lips. "Nice one, kid. I knew you would."

* * *

"Boarding teams across the flotilla are reporting all forty-seven passengers have been documented and settled," Technician Syl said.

"Very good," Raffa replied, his eyes drifting to the main screen. An organised mass of icons lingered around the station, pointing towards the Transit point back to Windan. He'd organised the flotilla into a rough sphere, with the merchant ships at the centre, where they'd be best protected by the F.A.C.s, the Thanatosian frigate, *Vypka* and *Mambaka*.

He tapped the button on his seat arm. "To all vessels in the Investigation Flotilla. I am extremely happy with all we've accomplished here, and I have no doubt that the information we have recovered, the things we've experienced, and the vessel we have taken temporary custody of, will give us plenty to study. For the time being, however, I am happy to say it's time to go home. *Mambaka* will shortly begin accelerating. All vessels are to maintain relative position to *Mambaka* as we navigate to the Windan T-point. That is all and, again, thank you. Comcap Raffa, outsign."

He sat back and closed his eyes, a slight smile on his face. He opened them again a few seconds later, when Elise cleared her throat.

"Specialist?"

"I was just thinking... it's weird, Winters not being here to give you his feedback on your talks."

"Yes. It's a small blessing, I know," Raffa replied, then got to his feet and approached the command deck. "Alright people, this is it. Bring *Mambaka* up to ninety-percent of what the merchants are capable of and get us home." He grinned. "Our work in this sys-

503

tem is complete."

There were various murmurs, smiles and sounds of approval as the noise from the engines grew louder.

Raffa went back to his seat, taking a moment to look over at Elise. "It *is* complete, isn't it?" he asked. "There's nothing we've overlooked or forgotten?"

She nodded. "I think so. I can't help but wonder what other questions we're going to find in amongst all the answers, but we've got people to talk to now, another ship to investigate and potentially use, even if only as a bartering device. It came at a heavy cost, but their sacrifices... all our sacrifices... made this possible."

"There's still the question of who did this," he said. "Not to mention that ship..."

"It'll keep. If it was a group of Reclaimers, there's not a lot we could have done in any case, most likely even with *Vypka*." She eased back in her seat. "And on the bright side, we've taken down a load of pirates, helped to liberate Freedom One, and potentially saved the lives of everyone on board Grinda Station. I'd call that a success."

"Indeed. And once word gets around of what we've done here, hopefully we'll have made our neighbouring systems just a little bit safer too."

Mambaka steadily increased speed, leading the formation away from Grinda Station. It was a sight to behold for Raffa, and he could barely imagine what Commissioner Zeled would have to say when they returned with everything they'd discovered.

CHAPTER TWENTY-SIX - MINING COPPER

Kaska's datapad hummed for barely a second before she snatched it off of the pillow beside her and answered it.

"Stone."

"Woah!" Coda Trast replied. "At least give it chance to beep!"

"I couldn't sleep."

"Well, then you might be relieved to know eleven ships appeared in-system a few kiloseks ago."

"Eleven?" Kaska sat up, alarmed

"Hey, hey, relax! It's them, Kas; it's *Mambaka*. They're home."

Oh, stars! Joseph... Thank the Void!

"We're still waiting on Comcap Raffa's report," Trast continued, "but... they did it, Kas they made it."

Kaska was already on her way to the clean room. "I'm coming to Command. Are you there now?"

"Yeah, about to get a snack. Meet you at the vendor?"

Kaska nodded. "Sounds good."

The hurried journey through the dimly lit corridors took barely a few minutes, and Kaska was almost jogging as she arrived outside the entrance to the command core.

"Hey!" Trast called out, a packet of grilled vegetables in her hand.

"I didn't notice the time, otherwise I'd have asked, but what are you doing here so late?" Kaska asked, catching her breath.

"Working extra time. I fancy a holiday, need the creds." She motioned for Kaska to follow her back inside.

"Anywhere nice?"

"Thought I might take a trip to Oceanside City in Gaitlin. I think I need to get away from all this for a while."

"You and me both," Kaska replied. "Been pretty stressful recently..."

"We all deserve a break, but you know what'd happen to this place if we all decided to take off for a spell."

"I dread to think."

"Hm. It's we Specialists who keep this place running, right? Without us, all the Commissioners and Arch-Commissioners in the galaxy wouldn't know what to do."

They passed through the door into the command core proper. A few of the other specialists on duty nodded to Kaska before returning to their work, while Coda settled in at her console and tapped the screen.

"Here."

A map of the system popped up, showing ten Kau D'varza transponder signals heading for the station along with one unknown.

"No doubt about it," Kaska replied, "those are ours. And with a prize, too."

"Yep. We should receive a report soon. It'll be interesting to hear what happened."

"I'm glad Comcap Teq is with them. I worried we were sending them into a trap."

"A trap he'd have been prepared for. And look, they're not completely unharmed. Looks like some patch repairs on both *Mambaka* and *Vypka*. They've evidently been in a scrap or two."

Kaska closed her eyes. "They already lost someone in Exen, I'd hate to hear of more…"

Trast sniffed. "Obviously it's never nice, but… well, I don't wanna sound cold, but when they signed up we made it as clear as we could that they might end up giving their lives to protect Kau D'varza, and we did our best to dissuade anyone not fully committed to that idea. Their families will be greatly compensated, they will be honoured, and their sacrifices remembered whenever we celebrate our freedom, but ultimately, they knew the risk; the choice was theirs. Besides, we lost one. The pirates lost a fleet."

"You're looking at this like it's just numbers," Kaska replied, "Laniz Rotik was a person, and anyone else they've lost were people."

"I know. But we've got to look at this professionally. When we're at home, behind closed doors, that's when we can process it properly." Coda's eyes narrowed. "You taught me that, Kas. Please don't start getting sentimental just because you and Raffa are seeing each other now."

"I don't-"

Coda raised her hand. "You told me before they left that this mission only worried you a little bit, yet you've been overusing the Krash beds, which means you've been having a lot of trouble sleeping, and I dare say Ikarus has been covering for you, too. But Raffa goes on lots of missions. The question is, can you really handle that?"

Kaska sighed. "That's not the real question, though, is it?"

"Oh?"

"The real question is, am I willing to end things with him just so I can put up with this?"

Coda shook her head. "Damn, girl, you got it bad."

Kaska said nothing. What else could she say? Up to now, her duty to Kau D'varza had been all: all she wanted, all she needed, and now... Now there was something more, and unexpected. Now, suddenly, there was Joseph, not merely Comcap Raffa, not merely just another soldier at her - and therefore Kau D'varza's - disposal. Because that was the real root of the problem, wasn't it? In her eyes, Comcap Joseph Raffa no longer was disposable.

And I either have to find a way to balance duty and my feelings out, or quit one or the other.

The screen flickered and the image updated.

"Hey, what's that?" Kaska said, pointing, thankful for something to change the subject.

Coda tapped the screen, zooming in on the newcomers. "Two unidentified ships at the designated 'safe area' from Munry."

"Munry? There's nothing there. It's a dead-sys."

"Don't see many come that way, that's for sure."

"You think they could be pirates? Their turning up so soon after the arrival of our ships..."

"Yeah, I get you, but it's very, very doubtful. For one thing, how could they have known?"

Kaska shook her head. "I still don't like it. Have you got a profile, a type?"

"Negative. Sensors aren't receiving information for a profile." Trast tapped the screen, marking it up. "I'll keep an eye on them and get in touch when we can."

"Make it a *close* eye, Coda."

"Of course. We gotta be careful not to start seeing monsters everywhere though, Kas." A notification popped up on the screen and she smiled. "Ah! You'll find this more interesting; Comcap Raffa's report just arrived."

"Thank the Void..." Kaska whispered. "Run it."

Coda didn't hesitate. Barely a second later, Raffa's face appeared.

"This is Comcap Raffa of the Kau D'varza Investigation Flotilla, reporting."

"He looks worn out..." Coda murmured, to which

Kaska frowned and nodded.

"I am happy to report that our mission was mostly a success," Raffa's message continued. "I have many things I need to explain, but... now is not the time, and I will try to be as brief as I can. Following on from my report from Exen, we arrived in the Grindan system to find hostile forces waiting on the default Transit point from Windan. We sent them footage of our work in Exen, and this angered them enough to pull away from their ambush point. Shortly thereafter, Comcap Teq arrived, and the pirates ended their pursuit and ran for the Transit point to Exen, their systems having been compromised by a version of the virus that had been uploaded to our ships' mainframes. We gave chase, and were eventually made to split our forces to engage the pirates. *Mambaka* and *Vypka* took part in that engagement, while the F.A.C.s formed a group of their own."

Kaska sighed. "So there was another fight..."

"We took casualties and suffered some fairly extensive damage. However, the pirate presence in Grinda has been eliminated, at least for now. Furthermore, we were able to confirm the existence of a debris field, and while we were unable to confirm the precise cause, we detected a Reclaimer style vessel leaving the field under cover of an interference field. Given the damage we had already sustained and the unknown capabilities of the suspect vessel, we allowed them to believe their attempted 'silent run' had been successful. We also believed the inhabitants of Grinda Station to be under threat, and approached them with an offer to ferry them to Kau D'varza, where they will shelter until their home is stable and free of danger once more. I will send additional details with this message."

Coda coughed. "Refugees? I'll make a note to have habs prepared."

Kaska shook her head, slowly. "Zeled's gonna love this..."

Raffa's message continued. "It should be noted that the action I have taken is not merely humanitarian. We believe that these rescued civilians will be able to provide valuable information as to what happened in their system - something they were unable to do safely while there. However, even if every single one of them refuses to talk, we still managed to recover a vessel, intact. I am informed by our systems that it is of Thanatosian design, but we haven't discovered much more than that. It is, however, clearly an advanced vessel, even by *Kobra*'s standards. Once we are in range, we will establish communication for further orders. Comcap Raffa, outsign."

"By the Void, they've been busy!" Coda finally said after reviewing some of the attached details.

Kaska smiled, faintly. "Yeah, I got that impression. How many refugees are we looking at?"

"Just shy of fifty."

"*Fifty?*" Kaska gasped, unknowingly echoing Raffa's

response.

Trast raised her eyebrows and nodded. "I know. But don't worry; I'll have the habitats set up before they arrive."

"That's not the point. Can we really sustain that many extra people?"

Trast was already calling up stock inventories on her screen. "Our food stockpiles are looking good. Might take the system a while to adjust, and we'll have to put those who are able to work, but according to this, we've got enough of a buffer to delay any problems until we can resettle them."

"Either way, Nevos will have to be told..." she said, doubtfully. "Did he send anything regarding the suspected Reclaimer ship?"

"Unknown. We're still downloading everything he sent. I'll let you know as soon as we can view it."

Kaska nodded. "Thanks, Coda."

She turned away and tried to settle at a console of her own, but her mind was on anything but work. She frowned, annoyed at herself for her lack of focus. It had always been the thing she had prided herself on, yet now... now she was distracted, troubled, but she couldn't figure out why. Was it some kind of delayed reaction to the incident in the engineering bay? Was it down to her hopes and fears about the mission, and Raffa's part in it?

No, that can't be it. The mission has clearly been a success. Joseph is safe and as good as home. So why do I still feel as if there's something left undone?

She glanced around the command core, where the other Specialists and Technicians were going about their regular duties without a hint of worry, let alone panic, and replayed Raffa's message, electing to have the audio fed to her headset. Maybe she'd spot something in there, maybe something he said might trigger an association.

Or maybe, she thought, with a tight, almost bitter smile, *I just want to hear his voice.*

* * *

Kau D'varza grew steadily larger on the main screen as the flotilla made its approach, and Elise watched, anxiously.

"Six hundred sekunds to dock," the pilot called.

"Acknowledged," Raffa replied, in a tone that was almost off-handed, then hit a button on his chair arm. "Raffa speaking. We have just entered final approach. All stations, make final prep and stand ready to disembark. Let's make sure those damage reports and maintenance logs are ready for the repair crews in the engineering bay. We'll need these ships on a fast turnaround, so I don't want to see any of us getting blamed for delays. And on a personal note, well done to each and every one of you. As always, it has been an honour and a privilege to have you under my command. You are a credit to yourselves and Kau D'varza, and I shall be sure to enter that in my final report. Comcap Raffa, outsign."

"Well said," Elise said, smiling.

Raffa made no reply, instead preferring to sit back with his eyes closed while the pilots conferred with each other and the station's traffic control specialists in low voices.

She eyed him enviously.

How can he be so calm? How can he just sit and wait like that, when I feel as jumpy as a litter of varka cubs?

Her eyes went back to the main screen, where the ship icons were edging ever closer - but ever more slowly - towards the station. As she watched, the icons began to move into their final positions, ready to enter their assigned bays. All apart from the Thanatonisan ship that they had temporarily named *Wanderer*, which slowed to increase the gap between themselves and the rest of the flotilla.

"Hey! What are they doing?"

Raffa opened his eyes and glanced at the screen before turning his attention to her. "Commissioner Zeled has requested we leave *Wanderer* outside blast radius until his engineers have inspected it and ruled out any possibility of a booby trap or overload. Why, something the matter?"

"I... no..." She shook her head. "We should have more than enough data to go through already. That'll give them time to run their checks."

Raffa grinned. "Wanted to get your hands on it straight away, eh? You're not the only one. But Commissioner Zeled is right to be concerned; we can only check so much with the equipment we've got, and while it's unlikely we'll have missed anything big enough to pose a major threat, it'll still need proper engineers and technicians to make sure it's one hundred percent safe. Once they're done, you'll be able to get at that info."

"What's going to happen to Winters?"

"Force-Commander Winters will be transferred back to Kau D'varza once a relief team has been deployed. Command will want to talk to him as soon as they can. Out of all of us, he's had the most experience with the ship."

"Surely the other information is more valuable to them?" she replied, her forehead creased in a frown. "*Wanderer* is really just a distraction until we can crack its data-stores."

"It will still take some time to assemble and deploy the relief team, so we'll have plenty of opportunity to share our findings." His eyes drifted back to the screen. "Besides, I get the impression Command is as confused about what to do with it as we are. Do we send a delegation to Thanatos? Do we keep the ship? Are we legally allowed to keep it? Is it a threat? Are the Thanatosians looking for it and will they assume we were the aggressors if they Transit here and find it?"

"Thanatos is..." Elise stretched her arms in despair. "Well, it's an inconceivably long way from here. You know how long it takes to get to Ar-Kaos? Well try to imagine that, then tag several more systems onto your journey. Whether they come looking for it or we go to them, it will take time. And it'll take even longer if we can't fix the 'default-only' transit issues. It's not like we can send *Wanderer* alone."

Raffa rubbed his chin thoughtfully. "Time enough to get the info off it. Time enough to work out our response."

"Yes, we do have some time, but what I meant is, it's not very likely that the Thanatosians will bother coming all this way. I say Kau D'varza might as well keep it and use it to our advantage, so the sooner-"

"Sorry, Specialist, but you'll have to take it up with Command. For what it's worth, though, you might as well resign yourself to the wait. Zeled will want to make sure it is safe, then he and the other Commissioners - including the Arch-Commissioner - will weigh up all the pros and cons. If they decide to return it as a gesture of goodwill, it's more than likely that they'll choose to do so with everything intact - data included."

"But-"

He raised a hand. "I understand why you'd get frustrated, but look at it this way: what's the point of returning a ship like that as a gesture of goodwill or friendship if the first thing they'll notice on checking it out is that the data core has been hacked? What kind of friends would we seem to be then?"

"Cautious ones? *Sensible* ones?" she said.

He smiled. "Or suspicious ones, untrustworthy ones. The Thanatosians would probably start to wonder whether we'd done anything else, like leave a little surprise in an obscure, secondary system perhaps, or program the core to transmit a virus to the command centre after a certain amount of time. Any hint of data access, let alone tampering, could in itself look like an act of aggression, if not actual war."

"So when will the Commissioners decide?"

He spread his hands. "Cycles. Tens of cycles. Hundreds. Thousands. Who knows?"

Elise slumped in her seat. "Bureaucrats!"

"*Mambaka* has been allocated bay sixteen, Sir. Adjusting course... course set. Guidance systems engaged," the co-pilot announced.

"Acknowledged." He hit the button on his chair arm again as he strapped himself into his seat. "Raffa speaking. All hands prepare for docking. Let's buckle up, people. Comcap Raffa, outsign."

The command centre crew immediately adjusted their harnesses and Elise followed suit, watching her screen as Kau D'varza loomed to take up the whole image. As they drew even closer, she was able to pick out movement in certain areas and sections and fine detail in others. It was spectacular, and beautiful, and terrifying all at the same time.

Damn... if I'd never had that conversation with Nevos... I'd still be rotting in a jail cell... dodged a bullet there, for sure...

The outer ship airlock door slid open painfully slowly. For a few seconds, Elise thought they were going to hit it, but the pilots quickly allayed her fears with professional announcements and distance readings. They slowed, slowed, and finally - after what seemed like an age - came to a stop. There were a few tense moments while they waited for the outer door to close, lock, and the pressure to normalise before the inner door ground open. Then a gantry swung down from the walls, *Mambaka* shook as the clamps took hold, and the ship was guided gently to Bay Sixteen.

"Ten sekunds to docking completion," the pilot announced. "Nine... eight... seven... six..."

The countdown went on, cutting out at one, whereupon the hull kissed the station with a loud, metallic *clunk* and *Mambaka* came to rest. A loud cheer erupted in the command centre, and Elise imagined it being echoed throughout the ship.

Raffa turned to Elise with a smile that engulfed his face. "Mission accomplished. Home at last."

* * *

Kaska held her breath as *Mambaka*'s cargo ramp

lowered just ahead of where she stood.

They're here. He's finally home!

She felt as much as heard Nevos draw himself up to attention beside her and did likewise, knowing that Commissioner Zeled - standing to the Arch-Commissioner's left as she was on his right - would be trying to outdo them both.

The ramp clanged into the place, the sound seeming to ring throughout the bay, and a sigh of relief escaped her as Raffa appeared in the opening, flanked by Elise and a handful of soldiers.

Gierre Nevos gave the salute and smiled widely. "Welcome home, honoured ones."

Raffa and his soldiers returned the salute, while Elise at least tried to mimic the gesture. She didn't do an entirely bad job, but it was enough to make Kaska smile and Nevos laugh as he waved them to ease.

"Permission to disembark, Sir," Raffa said, formally.

"Permission granted, Comcap," Nevos replied, upon which Raffa led the way down the ramp toward them. "I understand you have had an extremely interesting time," the Arch-Commissioner added, nodding in acknowledgement and greeting to the soldiers and technicians as they passed.

"Yes, you could say that, Sir."

"Well, we will hear all about it in due time. But first, you and your forces are to take the following cycle to recuperate and re-adjust."

Zeled's mouth fell open. "But, Arch-Commissioner! Surely we should start the debriefing as soon as-"

Nevos waved him to silence. "The debriefing is important, Zeled, I agree, but how much use is it likely to be if Comcap Raffa and Specialist Rivera are out on their feet? No, we already have enough data to work through, and with all they've been through the least we can offer them is a few kilosekunds' rest."

"If you insist, Arch-Commissioner," Zeled grumbled.

"Yes, I do," he replied, and turned his full attention to Raffa and Elise. "I have no problems with you using this down-time to finish reports, but after speaking with some of my specialists, I am also minded to instruct you to make sure you get plenty of rest. Commissioner Zeled is correct; we do need to start your full debriefing as soon as we can, or at least as soon as is... decent. In any case, given that we will be kept rather busy with the vessel you found, I believe this arrangement benefits us all. However, since there is a lot we will need to discuss it would be remiss of me not to warn you that the debriefing process is likely to be a lengthy one."

Kaska noticed Raffa's eyes flick to her. She read the question in them and tilted her head slightly in response, though Nevos apparently caught the exchange and cleared his throat.

"I believe it would also be appropriate if this... er, rest period... was spent in one's own quarters. Alone," he said, and offered a conciliatory smile. "Though of course, what you do afterwards, or what you choose to do now, is really not of official concern. It is merely my... recommendation."

"I will see to it the troops are informed. Thank you, Sir," Raffa said.

Nevos couldn't suppress a slight chuckle. "I'm sure you will, Comcap Raffa, and it is we who should be thanking you. I have already had the chance to review some of the information you sent, and I am stunned at what's been happening around us. I can't stress how badly we needed to be made aware of this, and your choice to go to Exen prior to Grinda... well, we've been discussing that, and have concluded you truly are an asset to this station."

"It was a bold choice, and ultimately the correct one," Zeled agreed, albeit in a tone that made it clear he didn't find it easy to hand out praise. "However, I have to say I am disappointed at the damage sustained-"

"I swear to the Void, Zeled-" Nevos began, but Zeled raised his hand.

"If you'll allow me to finish, Arch-Commissioner?" he said, before continuing when Nevos nodded. "Yes, I *am* disappointed at the damage sustained, not least because it will take several cycles to repair and it is extra work the engineering crews didn't need at this moment in time. But nor can I deny how impressed I am by what you've discovered, how you handled the situation and how you returned with all vessels present if not entirely intact, and it is... will be... an honour... my honour, Comcap Joseph Raffa, to present you with the Scroll of Kau D'varza, awarded for your exceptional leadership, tactical foresight, and conduct during extreme conditions. An official ceremony will be held two cycles from now to officially recognise this achievement. Congratulations, Comcap, and well done."

Raffa seemed stunned, then drew breath to reply, stopped, and finally found his voice. "Will Comcap Teq and Force-Commander Winters receive this award as well?"

Nevos cleared his throat. "Their actions were in no way equal to yours. We do, however, recognise their contribution, and will reward each of them appropriately."

"I...I don't know what to say, except..." Raffa came to attention and saluted. "Thank you, Sirs."

Zeled immediately returned the salute, his movements as sharp and practiced as those of any soldier, then nodded, turned on his heel and left, all in the time it took for Gierre to pause, glance at his hand, then raise it in his own salute. Of the two, there was no doubt in Kaska's mind which Raffa valued more.

He looked at her, and she beamed at him.

"Well done, Joseph. You deserve it," she said.

"You do," Elise echoed, grinning her trademark grin. "All these people, all those ships... we wouldn't be here without you. We wouldn't know what threats we faced. I don't know what this Scroll is, but it's obvious it means a lot to everyone here. Congratulations. Well done."

"The Scroll of Kau D'varza..." Nevos replied, "is a symbol of our station's humble beginnings. An announcement, an official decree of our independence from the surface. We award a special copper coin to our most outstanding citizens."

"Copper?" Elise said, confused.

"From the first asteroid mined after Kau D'varza became independent. It represents our freedom from the surface."

Elise glanced back to Raffa. "Damn... I think even I'd be offended if you turned it down after hearing that."

"I was only doing my job. Really," Raffa said.

"And it is for that job, as well as you consistently displaying that kind of attitude, that we have decided to give you this award," Nevos said.

"You have to accept, Joseph. No one has ever turned down such an award before. You can't - you don't deserve to be - the first," Kaska added.

Raffa looked at the floor and shook his head. "Alright. As much as I don't see what I've done to deserve it..." He looked back to Commissioner Zeled. "Sir, it would be an honour to accept the award."

Nevos grinned. "Excellent. As Commissioner Zeled indicated, we shall make the formal presentation in two cycles. In the meantime, what say we all retreat to my office and celebrate?"

"I would be happy to, Sir," Raffa said. "However I should attend to and complete my duties here first."

"You can unpack *Mambaka* some other time. In fact, we'll have the engineering staff do it. As of right now, you, and everyone else involved in this mission, are on rest, effective immediately."

"Thank you, Sir!" a passing soldier said, while another shouted, "Gierre Nevos is a legend!" Then, after a pause, added, "Sir!"

Nevos laughed, and the others joined in before Raffa turned and called to his troops.

"Spread the word, then. Make sure everyone knows, then go enjoy yourselves. You earned it."

Nevos smiled at each of them in turn and extended a hand in invitation. "Alright, then. Shall we?"

The Arch-Commissioner turned and walked away, Elise following not too far behind. Raffa held back, and Kaska went to stand with him. She noticed Elise glance back once, her initial frown turning slowly to a smirk of support and understanding, then turned away to engage Nevos in conversation.

Thank you, Elise.

"So-" Raffa began, but got no further as Kaska grabbed

his uniform by the collar, whispered, "Welcome home", and pulled him in for a kiss that landed like an explosion.

EPILOGUE

Kaska woke as the light bloomed, indicating the start of another cycle. For the first time in a long while, she felt refreshed and well-rested. Even her spell in the Krash bed hadn't managed that.

She looked over at Raffa, who was still fast asleep with his mouth slightly open, smiled, then got out of bed. She dressed quickly and quietly, slipping into the same tunic as she'd discarded the night before, a pair of loose-fitting trousers, and her work shoes before heading out the door.

Her stomach growled at the various smells as she stepped into the empty food court. It was still early on the station, meaning there were plenty of seats available and little chance of her being bothered by anyone. Better yet, she wouldn't have to sit wondering whether people could tell she hadn't visited the cleanroom yet. She took a few seconds to enjoy the quiet peacefulness of it all before walking through the jungle of chairs upturned on tables towards Miranda's Grill.

She stepped through the door and approached the counter, immediately noticing a group in one of the booths. They looked seriously out of place, mostly wearing the style of clothing that Kaska associated with some regions in Gaitlin, though other items were clearly from elsewhere and some were utterly alien to her. Even their hairstyles were different, not only to those of Kau D'varzans, but also to each other. The only thing everyone in the group had in common was a look of deep concern, though one of them - a woman - looked more intense and highly-strung than the others.

She looked away quickly when one of the group nudged another and muttered something, drawing the other's attention. She didn't need to glance over again as she heard a hurried, whispered conversation and the rasp of fabric sliding off a seat covering.

They must've recognised the tunic. Damnit, why couldn't I have taken a bit more time and chosen something else?

"Uh... excuse me?"

Damnit. Standard. I wish Elise was here... or that I at least had an earworm.

Kaska turned to the intense-looking woman and studied her for a few seconds while she tried to scrape up a response.

"Help you with something can I?" she tried, drawing a frown from the other woman.

No, I know that wasn't right. Damnit, I always did struggle with the right word order...

"Have you... er..." She motioned to her ear, signalling that she meant to ask if any of them had a translation device.

"Are you asking if I have an Earworm?"

Kaska grinned in relief. "Yes! Yes, Earworm. Have you one?"

But the woman was already shaking her head, looking genuinely regretful.

"Sorry, no. And I know no Kau D'varzan. But your... You... an administrator here?"

Kaska frowned, hearing what she recognised were words and separate sounds, but failing to translate them.

"Yes, I'm a..." She struggled for the word for 'Specialist', couldn't find it, and gave up. "Yes. But I'm not this... er... this time... worker ." She grimaced and shook her head, knowing from the other woman's expression that she was getting it wrong, but not knowing or remembering enough to get it right. "You should with to talk your receive-person if you are... er... *Oh, damnit...* doing-pains or thought-ideas."

Kaska watched the other woman frown and mouth *Doing-pains and thought-ideas?*

The woman glanced at her companions, who did their best to hide their smiles and shrugged. She shook her head, dismissing them, and stood thinking for a moment or two more until her expression suddenly cleared.

"Ah! Er... I'm sorry," she said, "but did you mean to say 'complaints and... suggestions'?"

Kaska recognised the words instantly, and smiled, nodding. "Yes, yes. That's it."

"Oh... No, it's nothing like that, and we don't have a 'receive-person'," the woman said, clearly making an effort now to use the simplest words she could find. "We wanted to talk about the... er... investigations? Do you know that word?"

I wouldn't have said so, but I recognise it now!

Kaska nodded, much to the other woman's relief.

"Yes, that's it, then. We wanted to talk about the investigations in Beyema."

"Beyema? We have in Beyema no investigations."

"No, I didn't mean *your* investigation. I meant... the investigations of others. We have information regarding ship disappearances in the region. I was led to believe that the source of the problem most likely lay in Beyema."

Kaska tried to control her reaction to those words, but failed. "Who are you?"

The woman smiled. "I'm Mira. This is Rolo and Kiki. We recently arrived from Munry."

"Oh! From the ships you are! I'm sorry. You were from Grinda, I thought."

"Grinda? No."

Kaska ran her eye over the group once more. The eclectic clothing, the fact that some of it was in clear need of repair if not replacement... they certainly *looked* like potential refugees.

"So, you are from where?"

Another smile. "I told you; Munry."

Kaska shook her head. "No. Munry is a dead system. You passed there through, maybe, but from there, no one is."

Mira's smile fell away. "Does it really matter where we're from?"

"Yes."

Mira sighed. "Very well. We're from..." Another quick smile. "Everywhere and nowhere. How's that?"

Kaska flashed a smile of her own. "So, mercenaries you are."

"Something like that..."

"Mercenaries," Kaska repeated, firmly. "And what want I to know is, why is a bunch of mercenaries in that so interested?"

"All I'm going to say is we ran into someone who gave us a bunch of info about what's going on. We've seen it for ourselves, and we want to put an end to it."

"You saw it where? In Munry?"

"No, we only passed through there. It doesn't really matter where we saw it, does it? And I'm sorry, but I'm not at liberty to say where the info came from, either, only that it came from someone who's been investigating kidnappings in the region around the Void Cloud. We were hired to come here, deliver some data, and help if we can. We're trained. Oceanside certified."

"Oceanside. Gaitlin, huh?"

Mira nodded.

Kaska thought it over for a few seconds while she checked the contents of the steaming bags that were placed on the counter and, finally satisfied, gathered them together.

Mercenaries. Might be bad news... but still, they're trained. And if what Raffa and Elise found is the work of Reclaimers, we'll likely need every spare ship and trained hand we can get.

"I'm Kaska Stone," she said, and just like that, the word for 'Specialist' popped into her head. "*Specialist* Stone. Command Core is where I work. Where stay you, exactly?"

Mira's mouth quirked into a smile again, making Kaska feel hot and self-conscious.

"You can find us on our ship. It's in the civilian docking bay. T.S. *Resolve*."

"*Resolve*," Kaska repeated, nodding. "I will this to my superiors bring. They will as soon as they can contact you. I..." She frowned again. *How in the Void do you say 'recommend'?* She couldn't remember, if she'd ever known, and shook her head. "Stay with device connected to your ship, or better, leave not as if someone comes looking, maybe."

Mira nodded. "I think I understand. Thank you."

"My pleasure. She started back towards the entrance, relieved that the torture was coming to an end. "Meet you all was it good. l hope we be speaking again soon."

The mercenaries smiled their goodbyes, leaving Kaska to be on her way.

And next time we speak, I'll make damn sure Elise is present, Kaska thought, gritting her teeth against the lingering stress and embarrassment as she headed back to her quarters.

* * *

Joseph Raffa opened his eyes to find Kaska sitting over him, smiling.

Now that's a beautiful thing to wake up to...

"Good morning," he mumbled, groggily, and shifted so he could prop himself up on his elbows.

"Morning yourself," she said, leaning down to give him a playful kiss before straightening up again.

"Void, you're too awake for me," he complained. "Been awake long?"

"Hm... long enough. I got breakfast. Here." She unceremoniously dumped one of the bags on his chest, and laughed as he recoiled.

"Mmm... Smells good," Raffa said, as he sat up properly, sniffing the air.

"It's bora steak wrap."

"For breakfast?"

She grinned. "For anytime. Anyway, you were the one who said it smelled good. Now, we can eat in bed, or at the table. It's up to you."

Raffa nodded to the table and got out of bed, squirming into a pair of trousers as Kaska carried everything over.

"I met some rather interesting people while I was getting this," she said, nonchalantly, as he hobbled over and sat down.

"Oh?"

"Hm. Mercenaries from the looks of it. Their leader... at least, I assume she was their leader... says they've got information on the disappearances."

Raffa studied her with a curious frown. "They've lost people too?"

"No, no, nothing like that." Kaska sat down at the table and began unwrapping her meal. "Stranger, actually. They say they ran into... someone, and this 'someone' hired them to come here and deliver some data."

Raffa blinked. "Data, here? Why?"

She smiled and spread her hands. "I don't know."

"Well... what else did they say?"

"Not much. The conversation was a little... difficult."

David Noe

"They were being evasive?"

"No, it was in Standard."

"Oh. Did you think to call Specialist Rivera?"

She made a show of being shocked by the suggestion. "Oh wow! I mean, I never..." She gave him a look. "*Of course* I thought of Elise. I also thought of what time it was and how you're all supposed to be on a rest cycle. If she's anything like you..."

"Yes, yes. Alright." He bit into his wrap and chewed thoughtfully for a few moments. "I wonder, though... this info these mercenaries were hired to bring, if it really does relate to the abductions, that isn't information you just stumble upon. They might have dug it up themselves and are looking to cover their involvement, could have been a pirate who came across something they couldn't use themselves, some random corporation, a data-jockey... Or it could be the people doing all this trying to throw us off the scent. I'll have Ikarus go through it extremely thoroughly, see if he can determine the source."

"Hold on. Data-jockey?"

"Oh. I don't know much about them, just bits and pieces I've heard during my travels-"

"Ah, I forgot, you're the brave wanderer of the universe..." Kaska teased.

"Hush, you," he said, grinning before becoming serious once more. "No, these data-jockeys... they've been around a while. They take in bits of anything - raw data, information, partially-substantiated rumours, and..." He spread his hands. "Well, save some of it until it's needed, I guess. And of course, what they can't simply gather, they try to obtain."

"So they're basically data-pirates?"

Raffa shook his head. "No... I think they're more legitimate than that. I'm not saying they're above that kind of thing, but it's more in the way of business, for them."

"Hmm. Well, one potentially gave these mercenaries some information and sent them here specifically, for some reason."

He took another chunk out of the wrap and frowned while he chewed. "What are they getting out of it?"

"Hmm?"

"It's the first question I always ask when dealing with mercs; What do they get out of it?"

"Credits? Favours? Either way, we'll need to see if their information is legitimate."

"Hm. I'll have Ikarus go through it carefully. Let me know once it's been transferred to the station."

"I will, but for now... eat up. I've got a long cycle of doing nothing planned."

"Doing... nothing?"

She grinned. "Well, I *can* think of a few things."

* * *

Elise woke with a start, and only then realised that she'd fallen asleep on her sofa. Wiping the dribble off her chin, she smiled and sat up.

It's good to be home.

She stretched, yawned then got to her feet. The processor spluttered the usual brown concoction into her cup while she staggered to the clean room. When she emerged a few minutes later wearing some loose fitting clothes, her habitat glowed with simulated sunlight.

As much as this place feels like home, it's not perfect. That light's all wrong, for a start. She sighed, and took a long swig from her drink. *Damn, I miss Paradise sometimes...*

She closed that line of thinking down before it could get her moping about her family and headed for the door, the remains of her drink still in her hand.

The door to the public observation lounge hissed open and she stepped forward tentatively, before sighing and smiling in relief as she saw the room was empty. She made her way to the bench at the front and settled into her usual spot, looking out at the Void Cloud.

She watched it bursting with stunning deep azures and aquamarines for a few moments. Its beauty was beguiling, entrancing, the colours swirled and shifted, patterns formed and just as quickly disappeared, never to be repeated, at least not in quite the same way. Next time, it might be subtly different, or the colours would be different, or the patterns would hold together for as long, though some might last longer. Constant motion, constant shifts, constant changes...

Elise was captivated, and was so lost in appreciation and daydream that she failed to see a shadow walking up to the window.

"Hello, Specialist," Nevos said without looking.

Elise glanced over and grinned. "Arch-Commissioner."

"I hope I'm not interrupting."

"No. I think I was hoping you'd join me."

"Oh?"

"This isn't a coincidence, is it?"

Gierre turned to her. "No. I saw you heading to this sector, and made an educated guess that you were on your way here."

"I don't mind." She motioned to the bench, inviting him to join her. "But I am wondering why you wanted me."

He smiled his acceptance, sat down and leaned back, looking out at the Void Cloud. "It is beautiful, isn't it?" he said. "I've seen it... well, you know how often. Yet every time is different, every time is like it's my first."

"Yes," she murmured in agreement. "But…"

He glanced at her and smiled. "Oh, don't worry; I promised you the cycle off and you've got the cycle off. I'm not here because of work. I simply had a while before I have to be at Command and thought I'd enjoy this… and your company, of course."

"Of course," she said, "and you're always welcome. But, what did you wanna talk about?"

Nevos shrugged. "Nothing, really. I admit I was curious, but…"

"Curious? About what?"

"Well, I wondered… Just between us, how was your trip?"

"Whew, is that all?" Elise replied. "Well, I guess it was good in bits, and terrifying in others."

"Oh?"

"Yeah. I mean, it was interesting seeing some of our neighbouring systems, and it felt good clearing out the pirates, but space battles? They're pretty scary."

"I can only imagine." Gierre's gaze drifted back to the Cloud. "You're very brave, you know."

"Brave? Nah, I just didn't know what I was getting into. I thought we'd be popping to the next system and getting information. It wasn't until the missiles started flying that I really understood what I'd signed up for. You want brave, Raffa? Winters? They're brave. They knew what they were up against and went anyway."

"Would you do it again?" he asked.

"In a heartbeat," she replied, grinning.

Gierre laughed. "Very good. Well - and I'm sorry here, because I don't mean to drift onto work talk -but I daresay plenty more such ventures will be available to you in the near future. If you want them, of course."

"I look forward to it."

"Good."

Silence hung between them for a few seconds before Elise drew breath to say something, then paused.

Gierre tilted his head towards her. "Something on your mind?"

"I just... It's... I'm worried."

"Oh? Why?"

"When we were flying around... especially after Comcap Teq joined us... I felt the strength of the flotilla. It scared me, the idea that we had so much power, and yet..."

"And yet, despite this, we're still at risk from pirates and the Reclaimers." He shook his head. "We *are* powerful, but it's not overwhelming. Whatever power we wield alone would never be enough to turn back all those who would do us harm."

"Then we are not yet powerful enough. We should look to build it until no one would dare to hurt us."

"*Elise,*" he said, softly. "Such sentiments do not become you. I've only known you a short time, but I know you're a good person; you have always spoken and acted out of courage, not fear, yet thoughts like the one you've just had? They're for small people, selfish people, fearful people. Like the people you encountered, the pirates? They use their power to steal and murder. You would use the same power to help people, solve problems... That takes courage, as does trust. We could build up our power and exercise it through our fleets, it is true. But the stronger we became, the more likely it is that we would find ourselves at war. Regardless of our intentions, we would become a vast and terrible thing in the eyes of our neighbours... and they would combine their forces to stand against us, or strike us before we could do it to them." He paused and shook his head. "That's the thing about power, Elise; you argue that it is necessary, that you will never use it... but once it is there, once you have all that power in your hands... why, you might think to yourself; what is the point in having all this power, if I never get to wield it?" He looked at her and smiled. "You have to remember that there is a balance to be found, that power is only a tool, and it is the mind behind the hand that controls that tool which decides. Yes, respect it, perhaps even fear it, but as long as it is only used for the benefit of others, then you are worthy of wielding it."

She stared at him thoughtfully, and eventually her mouth formed something like "Thank you".

He gave her a reassuring, even fatherly smile and turned his attention back to the vast glory of the Void Cloud.

After a short time, he pulled out his datapad, read the message there, and stood. Elise automatically went to rise too, but he waved her back into her seat.

"Unfortunately I must go. Duty calls, and all that."

"Is it..." She stopped and smiled. "Sorry. I was about to ask if it was anything important. What I mean is, is it anything I can help you with?"

"No, no," he said. "As I said earlier, you get the full cycle. Enjoy what remains of it." He turned to leave, then stopped. "Oh, I forgot! For this cycle only, all your meals in the food court are free. Just a little part of the thank you we are preparing for your work. I recommend the crabster in Miranda's Grill. Delicious. Anyway, have a good cycle!"

"You too, and thank you, Sir."

He waved a hand in acknowledgement and was gone. Elise closed her eyes as the door hissed shut behind him.

Free food, eh? I'll have to go and check that out. And what's this 'thank you' they have in mind? Ah, never mind... I don't care.

She sat for a few moments longer, savouring the silence, remembering what Gierre had said and wondering where it all might lead.

I never thought for a sekund that I'd be doing this sort of thing... Never crossed my mind I'd be wearing a uniform for the leader of a station... And I've taken part in two space battles. Two! Back in Paradise I would have been lucky to see the edited highlights!

Elise opened her eyes and focused on the mass of vibrant colours that seemed so deceptively close.

And despite how scary all that is, I can't shake the feeling I'm exactly where I'm supposed to be...

23096702R00310

Printed in Great Britain
by Amazon